A MEMORY IN THE BLACK
BOOK TWO OF THE NEW AENEID CYCLE

MICHAEL G. MUNZ

RED MUSE PRESS

Red Muse Press
Seattle, WA 2016

Cover Design by Amalia Chitulescu

Previously self-published 2013

This is a work of fiction. Names, characters, places, brands, media, and incidents are either the product of the author's imagination or are used fictitiously. Any resemblance to similarly named places or to persons living or deceased is unintentional.

PRINT ISBN 978-0-9977622-2-8

Library of Congress Control Number: 2015903658

ACKNOWLEDGMENTS

A big thank-you to all the fans who loved the original 2013 e-book release of *A Shadow in the Flames* and clamored for more until I let them see what, at the time, was its written but unpublished sequel. Thank you also to Brian Rathbone for his publishing guidance, to Amy Herndon and David Taylor for their help in getting the word out, and of course, once again, to my parents and sister for all their encouragement.

Special thanks to beta-readers Brian, Linda, and especially Joe, who was always great with the detailed notes and unrequested puns.

For everyone who kept asking,
"What happens next?"

I

NORTHGATE. THE CITY was a cesspool. Though it served Joseph Curwen's needs, its heat always flared during his visits. Its pollution choked him and stung his eyes. Even the jet lag he felt upon arrival always refused to let him go until right before his departure. It was as if Northgate itself believed he didn't belong there. Crazy as the idea was, the loathsome city was right. This wasn't even his hemisphere.

It was August of 2051, and he was running out of time.

Curwen passed through the security point at the monorail station's exit. The lights, the crowds, and the pressure of the security scanners that checked him for weapons and explosives added to the heat. The sweat that rolled beneath his suit made him further aware of the extra weight he'd put on over his usual bulk since the whole clandestine affair began some months ago. The snug material around his waist gave his skin little room to breathe. When he returned to Europe, it would be time to give his long-suffering tailor some more business.

The concourse doors slid open. Curwen passed through them into the suffocation of the late afternoon swelter. He popped a second dose of antacids and made his way toward the crowded escalator that would bear him down to the street. Too much stress, not enough downtime. Especially with the risks he was taking lately. At least those risks would pay off soon, if he could just carry on a bit further.

Other travelers packed around him and forced him to restrain nerves that would otherwise have sent him bounding down the escalator after being stuck rigid on the monorail. The corner of a briefcase ground into the small of his back as its owner's lung-rumbling cough shook the city air. Ahead of him stood a woman whose perfume trailed in a wake behind her. As his eyes dropped to study the way her skirt fell over her hips, he tried to hold his breath and wondered if he would be sick from the fumes.

Frogs' balls, he wanted this day over with. He reached the bottom of the escalator without passing out and turned onto the sidewalk toward his destination: the Nexus Tower Hotel and the restaurant housed on its twentieth floor.

This was his fourth visit to Northgate in the last six months. He should not even be there today, but the deal he originally brokered with Raven Defense Technologies Vice-President Ken Wallace had proven fragile and, ultimately, disastrous.

Wallace had stolen equipment from his own company, hired someone to cover the theft with arson, and then tried to sell the spoils to pay Curwen. When evidence surfaced of Wallace's crimes, he turned up dead soon after. Curwen felt no guilt from knowing that Wallace died trying to raise money to buy the secrets he was selling. Wallace was a business partner, not a friend—one who'd made poor decisions and failed to live up to his promises.

Yet the mistake of approaching Wallace at all was Curwen's own. Dealing with Wallace—one man working secretly within his own organization—was too unstable of an arrangement. Curwen was already doing such a thing himself. So when Wallace died, Curwen sought to partner with an entire company.

The wisdom of hindsight allowed him to realize that he'd hurried that first time. When he'd first contracted with Wallace and offered him a line on the secrets of an actual alien spacecraft the European Space Agency had found on the Moon, Curwen had deemed it prudent to move quickly. As time went on and ESA erred on the side of caution, it became clear that he would be afforded more time. And so this time around, he had taken his time feeling out Marquand Cybernetics and negotiating a deal for the soon-to-be-stolen technology that would leave him set for life. He was certain he had hooked their interest. Today's meeting would close the deal.

As far as he had told his contacts at Marquand, however, he had found another partner and they were about to lose a deal that would otherwise rocket them to the forefront of the industry. It was only a negotiating ploy to make them increase what was already a very lucrative offer. He would listen to their new offer—they had called the meeting, after all—and he would, after feigning apprehension, agree. Curwen smirked.

And yet, what if they called his bluff? *Easy now. Things are nearly done.*

He strode past the Marquand building while trying not to look at it, though maybe that was being overcautious. Even if anyone was watching him, how much could they glean from even a long glance? Curwen looked over his shoulder regardless. No one was following— at least, no one he recognized. He quickened his pace anyway. The Nexus Tower loomed a block away. A crosswalk light changed ahead of him. Curwen stopped short on pins and needles and waited for the traffic to clear.

For him, it never did. Two bullets ripped through Curwen's heart. He had only a moment to blink before he collapsed on the pavement.

*   *   *

Diomedes watched the fat man collapse from a room on the nineteenth floor of the Nexus Tower Hotel. He raised his eye from the scope of the rifle. People scattered from the body. A few fools crouched by the mark, perhaps trying to help him. But the shot was clean. There would be nothing they could do. The man on the pavement was lost and gone, like all the rest.

Sirens rose from below. An ambulance appeared on the scene almost too quickly. Diomedes moved back from the window. His job was over.

As quickly as he could, he broke down the rifle, folded up the tripod, and slid it all under the bed. The rifle was a RavenTech HG-113. It was powerful, and among the most accurate he'd ever fired. Both bullets hit the mark perfectly. More than once he'd considered taking it with him. It had been waiting for him in the room. It was provided for the job. His instructions: leave it under the bed. Taking it would complicate the prospect of future jobs from this employer. Still, if he could have thought of a way to get the rifle out of the hotel undetected, he might have risked it.

He let the weapon go. There wasn't much choice.

The rifle was only one of the things provided for the job. The other was the security grid suspension.

Scanners were heavy throughout the Corporate District. A sensor screen able to detect any objects passing through it above a certain velocity netted any building taller than four stories. The point of origin would be determined within a second. Alarms would sound. Guards would respond. Or so it was said. The grid was rarely put to the test.

His employer—a blond woman, dressed in upscale business attire—had approached Diomedes on the street. Though she looked familiar, he didn't know her. He'd been leaving the freelancer bar that he and countless other mercenaries frequented. She gave him the job's time and place in a way that made him think he was the first she'd ever hired. Yet she'd been determined. The rifle, the grid suspension—both would be taken care of. Even disregarding her clothes, she was obviously corporate—from Marquand or Aegis Security if she could disable the grid.

Diomedes didn't ask. She paid him in full and promised further jobs. The money was good. The rifle was there. He took the risk that she was lying about the grid.

Or had he even considered it? The prospect of future jobs and steady money persuaded him not to care.

And it was easier not to argue.

Now Diomedes took the elevator to the twelfth floor. No alarms had sounded inside the building. He exited the elevator in front of a group of suits. They ignored him. He looked down on them as he passed. A little over a minute later, he crossed to the other side of the building and swiped the keycard on the door to his room. He would stay there for the evening. Security would scrutinize anyone leaving the building now. Though no grid alarms had gone off, the dead mark outside wouldn't be ignored. A room reserved under a fake name on the opposite side of the building would be the safest place. If security did contact him, his statement would be brief and dull. He locked the door, drew the shades, and turned on the news to pass the time.

This job was nearly done. It was only a matter of time. Two bullets, then wait. More straightforward than the other job he had going. He checked his messages: nothing yet from his contact on that one. The man had told him to wait, but Diomedes wouldn't wait forever. The man was powerful, yes, but he didn't hold all the cards. They had worked together before. The first time had gone bad, and Diomedes wasn't about to let him jerk him around a second time. As soon as he got out of the hotel, he would have to see about that.

*   *   *

From a window table in the Skylark Restaurant on the twentieth floor of the Nexus Tower, Ondrea Noble watched events unfold on the streets below with bittersweet satisfaction. Diomedes had done his job, and the man from ESA would never make the lunch meeting to which her superiors had invited him. As panicked pedestrians ran from the fallen man, the waiting EMTs heroically swooped in and gathered him into their "ambulance" floater.

He would never reach any hospital. Marquand's plan—her plan—was going as devised. The secrets he had turned around and promised to another company would belong to Marquand, or they would belong to no one. She had told her project leader the same when she proposed her idea. The technology she designed would do what they needed; she had insisted it.

Confidently.

In truth, Ondrea was only partially convinced the procedure would allow them to recover the information Marquand needed, but she didn't care. The possibility of its recovery merely got her the approval she required. While Curwen's promise of alien technology certainly interested her, the procedure would allow her a much more personal accomplishment.

Getting Diomedes for the assassination was a further boon in the mix. Trusting her at her word that she knew someone qualified to do the job, Marquand allowed her to set up the details herself. It was their way of separating themselves to protect the company, but it worked to her advantage. She found him. She hired him. It was utterly poetic in its justice.

Ondrea sipped her ice water. Her gaze drifted across the intersection to the nineteenth floor of the Marquand building. There, almost directly across from the hotel room set up for Diomedes to take the shot, Ondrea had placed a camera. No one else knew. When footage from that camera reached the authorities, Diomedes's life would be over.

She smiled ruefully. It would be a fitting end for the man who six months ago pulled the trigger on her brother.

I I

ON THE OTHER SIDE of Northgate, no less than an hour before Joseph Curwen collapsed on the pavement, Marc Triton plugged the wet-link into his mind and launched his perception elsewhere. Reality fell from his world like a discarded cloak.

He could still feel, of course. The support of his chair remained beneath him and held his body in its cushions just as it had moments before. The rise and fall of his breathing remained a steady rhythm in his chest. Yet such sensations now retreated to a place somewhere behind his consciousness, to make way for artificial mental images and the knowledge of the datastreams that became his mind's focus.

The virtual space seemed to form around him, though more accurately it was he who made the entrance into it: a final destination after slipping through layer upon layer of encryption-stealth protocols that boggled even Marc's mind. The Agents of Aeneas Council sat in the center, their seven avatars arranged in a circle at a virtual table. Around them sat the others, hidden in a shadow of data that was indistinct unless focused on. Marc formed within that shadow, one of many members of the secret society from across the globe, and turned his attention toward the center.

The session was already underway, though only barely. Feeling too preoccupied that morning for any pre-session mingling with his fellow agents, he had connected late on purpose. Besides, today Marc anticipated a need to leave early, and he wished to observe quietly on his own.

" . . . already running a dangerous risk of exposure." Councilor Knapp was in mid-speech as Marc began to listen. The oldest member of the Council at sixty-two, Marla Knapp had always seemed a matriarchal figure in the AoA despite having never served as Arbiter. Her British accent echoed in the chamber's virtual space. "Knowledge of the crater site continues to filter through the European Space Agency at an alarming rate. Precisely how long do we let this knowledge spread?"

"Councilor, the 'alarming' rate you refer to is negligible for our purposes." The genial reply came from Councilor May Lin, half Knapp's age but no less confident.

"Secrecy is paramount. If what we have found—what *we* led ESA to—was to become common knowledge, then the Exodus Project is compromised and all of our effort is for naught!"

"A necessary risk." Lin continued to speak, as gently as Knapp was stern. "We do not have the resources to carry on the research ourselves from its current state. We should continue to work behind the scenes, as we've always done."

Arbiter Nicholai Szendroi, the head of the Council, cleared his throat. "I feel it necessary to remind the group that our detachment scenario remains viable—but only if sufficient progress is made to allow autonomy at the site. To move too soon would leave us unready to capitalize on whatever security we may create."

"And if we don't move soon enough, there won't be a thing to capitalize on!" Knapp declared. "Working behind the scenes is not at issue here. We're talking about a critical security problem! Or have we forgotten the ESA mole?"

"Ah, the mole is being closely watched." Another councilor had broken his silence—a rapidly-speaking American named Samuel Ramis with whom Marc had worked personally. "He's made no attempt to initiate any new deals since his Northgate failure six months ago."

"Watched is not good enough. I've said so before. We've seen already that our surveillance is imperfect. What if he should slip through the cracks again?"

The arbiter turned to face Knapp. "That matter has been discussed previously, Councilor. I stand by the decision of this council that he would pose a greater risk if cut loose from ESA. We could not watch him so easily. I see no cause to reopen the issue."

"No cause? Arbiter, Joseph Curwen's attempt to sell ESA's secrets—"

"An attempt that occurred six months ago—," Lin tried.

"—is an attempt to sell our own! He is a clear and present threat to the entire project and must be neutralized, one way or another!"

Chaos erupted as three others tried to speak at once, and the arbiter cut the audio to keep order. "Councilor Knapp," he began cautiously when the others had settled, "Are you implying lethal force?"

Knapp remained silent a moment, as if choosing her words. Her virtual face became a mask of resolve and regret. "Perhaps I am. But only as a last resort. Certainly you—"

Again the Council erupted in shouts, and again the arbiter invoked silence. "I should not have to remind the councilor that such a thing has not been done since the days of the Illuminati." His voice, though measured, carried a trace of warning.

Knapp's response was just as measured. "We have never been so close to one of our objectives, Arbiter."

For a time, no one spoke. Glances were traded across the table as the multitude of others in attendance watched with interest, no doubt considering their own votes on such a matter. Marc was sure it was a mistake. It would be a start down a path that would make them no better than those who had already set humanity on the self-destructive course AoA had sworn to fight.

Councilor Ramis broke the silence first. "If I may offer a suggestion, as it were?"

All attention turned toward him and he continued, speaking as if he feared his words might explode on his tongue if not said fast enough. "If you'll pardon the melodrama, the very thing that we're afraid of may in fact be something we can use to our advantage. Consider: the more word spreads, the more difficult it becomes to control. Things get chaotic. But what if we harness this chaos—to the best of our ability direct it—assuming it does actually occur? We create a haze of action and reaction around those who know too much, and in that haze our own movements will be concealed."

"What exactly do you propose?"

"Sleight of hand and misdirection. Use the mole against ESA. Give them an adversary to focus on and direct them away from our own actions. We orchestrate everything into a moment of chaos, and in that moment make our move."

"Takeover of the site, you mean," Knapp stated.

"Yes."

"It may be viable," observed another councilor. "Given the success of the Denver situation, such chaos could certainly create the opportunity we need."

As the Council debated, Marc heard the distant tone of an alert sounding in the real world, where his body waited. It was the one he was waiting for. While he'd been observing the forum of the Agents of Aeneas, some of their designs had come to fruition. He left the forum in a subtle blink and opened his eyes to the reality of his apartment.

Expecting he already knew the answer, Marc asked the question anyway. "What have you got for me, Holes?" Holes's matrix was still developing, and still at a point where additional stimulation would help it mature.

"You have two new messages, Mr. Triton," Holes remarked. "As per your instruction, I have alerted you for a message from the European Space Agency, and assigned it first priority."

Barely a few weeks old, the artificial intelligence Marc named "Holes" still retained the original, unremarkable, and just barely male voice and tone Marc had programmed into him. As it matured, it might yet choose another—a common side effect of an emergently-designed A.I., and Marc himself looked forward to the prospect in the same way the parents of a human child might look forward to the child's first words. Of course, a human child could not be reset to an embryo if it started cursing too much.

"Any video or audio with that ESA message?"

"No, Mr. Triton. The message is text only."

"Display on the main monitor if you could, please."

"I am fully capable of doing so, Mr. Triton." An email appeared, emblazoned at the bottom with ESA's circular logo. Marc stepped over to the monitor to see if it said what he expected.

It did.

The smile on his face was a satisfied one. "What's the second message, Holes?"

"Voice message only, identified as from a Mr. Felix Hiatt."

Marc winced in memory and checked the time. He'd completely forgotten about meeting his friend for lunch.

"Play it?"

Felix's voice came over the speaker against a background of mingled voices and dish clatter. "*Penguins!*" he cried. "*There's penguins everywhere! They're storming the café and holding the waitstaff at beak-point! They're demanding to know where you are! So, um, hey, where are you?*"

Marc laughed and shook his head. At least Felix could be counted on to be reasonably good-natured about having to wait for him. "Call Felix for me, would you, Holes?"

"Placing the call, Mr. Triton." Marc waited as it rang. "I find it highly improbable that hostile penguins have captured a restaurant of any sort."

Before Marc could respond to Holes, Felix picked up. Marc answered his greeting with, "Holding the waitstaff at beak-point, eh?"

"*Yeah. Plus now they've gotten into the espresso and it's not pretty. You ever see a flightless bird on a caffeine buzz? They're flapping like crazy and getting nowhere. Waitresses' skirts blowing up left and right, some guy's toupee shot right across the room—*"

"You ate a whole bag of coffee beans again, didn't you?"

"*Hey, if I'd done that I'd be running around flapping, myself. You know what that much does to me.*"

"True."

"*So listen,*" Felix put pleasantly, "*did you forget about us, or what? I mean, I'm okay with it, but, you know, Caitlin'll kill ya.*"

"Ah, she made it, then?" The two had been dating for nearly six months, but Felix said earlier that she might not be joining them for lunch.

"*Yeah, she's—Ow! Hey! I'm getting elbow jabbings for that 'killing you' comment, too.*"

Marc grinned. "You can tell her I was pretty sure you were kidding."

"*I'm trying, but I can't get a word in between the jabs! Hey! No tickling!*"

"Um, listen, Felix," Marc broke in, "I'm sorry but it doesn't look like I'll be able to make it."

"*Something up?*"

"A job I was waiting on just came through. I need to pack."

"*Pack?*" He could hear the interest in Felix's voice. "*Where're you off to?*"

"I can't tell you," he answered, as if that answer would work. Felix knew full well that he worked only for the Agents of Aeneas. His friend was a former member of the secret society himself—one of the few former members that existed.

"Yeah, I know. So where're you off to?"

"Antarctica," he joked. "Why do you think all those penguins are looking for me?"

"Ah, yes. Should have known."

"I'll make sure to give you a call when I get back in town. Say 'hi' to Caitlin for me."

"Will do. And, hey. Be careful, whatever it is."

"Hey, I sit behind a keyboard for a living. The most I've got to worry about's carpal tunnel syndrome."

"And bad posture."

"That, too."

"Eye strain."

"Yes."

"Keyboard gnomes."

"I'll talk to you later, Felix."

"Have fun!"

Marc said good-bye and sat thinking. He had never been in space before, to say nothing of going to the Moon.

Hell, he didn't even like to fly.

Marc paused a moment to collect himself and study out of habit the various readouts on the heads-up display of the sunglasses-like data visor he habitually wore. The time read 1:17 p.m. Four wireless networks in the area. Room temperature was 70.5 degrees.

Space travel wouldn't be so bad, he supposed. Might even be fun.

"Holes?" he said finally.

"Yes, Mr. Triton?"

"I'm going to need to make some travel arrangements." After a moment, he added, "And probably some motion-sickness meds."

III

TWO DAYS LATER, Marc jerked awake as the passenger shuttle fell into orbit around the Moon. Remembering where he was, he stirred in his seat, stretching cramped muscles and yawning wide. He'd left his data visor on while sleeping, and its clock told him that he'd slept just under seven hours. Marc grunted, surprised. The seat wasn't as uncomfortable as he'd first expected.

Then again, he was in space. A wooden plank might have been just as comfortable in an environment that involved constant weightlessness.

He had felt that sensation for the first time on the first shuttle from Earth. Once he'd gotten used to it with the help of a friendly motion-sickness bag designed for just such a purpose, he found the sensation surprisingly marvelous. He once went snorkeling in Hawaii and had spent hours just drifting in the water. Actual weightlessness was even more liberating. He had just begun to enjoy it when the first shuttle had docked at Sunrise Station in Earth orbit. Designed to spin constantly to create artificial gravity, the station robbed him of his new fix.

Once he had boarded the lunar bound shuttle and felt that weightlessness again, he'd found himself wondering if there was such a thing as an anti-grav junkie. He also wondered if anyone would mind if he slipped out of his seat and did a few somersaults in the passenger cabin. Unfortunately, his stomach had done a few somersaults of its own at the thought and forced him to abandon the idea. He'd likely have made a fool of himself anyway.

Outside his window, the broad, gray landscape of the Moon had replaced the endless starlight, though he couldn't tell if their orbit was stable or if they'd begun their descent toward Alpha Station on the lunar surface.

Millions of years of cosmic bombardment rolled by below. Craters upon craters dotted the landscape in crowded formation amid mountains untouched by erosion. The shuttle continued in its orbit, and soon the scenery changed to darker, flatter expanses of lava fields long since cooled.

Marc watched it all beneath him and, wishing for a spot of color, set an orange packet of peanuts spinning in mid-air above his lap. It drifted out over his thigh and hit the seat in front of him before he decided to stop it.

He glanced out at the Moon again, and as he watched it float he began to hear "The Blue Danube." It sounded in a patient tempo, drifted in flow with the gray outside, and then repeated.

It didn't take terribly long to get on his nerves.

Marc released his seatbelt and allowed himself the indulgence of floating upward and turning around in a slightly dizzying spin. "Um, I don't suppose I could persuade you to stop whistling that?"

The young man behind him laughed. "Heh, yeah. Sorry, didn't even know I was doing it. Just kinda popped in there, you know? Yeah. You want another game while we wait to land?"

"No thanks. I'm still seeing lasers and plasma bombs when I close my eyes."

Playing *Darkstalker* on the seat consoles had been his only real contact with the man thus far. Their last session ate up over three hours, during which time Marc learned that the younger man's name was Nick, that he was also going to the Moon for ESA, and that he spent considerably more time playing first-person shooter games than Marc did.

"Yeah, you're just tired of losing, I think," Nick teased.

Marc laughed. "If I was tired of losing, I'd have stopped after the first hour."

"Hey, you managed to do okay after a while, though, yeah. I can't help it if I'm good. 'Sides, I bet you got a job that keeps you from playing all day like me."

"I tend to stay busy." Marc continued to float, steadying himself with a hand and enjoying the freedom. "So, um, how'd you get involved with ESA on this if you're unemployed? You don't even seem like you're from Europe."

Nick chortled. "Yeah, neither do you."

"No, they got me out of Portland," he lied. "But I have a resume."

"Yeah? Portland? I'm from Denver. And I didn't say I don't have a resume. Ask ESA. Hacked right into their satellite control center in Germany and gave it to them."

Marc blinked. "Gutsy. You're what, twenty?"

"Twenty-one. I didn't get too deep or break anything. Just enough to show 'em I got the skills, yeah?"

"What if they came after you?"

"Ah, why would they? I told 'em crystal how I got in, left a log of the whole hack, even said how to plug the hole. 'Sides, I didn't do it from my own rig."

"Oh?" Was Nick foolish or just a risk-taker?

"Snuck into one of the U of Colorado comp-sci labs and 'borrowed' an account. If they ever did try to ice me, one Leland T. Whitman would have had a *lot* of explaining to do." He grinned.

"So you hacked them, told them how to contact you. Anonymous email, I'm sure."

"Natch," Nick agreed. "Took 'em a few months, but yeah."

"How'd you know it wasn't a trick to find out who you were?"

"Nah, no chance. I wasn't worried." Nick leaned closer. "So part of me was scared shitless it might be. But if it was, why wait so long? No pain no gain, right?"

"So they say."

"Still good to know they tapped someone else for this job. I mean, you didn't hack 'em, too, right?"

"Me?" Marc chuckled. "No, never hacked them myself." Picked for the job via the machinations of a secret international society with ways to manipulate ESA from the inside? Sure. But he never actually hacked ESA himself.

"Yeah, see? I doubt they'd spend the cash to fly me all the way up here just to bust me." Marc considered telling him that it would be easier to hide a body that way, but opted to bite his tongue on the joke. Nick looked out the window. "Yeah, so now I'm up here spinning around the Moon and waiting to test some sort of new base computer or something."

The Moon turned dark beneath them as they crossed the Lunar terminator onto the far side.

"They give you any details?" Nick asked. "Like just what we're supposed to be testing?"

"ESA's not told me anything like that."

"Yeah, everything's some big secret nowadays. Like back in Denver, you hear about that? They evacuated part of the city around some office building and said it was a gas leak. Word on the 'Net got out that it was really some secret lab where a gray goo experiment got out of hand."

Marc feigned ignorance. "Gray goo?"

"Yeah, self-replicating nanobot stuff. They break down all the stuff they can find and build more of themselves. Spreads exponentially. They get out of control and pretty soon the whole city'd be a gray goo."

"Ah, I think I read a sci-fi story or seven about that. They can't really make that kind of thing."

"Maybe, maybe not. But that's what they say really happened. They had a breakthrough and nearly couldn't contain it. Got the government and corps pretty worried."

"Or so you heard on the 'Net," Marc said. He'd have to mention this in his AoA report; they'd be eager to know that rumors had spread. Marc made a mental note to encourage Nick to spread it around further while he was on the Moon.

"Like I said, everything's a cover-up." Nick sat back in his seat. "So you don't know what they want us to test up here, huh?"

Marc turned to watch the window and shook his head. "Not a clue," he lied.

* * *

Marette Clarion's brisk stride down the corridors of Alpha Station took her from her temporary quarters to the primary landing concourse. The exercise also served as a reminder that the Moon's gravity was making her soft.

She had been lunar-bound for over seven months now in her duty to the European Space Agency. Though that duty did allow her some precious little free time to keep in shape with the available—and recommended—increased-resistance exercise machines, she was often loath to do so. She possessed the capacity to focus on rising to her position in ESA and enough determination to remain undiscovered as an operative for the Agents of Aeneas, yet somehow she could not find the discipline to stick to an exercise regimen that involved any stationary machine.

Sitting in place and spinning her wheels felt too much like waiting.

Alpha Station's racquetball courts were the only real place she could get any satisfying exercise. There she could play using wrist, ankle, and hip weights. Yet her work at the excavation site made such indulgences few and far between. Her shortest time between games was eight days.

She rounded a corner and caught sight of the shuttle's final approach. She would be slightly early. More waiting. Ironic that she'd spent so much of her time in the past year waiting. Perhaps, she mused, it added to her reluctance to use the machines.

Though a great deal of progress had been made, such progress came in surges. First, the AoA found evidence of something in the Aristarchus crater, led ESA to that evidence, and then waited for them to react. Six months ago, ESA sent a commercial mining crew to the crater, and then waited for them to discover the craft. ESA cleared the immediate area within the ship of the lethal security drones that had slaughtered the first team sent inside, and then the AoA waited while ESA constructed an on-site base of operations. They learned that the strange black liquid "skin" coating the ship inside was some sort of computer, determined a way to access it at the simplest level to open a few doors, and then had to wait again for some deeper means to interface with it in order to go any further.

Now they had found such a means, and still found cause to wait. While there was always work to be done, and caution was a prime concern in order to safeguard lives, Marette was always aware of the waiting.

It took about five minutes for the shuttle passengers to disembark once she arrived at the terminal. The majority were workers for any of the various mining companies that the Space Agency allowed lunar contracts. A few might have been tourists. Mixed among them all were the three she came to meet, one of whom would be another AoA operative.

Marette first greeted the woman: an Asian with a cropped hair dyed red and an English accent whom Marette knew to be an encryption expert who sometimes contracted with ESA. One of the first out of the tunnel, she spotted Marette's uniform and made a beeline toward her to introduce herself as Suzanne Namura.

Marette shook her hand but detected nothing.

The others arrived together. She guessed by the data visor over his eyes that the older of the two with the darker hair was Marc Triton, a network specialist and artificial intelligence programmer from Portland in America. The other, who would therefore be Nicholas Boyd, looked much too young to be there at all.

"Good day, gentlemen," she offered. "Mr. Boyd and Mr. Triton, I presume?"

They both nodded, offering their hands, and Marette shook Nick's first. Again, nothing.

"I am ESA Field Chief Marette Clarion."

She shook Triton's hand. The small hum against her palm confirmed her supposition: he was the one. A knowing look passed between them and Marette tried to hide from the others the extra welcome she felt for a kindred spirit after being on her own for so long.

"It would seem you two have already met," she continued. "This is Ms. Namura, one of the others with whom you will be working on this project."

She waited as the three said hello.

"Yeah, so are we it?" Nicholas asked with a glance behind him.

"You are the last to arrive. The others are housed in the habitat wing where you will be boarded for the duration of the project. There will be time to meet them tonight if you wish, though I recommend you spend the evening resting and adjusting to the lunar clock. We depart for the project site tomorrow morning at 0800 hours. If you come with me, I will show you to your quarters."

Marette led them out of the main concourse down corridors lined with narrow windows that allowed a view of the vacuum outside. Beneath the windows, tiny ferns bordered a thin stream built into a shelf along the walls. The ferns grew in soil brought from Earth, took their water from the stream, and took the light they needed from the full spectrum lights that illuminated the corridors. It was designed to help visitors from Earth feel more at ease, and after having walked such corridors for over half a year, Marette barely noticed them herself anymore unless escorting visitors.

Namura increased her pace to walk beside her. "Can you give us a rundown of the project? I'd like to get a jump on things if I could."

Marette shook her head. "For security reasons, ESA wishes to hold any briefing at the project site."

"0800 hours, security reasons," she heard Nicholas quote behind her. "Look out guys, we've been drafted."

"Is that a complaint, Mr. Boyd?"

"Heh. Just observing." He flashed a puerile grin.

"Good," she told him. "You have not been drafted, but will be expected to adhere to all guidelines set by the Space Agency and myself." She opened the door to the habitat wing and turned to face him. "Such guidelines are in place for ESA security and your own safety. We *are* in space, Mr. Boyd, as a man of your intelligence has certainly determined."

Nicholas chuckled and gave a show of saluting. "Aye, aye, ma'am. I can be good for awhile."

"If you have a problem doing so, ESA is perfectly willing to allow you access to a space suit so you may walk home to Earth." Marette allowed herself the luxury of a smirk.

Nicholas laughed aloud. "Hey, look, Marc!" he cried, clapping Marc on the back, "Our boss has a sense of humor! Ya know, kinda."

Marette merely smiled. Humor or no, she hoped he would take the warning for what it was. She ushered them through the doorway in silence.

The silence didn't last long. "Shit!" Nick declared. "We're on the fuckin' *Moon!*"

"Just clued to that, did you?" Namura asked.

Nicholas laughed again. "Yeah, hey, I've never been off-planet. Takes a while to sink in."

Marette sighed inwardly. As one once drawn to the wonder of space herself, she could not blame Nick for being excited. Yet the prospect of having to deal with a boisterous juvenile did not please her. It was some comfort that he would not have been there if he were incompetent, but he was so young.

The first team she had sent inside the ship had met with a massacre.

For what might have been the thousandth time, she saw their lifeless bodies on the midnight floor of the entrance. She saw their faces, burned into her memory.

"Much too young," she whispered.

Nearly half an hour later, after getting the three settled in their quarters and filing the appropriate reports, Marette touched the signal key on Marc Triton's door. He opened it a moment later.

She nodded to his greeting and then stepped through the hatch as he retreated to make room. His luggage and equipment lay out across the compact chamber, covering his bunk and a small countertop that served as a desk. She caught a glimpse of his more personal wardrobe choices before turning to seal the door behind her. Marette rested her back against it a moment later and released a long sigh.

"Rough day?" Triton asked.

"*Oui.* Rough month." She opened her eyes and caught the sympathy in his smile. "Have you ever been the sole operative on any AoA mission, Mr. Triton?"

"Just Marc works fine," he said. "And, no. Most of what I do's in the privacy of my own home." He closed his bag and sat down on the edge of the bed. His hair was slightly wet; he must have showered after arriving. "I'd guess it's pretty draining being on your guard so much."

"Very much so. I see others of us from time to time, but I am the only one constantly here."

"I don't imagine you can attend the Council meetings from here, either."

She shook her head. "Even without the difficulties it causes the AoA encryption protocols, the transmission delay itself would make real-time attendance problematic at best. I receive transcripts."

Marc nodded. "We can connect loads of people all around the world to a virtual meeting, but go off-planet and that damn speed of light gets ya."

"I often consider it a reminder of why we are here. Breaking the barrier," she told him. "You are from Portland?"

"Actually, Northgate. The AoA figured it'd be best not to give my real address when they got me into this."

"A wise precaution."

Marette studied him for a moment. He was not much taller than she, with a lean, comfortable frame topped with a head of dark brown hair. His hair was trimmed, though she could see the hint of a curl where it grew thicker toward the back. A gentle face was set off by a neat goatee around his mouth and the oblong data visor that formed a shield over his eyes. She wondered what color they were beneath it.

Marette moved closer and took the seat at the tiny desk. "How much do you know? My briefing was incomplete in that regard."

"Well, obviously not everything makes it to the rest of us, detail-wise." He pulled something from his pocket. "Lifesaver?" She thanked him but declined the candy, which he put away before continuing. "Long story short, I know the black lining inside the ship is some sort of computer, I know ESA managed an interface of some sort, and I know I'm here to keep a closer eye on things while we try to figure out what's inside. Anything I missed?"

"Just, as you say, detail-wise." She clasped her hands and tapped her chin. "The ship—ESA has codenamed it *Paragon*—would appear to be a product of organic and inorganic engineering. The black material is obviously organic. It effectively breathes carbon dioxide, changing it to oxygen like a plant. ESA believes it may also be part of a complex life support system."

"Pretty ingenious."

She nodded. "Except thus far we have encountered no trace of life to be supported. I expect such traces may be found once we have gained access to the rest of the structure."

"Do you know why the touch gooey stopped opening doors?"

"I am sorry, 'gooey'?"

"Acronym," Marc said. "Graphical user interface."

"Ah, G-U-I, *oui*." She should not have had to ask him. Technical acronyms in another language. "No, we know not why. There is a debate over whether it is due to our not knowing some code sequence, or that further passages are simply designed to be opened by other means."

"What do you think?"

"I think we do not know enough about the language of the interface to be completely certain of anything. Linguistic analysis is still incomplete and is lacking in some key details."

"So we need a Rosetta Stone."

"*Oui.* That is one objective you and the others will attempt to accomplish, though they will be unaware of this. But any data you find is likely to add to our knowledge."

"And our other objectives?"

"Data about *Paragon* itself. Technical or operational. We have discovered that the organic computer interfaces with the inorganic structure of the craft. There are access ports distributed throughout the walls: small cylindrical sockets that the black material fills in order to interface with the physical structure and control systems. Theoretically. New Eden Biotechnics is working on a synthetic replacement that will allow us to bypass the, ah, alien material by using our own, but it is not yet ready. And without more knowledge of how the two systems relate, it may not be of much use."

"You hesitated on the word 'alien' there," he said. "It's a pretty fitting word, isn't it? This thing didn't come from Earth."

"It is fitting. But here?" She shook her head. "The drones inside that ship have killed ten people, Marc. I try not to hurt morale with terms that conjure images of science fiction and horror. There are those who believe that the reason we are unable to open more doors is that something does not wish us to."

Marc nodded, brows furrowing. "And what do you think?"

Marette paused to throw her gaze out the room's narrow window. She recalled Alberto, the Agents of Aeneas operative who was with her during the initial exploration. She heard him scream with the rest of the team when the first drone exterminated them. Marette quickly blocked it from her mind and turned back to Marc. "I think that ESA should not have sent a child to us."

"Nick?"

"Nicholas, yes. Your group will be working in the base outside of the structure. There should be minimum risk." Was she trying to reassure him, or herself?

The worry that had haunted her since the incident swelled up from inside. She pushed it back down out of habit and let out a silent chuckle. "I am used to not talking about this. As you said, it is difficult to be on guard so much. It has become almost automatic." She cursed softly in French, shook her head, and tried to explain. "To speak of feelings is to let the listener in. If someone gets in a little, they could go further. I cannot risk exposing the AoA's position here." She looked for understanding in his eyes, but could not see beyond the visor.

"Er, well." He shrugged with a smile. "I mean, we're both AoA, so, you know, talk away. If you want." He shrugged again.

Marette considered it. She trusted him as she would any member of the AoA; the affiliation connected them intimately. Yet her thoughts were too jumbled in the cage she kept them in to come out smoothly.

"I would not know where to begin. I have been on my guard so long. It is like . . . " She paused to get a handle on the feeling and then decided on impulse, stepping a bit closer. "Like many things, I suppose. A breaking of the ice, or the first time undressing before another. "

Marc chuckled. Was he uncomfortable? Again, she looked in his eyes out of instinct only to be blocked by the visor.

"May I ask you a question?" she tried.

"Go ahead."

She reached out and traced the edge of his visor. "Does that thing come off?" He was the first fellow agent she had been face to face with in over a month, and the first man she didn't have to be on her guard around in nearly four times as long. She wanted to see his eyes.

"Er, it comes off. Though I'm used to having it on. Functional fashion, I guess." He brushed his fingertips along the edge of the reflective covering. He had very nice hands.

"We all have our walls to hide behind."

He nodded. "Outside of a few friends and the AoA, I guess I'm not really what you'd call a 'people person.' Mostly I'm behind a computer, so I've usually got it on." He shrugged and then seemed to realize something. "Not that I'm ignoring you, I mean, it's just, background or—it's hard to explain. But if it'd help, I could take it off."

Marette smirked. "You take off your clothing if I take off my own, so to speak?"

He laughed. "If you want to put it that way."

Was he oblivious? "That is a dangerous topic of conversation, Marc."

His eyebrows furrowed again slightly. "Er?"

She smiled once more at his . . . Was it discomfort or merely confusion? It would not be so difficult to slide over onto the bunk where he sat. Not entirely wise, perhaps, but not difficult. "It is curious what an oasis of trust can do when one has been keeping watch in the desert," she whispered.

"How do you mean?" He was forming words again, at least. Would it be so unfair to indulge in a physical impulse after so many months discipline? Human comfort, that's all it was, but if he was uncomfortable . . .

"There are racquetball courts here at Alpha Station," she said suddenly. "Do you play racquetball, Marc?"

Eyebrows raised above the visor preceded a reply of, "Not often, but I've played before." He was getting quicker, though still struggling slightly. "Are you suggesting a game, or . . . ?"

"I am suggesting a game," she answered as she stood. "This is my first time away from the site in two weeks, and I am needing, shall we say, exercise."

"I've got a bit of energy left in me yet tonight." Marc slapped his hands on his jeans-covered thighs. "Let's go."

"*Bien*." She smiled. It was either racquetball or something more private, and perhaps it was for the best that the door opened to her touch before she could say so. "And you already have the eye gear."

I V

MARC AWOKE with a stretch the following morning to find his thighs burning. The sky was just as black as when he'd gone to bed, but at least the clock told the right story. Well, mostly right. His alarm wasn't set to go off for another half hour.

After putting on his visor to check the familiar readouts of his primary computer—a book-sized "hip rig" he felt naked without—he hugged his thighs up against his chest and counted to thirty. Marc liked racquetball, but he hadn't played in over two years. The constant bursts of running and stopping on the court had taken their toll. The wrist and ankle weights he'd worn to counter the low gravity likely hadn't helped either. Marette wore them, and he'd told her—and himself—that for him to do otherwise wouldn't be fair; he wanted to play on even ground. Okay, so there was likely a bit of macho pride involved too, but normally he was far from the macho type. A small dose in the name of a fair game wouldn't hurt, right?

They had played four matches in just under an hour, during which time Marette beat him just under five times. Except for the third game, when Marc only managed three points, the matches were reasonably close. He'd wondered if she was going easy on him.

They'd talked, then, of simple things unconnected with the AoA or their mission, as if they were just two new friends sitting against the court wall getting to know each other. She told him what drew her to ESA. He shared the details of his life on Earth. Marc surprised himself with how easily he talked to her. Maybe it was the attention she'd shown him, or purely that she seemed to need the connection with a fellow agent.

Or heck, maybe he just liked her. There was something about her that made him more comfortable than he was around most women.

The two of them talked for he didn't know how long and then walked, tired, back to his quarters.

It was then that they'd said good night. In truth, he almost invited her in. Somewhat. On the racquetball court, watching her dash in front of him, muscles pushing hard beneath her workout gear, the thought crossed his mind often. But that was hardly appropriate, was it?

After all, he'd gotten no clear signals of anything physical from her. If he invited her to act on those feelings when she wasn't receptive . . . Well, it would put a kink in their working together, to say the least. He wasn't used to making such invitations anyway. It was more than likely that he would have just made a fool of himself.

And yet, lying there with the benefit of a full night's sleep to help his thinking, previously-missed signals began to show themselves. Were they really signals, or merely the product of her being from another culture? Or her relief at seeing another soul from the AoA? When they had said good night at his door, she had offered to wake him in the morning. There was a look in her eyes then. Maybe. Was there? She was rather tactile with him all night when they'd played and chatted. Not overwhelmingly so. But it could have been something.

Maybe.

Or maybe she was just that way with everyone. She didn't seem to be when she was with the others, though. The conclusion he'd drawn in those few moments in front of the door was uncertain enough to keep him from doing anything about it. Besides, he'd only just met the woman.

He lay there a while longer while the issue chased itself through his brain, and then he found himself doing some idle computer maintenance via his visor. Fifteen minutes later it became clear that he wasn't going to be falling back asleep in time for it to matter when the alarm went off. Marc tossed the sheets away, swung himself out of the bunk, and crossed the cramped room to the shower.

"I'm about to hack into an alien computer and I'm worried about a woman," he muttered. "Stick to what you know, Marc."

Standard lunar water rationing made for a brief shower. He was dried and stepping into his pants before he would have normally even turned off the water. The door signal chimed a second later. It was her.

"Just a sec," he called. Modesty made him reach for his shirt before he stopped to think for a moment. Answering the door shirtless wouldn't be completely unusual, would it? *Oh, what the hell.* He unlocked the door and opened it. In the fraction of a second it took to slide open, he realized that Marette might not be alone, and he felt very underdressed.

She was alone.

That previous bothersome thought lingered just long enough to make him hesitate. It was Marette who spoke first. "*Bonjour.* Up already, I see?"

"Good morning," he said with a nod. "I woke up early and couldn't get back to sleep so . . . " He shrugged. He also realized that in his hesitation he'd completely missed noting her first reaction when she saw him shirtless. So much for his test.

"It would seem you did not need a wake-up after all."

"Still nice of you to check," he managed. "Come in." He turned from the door to get a shirt. She came in silently. The door closed behind her. "Any new developments?" He couldn't think of what else to say. Falling back on work seemed best. Work was good. Work was comfortable.

"Nothing new since last night, Mr. Triton. To my knowledge."

He pulled the shirt over his head and turned back toward her. "'Mr. Triton?'" He tried to mask his disappointment.

"After last night, I thought the less familiar was more appropriate."

"I had a good time last night."

"As did I."

Okay? "So . . . "

"So."

He shook his head. "Forget it." He moved back to grab his watch. When he turned to face her again, she was a step closer.

"You gave the impression of being eager to end it."

"I wasn't," he said, and managed to meet her gaze. "I wasn't sure how you—what you . . . "

Something flashed in her brown eyes that might have been amusement. "Are all American men so thickheaded?"

"Ah, just me, I think. I'm not really, uh . . . "

"Take off the visor, Marc," she told him. He didn't say anything. He just did as she asked. She took the prosthetic from him and stepped softly into his space. "You have very nice eyes," she whispered. Her own gazed back at him, dark and deep.

"So do you."

"If I had told you such a thing last night, would you have been sure?" Her body was close. The heat of his shower still hovered above his skin. He could feel her brush against that aura. He let go of his thoughts and kissed her.

It was just a light touch, just the barest whisper of his lips across hers. One brush, then another. His fingertips drifted over her hand, and she took his in a way that pulled the kiss deeper. He breathed her in. Their bodies melted together. Arms tightened. He could feel her heart pounding his.

Something was beeping.

Muffled between them, something was beeping. Marette broke away with what sounded like a curse and pulled a communicator from her belt. "This is Clarion."

He watched her as she talked. Her eyes avoided his until she signed off.

"*Je suis désolé,* I am needed," she apologized.

Marc watched her breathing slow. "Problem?"

She shook her head. "*Non.* But there are things that must be done before you and the others assemble." She kissed him again firmly and lingered just a moment. "This is why you must not hesitate," she told him before heading for the door. "Assemble with the others in Shuttle Bay Two at 0800 hours."

And with that, she was gone. Marc sat down on the bunk, pulled out a laptop, and kicked himself.

V

THE ARISTARCHUS CRATER SITE loomed on the hackers' horizon, and Marc spent the cramped, fifty-minute shuttle trip meeting the rest of the team. He talked with them, he listened — well, mostly he listened. There were others, Nick and a blond German by the name of Gunther, who did most of the talking. Marc was content to listen anyway.

Gunther did not particularly look like a "Gunther." To Marc, the name always seemed like it should belong to a muscular bald man with a multitude of scars who didn't talk much. He didn't know any other Gunthers, to say nothing of one who matched that image, but the association had always been there nevertheless. This Gunther was thin, unscarred, and pleasant, with what seemed to be a friendly intelligence behind his chatter.

Along with Suzanne Namura, the Asian woman with whom he and Nick had arrived, there were three others: two women and one man. Unlike Namura, the other women were of European descent. One, named Elsa Litzenburg, was tall with short, dark hair. The other, who only introduced herself as Maria, was a foot shorter, with hair just as dark in a tight ponytail, and a data visor similar to Marc's own. Elsa seemed the more sociable of the two and often got a word in between Nick and Gunther's banter. Maria kept as quiet as Marc did.

Still quieter was the man, a Brit named Nigel Marley. He took the rearmost seat and, aside from his introduction at the beginning, didn't say much at all. To Marc's surprise, it was Nick who finally tried to get him involved.

"Yeah, you're pretty quiet back there, Nigel. You get all your sleep?"

Nigel's eyes flicked up to look at them all. He shrugged, began to say something, and then paused on the edge of a stammer. "Bad dreams," he said finally.

Gunther went on to talk about previous odd dreams he had experienced over the course of his life, and Maria turned around in her seat to say something more to Nigel. Marc couldn't hear what was said.

Marette spent the flight in the cockpit beside the pilot. Before boarding the shuttle, everyone asked more about the project. She dismissed the questions as she had the previous night and assured them that she would give a full briefing when they arrived at the site. Once in flight, her seating position served to keep her out of the circle of conversation. She wasn't avoiding him, but Marc did wonder if she was intentionally distancing herself from the others.

He also wondered if being a double agent was taking its toll on her. Their talk the previous night obviously indicated that she found it difficult. But then, who wouldn't? Each day here in the service of ESA was at least partially a lie for her, and now ESA was making her lie to the hacker team on top of that. Marc worked only for the Agents of Aeneas, with no cover affiliation. He still had to keep secrets, yes, but Marette's duty was far beyond that. Undertaking this mission added to his life a small fraction of the stress Marette dealt with every day, and he was already feeling it. How did she cope?

The question remained unanswered as they made a final approach to the crater site. The pilot banked the shuttle and kept their approach vector such that none of them were given a complete view. Marc was sure it was intentional. Based on what he'd learned from AoA reports, he knew that ESA had expanded the originally excavated sub-lunar tunnel along *Paragon's* side to create an oblong, concave depression that extended outward and was now open to space above. They then constructed the complex at which they were landing up against the side of the alien ship. *Paragon* itself was not supposed to be visible from above. Tarps concealed parts of *Paragon* not hidden by the complex or still buried under the lunar surface. The pilot's care ensured that Marc was unable to see for himself if the reports were accurate.

After their landing, Marette led them out through a gantry and down a short series of corridors more visually sterile than any hospital Marc had seen. They wound up in what appeared to be a control room. A second door sat in the center of a bank of terminals across the room.

Inactive video screens framed the two shorter adjoining walls, and a large conference table strewn with a myriad of interfaces dominated the room's center. Marette motioned for the seven of them to sit. As they all deposited their equipment on the table, she moved to one of the screens.

"Welcome to ESA Lunar Research Complex Omicron," Marette announced. The display screen flickered to life to show the ESA logo within a crescent moon. "This complex, when complete, will house the bulk of the Space Agency's classified lunar research. Your purpose here today is to test the security of the base's encryption and data storage network in accordance with a number of worst-case scenarios."

There was a slight murmur of anticipatory body language around the conference table. Nick shot Marc a grin.

"The Omicron Complex is connected to external ESA networks through a series of redundant links, the nature of which I am not permitted to discuss with you. The integrity of these links is being tested by another group, which, for security purposes that are no doubt clear, will function independently of your own. Your group will operate under the scenario that external security protocols have failed. You will therefore have full access to the complex's internal systems."

Though Marc nodded with the rest of them, like Marette, he knew there was no other team, or even an operational external link. Though a data link via standard radio *could* be established in an emergency from within—and only from within—Omicron, any data leaving the complex otherwise would need to be physically carried out. But for the cover story to fit, they needed to say there was an external way to connect to the complex. Why hack-test a mainframe that was physically inaccessible? ESA certainly wasn't going to tell them what they were truly hacking into.

He supposed there really was another team of sorts, once. After all, ESA had managed to create the link to the ship via an interface they'd reverse engineered from the ports lining *Paragon*'s interior beneath the black substance. They uncovered one of the ports and installed their own construction atop it. When the black stuff was allowed to consume the area once more, it accepted the artificial port for the one it was covering, and an active connection was made. But now that the door to the metaphorical crypt was unsealed, after the tragedy of the first physical entry six months prior, they were sending in the expendable diggers first.

Charming.

"Your first objective is basic," Marette continued. "Get in. Once — or if — you obtain access, you are to test the limits of that access. We have deposited a selection of junk data into the mainframe of the complex. Get out with what you can."

Gunther raised his hand and spoke. "So there will be no particular data we're looking for?"

"Not at first. Initially, get what you can. The junk data will be encrypted. In subsequent stages of this operation, you will test the individual file encryption."

"What sort of encryption are we talking about, exactly?" It was Namura this time.

Marette smiled. "That will be part of the test, Ms. Namura. You are the encryption expert. I am told that you may expect a challenge."

The Asian woman grinned. "Something new then?" Her British accent still threw him.

"Most definitely."

It was Marc's turn to ask a question. "Is there a time limit?" An ESA imposed time limit would be illogical under the circumstances, but asking helped Marette point out that they could take time to be cautious.

"There is no operational time limit for this phase. The Space Agency wishes to determine *if* you can crack it, not how fast. Our computer scientists do not expect you to succeed."

"Ja, and where are these scientists so that we may rub their faces in it when we prove them wrong?" Gunther asked. The table chuckled collectively. Even Nigel managed a smirk.

Marette smiled but let the question go unanswered. "You have all brought your personal equipment with you. As promised, you will be supplied with any additional resources you feel you may need. Connections, of course, will be achieved through the interface table before you . . . "

Marette continued to detail the technical elements of the operation — the few ESA knew, anyway. As he listened to the cover story, Marc examined the table before him, planning. He already intended to ask for an artificial intelligence matrix: something simple to handle the data switching and analysis. It felt strange to think that when he plugged in, the thing on the other end would be an alien computer.

As he made a show of listening to the superfluous briefing, the thought continued to occupy his mind.

The remainder of the briefing, questions and all, took another twenty minutes. Equipment requisition and set-up ate another forty. Then they began to cook. There was much discussion of strategy. Most of the hackers seemed unaccustomed to working in a group. Egos and ideas rubbed up against each other, but fortunately didn't collide. After the first hour, the group managed to agree not only that they needed more information about the system, but, more importantly, just how to go about acquiring it.

The tests began. Virtual feints were used to test the system: delicate, minor incursions just potent enough to trigger an alert response that could then be measured, analyzed, and modeled. Nigel, seeming to be both the most cautious and the most patient, coordinated the tedious process. The entire group handled the analysis, though Elsa and Maria appeared to be the most practiced at it. Marc handled the data management and, with the help of the junior A.I. he'd requested, created a rudimentary construct of what might be the inner workings of the alien system.

The A.I. was also secretly recording and transmitting every moment to an AoA link Marette had prepared.

Just after three-thirty in the afternoon, Marc was attempting to sum up what they had figured out so far. "So what we're looking at," he started, "is a level-five-equivalent security grid supported by either a human sysop with A.I. assistance or a fully automated A.I. that appears to outclass third-F capabilities."

"They don't have a sysop," Maria said. "The data's just not right for it."

"But you can't quantify that," argued Gunther.

"Not specifically, no. It's just not reacting the way a human would. They've come up with a revolutionary A.I. It must be."

"Yeah, Marc's the expert on that," Nick said. "What do you think?"

Marc knew it wasn't anything human on the other end. "Maria's right. What we're seeing might be the result of a few first-Fs in tandem somehow, but ESA's proud of something. I'd say they've come up with a new class. Something experimental."

"Yeah, makes sense," Nick agreed. He let out another of the exasperated sighs that had punctuated most of his arguments for the past hour. "So now we've gotta do even more tests to figure out what this—what, it'd be a first-G, yeah? What this first-G can do?"

Elsa stood by the wall monitor, rubbed her temples, and sighed. "I don't know that there are more tests we can do. Not that I'm aware of. Not without just going in."

Marc looked around the room. "Like I said, it behaves most like a few first-Fs in tandem. If we have to, we can proceed on that. Unless anyone knows any more tricks we can run on it from outside, it might be time to go in." He waited. Gunther opened his mouth but shut it before saying anything. No one else offered any suggestions.

"Great!" Nick grinned. "So we go in!"

Marc's stomach knotted.

V I

THE FACT that Nigel Marley chose not to use a wet-link both frustrated and relieved Marette. Direct neural links were widely accepted as more efficient and effective for the sort of intrusion the team was to attempt. This group had been picked to get results, and they should all be using the best tools for the job. Even so, the lack of one would make for an interface more separated from whatever they were about to tap into.

There was no danger that Marette could consciously name, but the total destruction of the first team that physically entered *Paragon* continued to haunt her. Nigel's separation provided a small measure of comfort for which she was both grateful and resentful of her own need.

"Call me old-fashioned," Nigel said. "I prefer to use my hands."

"Yeah, that's what she said!" Nicholas called out with a snicker.

Gunther slipped an interface cord into his bio-port. "You don't think you could handle things faster if you jacked in?"

"I've never had cause to complain before. I've got a custom interface. Optics based." He pointed to his eyes. "It's fast enough."

"Yes, but there's more than just speed at stake," Namura said. "Perceptions of your environment. I know I just plain understand things better. Especially doing encryption work."

Nigel shrugged. "I don't like having the world's finger in my brain."

From beside one of the wall monitors, Marette decided that she disliked that particular metaphor.

"Everybody hooked up?" Marc asked.

All answered affirmative save Nicholas and Namura, who awaited a go signal. The team's plan was to use the bulk of their energies to run multiple decoy attacks against the system in an effort to draw on its resources and, essentially, distract it. The other two would then attempt to slip into the protected areas and come away with data. Marc appeared reasonably confident in the idea. She was pleased with his attempt to provide the group with some leadership. He was doubtless more comfortable in this arena than in that of the previous night.

And then, as Marette observed them from her position beside the wall monitor, the first group was in. Eyes closed to block out distractions, the hackers slipped into a world of code and altered perception. Nigel remained engrossed in his own rig's screen. His fingers clicked as his gaze darted across the readouts. Nicholas and Namura sat waiting, eyes on the wall monitor. Nigel had devised a way to gauge the percent of system resources directed toward the first team's distraction. It was estimation only, based on theory and assumption, but it was the best indicator they had to work with. The remaining two hackers would wait until the percentage had reached a certain point, and then make their runs.

It was an uphill climb. The first diversionary hits raised it to 20 percent before it leveled off. They set more intrusion programs running, all designed to eat up system resources with tests and tasks. Marette did not understand every detail, but she understood enough to know that they were feeding more and more into the system, piling their own processing power atop it in an attempt to make it buckle, and constantly adjusting existing attacks while sending in new ones. Marette quietly linked one of the main ESA computers into Marc's already augmented rig and added its power to the onslaught.

The readout reached 85 percent and Nigel spoke without looking up. "I think that may be as high as we're going to get it. Go."

Nicholas and Namura acknowledged. Their eyes shut. They were in.

Marette wished she could see what they saw or do more beyond standing by the wall. The two hackers called out instructions and status to each other as they began their intrusion.

"We can't make a dent in this sodding thing yet," Namura said after the first few minutes. "Can you punch it up a bit, Nigel?"

"No promises."

Marc turned his head toward Marette. His eyes might have been open and focused on her, but that cursed visor prevented her from being sure until he motioned to the A.I. sending data to the AoA. His eyebrows raised in a question. She could guess at what the question was. Allowing the A.I. to discontinue the transmission and add its full resources to the effort might give the second team some breathing room.

She nodded. Marc made the switch. ESA was making its own records. The AoA would have to get its copy later.

The system readout reached 90 percent.

"Yeah, I got something!" Nicholas called a moment later. "What the hell, this is some screwed up structuring in here."

Marette watched the storage disks fill with a few hundred megabytes of data that would instantly be copied and shunted to protected storage.

Namura shouted in triumph and the storage increased by a factor of one hundred. "Ha! You got the first bite but I got the big one!"

"Yeah, we'll see about—Ah, shit!" Nicholas shouted.

"What happened?" Marc shot, giving voice to Marette's own thoughts.

"I'm kicked out!"

"Same here," Namura said.

"We're all still in over here," said Nigel. Everyone providing the distraction remained connected.

"Yeah. I don't give up that easily."

"Right behind you," Namura called. "Arseholes and elbows."

Marette glanced at the system readout: 92 percent.

"Uh, hang a bit there," Nigel warned. "I'm getting some odd readings."

"Define odd?" Namura asked.

The readout jumped to 98 percent.

"Uh, Marc?" Nigel sounded confused.

"I'm getting it, too," Marc said. "Hang on."

"Yeah, getting what?"

"Guys, I'm showing 107 percent system operation. Something's not right."

"So your estimator's off," Elsa said. "We're still good to go."

Namura licked her lips. "Closing in on another big file here."

"Sure, take all the juicy ones yourself, yeah?" Nicholas told her.

"You got it, love."

They both forged ahead. The readout jumped to 130 percent.

Marc shot Marette a look that she felt through his visor. "Suzanne, back off! This A.I.'s—Shit, something's not right."

"Marc's right, something's bollocksed," Nigel called.

180 percent.

Marette took a step forward and then stopped herself. She'd have to wait for Marc before she could act without blowing cover. *Merde.*

"Hang on, yeah? She's almost got it."

"We're supposed to be testing this thing," Namura said. "Just hang on."

"She's right." It was Elsa again. "Push it!"

"No!"

"I've almost got it!"

"Right behind you," called Nicholas.

The readout went blank.

"You don't understand!" Marc grabbed the link to Nicholas's rig and ripped it out of the socket.

The young man's eyes snapped open. Surprise flashed to anger. "What the hell!"

Marc's action freed Marette. She rushed to another terminal as he dove toward the table's control hub. A second before either of them made it, Namura screamed. Her rig flared in a blaze of electric fire a moment before Marette cut the power and the lights went out.

The glow of the flame died quickly in the darkness. There was just enough silence to let it fade before everyone started shouting.

VII

FELIX HIATT SAT in a lab in Horizon Research's Northgate facility and, gingerly, touched a diagnostic cable connected to the memory implant behind his right ear. It still wasn't a sensation he was used to. "Sometimes I wonder about what happens to me if this thing borks out and I lose everything."

The tech, peering at readouts on a screen hidden from Felix's view, spared a quick glance up to ask, "Everything?"

"Yes, Neal, everything. *Tout le monde*, the whole nine yards. Hey, did you know 'the whole nine yards' refers to using the entire length of an ammo belt in World War Two?"

Neal chuckled. "Can't say as I did. You've got quite a bit in there, don't you?" He pointed at Felix's head.

"Oh, plenty. And more of it dealing with asparagus than you'd guess, too," Felix joked. "That's why I wonder so much. We know this thing somehow affects my own memory, so what happens to me if it all blanks out? You have to admit, it's an interesting question. At least I have to admit it; you're free to admit whatever you wish. Though I wouldn't admit you picked out that tie without a lawyer present."

"My wife bought me this tie."

"Say no more." Felix grinned. Feeling this chatty was hardly a unique mood for him, but sometimes during his checks he spent the time just trying to learn all he could about how his implant actually worked. By now, he figured he'd gleaned as much of the technical stuff that he could grasp without a degree, so lately he was usually content to try to drag Neal (perhaps kicking and screaming) into a philosophical discussion.

Apparently satisfied with what he saw on the screen before him, Neal leaned back from the terminal, clasped his hands behind his head, and asked, "So you wonder how you'd know where you live, who your friends are? Like that?"

"You're being too topical. I mean, what happens to Felix Hiatt. How much do my memories affect who I am?"

Neal shrugged. "I think even if you forgot all you know, you'd still be you. Amnesiacs don't suddenly take on different personalities."

"Ah, but what if this thing's different? When you guys stuck it in me you were just trying to add someone else's memories to mine, but then we find out it's augmenting my ability to remember new things, too. It's not just tacked on like you all thought it'd be, so if it goes, who knows how much it takes with it?"

Realistically, Felix hadn't had a blip of trouble since helping Diomedes and Flynn find the vigilante Gideon six months ago. Horizon had fixed it quickly enough then so that the search wasn't hindered. Diomedes also killed Gideon in cold blood shortly thereafter. Okay, so things didn't always turn out well, but that didn't have anything to do with the implant.

"You're in here for testing every month," Neal assured him. "It won't go."

Felix grinned again. "And don't think I don't appreciate it, even if you've got no choice." The project was long since shut down, but the Cybernetic Research Act of 2038 made researchers responsible for taking care of any lasting effects. The litigation that would result from failure to do so made it much more cost effective for them to not abandon their test subjects. In a world where the police were falling apart, it was the lawyers who enforced the laws. "But what I'm getting at here, if you'd listen, is the question of how much of who we are is dictated by our memories."

"That's philosophy." Neal smiled. "I'm a scientist."

Yep, kicking and screaming. "You ran a project on downloading the entire memory record of a human brain. You mean to tell me you didn't at least consider the question?"

"I didn't run it, Mr. Supposed Photographic Memory, just assisted."

"Close enough. You've never thought about it?"

"I've been doing your tune-ups for this long and we've never had this discussion before, either," he said. "So, no. Not in those terms, anyway. Did you become any different when you suddenly had another man's lifetime of memories added in with yours?"

"It's let me see someone else's viewpoint on things. I think it did affect me in some ways. But did it change me completely? No."

"There's your answer, then."

"Ah, but I know those aren't my memories kicking around in here. I knew who I was when they got put in. It's different."

Neal apparently noticed something on his screen and leaned forward again. "Probably better not to worry about it. And you check out just fine here."

Felix nodded and began to unplug. "I didn't say I was worried, I said I wondered. You can relate to that? Wondering?"

Neal gathered up the cables. "Yeah, but I'm not getting paid to wonder about this anymore. The project's shut down. The data's been sold off. You, my friend, are simply housekeeping as far as anyone here is concerned."

Felix laughed. "Nice to know where I stand."

Neal led Felix toward the exit. "I mean as far as the company is concerned. I don't want you to lose your memory any more than you do, but to answer the kind of question you're asking would take a psychologist or something. I'm just a humble neurological cybernetics research technician." He opened the door for Felix and smiled. "See you next month."

"I sure hope so!" He headed out the door, but then stopped and turned back. "You wanna tell me who they sold the data to?"

Neal chuckled. "Every month you ask me that, and every month I tell you I don't know."

"Oh, come on. I'm nice enough to come in here, let you test me every month, and irritate you with questions you don't have the answers to. The least you could do is a little sleuthing for me." Felix tried out his best grin.

"See you next month."

"Not even willing to risk his job to satisfy my curiosity." Felix made a show of sighing and teased, "I don't know. This may jeopardize our friendship."

The shrill ring of Felix's phone sounded before Neal could respond. It was Caitlin. "I'll see you later," he told Neal with a wave. Neal locked the door behind him as Felix stepped down the corridor a few paces to take the call.

"Caitlin, hi!"

"Hullo, ducks. Did your appointment go alright?"

The sound of Caitlin's Welsh accent was always a pleasure to hear, but something felt wrong that he couldn't quite put his finger on. "It went fine. You sound a little . . . off?" It was a routine check-up. She knew that. It wasn't like her to be bothered by such a thing.

There was a pause on the line.

"Felix, I may have just seen Gideon. He's alive."

VIII

THE OTHERS SAT on Marc's bunk awaiting his answer while he paced his quarters. The clock on his visor display read nearly 10 p.m., and Marette hadn't arrived yet. The signal at the door minutes earlier had instead turned out to be Nick, Gunther, and Elsa, come to ask his help a second time. It was two hours since Nick had first tried to get Marc's help with hacking into ESA's system at Alpha Station.

It was six hours since the incident.

Shouting and confusion in the darkness had filled the moments after Namura's aborted scream. When they restored the power shortly thereafter, she was collapsed over her smoking rig.

Instantly-summoned ESA personnel rushed into the room and swept Namura off to a medical bay while Marette ordered the rest to wait behind; they'd only be in the way. The hackers were left alone in the room, stunned into silence.

It hadn't lasted. Nearly everyone spoke at once. What happened? What went wrong? Did ESA know such a thing would occur? A lack of available answers led to a renewed silence before someone suggested they go find out, despite Marette's orders.

Marc was primarily in shock up to that point, unsure what to say and afraid of what had happened himself. But he rallied and managed to keep in the room those who wanted to leave. Be patient, he urged, someone would be back soon. He had no loyalty to ESA, but he needed to support Marette. Letting the hackers run unescorted through the complex would be a security risk on multiple fronts.

Marette returned soon after. The look on her face spoke before she did: Namura was dead. They would all return to Alpha Station while the Space Agency determined what went wrong and how to proceed, if at all. She was composed, solemn, and professional. Marc guessed she was as frightened and saddened by what happened as the rest of them, but she was used to dealing with a more disciplined group that would draw its focus and strength from that sort of leadership.

To the hackers, it had only made her appear cold. Shouts erupted anew, spearheaded by Elsa and Gunther. Demands came again for answers, for assurances, and finally, for just some visible show of emotion on Marette's part.

Marette had remained calm.

It was a reaction that had launched Elsa across the room at her. It took Maria and Nigel to hold Elsa back from actually striking Marette. In those moments Marc saw a pain slice through Marette that she hid before the others could see.

The confrontation had ended there. Guards escorted them back to the shuttle. Marette did not join them.

It wasn't until an hour after they landed at the station that Nick had approached Marc in his quarters; he, Gunther, and Elsa were going to hack the base computers and find out what they could, and would Marc help?

Now, two hours later and all the more weary, Marc gave them much the same answer as he'd given Nick the first time: "I can't help you with this."

"You can't," Elsa asked, "or you won't?"

"Both! ESA brought us here? If they catch you hacking Alpha Station—"

"Yeah, but if you're helping us, we won't get caught!"

Marc sighed. Nick had said the three had already tried within the past hour. Marc's initial attempts at dissuasion hadn't been enough, but they'd only gotten so far before hitting a wall.

"You've already been in there once," Marc said. "You didn't find anything, and from what you tell me, you barely got away undetected."

"That's why we need you!" Gunther said. "With a fourth we can do it. I already know how."

"But you don't know if there's anything there worth the risk! ESA's just as shocked about what happened as we are. They wouldn't send us to test something like that. And they couldn't kill someone through their own rig, even if they wanted to!"

"Oh, there's *something* in there." Elsa shot to her feet. "The three of us found a whole partition about the complex that's blacked out with cryptog. You can't tell me they're not hiding something! And you can't tell me that ESA bitch felt anything for Suzanne! You saw her when she came back in the room!"

Marc's fists clenched. He faced her down. "She's in command of the whole place, she can't wear her heart on her sleeve! If you'd looked in her eyes instead of taking a swing at her maybe you'd have figured that out!"

Gunther stood up as if to step between them. Elsa just stared Marc down, and he broke under the weight of her gaze.

"Yeah, okay, come on, Marc," Nick tried. "We need you. Maria's too spooked and Nigel won't risk it, either."

"Sounds like they've got the right idea." Marc didn't know how much about *Paragon* ESA kept in the Alpha Station computers, but he needed to do his best to keep the information secret.

"We need a fourth," Gunther repeated.

"We *need* a cryptog specialist," Elsa growled, "but the best one we had is dead. Or is that just coincidence?"

"Elsa," Gunther warned.

Marc scowled back at her. "Oh, come on, you can't think that—" The door signal cut him off. He put off Elsa with a wave of his hand and checked the door. "It's Marette."

"Chief Clarion?"

"On a first name basis, I see," Elsa muttered.

Marc shook his head at Elsa's comment as much as his own. Using Marette's first name was likely harmless, but still bad for appearances. "Just hang on. I'll see what she wants."

What should he do? He needed to talk to Marette, but what would the others do if he let them go now? Yet how persuasive could he be against Elsa's anger? Could he trust them not to make another move without a fourth?

He moved so Marette would see the others behind him and opened the door.

She stood there, perceptively drained but still composed. Her eyes flicked from him to the others and back. "Mr. Triton. I need to speak with you."

"He's busy," Elsa said. "Come back later." Marc glanced back at Elsa, hesitating.

"It has been a long day," Marette said. "We are all tired and saddened by the loss of Ms. Namura—"

"Are you?"

Marette bristled. "I will need to speak separately to all of you, and I wish to begin with Mr. Triton. Now."

Elsa stepped up behind him before anyone else could speak. "*We* are speaking to Mr. Triton now. Go talk to Maria or Nigel," she hissed. "They're not doing anything."

"Look, maybe you guys better go," Marc said. "We can finish this later." Maybe they would wait to do anything if they thought they could still get him on board.

Elsa's comment was not encouraging. "So *that's* how it is."

She left without another word. Gunther and Nick followed, with Nick pausing just long enough to leave him with, "Yeah, um, we'll talk to you later."

Marette stepped into the room as Marc watched the others disappear down the corridor. He let the door close and turned to rest his back against it. "God, Marette, things aren't good."

"No," Marette leaned her hip against the edge of the desk. "They are not. But they are better than they might have been. I saw you cut Nicholas's interface before . . . things happened."

"I—Yeah." Arms crossed, he stared at the floor. "I tried to reach for the connection hub. I keep asking myself if I couldn't have reacted sooner. Maybe if I went for the hub first instead of pulling Nick's cable. It probably wouldn't have made a difference, but . . . " He shrugged and shook his head before meeting Marette's gaze. "I don't know."

"You acted. You saved Nicholas. You can rethink it all you like, but that gives no second chances." She faltered for a fraction of a second before continuing. "You did not stand by. Remember that."

"You didn't either. You cut the power."

"Yes, I acted." It seemed to give her no comfort. "This time."

She clasped her hands and tapped her thumbs to her lips. Marc opened his mouth to say something before realizing that he didn't know what to say. He let his gaze follow Marette's to the floor instead. He'd acted, yes. So had she. But he couldn't just leave it at that so easily—just turn the guilt off like a switch—no matter how healthy it might be to do so.

As if echoing his thoughts, she said, "I find it difficult to follow my own advice." He looked up in time to catch her shake her head once as if to clear it. "We do not have the luxury to dwell on such things. ESA is weighing its options and I have orders to determine if your part of the project can be salvaged. They will likely attempt to continue if your group is willing. I shall be speaking to each of you tonight, though I will obviously not tell the others these details."

"I think I can tell you what they'll say."

"Based on Ms. Litzenburg, I am not optimistic."

"She hates you, and I don't know her well enough to say whether or not that'll boil off. I can tell you that they're all three suspicious of ESA now. Maria and Nigel, I haven't talked to them myself, but it sounds like they're nervous at the very least. I hear Maria's downright scared." He stopped and weighed how to tell her about the hacker's plan. "What's more, we might have a security issue. Elsa and the rest were just here to enlist my help hacking Alpha Station. They've already gone in once, which made them think they needed my help."

Marette froze. "Did they find anything?"

"I don't think so. Nothing specific, anyway. But they said they found a bunch of encrypted data and they're convinced it's got something to do with what happened to Namura."

"It may well have. Most of the critical data is kept at the Omicron Complex, but they could find a hint of what *Paragon* really is." She waved a hand. "Or it could be unrelated."

Marc nodded. "Well, I'm sure things are contained so far. They think ESA may have known about a fatal risk, but they don't have cause to think the crater is anything other than a new research base. I don't think that they'll risk going in again without more help, though. They seemed pretty sure they'd be caught without a fourth."

"They may have already placed themselves in danger."

"What do you mean?"

"Marc, if ESA thinks there is a possibility they know anything about what the site really is, they will do their best to make sure that information does not get out."

"You think they'd arrest them?" Marc asked.

Marette shook her head. "Someone in prison may still contact the outside world, Marc. *Non*, I do not think ESA would arrest them."

Marc blinked. "You mean they'd kill them? Just like that? This isn't some shadow conspiracy group we're talking about, this is a visible, public organization."

"A visible organization that has so far concealed a major discovery from the rest of the world. ESA has quarantined the mining crew that uncovered the site for the past six months. And you and I are *part* of 'some shadow government conspiracy.' One that does *not* believe in taking lives. I have been in the contingency meetings, Marc. ESA is prepared to use deadly force to conceal their secrets." Her fists clenched, her face flushed, and suddenly she was glaring at him. "I reported this to the AoA! *Mon Dieu*, how could you come here and not know what was at stake!"

"I came here to help with the hack!" he stammered. "I only had time to read what was important!" Well, that came out wrong.

"What was important? This is important! Conserving lives is *important!*"

"That's not what I mean!" Damn, he didn't want to be yelling at her!

"How could you not know this?"

Marc heaved a sigh and sat down on his bunk, rubbing his forehead. "I didn't mean lives aren't—I meant 'important' to the immediate details of the hack. I heard at the Council meetings what ESA would do to keep things secret. I just thought they'd need more than suspicion. Detain, publicly ruin, yes, but kill? On suspicion only?"

"I believe they would."

He sighed again. "I don't know, maybe I just didn't want to think they were capable of that. I'm behind a screen for most of what I do. It's not something I usually have to deal with like this." He shook his head and looked up at her again. Would she now think him heartless?

Marette regarded him in silence for a time before she finally spoke. "I think about it every day," she whispered. The chill was fading from her voice.

"I'm not naïve," Marc said. "I'm just . . . focused. I didn't know it'd got to that point yet."

"It may not yet be. But I fear the possibility."

"Aside from the hackers, we're the only ones who know about it. That's as far as it has to go. I'll find a way to keep them from doing anything stupid."

Marette frowned and crouched low to the floor, elbows on her thighs. "My position in the Space Agency would demand that I report their first attempt," she said. "But I will not. Necessarily, we did not ever have this conversation."

Marc nodded. "There's no way they could prove you knew, even if they did somehow find out about the hack. I'll make sure the others don't risk a second try."

"But another of endless secrets." She continued before he could comment on the burden in her voice. "Do you believe there was a consciousness behind what happened today? To Namura? An intelligence?"

Was there? "I can't be sure. I mean, there seems to be an A.I. overseeing a number of automated systems, but I can't be sure of the relationship. This is an alien computer. So much of my analysis involves guesswork that I can't be sure of anything. Did the A.I. target Nick and Namura specifically when it saw them copying data, or was it completely automatic? I don't know."

"And what about your—What is it? Gut feeling?"

"There's too many variables to consider. I can't be certain."

Marette straightened. "Nothing is certain, Marc. If you had to pick, which would it be?"

He started to protest again, but then he recalled the sudden change in readings right before the surge and the uneasy feeling he'd had while monitoring the matrix. "It felt like a trap. In hindsight, I mean. It was testing us as we were testing it. It didn't move on us until we'd managed anything beyond a distraction. I don't think the attack was automated. Good news, in a way."

"You refer to the hope that it may be reasoned with?" It was an idea the Agents of Aeneas had once discussed that, if possible, might spare them the difficulty of having to decipher or deactivate the entire system.

"Yeah. You sound skeptical."

"It would be a great help if it were possible, Marc, but I am not optimistic. When the first team entered the structure, it made no attempt to reason with them. I stood by and watched that first drone slaughter them all. It appeared. It killed them." Her fists clenched. "That was it."

Marc watched the pain twist in the shadows behind her eyes. And Elsa thought her unfeeling?

"Namura's sacrifice bought us two terabytes of data," she whispered. "We will make that count."

"You got a copy for us? I hope there's something in there we can use."

"There will be."

The hard look she fixed him with made Marc realize how much she needed it to be true. He saw Namura's lifeless body slumped over her rig, and he realized how much he needed it to be, too.

"I ought to speak with the others now." Marette stood and drew a deep breath. Marc stood with her.

"Ah, it might work best to talk to Nick or Gunther or Elsa first. Make them wait that much longer before they can try anything."

"I will speak to Elsa first. Do your best to keep them from acting further." She straightened her uniform.

"I really doubt they'll go without a fourth, but I'll keep trying to make sure they don't. Good luck with Elsa."

"*Oui*, and you. I do not believe she has any love for either of us now." She moved to the doorway, but turned back to him rather than key it open. "Marc, I am sorry to have gotten angry with you. I—" She paused, her eyes searching his. For just a moment she reached for him, but then stopped and withdrew the gesture before he could respond. "I am sorry."

He nodded, welcoming the apology but suddenly unsure of what to say or do. Their gaze held for a time before she opened the door, and was gone.

*   *   *

Marette heard the door close as she strode down the corridor. Her impulse had been to touch him somehow. A kiss. An embrace. Some form of physical comfort. But it was her grief to deal with. Marc's was only a transient presence, especially given the day's events. She must not get used to relying on anyone but herself.

Merde.

IX

UNDER NORMAL CIRCUMSTANCES, Felix viewed a mystery like a kid viewed a Christmas present: an exquisite package of surprises of which the unwrapping was nearly as enjoyable as the contents themselves. Though he also made a passable living finding things out, it was the hunt, the discovery, and the challenge that drove him.

But these weren't normal circumstances. Indeed, if anyone but Caitlin had told him that Gideon could still be alive, he might have felt that same rush of anticipation. To hear it from her left him unsettled.

She couldn't talk long when she first called, and so they had agreed to meet in a couple of hours. Felix occupied his mind in the time between with not only the miniscule probability that the vigilante still lived, but how his survival might affect Caitlin. Six months ago, her grief for Gideon was mixed with relief that he was gone. The combination had plagued her conscience, and she'd beaten herself up over it for a time. Felix was unsure of the feelings it would stir up in her if he was truly still alive.

Yet how could Gideon have possibly survived? Felix could still see in his mind the sudden violence, the flash of a muzzle in the pouring night rain, horrifying and wasteful: Diomedes putting a gun to the back of the man's head and firing in cold blood. Cybernetic advances created a number of medical miracles in the past two decades, but the man's brain was obliterated. Some things you just couldn't fix.

Had Caitlin imagined seeing him?

Felix stepped off the bus with the worry that Caitlin's guilt might be affecting her more than he'd realized. She'd left the city for a time after the shooting and had rarely spoken of it since her return. He should have asked how she was handling things, instead of telling himself that she'd talk about it when and if she needed to. Perhaps he'd made a mistake.

The place at which they chose to meet was a combination of pub and café where Caitlin once perplexed the waitress speechless by ordering a "kiddie-size beer." It was a joke, of course, but her straight face and deceptively aristocratic accent fooled the woman into taking her seriously. It was, Felix found, a game she loved to play, usually with sales clerks. Yet it was always good-natured, and they'd left a generous tip.

It was those little quirks that fascinated him about her, and one of many things that made him care.

Felix spotted her at a table in a corner. She had ordered tea this time and was staring with furrowed brow into the orange liquid as if it were a crystal ball. To anyone who knew her, she was brooding.

Her light blue eyes rose at his approach. "Hullo, Felix."

"Hi there."

She stood and kissed him before he could say more. "How are you?" she asked as they broke away.

"Oh, fine, more or less." They sat down together. "A little worried about you. Been brooding?"

She nodded. "Just a little, I fear. I'm sorry to have worried you."

"Don't need to apologize for that. Can you tell me what you saw?"

She took a moment, sighing slightly, before she began. "I was in the University District, returning from a visit on campus. On my walk to the bus, I happened by his old flat. He was there. Outside."

"Did you speak to him? Face to face?"

"Am I certain it was him, you mean?" She shook her head. "I didn't speak to him. I was across the street, and when I saw him I just rather stood there, gaping. He was with a woman—platinum blond hair, just above shoulder length. They were arguing at something. I was too far away to hear clearly, but you know how you can still tell." She shrugged helplessly. "I just stood there. I suppose I should have tried to get closer and listen, but I was just . . . "

She trailed off and took a sip of her tea. Felix just listened. "Have you ever seen a ghost, Felix?" she asked finally.

"Nope. At least not that I knew was a ghost."

"I have. In a castle one night in Scotland. I just stood there, watching it. Today was the same, only this wasn't a ghost. I know it. And ghosts don't punch holes in walls."

"He did that?"

It sounded like Gideon. Punching a hole in a brick wall took a cyber-assisted limb, and Gideon had four. Felix always wondered if such levels of cybernetic enhancement were to blame for the man's instability. Gideon had lived on the edge of sanity, tormented by his own private demons. Basic cybernetic-induced psychosis, or something else? Or both?

Caitlin nodded. "Toward the end of the argument. He was angry at something, but I don't think at her. He let her hug him after that. Two other blokes ran up once he hit the wall, perhaps to help, but the woman waved them back."

"Just people on the street, or were they with her?"

"They were with her. With them. They all left in the same car soon afterwards. Gideon tried to go in the building, but she stopped him again. I believe she told him something. If they'd lingered much longer, perhaps I'd have gotten my brain back enough to move closer and listen, but I missed my chance."

"Can't say I blame you for being a little shocked, Caitlin," he told her, stopping short—again—of bringing up her trouble with Gideon's death.

"I did manage one thing. The plates on the car. It's registered to Marquand Cybernetics." She gave a little self-satisfied smile.

"Marquand?"

"Mm-hmm."

"Marquand," Felix mused. He spent time there now and again, trying to overhear random tidbits of interest. He knew a few faces. "The blonde, how tall was she?"

Caitlin sipped. "About one hundred seventy centimeters, if I had to guess."

He chuckled. "Oh, you're going to make me convert again, aren't you?"

"The rest of the world is metric, don't blame me if you Yanks haven't caught up. It's 2051 for goodness' sake." She flashed him a welcomed smile, though there was still a hint of brooding in her eyes.

"Hey, I just live here. And I happen to know distances in Wales are measured in miles."

"Roads, not people." She gave another quick smile, considering. "About your height, perhaps."

Felix nodded and concentrated on memory. One particular woman came to mind, though it was only a vague description. Who knew how many five-foot-six platinum blondes Marquand employed? "Would you recognize her if you saw her again?"

She nodded. "I believe so."

He pulled out his phone and searched the 'Net for a picture he had seen months ago. It didn't take long. "This would probably have to be too much of a coincidence to actually be her, but . . . ?" He leaned in and showed it to Caitlin.

Her eyes dropped to the screen and then rose back to his, eyebrows raised. "It must be a day for coincidence. That's her. Who is she?"

"Really?" Felix blinked. "Her name's Ondrea Noble. Marquand hired her maybe eight or nine months ago. She's an engineer, used to be independent, did a couple years of contract work for RavenTech that somehow got her noticed at Marquand. I was in the Marquand building not six months ago trying to find out what they had her working on. Didn't find anything out, though."

"Nothing at all?"

Felix shook his head. "In defense of my skills, my quest got interrupted by a certain freelancer we both know."

"Diomedes."

"Hiring me to help find Gideon, even."

Though it had been Felix's first step on the shared path that eventually led to Gideon's death, Felix was at least able to take comfort that the two men would have met with or without his help. Gideon, having discovered a common enemy was pitting them both against each other, was already looking for Diomedes. Once united, the two worked together toward that enemy's downfall before Diomedes finally killed Gideon over a stupid matter of money. Felix's protest immediately afterward nearly got him shot as well.

Caitlin tensed. "It must truly be a day for coincidence."

"His including me in that did end up bringing you and me together." Silver lining and all that.

The search had led Felix to a group called The Scry: information hunters who did in a group what Felix did on his own, and of whom

Caitlin was a part. Gideon had declared himself The Scry's protector in exchange for their being his eyes and ears in his fight against more violent groups. Fearing Gideon couldn't protect them from all the retaliation they might incur from those groups, Caitlin spoke to Felix when the other Scry would not. Her hope had been that Gideon would suspect The Scry gave him away and dissolve the relationship out of mistrust.

She couldn't have anticipated the outcome. When Diomedes pulled the trigger, it solved Caitlin's problem, but in a far more tragic way than she wanted.

"Natural disasters bring people together, too, Felix. That doesn't make a hurricane a good thing."

Felix nodded. "Kind of beside the point now anyway. I guess the question is, what does Ms. Noble have to do with Gideon?"

"One question, at least." Caitlin slipped away in thought for a moment before asking, "Do you know where she lives? What she might be working on now?"

"Afraid not." He grinned. "Well, not yet, I don't."

Caitlin returned the grin. "Not yet *we* don't."

"I'm sure we can find out where she lives if we apply ourselves. But then what?"

Caitlin's smile faded a touch to match the distemper in her eyes. "I don't know. But, Felix, I have to find out what's going on." She sighed again. "Oh, I can't even be sure it's him. How can it be?"

"You thought it was."

"I know." She nodded. "Jesus, we left him out there. Lying there, like garbage."

"Caitlin, we talked about it then. We all agreed it was for the best."

Gideon had clearly been dead. There was nothing they could have done for him. To avoid having to answer questions they couldn't afford, they summoned an ambulance and left before it arrived.

"He wasn't left out there," Felix went on. "And remember what you said. If he had any family, if we'd buried him ourselves, they'd never know what happened to him."

She nodded again and hugged the cup of tea in her hands. "You're right," she said finally. "I suppose. I thought I'd accepted that it wasn't my fault. That being relieved he was gone wasn't the same as wanting him dead. As causing his death. Now I wonder if maybe I just managed to ignore the guilt."

"Caitlin, before, it was over and done. Today everything you'd come to terms with was shaken. I don't think you ignored the guilt. I think it's just a second wave." He reached out and helped her cup the tea, his hands with hers. She let him.

"I'm not sure of what really happened that night anymore. It makes me doubt what I remember. Felix, I have to find out if it's him."

"We will." Even if he hadn't loved a mystery, he'd have promised her that.

She nodded with thanks in her eyes. "Oh, bloody right we will."

X

"I DON'T WANT anything more to do with you, bitch."

That one sentence from Elsa told Marette all she needed; the hacker team would not help further. Nearly all expressed their unwillingness in the form of fear, uncertainty, or, in the case of Elsa, naked rage. Except for Marc, none would agree to go back in. Elsa was merely the most succinct.

Marette's racquetball sprang off the wall with a reverberating smack that filled the court that she alone occupied. She rushed to get her own volley, swung, and missed a fraction of a second before her momentum slapped her against another wall. The tiny blue sphere bounced off the rear wall at an obtuse angle and dropped into a bouncing roll that took it to the front corner. With a curse, she sat on the floor to catch her breath. It was nearly nine hours since she had sent the surviving members of the hacker team home to safety. She had been on the court for over an hour.

Once she had made her determination, Marette ushered the hackers off-Moon as soon as possible. They created both a security risk and a risk to themselves. It mattered not how little they might achieve in a second hack on Alpha Station, or how few of the group made the attempt. If they were caught, action would be taken against them all. To speed their departure, Marette reported her decision to Command at a late hour when there would be less argument. She had not expected her decision to be questioned, but she had not wished to take chances. She wanted them away and out of danger.

Except for Marc. And especially for Marc.

It was that dichotomy that led her to allow him only an aborted farewell.

"If fortune favors, you will be returning," she had told him early that morning. "I have reported you as the only team member willing."

"I can't stay now?"

"It is not how they wish to continue. I am not even certain ESA will proceed in the same manner."

"They might not send in independents again, you mean." There was disappointment in his tone.

"The decision is not yet made. And you are in danger here."

"I won't be for long, once the rest leave. I'll be back, I think." He paused. "But, if I'm not—I mean, that is, if—"

She watched him try to stammer out an *adieu* a second longer before taking his mouth in a kiss. It was pointless for him to say more, and she didn't want to hear it. Wrapping him in a tight embrace, she drew as much companionship from that kiss as she could.

She wanted him safe. The death of Alberto, the AoA operative she had sent with the first team to enter the structure, still weighed on her beyond the grief she already held for the rest of them. Yet while Marc's departure would further him from danger, it also meant she would be alone with her secrets once more. Neither feeling was something she could afford. She needed to remain strong, to stay comfortable working alone for as long as it was required of her. Was that the only reason she cared about Marc?

Marette picked herself up from the floor. It was time for a break.

The walk back to her quarters was brief. She slipped off the wrist and ankle weights, removed a silver necklace that was the one piece of jewelry she allowed herself, and was about to strip for a shower when the comms-channel sounded.

ESA Command.

She keyed up voice only. "This is Clarion."

"Chief, something's happened. Have the hackers left yet?"

* * *

The Earth waited outside, large and quiet. Elsa kept watch on it as her heels struck harshly on Sunrise Station's concourse floor and took her toward the gate where her shuttle waited. She was returning to Earth, on the last leg of the journey planetside, and hardly too soon.

Though they had not yet managed a second hack on Alpha Station, and though they had zero answers, she'd snatched the chance to leave the moment it was offered. The ESA witch didn't want them anymore once they refused to be used, and Elsa had no wish to stay.

Elsa was certain they thought to be rid of her and the rest by sending them off with that bonus of hush money that they tried to call "hazard pay." If ESA thought it was over, they were wrong. She would make certain of that. ESA was cowardly—cowardly in lying to lure her and the others to their deaths, cowardly about sending them away without an explanation. She would see them pay.

She'd not known Suzanne Namura before a few days ago, and in that time they hadn't spoken in a nonprofessional capacity. But the ease with which ESA had used her life was offensive. It was infuriating! And had it gone differently, it might have been Elsa lying dead on the table. Bastards! Lying bastards. No one used her. No one.

They would pay.

None of the others would talk of a plan on the shuttle to Earth orbit. Their reluctance had finally disgusted her. She'd spent the two-hour layover on Sunrise Station apart from them all. In that time, she came to realize that perhaps they were prudent not to discuss things in such an open place. She would speak to them again of plans on the shuttle to Earth.

Except for Marc and Nick, she amended. The shuttle to the United States had left shortly after they arrived, and the two men with it. Nick she would find a way to contact later. Marc was useless to her.

And good riddance to him, anyway! He refused to help when they needed him. Maria and Nigel refused, too, but their reluctance was born of wariness. Marc was simply against them. She'd seen it in his eyes when Clarion had shown up the night before. In his voice. If he wasn't fucking her, he wanted to. Spineless. He was as bad as Clarion. Worse. He'd betrayed them.

The boarding light was off above the gateway. She was early, and none of the others had arrived yet. She was scowling out the window at the crescent of the Moon, planning, when the man spoke up from behind her.

"Ms. Litzenburg? There's been a problem. Will you please come with me?"

She turned.

XI

A BANSHEE WIND tears through darkness and hurls rain against the stone fort like a living thing striving to rip the structure from its vigil atop the cliffs. The crash of waves rolls up from the sea far below, heard yet unseen but for momentary lightning flashes that shine across its depths and then vanish in the dark.

Shielded by the battlements, Michael Flynn weathers the storm. He stands watch for the enemy that approaches and takes solace in the strength of the fort about him: a stronghold of the Agents of Aeneas. He is one of them now, lending his strength to their whole. That whole will support him. Together they stand as secret sentry, defending those who need it, those who live in the shelter of their guardianship, those who cannot defend themselves.

Michael walks the length of the ramparts, thankful for the shelter the stone gives from the elements that rage only feet away. He helped build this fort. Or had it been there before he came? He suddenly cannot recall. Perhaps both? But it is there, strong beneath his feet. Without a doubt, he belongs.

There comes a rumble. He feels it in the air and in his mind. A sickening creak of rock cuts through the wind outside. The fort begins to tremble. Michael presses back against the inner wall, his hands bracing against the stone as the wind whips inward to sling bullets of rain across his face. Lightning flashes in an assault of power. Thunder rolls in on its heels.

The storm rips the ceiling away in an instant. Buttresses crumble, fall, and with them tear away pieces of the cliff. Michael yells an alarm, barely able to hear his own voice, barely able to do more than hunker against what wall remains as the fort breaks apart around him. The deluge strikes with all its strength, drenching him, chilling him. It claws at the foundations of his fortress, ruining the cliff side until it buckles under its own weight and stone after stone falls. Streams of mud carry them down into darkness before they crash and splinter far below. Michael scrambles for footing as his perch begins to slide, broken beneath him, and then is gone.

Somehow he remains. Michael struggles against the torrent of rain, mud, and wind that twists about him like a thing alive. The fort is no more. He is alone, exposed. Water and darkness blind him as he fights to gain another handhold and keep from being dragged down with the rest.

Lightning flashes.

Diomedes is there.

The older man stands atop the cliff, cold, hard, and seemingly immune to the storm that assaults Michael's senses. He regards Michael like a priest on a pulpit. Mud washes over Michael's face, spills into his clothes, yet Diomedes makes no move toward him, gives no sign of acknowledgement beyond a cold gaze that grows harder with every thunderclap.

Rain continues to pour: rain like daggers, rain like fear, rain like the night Michael pointed a gun at the man he'd once called mentor and told him to get out of his life—at the man who stands there now.

A chunk of earth gives way beneath Michael's feet and only a blind, lucky grip on an exposed root saves him from falling after it. Diomedes rushes forward and reaches for Michael's free hand. Diomedes now struggles against the river of mud himself, trying to pull Michael up the cliff to safety, but even as Michael's grip on the root weakens, he beats away his mentor's hand with all the strength he has remaining. Diomedes stumbles back, off balance, until the mud sweeps his feet out from under him and takes him into open air.

Michael watches him fall.

Then the cliff gives way. Michael loses his grip. Rain bears him down into darkness.

The dream's end jolted Michael up in his bed. A crash a moment afterwards jerked his attention to the side, where the aloe plant had fallen to the floor from the far edge of his nightstand. He must have knocked it down with his waking movements, though it seemed strange that it should have toppled so easily from so far away.

He swung his feet out of bed, sat on the edge of the mattress, and tried to shake the nightmare's residue from his thoughts. Fading adrenaline still thrummed through his body as he stared down at the plant. The soil was spilled out across his tan carpet, but at least the pot remained intact. Michael moved to the floor, righted the pot, and then set to returning the dirt to its place. He tried not to think of the dream, or the man.

The small chore was little distraction. He set the pot back in its place. What did the dream mean? Even as the details faded, the look on Diomedes's face as he fell was still fresh in his mind. Betrayal. Pain. Loss? It was the same the night Michael turned from him. He'd done his best to forget that night, to move on. Michael had been blind to what the man was, blinded by fear and his own need of support. It still shamed him.

His palm was vibrating.

The hum from the paper-thin chip implanted under the skin of his right palm buzzed against the side of the pot where his hand rested. Michael caught his breath. It was the first time it had activated for him since the Agents of Aeneas had installed it upon his recruitment. It was an identifier, a means of access to any AoA facilities, and a method of recognizing another agent via handshake. And, in emergencies, it would vibrate.

Something was happening.

Check your email first, he told himself, recalling procedure. He went for his smartphone, propelled by the purpose of being needed. He opened his email, activated the encryption, and scanned what awaited him.

The message, broken into two parts, was relatively brief. The first part was a protection order for Marc Triton, one of their own. Marc had returned from the lunar crater site within the past week, one of six survivors of a seven-member team. According to the email, the AoA had just discovered that the other five were now either missing or dead. Michael was the closest qualified and available agent. Michael would be the one to protect him. Additional details were promised when he rendezvoused with Marc. For now, time was of the essence.

He hurried through his apartment to gather up his gear, anxious to prove himself, to help, and to learn those additional details. He was trained to protect. His desire for such things was one of the reasons the Agents of Aeneas had recruited him. Serving as a bodyguard didn't worry him. What did was the second part of the message, the part that listed his additional assignment.

The part that contained the name Diomedes.

It took Michael nearly twenty minutes to reach Marc's building. The apartment in which the Agents of Aeneas had placed Michael was across the city, and the late morning rush hour only lengthened the trip. When feasible, multiple agents in a city were geographically dispersed to cover a wider area. In this instance, Michael noted painfully, it worked against them.

A quick phone call to Marc from the cab had alleviated Michael's worry that his comrade was in any immediate danger. Marc was calm enough, if a bit on edge, and for the moment, safe. The cab's lack of privacy kept the conversation too short to learn more.

Make contact with the freelancer Diomedes. That single line of text beginning the description of his second objective was the focus of Michael's thoughts as the cab forced its way through traffic. He knew Joseph Curwen, the ESA mole, had been shot a week and a half ago, but until now Michael was uninvolved with what the AoA called the Exodus Project, and other duties had kept him from following the details closely. It wasn't until reading the email that Michael learned that Diomedes had pulled the trigger. Yet the brief message offered no evidence. Michael trusted his AoA fellows enough to guess it was more than a hasty assumption, yet he found himself hoping they'd made a mistake.

Soon after he arrived at Marc's, it was clear there was no mistake.

"I just—I just don't know that it's a good idea."

Michael sat beside Marc, talking to a screen they both were watching. A minute earlier it had shown a video of Diomedes firing the shots that brought down the mole. Now it held the live image of Abigail Brittan, a captain on the Northgate police force and the current AoA area coordinator.

"He knows you, Michael," Abigail said. "We had our eye on you when you were still under his wing, and we know that he's violently untrusting of others. The video's release will only exacerbate that, given the anonymity of its source. It wasn't from a district security camera. It was privately placed, likely by someone who knew he'd be there, and we need someone he knows to make contact. I gather you have a different take?"

Michael had been with the AoA long enough to know that they rarely issued an assignment that wasn't open for debate. Though it was still taking him some time to comprehend, the AoA philosophy was a communal one that valued input from its members. Leaders and coordinators were, in most cases, an organizational necessity rather than generals leading mindless troops. Michael had no idea how to find his old mentor and even less of an idea how he'd handle the man's sure negative reaction if he did. If he could persuade them that this was a bad idea, maybe they'd reconsider.

"He knows me," Michael started. "That might make it worse. The last time he saw me I stuck a gun in his face. I don't guess he'd react well to seeing me again."

"Unfortunately, the only other agent he's ever had direct contact with is Marc—and you'll be his shadow for a while now."

"Well, I helped him before," Marc offered. "Maybe the two of us can get him to talk."

"If we can find him. You said he's gone into hiding?"

"As far as we can tell, yes." Abigail regarded him a moment. "Michael, we need to learn what, if anything, Curwen told anyone. To find that, we need to know who ordered the hit and why. Diomedes can tell us."

Michael took a deep breath. "There's no other leads?"

"Not many. The fact that the corporate security grid was disabled indicates some tampering, but thus far they covered their tracks. What's more, the video footage records Diomedes firing two shots only. The body arrived at the morgue with three wounds. One in the head, two in the chest."

"So there might have been a second shooter," Marc said, echoing Michael's thoughts.

"One of a few possibilities. None of the district cameras were focused on the mole at the time, and we're having trouble reconciling eye-witness accounts. I'll report your concerns. Possibly there's another option. I don't see it, but we'll look. Expect to hear from me within the hour."

The transmission ended. Michael let out another long breath. Nearly any other assignment would have been welcome. Was contacting Diomedes doomed to failure, or did he just not like the idea?

"So," Marc asked suddenly, "how've *you* been?"

Michael laughed. "I guess I can't really complain."

What news did he have to tell? Marc was the first AoA member he'd met. He already knew about the three months of training Michael got after joining, and about the apartment and security job they'd placed him in. The position was only with a small security company—almost like additional training before he could be moved to Aegis, the industry leader. Few freelancers had the values and psych profile that the AoA was looking for, he'd been told. Most were too violent, too selfish. Too much like Diomedes. The Agents of Aeneas needed more people in Aegis, and Michael was to be one of them.

But Marc knew all of this.

"The job's been fine," Michael said. "I've had a couple AoA protection assignments, watching over one or two people for a few days without them knowing it. You've had a more exciting time from what I've heard?"

"I guess I've got my own briefing to give, huh?" Michael listened as Marc recounted his journey to the Moon. He filled him in on what details of the project's progress Michael didn't know, and then told him of the cryptologist's death and the effect it had on the rest of the team.

"They sent us home quickly after. Before Elsa and the others had a chance to do more. But ESA found out about their first attempt to hack Alpha Station. They didn't get anything useful, but they still left traces. Everyone from Europe—there were four—disappeared. Records show they left Earth orbit, but no one saw them after that. It's like they just hit the planet and vanished. No one noticed until Nick—the one I told you was from Denver, he was barely twenty-one—he was killed yesterday in an execution made to look like a carjacking."

"And now you're the last one left. If it's ESA, shouldn't we have seen it coming? I thought there were agents in there?"

"There are. But ESA's keeping this quiet. Marette is one of the highest placed of us there, and all she knew was they'd found evidence of the first hack. Other than that, they kept her out of the loop."

"So she's in danger, too?"

Marc sighed briefly. "Maybe. But she thinks it's more a case of plausible deniability. She doesn't need to know, so they don't tell her. Chances are, if her cover was blown, she'd be gone already." He frowned and then added, as if to comfort himself, "But she's able to take care of herself."

Michael nodded and wondered if there was more between Marc and Marette Clarion than he was saying. Though they were friends, Michael didn't feel comfortable posing the question.

Besides, there were more immediate things to worry about. "If ESA's looking for you, do you really think it's wise to stay here?" He glanced around again. The shades were drawn. The door remained locked.

"ESA doesn't know where I live. The records are falsified. They think I'm from Portland. That'll buy me at least a little time. And I need to stay here where I can work on Holes and maybe do some good for the cause. From the intelligence we have, the ESA'll try to make it look random like with Nick. Poor kid."

Michael bristled. Despite the training and responsibility he was entrusted with, he still felt young. Marc was near thirty, and at twenty-two, Michael wasn't much older than the "kid" to whom Marc was referring.

"I've also got Holes tied in to the building security and cameras," Marc continued. "He knows what the tenants look like and can alert us if something unusual's going on."

"So you're most vulnerable when you're not here."

"Yeah."

"Another reason not to go looking for Diomedes."

Marc heaved a sigh as he stood up. "I can't say I wouldn't feel safer holed up here. But . . . " He trailed off and headed for the kitchen. "You want something to eat?"

A crashing smack of metal sounded outside and Marc cursed, throwing himself to the carpet in an instant. Michael's hand was on the auto-pistol in his shoulder holster without thinking about it. It sounded like a car had hit something, but he dashed to the blinds to check.

"Shit, what was that?" Marc asked, flat on the carpet. "Holes?"

"A white sedan has impacted the side of a sports car, Mr. Triton," the A.I. answered.

Michael looked out between the blinds to find the scene that Holes described. "It's right. Doesn't look too bad, but we'd better call 911 just in case."

Visibly sweating, Marc crawled to a sitting position against the wall beside the kitchen doorway. "Take care of it please, Holes," he murmured.

"Please specify your reference to 'it,' Mr. Triton."

"Call 911!" Marc swallowed and calmed. "For the accident, I mean. Make it anonymous. Please."

The A.I. acknowledged, and Michael walked over to his comrade and crouched down. "You okay?"

"Yeah." Marc nodded. "Yeah, I'm okay. Just a little tense. First time an international organization's tried to kill me." He gave a weak smile.

Michael returned a smile of his own, unsure of what to say to comfort someone older than he was. He sat there as Marc got up and continued to the kitchen. Marc had done his job and his duty for the AoA. He went to the Moon, risked his life multiple times, and now his life was in danger again because of it. And it was his own duty to protect him, Michael reminded himself—to protect Marc, not to protect himself.

With a swell of honor, Michael realized that he would hate himself for doing any less. He was making excuses not to go after Diomedes and trying to pass them off as wisdom. His issues were his own. His commitment to the AoA would not suffer for them.

"So, assuming you're up for finding Diomedes," Michael said finally, "let's do it."

Marc stopped in the kitchen doorway and turned. "Holes, get Abigail Brittan for us again, please. Coded link."

XII

THEIR SEARCH CONTINUED.

Felix returned from Caitlin's kitchen with a half-full glass of water and stood behind her chair. She sat, one foot tucked under her, searching the screen of her laptop. Felix watched her silently for a moment and took a sip. The screen displayed six-month-old news features. She chose one, shook her head, and then went back to choose another.

Felix took another drink, this time holding the glass to his lips so that his voice burbled through the water. "Ahnd now," he whispered in a mangled French accent, "vee join zee intrehpeed Caitlin Danae een her undahr-sea search forr zee eeloosive projects ahv zee great white Mees Ondrea No-bel."

Caitlin turned, one eyebrow raised. "Oh, dear. Gone daft, have you, ducks?"

"What makes you say that?" Felix burbled.

The corners of her mouth turned up in a barely unhidden smile. She caressed her fingertips along his cheek and down to his knuckles on the glass. Then she grinned like a pixie and tipped it to dump its contents over his chin.

"Hey!" He laughed. "Not a Jacques Cousteau fan, are you?"

"I fear I don't even know who he is. Frenchman?"

He nodded, fruitlessly trying to dry his shirt. "Twentieth-century oceanographer. Did a lot of narrating."

She leaned back to smirk with one elbow behind her on the desk. "You're charming when you make references nobody gets."

"Charming enough to get me soaked, it would seem. Look at this! *Nothing* gets water out!" he joked before rubbing her shoulders. "You're going to pay for that."

She turned back around. The screen reflected her subtle grin. "Oh, I'm quite certain."

He continued the massage a little longer, still smiling. As tempting as it might be to distract her further, he'd feel bad for taking her away from the search. Then again, she was relaxing a bit. Was he ascribing more distress to her about their search for answers about Gideon than she felt? Maybe he was treading too lightly.

Caitlin sighed.

"What's wrong?"

"We're really not making much progress, are we?"

"Searching?" He sat down beside her. "Well. No. But you've had a real job taking up your time and I've, well, I've just been unlucky."

"You've done alright. I don't know that I'd call riding horses a 'job' when I enjoy it so much. I should have passed."

"Movie opportunities don't come up often, Caitlin. You know you'd have kicked yourself later for turning it down."

"We might know more now if I hadn't taken those few days, Felix," she said, staring at the screen. She was kicking herself now, too, it seemed.

"Maybe. But you are new to this stunt rider thing. Like you said, you have to take it when it comes. And we've turned up a little."

"Not much."

"Some."

The first thing they had done was try to verify Gideon's death. Caitlin had kept an eye on his body in the days immediately after Diomedes shot him. At the time, Gideon had been buried and his next of kin notified, though their identities were kept confidential as normal. She never knew his full name, but there was only one body found at the site where he'd been shot that night, and it wasn't difficult to infer it was his.

Just to be safe, in the past week they'd double-checked her findings and gotten the same results. There was no extra evidence that Gideon was dead, but nothing to show that he wasn't. Again, the severity of his wounds made it hard to believe otherwise. If Caitlin hadn't been the one to see him last week, Felix wouldn't have believed it.

As for Ondrea Noble, they had managed to turn up a few things around Marquand. One of Ondrea's first projects there involved helping to develop cyberware utility upgrades. Since then, they'd moved her to something in biotech. According to a gem that Caitlin overheard while tailing a Marquand employee on lunch, Ondrea spent a great deal of time in the biotech labs recently.

Yet further information had eluded them. Even Noble's home address seemed out of reach and, according to their observation (which Felix had to admit wasn't constant), she'd not even left the Marquand building at all. They'd yet to see her, at the very least.

And so they sat, for the moment, sifting through old news reports and looking for a needle in a haystack until they could think of another plan. Felix had a favorite saying about needles and haystacks, but he'd already used it on Caitlin last week.

"Are you searching for stuff on Gideon, or Ondrea?"

"Ondrea." Caitlin shifted in the chair to switch the leg crossed beneath her. "Crikey, I'm starting to think we should just track her down and talk to her personally."

"Wait, wait, wait. You mean just come right out and ask her what she's up to? No snooping? No research? No deceptive midnight alley-crouching?"

"Well," she put with growing appraisal, "why not?"

"But—I mean . . . That's so boring!"

She turned, one eyebrow raised again.

"You're so dull," he teased, not without irony.

Her grin showed itself a moment. "This is assuming we can get in to see her. You may get to be devious after all."

"Ooh, how about clever? Can I be clever? I've heard it's less fattening."

"You're a strange one, ducks." She stood. "Shall we be off, then?"

* * *

The tiny neon sign outside the place read *The Flaming Pyre*, but its regular patrons just called it "The 'Pyre." By and large, it was a freelancer bar, close enough to the Corporate District to attract the ones who swore fealty to a particular company, yet far away enough to draw the unaffiliated guns for hire. The latter were freelancers in the true sense of the word, Michael supposed, but the term extended to anyone, affiliated or not, in the unofficial caste of modern knights.

Knights, Michael mused. There must be a better word. "Knights" conjured thoughts of honor. Of valor. Of nobility. Michael had once bought into that dream. "Freelancer" had been a glorious label he'd put on his own dreams of making a positive contribution to the world, before he found that few freelancers bothered with such ideals.

Michael glanced about the area as they approached the building. No one seemed particularly dangerous or out of the ordinary, much like the exterior of the building itself. The glowing orange sign was the only thing remarkable about the outside. Gray, windowless concrete, dirtier for the cloudy, late-morning daylight, hid the interior of the place. There was little to catch the eye or draw customers inside. It was just one of those places that everyone knew.

"I've never been in there before," Marc told him, wary.

"It's better inside. Or different, anyway. I haven't been in here since I left Diomedes."

"That's a while. Maybe he doesn't come here anymore?"

"He comes here," Michael said. "He's not one to change."

"He changed his phone number."

"Well, not most stuff, I guess." He took hold of the heavy door, pulled it open for Marc, and gave the street another glance for any trouble.

"Windows or not, I'm glad we're here in the daylight." Marc stood at the open door for a moment, and then entered.

"It's not too bad," Michael told him when the door closed behind them.

Michael recalled the first time Diomedes allowed him to join him here, and the warnings Diomedes had given him. "Usually people will leave you alone if you leave them alone. Just try not to make eye contact with anyone unless you're prepared for them to hassle you. Try to use your peripheral vision if you—" He stopped as Marc turned back to listen. "I guess that visor of yours'll be good for that."

"That's what I'm hoping."

"You don't take that off much, do you?"

He shrugged and tapped the book-sized computer at his hip. "Makes it easier to use the hip rig without drawing attention. Plus it's just, I don't know, comfortable."

"Come to think of it, Felix wore sunglasses in here when I first met him. I wonder if the bartender remembers me." Michael led the way toward the bar at the center of the room.

The late-morning crowd was sparse, and though conversations in the place had always seemed muted unless there was about to be a fight, it felt quieter now. Most were drinking alone. What talk there was got drowned out by the white noise of the metal rock that was as pervasive as the brown-orange light that dominated the establishment. The bar was one of the few spots in the place where a bit of white light shone. Portioned out by a few fluorescents tucked away in the rafters, it barely managed to permeate beyond.

The two men each took a stool and waited to catch the attention of the bartender, who seemed content to take his time pouring something for a sullen man on the other side.

Daylight swelled from the entrance as the door swung open and a man and woman strode in wearing leisure street armor tagged with Aegis Security insignia. Michael gave them a sidelong glance and noted the stun grenades and auto-pistols at their belts. They looked over the area briefly and then made for a table.

Marc heaved a sigh. "Guns make me nervous when there *isn't* someone out to kill me."

"Relax," Michael whispered. "If anything, you're safer in here. Diomedes told me people here don't like to have their drinks interrupted by gunfire. I saw a brawl once. No one much cared until one of 'em pulled out a gun and I guess at least a dozen guys drew on him until he holstered it."

"Yeah, I figure no one likes a ricochet. Good news, I suppose. Hopefully ESA won't come at me with a crowbar."

Michael expected he could probably handle a crowbar, but the bartender approached before he could say so.

"What can I getcha?"

"Yeah, um, a pint of whatever's on tap," Michael ordered, guessing it was probably better to do that before asking for information.

Michael took the opportunity while Marc ordered to glance at the two freelancers who'd come in. Something familiar struck him. Was that? It was. They were in the booth he and Diomedes had shared on the last night he'd been here. It was there that his old mentor had first dubbed Michael a freelancer and allowed him to join him on a job. Then so much had happened in the few days that followed.

His eyes had been opened.

The bartender returned with the drinks and broke Michael from his reverie. He took a little time rummaging for his wallet in order to stall while he tried to think of just what to say to the man. He put the cash down on the counter, plus an excessive tip. "Keep the change."

The bartender scooped it off the bar with barely a glance. "Who're you lookin' for?"

"How do you know we're looking for someone?"

The man shrugged. "Cause I ain't blind, and I ain't stupid. That's the kinda tip that either says yer lookin' for someone or ya broke somethin'." He glanced at Marc. "And I been wrong before, but you don't quite look in a breakin' mood."

Alright. "We're looking for Diomedes. I know he used to come here a lot. Any sign of him lately?"

"Diomedes?" The man said the name as if it meant nothing, with an expression and shrug to match.

"Don't know him?" Michael asked, doubtful.

"Why, he famous?"

Struggling to not scowl, Michael changed his approach. "I don't suppose you remember me? I used to come here with him sometimes."

The bartender sized him up. Marc sipped his beer and turned to look behind him while Michael waited.

The bartender stood a bit taller to look down on him. "Yeah, I think I do at that. You ain't been here in a while, huh?"

"So you do know him."

"Lots of freelancers come in here, kid. Freelancers got enemies. I start tellin' every punk that asks about one of 'em, pretty soon I either got no business or a slug in my gut." He wiped the counter absently. "Ain't seen Diomedes in a week or so. Maybe more. I don't keep count."

"Think you can do me a favor and get a message to him if he comes in?"

He scowled. "I ain't a bulletin board here, kid."

Michael scowled back this time. "Kid?"

Marc slid some more cash across the bar at the man. "It's just a message."

The bartender sucked his teeth, watching them a moment, and then took the money. "A *short* message."

Michael wrote his number down on a napkin and gave it to him. "Just tell him his old roommate is looking for him."

He pocketed the number without looking at it. "He'll get it. If he comes in. Bounty on 'im, so who's to say?"

"I appreciate it. You sure you haven't seen him? You don't know where we'd find him?"

"'S'all I know, kid. Yer the one that lived with him. 'Scuse me." The man across the bar was waving for him. With a nod, he left Marc and Michael to their drinks.

Michael took his first swallow of the beer. "Well, it's a start."

"Yeah." Marc looked around. "Think he'll get the message?"

"I don't know. He's right; Diomedes is wanted, maybe he'll lie low. But I think he was wanted before this started. I guess it might depend on how much heat he thinks is on him."

Marc nodded and then held up his glass. "You know I don't even like beer?"

* * *

A short while later, Lars picked the half-empty glasses off the bar and wiped it down as he watched the two men leave. No one was trying to get his attention. He wiped his hands and picked up the phone. The number was dialed and ringing a moment later.

Someone picked up, answering only with silence.

"Hey, it's Lars."

"*Yeah?*"

"Two guys just came askin' for ya. One said he used to be yer roommate."

"*Was he?*"

"Could be. Been a while since I seen him, but yeah, think so."

"*And the other?*"

"Didn't recognize him. Data visor, kinda scrawny. Didn't say much. If he was a freelancer, I'm a damn nun."

"*Anything else?*"

"Just a message. Roommate left a number. Want it?"
Silence.
"You want it?"
"*No.*"
The line clicked dead.

XIII

DIOMEDES SET his phone down on the passenger seat. The car's engine rumbled. Idled. Traffic moved slowly, when it moved at all. He gripped the wheel and squeezed, waiting.

Paying off Lars had been smart. Diomedes needed assets. Eyes. Ears. He'd been betrayed. He was wanted. Lars would likely betray him sooner or later too, unless he took revenge on the one who'd sold him out. Only the woman who hired him knew. Only she could have placed the camera. She'd regret it.

Michael was looking for him. Why was Michael looking for him?

The voice came, deep and large like always, to guide him. **The same reason everyone else is looking for you,** it told him. **Just like the others, come to find you for the same reason: there's a reward. He betrayed you before. Pulled a gun on you, after all you did for him. Now he's coming back to do it again and cash in.**

Of course that was it. Diomedes nodded to himself, to the voice. He'd learned to trust it, so much so that when the second voice came, it was barely a whisper.

Michael let you go before, it said.

What?

He let you go. He could have shot you. He let you go.

Michael betrayed you! shot the large voice.

But he let you go. He's a friend. You need a friend.

That's what you said the last time. Protected him, taught him, and he betrayed you. Friends die. Friends betray. Friends invite weakness. Trust is weakness! You trusted the woman who hired you, and look what happened. You'll take care of her, find out what she knows. Then you'll take care of Michael, like you should have done already.

The traffic moved. Diomedes pushed the car forward.

No, came the small voice. *Not Michael.*

Why not?

No.

The voices drifted away to argue. The Marquand building was ahead. He'd seen her enter there, days ago. He'd guessed, he'd looked, and she was there. He couldn't take her in the Corporate District. Too many eyes. But he could watch. He could wait until she left it. Today, he waited.

Up the street, a delivery truck had crashed. Traffic oozed its way around it. He would find a vantage point nearby. He would wait. He would find her. And then, he would find Michael.

No. Not Michael.

*   *   *

Within an elevator inside the Marquand building, the lights changed as Ondrea waited to reach her floor. The procedure had been successful. Of that there was no question, and the part that mattered most to her was, aside from a few surmountable obstacles, complete. Yet what mattered to Marquand was proving more difficult to achieve. She'd told them this, of course. She had warned them that it would take patience.

Fine, so she may have oversold the possibility of success in order to accomplish what she wanted. But what did they expect? The more humanity learned about the human brain and the minds it could hold, the only thing that became truly certain was that it was far more complex than anyone could dream. Marquand wasn't working with muscle and bone anymore; neurons weren't so straightforward. Even if Mr. Tseng and the rest of her Marquand superiors were frustrated with the sluggish progress, they were committed.

Or perhaps they had known it was a gamble. By taking his alien secrets elsewhere, Joseph Curwen had forced them to choose between a gamble and nothing, but that didn't mean they would accept defeat any more lightly. Management was itching for more intensive hypnosis sessions, but they were patient enough to listen to her and the other specialists on the project team. So far.

She wasn't sure if Gideon could take any more right now.

He was still confused from time to time. It was definitely Gideon—in that, at least, she was confident—and in some ways he was actually more stable and willing to listen than he had been . . . before. Ondrea was tempted to say Gideon almost seemed like the person he'd been before his cybernetics pushed his sanity closer to the brink. But he wasn't yet confident in that identity, even as it struggled to assert itself.

Last week's outburst at his old apartment meant he was trying to regain the consciousness he remembered. He refused to believe it had been six months since he'd lived there, as if such a thing would invalidate his existence. Ondrea had barely managed to talk him down and get him back to Marquand.

The company hadn't wanted to let him go out there at all, but Ondrea had told them that it was necessary. She was certain that once he was satisfied with what she had told him, his subconscious would be more willing to share the secrets they sought. Trying to force things along might have catastrophic results, and she refused to lose her brother now.

The elevator doors opened onto a view of the bio labs and one of her lab assistants running straight toward her. She stepped out and he gripped her arm as if he might blow away otherwise.

"Where've you been?" The way he whispered it set alarms in her head screaming.

"Jesus, Beck, getting some lunch. What happened? Is he okay?"

"I don't know. He broke out. He's gone!"

* * *

Outside, a tow truck had somehow gained a spot ahead of the crashed delivery truck. Inside the main lobby of the Marquand building, its flashing hazard lights caught Felix's eye through the windows as he waited for the receptionist to check his computer.

"I'm sorry," he said, regaining Felix's attention. "Ms. Noble has not given permission to be paged for public visits."

"Well, that has to be a mistake," Felix tried. "How do I let her know I'm here?"

"I'm sorry, but if she's expecting you, she should have logged your appointment with the system." The man watched Felix patiently, his eyes apologetic, yet clearly hoping Felix would be satisfied with his explanation.

Not likely. "That's hardly my fault, I think. Look, I know she's in the bio labs. I'm sure she just forgot to say I was expected."

"I can't give you a pass for the labs, sir. If you like, I can take a message and see that she gets it."

"But she won't get it immediately."

"She'll get it as soon as she checks her messages."

"Right, but that will be when?"

The receptionist frowned. "I'm afraid I can't speak to that, sir. But it's the best I can offer."

"The best you can do."

The receptionist nodded contritely. Felix harrumphed, let him wait, and glanced across the wide foyer to where Caitlin stood. Marquand had sacrificed the space of four stories above ground level to aesthetics in order to create a spacious, open area accented with a mix of mirrored trim and cascading plant life that spilled down around octagonal support pillars. It was a mix of technology and life that matched the company philosophy. Along the wall, transparent elevator shafts rose up, met the ceiling, and disappeared into the structure above. At the moment, Caitlin was watching the shafts.

Felix turned back to the receptionist. "Alright, a message. Tell her a friend of Gideon's is here to see her. And him."

The receptionist dutifully took it down along with Felix's phone number. "And your name, sir?"

"Just tell her it's Felix," he said. "She'll know me."

She wouldn't, of course, but the message itself might get her attention if he couldn't find another way in before then. Temporarily unable to come up with a suitable smart-assed remark, Felix turned away from the desk. He would give the man a few minutes and then come at him anew.

Where had Caitlin gone?

A few glances revealed no trace of her among the small groups of people waiting near the elevators. Curious, he strode about the lobby. There seemed to be no sign of her inside, though he doubted she was in trouble. Caitlin was certainly capable of taking care of herself. He still owed her for coming to his own rescue once, in fact.

Felix crossed to the wall opposite the reception desk and took a seat in one of the plush couches he found there. He watched, he waited, and he glared at the receptionist who'd been keeping an eye on him since he'd left the desk. He tried to think of what he would say when he was ready to harass him again, but he couldn't stop wondering what interesting thing Caitlin had found to go off and do.

He should've let *her* talk to the receptionist, dang it.

His phone rang. It was Caitlin.

"Felix, get to the parking exit, hail a taxi, and wait for me."

He was up and moving for the door before she'd finished her sentence. By her tone, she wasn't in trouble; she'd found something. "Bossy, aren't you?" he teased. "You sure you don't want to come in here and play with my receptionist friend? He's all bureaucratic and efficient!"

"Felix, you need to hurry on this."

"Don't worry, I'm already outside." He jogged around the corner to where the parking garage fed out onto the street from below the building. "Where are you, anyway?"

"Don't worry, I'll meet you there. I need to go." A moment later, she'd hung up.

"That wasn't what I asked," he muttered with a grin. She liked keeping secrets too much. That was his job. Hardly fair of her to spoil his fun by making it her own.

No wonder he liked her.

Cabs were abundant in the Corporate District, and he had one idling just outside the garage when Caitlin raced out on foot, jumped in beside him, and told the driver to follow the gray sedan that had slipped out ahead of her.

"We got lucky," she explained with a grin.

"Is it them?"

"It's her. I spied her on a lift going down and caught the one beside it. She was making for the garage. She's with someone else, a man, and they're in a hurry. It wasn't hard to tail them."

Felix grinned back. "And you said we weren't making any progress."

*　*　*

Halfway down the block, Diomedes caught sight of the blond woman in a car leaving the garage. Headed his way. Gray sedan, passenger's seat. He'd nearly missed her, would have missed her if not for the hardware in his eyes.

Worth the price.

She might be leaving the Corporate District. Might make herself vulnerable. There was someone else in the car. He'd have to be careful.

He let the sedan pass and pulled out to follow. A few cars back, behind a city cab, he drove. He watched. He waited.

Soon . . .

XIV

"**I HATE THIS PLACE,**" Ondrea whispered.

The building still stood, couched in crumbling brick. Ondrea never cared for it, though that wasn't so much due to the building itself as the time in Gideon's life it represented. She had visited numerous times when he lived here to upgrade his old cybernetics, let him try her new designs, and just to check on him. It was something they could have done more comfortably at her place, but he hadn't wanted to put her at risk should anyone trace him to her home.

A turn-of-the-century apartment on the edge of the University District, it remained a centerpiece in her brother's memory of his old life.

Ondrea looked back down at the tracking receiver that she held on her thigh as her assistant pulled the car into an open spot on the street about halfway down the block. "He's in there."

Beck turned off the engine. "Assuming that thing's working. What now?"

"Will you have a bit of confidence in your own designs?" Beck was a definite engineering talent, but the amount of hand-holding his ego needed often overpowered her patience.

"It's not that. We just installed the beacon on the chassis. It's not fully tested."

Ondrea ignored the distasteful "chassis" comment. "We're getting *some* sort of signal. He's in there." It made sense that he would be. Had they no tracker, the apartment would have been her first guess, anyway.

"Like I said, what now? Still set on going in alone?"

She undid her seatbelt and tucked the receiver into her blazer. "Still, yes. If it's just me I can talk him down easier." She flashed him a warning glare. "And don't call Marquand. Not unless you hear from me first."

Beck accepted the order with a nod. Eager to please as ever. It was just as well; she didn't want to have to explain her fears to him. Marquand had invested a lot of money in Gideon, that was certain, but she didn't know how well they would tolerate a failure to cooperate. She preferred not to risk it.

Ondrea left the car, waited as a cab passed them by, and then crossed the street toward her brother's past.

*   *   *

The distance at which he tailed the woman had Diomedes rounding the block in time to spot her entering the apartment building. The car she'd arrived in sat parked nearby. One man remained with it. Was she going to meet someone? Was this her home?

Diomedes drove just around the corner to a spot on the edge of the intersection. He could still see the entrance. It was a key spot: good vantage point, easy to leave quickly. Might be illegal. He'd have to watch for cops.

He weighed his options. If she did live there, she'd be out soon. The man in the car wouldn't wait otherwise. It left little time to move on her. If she was there to meet someone? He'd have to find out who. How many. How strong. The man in the car would know.

But a car like that . . . Luxury car drivers were jumpy. Any move he made against the man, he'd call the cops. Hard to be sure how fast they'd come around here. Too risky. He could neutralize the man from a distance, but he'd be more useful alive, and his shot was blocked.

Familiarity nagged at him. He'd been here before, but why? It wasn't likely the woman lived here, either. Too run down, wrong place for her type. Half a block from the building to her car. If Diomedes was careful, he could intercept her when she came out. Pull her in and go. He could sideswipe the car against her if he needed to.

And if she's not alone?

Might be too risky. He could just take her out from the car. Line of sight would make it easy. But then she'd just be gone, without her knowing why. He'd have the rifle ready, though.

The minutes ticked by. Five, then ten. Maybe she lived there after all. The man in the car might be watching over her. Diomedes could wait longer, or he could break in a back entrance. But the building was big; she'd be hard to find. She might leave before he finished his search. He needed another set of eyes on the front entrance and cursed his lack. Assets. He needed assets. He would wait here longer.

The large voice began to crawl against the inside of his skull. Diomedes shifted in his seat.

She came out. He brought the gun higher, just under the window. He'd keep it hidden until he was ready to fire. His left hand was on the gun, his right on the ignition. As he waited for the best course of action to reveal itself, she stopped in the doorway and looked back.

Someone was coming out with her. Patience. Another man stepped into view behind her. At once it all made sense: he knew why he remembered this building! He'd left that man for dead six months ago! That night flashed in his mind. That man should be dead!

The vigilante! Gideon! They'd *both* set him up for revenge! The realization froze him. His weapon was heavy in his hands as the two descended the building's front steps.

Kill him! came the large voice. **Finish the job!**

Anger smashed his doubt. Diomedes fired.

The bullets struck Gideon's shoulder with little effect. Hard to kill. Instantly, Gideon dove to shield the woman. Diomedes adjusted, fired a second burst that shattered windows behind where they huddled, and then switched the weapon to full-auto a moment before a passing freight truck blocked his line of sight.

It passed in an instant. Gideon was gone. The woman stood, a foolish target, yelling.

Her turn.

He aimed at the bitch and fired again.

Felix and Caitlin were coming from the apartment building's back entrance and into a hallway leading to the lobby when they heard the first shots. Worried glances exchanged, they both rushed to the front as fast as they dared. Another burst rang out and found them staring out the front door at Ondrea and a man in sweats and a dark jacket whom Felix thought could only be Gideon. Shots burst around them again. Felix and Caitlin cursed and threw themselves to the floor inside the doorway.

"Felix," Caitlin whispered. She didn't have to say that it was Gideon for him to know that was what she was thinking, too.

But who was shooting?

A truck passed and shielded the building for a few precious moments. Felix watched as Gideon pushed Ondrea to safety behind a car and darted forward to jump onto the truck's rear bumper. Ondrea was back up in a blink and yelling after him. The truck continued down the street and passed a parked car up the block. Felix saw the shooter.

Felix hissed the name. "Diomedes!"

"*What*?" Caitlin burst.

She was up and dashing out the doorway before Felix could stop her. Diomedes fired again through Felix's yell as Caitlin rushed to Ondrea and pulled the other woman to cover again in a near-tackle. Felix moved to follow a second later, but gunfire cut across his path and forced him to take cover against the cement wall of the steps.

Caitlin was doing her best to hold onto Ondrea. "Stay down!"

"Let me go!" she yelled, struggling. "You don't know what you're doing!" Bullets sprayed into the engine block.

"Stay *down!*" Though momentum and surprise first helped Caitlin get Ondrea down, her smaller size made keeping her there a losing battle.

The gunfire stopped long enough for Felix to risk a look above the wall at Diomedes. Gideon had reached him. The two grappled through the car window for the rifle.

Tires squealed from the opposite direction as the sedan in which Ondrea had come pulled up and screeched to a stop in front of the building, its driver yelling. Ondrea wrenched herself from Caitlin's grip and scrambled out to it. Shots rang out again, fired blindly from Diomedes in his struggle a moment before Gideon flung the weapon to the ground.

Felix dashed to Caitlin's side, one hand slamming into the fender to stop his momentum and the other grabbing her arm to keep her there. Frantic looks exchanged, they both peered out at the road as an engine revved, tires squealed again, and Diomedes's car bulleted into the street with Gideon clinging to the hood. There was only enough time to see the latter raise a fist as if to smash the windshield before the car barreled out of view.

Ondrea's sedan took off a second later with a hard U-turn that scraped metal against a parked car and pointed it in the direction opposite Diomedes's escape. Rubber peeled and burned. Seconds later, Felix and Caitlin were alone on the block.

"Christ," Caitlin gasped. "Are you alright?" She turned to Felix and looked him over for any injury.

"I'm fine, fine. I should be asking you the same question! God, Caitlin—" He stopped as the words all bunched up trying to get out. He could hardly get angry at her for acting like the woman he'd fallen in love with but—"Damn it!" he finally burst. "Next time it's my turn to give *you* the heart attack!"

She grabbed him into a quick, tight hug. "I'm sorry. But I'm okay." She released him. "What the hell is happening? You're sure that was Diomedes? I couldn't see."

"Sure as I am about anything," he said. "But as for what's happening, I think the question is which one of those cars are we going to follow?"

* * *

Diomedes floored the gas, shooting the car past a blur of buildings. He swerved hard, he swiped it against parked vehicles, and still the vigilante hung on. A parking garage loomed on the right. Diomedes hooked the car into it. Gideon gripped against the force that flung him to the edge of the hood and refused to let go even as the car scraped bottom on the ramp to the second level. It catapulted off the ramp, landed again, and bounced on worn shocks with a loss of control that smashed them into a parked van.

The collision bruised a seatbelt line across Diomedes's chest and flung Gideon onto the concrete. Diomedes watched the body tumble like a rag doll and then stop. For just a moment, he lay there.

In another instant, the man was up. Powerful strides carried him away across the garage. Diomedes slammed the car into reverse, pulled back from the van, and then sped forward after him.

Gideon should be dead. Gunshot, point blank from behind! He should be dead!

An easy shot, and you couldn't do it right. You're incompetent! "Incompetent freelancer!" Kill him now or they'll all think that!

Gideon still ran. Fast, but it wouldn't be enough. Diomedes drove the car up behind him on the next ramp and clipped Gideon with the bumper on a turn that sent the car skidding and Gideon tumbling off his feet into a wall. Diomedes regained control, turned the car again, and saw his prey struggle to his feet once more.

Diomedes remembered Gideon's cybernetics. Implants, limb replacements, maybe more than Diomedes's own if he could take such punishment. He mashed the gas pedal. He'd pin the freak to the wall, crush him against cement!

Gideon sprang onto the hood a second before the car hit the wall. The impact threw him back but he didn't let go. Instead, the vigilante raised his fist to smash the already damaged windshield. Diomedes reversed hard again. It kept Gideon from doing anything more than cracking the glass and struggling to hold on.

Diomedes angled the car toward the railing at the edge of the level. He eyed the three-story drop as Gideon regained his balance, and then launched the car forward. Parked cars became a blur. The railing loomed as Gideon turned to look.

Diomedes stomped the breaks and bellowed. Tires screeched. The car slammed against the railing. Momentum ripped the vigilante from the hood and spilled him over the side as the railing stopped the car completely. It trapped the car in its punctured mesh. Front tires hung useless over the edge.

Trying to block the pain of the impact, Diomedes finally pushed himself out of the car and looked over the side. The body he'd expected to see broken on the street was not there.

His prey was gone.

XV

THE TWO TERABYTES of data that the hackers downloaded from *Paragon* were, so far, mostly incomprehensible gibberish. The ESA analysts called it fragmented code. They cited their understanding of the alien computer's principles as barely rudimentary and tossed around simile and metaphor in an effort to define their lack of progress: It was like trying to see the whole picture by looking at a few drops of paint. They were toddlers trying to comprehend Shakespeare with only half the alphabet. They were cavemen peering over Einstein's shoulder, and so forth.

Marette refused to believe that it was hopeless. After all, they had managed to interface with the computer in the first place. They were not powerless. They were not stupid. They could learn. She would not accept that the data was useless. Lost lives must count for something!

ESA had disappeared—and by all indications killed—the hackers to keep their secrets. The news reached her via an AoA communiqué, and Marette had nearly destroyed her quarters upon reading it. The hackers had posed no real threat. Their deaths were senseless! Needless! Wrong! Marc's survival was the one thing that enabled her to rebottle her rage enough to face her ESA comrades with a cool exterior that belied nothing of her knowledge of events that she was not supposed to know about.

But she refused to let it be for nothing. If she could not wring some modicum of meaning from the data personally, she could at least refuse to back off from those who could.

It was five days after Namura's death that ESA deciphered the map.

Though not the Rosetta Stone for which they had hoped, it did reveal something of the interior of the structure. Pathways, hallways, chambers—all appeared to be detailed, quantitatively if not qualitatively. Of special interest was an immense, centrally located chamber adjacent to the few areas they had previously entered. They soon tried to gain access to it via the black material's touch interface, working under the watch of mini-turrets and Geiger cannons to protect against the security drones that once killed an entire team. Coded sequences and symbols found in the captured data were brought to bear, but to no avail. There were no appreciable results for nearly a day.

It was then that they'd heard the rumbling. It lasted twenty seconds, something distantly faint yet still felt against the boots of everyone within the structure. Then it stopped as abruptly as it started, with no indication of its cause. No change was apparent in any of the explored chambers. No security drones appeared. No other sounds were heard.

It was a mystery that remained unsolved until a seismic scan near a still-buried end of the ship revealed a change. A wedge-shaped hatch had folded out from the structure and pushed soil away as it opened.

They had a new point of entry.

Marette descended the ladder that rose up the wall of the three-meter tunnel they had carved out to reach the opened section. The ship's hatch, folded upward, now formed the ceiling of a horizontal passage through the loose soil, beneath which a seven-meter walk led to the ship's new opening. Reaching the bottom, she checked the data recorder on her suit's computer, unsure if it would even function properly. Electromagnetic interference in the immediate area prevented communication with the surface, a fact discovered when they had sent the remote inside. It had rolled halfway down the passage when they promptly lost contact.

Marette called out to the tech in the suit just ahead of her. "Can you read me, Officer?"

"That's an affirmative, Chief. Looks like we're in a bubble. I can't raise the complex." Chief Petty Officer Levy stopped at the opening, turned, and pointed inside. "There's the remote. Looks like a dead end in there, ma'am."

Marette advanced to stand beside him near the edge of the opening. The slate gray of the outer hull continued inside. It formed a smooth, conical passage uncovered by the black material save for a small, rectangular space on the curve of the left wall.

It was the first time they had encountered an area without the material, and Marette wondered at the significance of its near absence here. The tunnel itself led only to a dead end formed by a grid of openings each barely large enough for a flattened hand to pass through. Midway down the tunnel sat the remote.

"Might be some sort of venting system," Levy said. Marette found herself in agreement. Did that have to do with the lack of black material? They had found no non-lunar debris outside the tunnel. If it was a venting system, then what had it vented?

"See what you can do with that panel," she ordered, and then she turned to another tech waiting at the base of the surface ladder. She gave him a hand signal to indicate that they were going inside, and he relayed it in turn up to the surface. Limited by space, only Marette and Levy would be entering for the moment. Ordinarily, Marette would be safely outside, directing the entry team from there, but the communication blackout made that impossible.

In some small part, she was thankful for that. Nearly every life lost in this venture was taken while she was safely elsewhere, observing. Directing. It was how it should be, she knew, how it must be in a chain of command. Her duty as one of the Agents of Aeneas further underscored her need to remain safe. Yet shouldn't she shoulder the same risks as those she commanded? The blackout gave her the excuse she needed to satisfy that question. Whatever would be found in that tunnel, the AoA would need a representative. This time she could not do that from outside.

The day was coming when the AoA would take over the site completely. Perhaps whatever she found here would be vital enough to bring that day sooner.

She followed Levy down the tunnel to the square of black material.

"The panel seems dead, Chief." Levy slid his hand over the blackness with the light touch that would normally activate the interface. "It's not responding."

Marette shifted the weight of the recoilless rifle she carried and turned her attention to the vent holes. "Keep trying. We have not seen one so small before. Possibly it works in a new fashion."

"They've never been picky about lighting up wherever we've touched—oh!"

Marette turned. A transparent panel was folding away from where it sat previously unnoticed atop the midnight surface. The cover became perpendicular to the wall, then slid itself inside as the black material swelled forward a fraction of a centimeter. "I pressed harder. It just started moving, like a catch release. Protective covering, maybe?"

"To protect from whatever it is that is vented here," Marette finished. They had discovered early on that the material was sensitive to radiation. The cover disappeared into the wall completely. "I want an analysis of that cover plate if we get another chance."

"Yes, ma'am. The interface seems normal now, though there's a few symbols here I don't recognize."

"Let the new ones alone for now. See if it will accept any of our opening sequences."

She waited as Levy accessed menus and submenus that they only half understood. It stood to reason in Marette's mind that an access panel in such a place outside any vessel could grant passage to the interior. She only hoped that it would be triggered by one of the previously discovered sequences.

The first few Levy tried were useless, lacking each time for a key symbol to touch. Marette eyed the vents once more. If it were her design, venting anything dangerous would be impossible when the panel was being accessed. But who knew if whatever creatures built the ship were subject to the same vulnerabilities? She stood with the rifle trained on the vents, aware of how useless the weapon would probably be against anything likely to issue from them.

"I think I may have something, Chief."

Levy's voice brought her attention back to the panel as he touched a symbol. For a moment, the borders of the panel flashed violet. Seconds later, the tunnel hatch swung down, sweeping fallen debris into the tunnel and sealing them inside. With suit lights shining dimly against the interior, they both waited and tried to prepare for what might occur next.

Marette became aware of a faint hissing. "Check your readings. Is that atmosphere?" Her weapon remained firmly pointed toward the vents.

"Affirmative. All the same, I'd prefer to keep my helmet on, long as we might be standing in an exhaust vent. Nearly standard pressure . . . now."

The surface they were standing on moved. The entire tunnel was rotating to uncover a seamless opening beside the panel. Marette turned her weapon on it as both she and Levy shifted their footing against the tunnel's motion. When it finally stopped, they were staring at a rectangular hatchway that led a short distance into a small compartment. Marette crept forward, able to make out a shaft leading from the compartment down into the ship. They held there at her order, weapons trained on the shaft and waiting to see what might rise up to greet them. Nothing came, but the fact remained: they were cut off from the surface.

"Officer," she said finally, "can you reopen the outer hatch?"

"I'd right better try."

"*Excuséz moi?*"

"Do my best, ma'am."

Levy returned his attention to the panel as Marette tried contacting the surface. "Omicron, this is Clarion, do you receive? Clarion to Omicron Complex, respond please." There was little reason to believe that the interference would be gone with the closing of the tunnel, but it was worth checking. She waited a moment in silence before abandoning the possibility.

Beside her, Levy was working at the symbols on the panel, slowly navigating alien submenus, when it abruptly went blank. He tapped it experimentally. "Well, what the hell."

"What did you do?"

"Not a thing. Nothing that should just shut it off."

"We have found no sequence to shut it off, Officer. Did you use a new one?"

"No, ma'am. I tried the one that rotated the tunnel, then I tried the one that we think opened this section in the first place. Midway through, it just . . . " He motioned demonstrably to the screen, and then tapped it a few more times. "Bugger doesn't want to come back."

Doesn't want to?

Marette inched closer to the shaft and peered down. Unremarkable but for rungs that jutted out from the side, it dropped a good ten meters into another chamber. Descending the shaft was an option. Holding back for those outside to figure out how to reopen the hatch was another. She frowned. The idea of the two of them moving alone through the ship did not appeal. Remaining trapped inside and waiting for rescue, while arguably safer, did not appeal, either. And there was the additional possibility of some unknown substance venting through the chamber with its next opening.

"Officer," she said, "we are going in."

They began their descent. Rung by rung, they lowered themselves, suits barely clearing the diameter of the walls around them. Levy led the way, as per procedure. Marette came after, regretting her decision to follow that procedure with every other step and trying to ready herself for the next disaster that might befall them.

The spacing of the rungs felt too close together, perhaps designed for a creature of slightly smaller stature. To her relief, they reached the bottom without incident and found themselves in a narrow passage. Like nearly everywhere else, the walls were coated in black. They reflected the suit lights at eerie angles. The passage was grim, empty, and deathly silent.

"Ma'am?"

"Officer?"

"Suppose we can get the lads back at the complex to work on figuring the code for the lights in here soon?"

Marette smiled in spite of herself. "So noted, Officer. Can you locate our position on the map?" She waited as he checked his screen. The passage led forward several meters and disappeared around the corner. There was no sign of movement.

"Based on where we estimated the hatch, I think so."

"I want the shortest route to the explored areas. The fewer doors we must open, the better."

"Aye, ma'am. There ought to be a chamber up around that corner. If we can get in there, there's another hallway branching off it that's our best bet."

"*D'accord.* Let us try." She checked her suit readout to verify *Paragon*'s air still showed as breathable, then unsealed her helmet and slid the faceplate away. "Depressurize your suit. We should conserve air."

Levy acknowledged and obeyed. They began their walk through the dark.

Their footfalls sounded lightly, the impact absorbed by the black material along the deck. As they neared the corner they became aware of a dim, bluish light ahead. Rounding the corner carefully, their searchlights played across the depth of a new chamber.

They stood on the left side of a narrow balcony that ran the width of the room. A low wall formed the balcony's railing, atop which was a broad, angled surface that, like much of the room, was covered in the black material. The angled surface was at a height that—while perhaps a little low—gave the impression of being some sort of control console. Compounding this impression was the presence of a small, glowing oval, the source of the bluish light, which sat waiting for them in the console's center.

Though the light was the first thing that caught Marette's attention, the chamber's lower level soon drew her interest. It stretched beyond the balcony level a likely twenty meters to the rear of the chamber. Five strange domes protruded from the lower level's floor. Coated in the black material, they loosely surrounded a slightly larger, squat object in the center. Nearly two meters tall and five meters wide, the object resembled nothing upon first glance so much as a great four-legged spider. The slate gray metal jutted with odd geometric protuberances, and though the rest of the chamber remained uniformly coated in the black material, only a single thin strip of each boxy "leg" displayed the stuff.

In the center of the object sat what first appeared to be a large, thick disk, though once Marette trained her light on it, she saw it to be shaped instead like a great cut diamond. Though the base had the dark metal sheen of the legs surrounding it, her searchlight glinted off of the flat top to show a surface of deepest green.

"This is . . . amazing . . . " Levy whispered. "What is it?"

They stood a while longer atop the balcony, taking in the sight while the blue light pulsed. For nearly a year Marette had been involved in this operation. The awe, the initial spirit-testing revelation that another civilization existed somewhere amongst the stars had gradually faded under the everyday pressures that she faced, overshadowed by the deaths of her colleagues. Up to that moment, all *Paragon* had afforded of itself was a distant sense of *something* hidden behind uniform black hallways and abstract computer systems. But there, in the previously unseen size and features of this chamber, the reminder of what they were standing in brought a renewed wave of that faded awe.

"People died for this," she whispered.

"Chief?"

Marette shook off the awe again. They were still trapped. She ran her light along the perimeter of the room, across the far end where the chamber's ceiling sloped into a downward curvature that reached the floor, and then back along the vertical sidewalls up to the opposite corner of the balcony. "I do not see any exits."

Levy followed her light with his and then checked his screen. "There ought to be one along the far wall up near us."

Marette nodded. Most of the passages they had found were hidden beneath the black material and revealed themselves only when the proper sequence was activated. She looked back to the object at the center of the room, then to the pulsing blue oval. No, they should find a way out first. They needed to secure their position. The oval continued to pulse. Why was it doing that? What had they found?

Later. "See if you can open the door."

Marette followed Levy to the opposite corner of the balcony where the door should be and then turned back to keep watch on the chamber. She could not let her awe blind her to the dangers and her responsibility to Levy. Previous encounters with the security drones had come silently and with little preamble.

Yet there were no drones. There was nothing to confront but pulsing blue light, the large, hunched object, and its cadre of black domes.

"Chief, I can't get a response. I can't even bring up the interface." Levy pushed his hand against several places on the wall to show her. The black material remained inactive. "Nothing."

Marette tried her own touch on the adjoining wall but received the same lack of result. "Keep trying until you find an area that works."

"What about . . . ?" Levy nodded toward the flashing oval. "Could be it activates the section."

"It may, *oui*. It may not. Check the walls first, Officer."

Levy did so, making his way across the rear of the chamber balcony and thoroughly testing the surface while Marette covered him. Nowhere did his touch have an effect. He tried along the slanted paneling on the balcony railing and swept the entire surface save for the immediate area around the flashing. Again, there was no response.

"Down below?" he asked.

Marette frowned and eyed the lifeless black domes with suspicion. "What do you scan down there?"

"Very faint energy readings, but nothing hazardous. Nothing that I can tell from here, at least. That crystal in the center, it's definitely not something I've seen before."

"Whatever that is, I would guess it is for a greater purpose than opening a simple door." What was it?

She returned her attention to the blue pulsing. Barely larger than the circumference of a human hand, it begged to be tried, yet the more she considered such a course of action, the more wrong it seemed. Or was it simply the pervasive mental image of each dome opening to release a drone? She stepped closer. "There are no other exits indicated? Nothing on the lower level?"

"No, ma'am."

That was it, then. Better to take action than fall victim to indecision. She motioned toward the oval. "I am going to try this. Make yourself ready."

With a nod, Levy slung his sensor equipment over his shoulder and readied his weapon. Though research on the salvaged drones had helped ESA to improve a defense against the killing machines, there was only so much the two of them could do against them on their own. One drone at a time they might stand against. Five they could not. With a final glance at the waiting hemispheres below, she pressed her hand to the blue.

The result was immediate. Across the panel, lighted symbols bloomed in a glowing symphony of color along the previously black space. The symbols and readouts continued across the walls in the lower section, lighting fully before falling to a more subdued state. The black domes themselves came to life moments later. As symbols began to ring their lower sections, Marette watched the black material atop each begin to peel back. Her breathing quickened and her fingers tensed on the trigger as a long cylindrical object rose out of the top of each dome. The objects started to pulse in sequence, emitting flashes of clean white light that grew more and more rapid until they blurred into a constant, brilliant glow.

Before she could think to take any sort of readings, the black material at the far section of the ceiling withdrew to uncover the metal plating beneath it, spanning nearly the entire width of the chamber. Moments later, the metal itself began to slide open. Marette braced herself. Startled by the size of the area that was opening and imagining the sheer number of drones that could be released through it, it wasn't until it had slid halfway open that she saw it was, in fact, opening to the outside. Lunar soil lay suspended above the hole: gray, pressed smooth, and refusing to be disturbed by any rush of escaping atmosphere as common sense told her it ought.

"Levy! Pressurize!" she called out. She shut her own helmet and reengaged the suit's life support. Every readout told her that the atmosphere in the chamber remained unchanged, that none of it was escaping, but she knew the lunar material on the surface to be loose and barely five meters thick. Even if it were massive enough to hold the ship's atmosphere in, some of it should simply fall into the chamber. It should not be motionless. Logically it had something to do with the glowing cylinders, but the very sight defied anything she knew.

"Levy, can you—"

A brilliant green flash flared from the crystal at the center of the object. Levy threw up his arms to shield his face as lightning arced from the center to strike one of the cylinders in an explosion of energy and chaos. The cylinders flickered and went dark. The crystal dimmed. The symbols throughout the chamber disappeared. As the light and sound faded, Marette's searchlight caught the first tumble of lunar debris into the chamber.

The chamber was about to decompress! She and Levy called out the same warning. With nothing to hold onto, they pressed themselves down on the floor behind the balcony wall as the lunar rock crumbled and the atmosphere forced itself past it into the vacuum outside. They lay there, waiting for the pressures to equalize and grateful that they had closed their helmets.

"Chief, the pressure is stabilizing," Levy reported finally with some surprise. "The atmosphere's back."

Marette stood and looked over the chamber, expecting the ceiling section to have closed again so that the place could refill with air.

It remained open.

Levy stood up beside her. "Now that's right peculiar."

Lunar debris lay strewn over the bottom rim of the opening, unevenly spread across the floor of the chamber where it fell. Above, the stars glowed in the sky beyond, but something was different. A faint shimmer across the open space caught her eye. A bit of rock, loosened by the blast, spilled belatedly down into the chamber from outside. When it passed the boundary between outside and in, slipping through the shimmer that appeared to be a semitransparent barrier, Marette began to comprehend what had happened.

"*Incroyable*," she gasped.

Levy looked up at the barrier from his sensor readout. His words were a confirmation of her suspicions. "That barrier?" he whispered. "That's the black stuff."

XVI

THEY WEREN'T FAST ENOUGH.

They'd hoped to track Diomedes and Gideon by the damage the car would do, but it wasn't enough for Felix and Caitlin to keep up on foot. The destruction was meager—though Felix realized that was probably for the best despite their immediate need—and the crisscross of streets and turns gave them too many options to be sure of where to go.

It was the sound of sirens that finally led them to the above-ground parking garage and the front half of the car hanging out three stories above the sidewalk. Spotting the flash of emergency lights reflected from inside, they rushed up to learn more.

They reached the third story and greeted what they found there with a mix of frustration and relief. No one was around save for a lone patrolman and an opportunistic tow truck. Upon confirmation that neither Felix nor Caitlin had witnessed the accident—a truth about which neither chose to elaborate—the patrolman ushered them from the scene with the reassurance that no one was hurt.

"They both got away," Caitlin surmised as they left. "The way he questioned us, I don't think he had any answers."

"No argument here," Felix said. "But then where'd they go?"

"I don't know, Felix." Concern colored her tone. "Do you suppose they got away together? One capturing the other?"

"I don't think so. I hate to say it, but in this kind of mood," Felix gestured to a smashed section of wall as they passed, "I don't think Dio was looking to capture anyone. But Gideon? Maybe. He's subdued Dio before. But, and this is just an impression, I think he was more—"

"Just trying to protect Ondrea?"

"Yeah. Distract Dio. Give her time to get away."

"She nearly ran after him. I had rather a time holding her back."

"You might have saved her life," he said.

Caitlin flushed slightly and shook her head. "I just. . ."

Felix stopped walking and laid a touch on her forearm. "What is it?"

"He shot Gideon. We both saw it. I just didn't want to see it again. Gideon, or anyone else."

They held each other's gaze for a time, and Felix was once again amazed at how she could touch him without physical contact. "You're not a bystander, are you?"

"Not a great deal," she admitted before continuing to walk. "I do hope he got away."

"Gideon was faster than Diomedes," Felix said with a nod. "Without the car . . . " He paused as things caught up to him. "God, Caitlin, that really seemed like him, didn't it? I hardly thought otherwise once I saw him."

"I know the feeling. I'm going to find out what's happening, Felix."

"We were close. We'll catch up again. And now we've got another piece of the puzzle. What was Diomedes doing there?"

"That would seem to be more of a question than a solution. There's a bounty for him, yes?"

"He's wanted. I've been concentrating on so much else lately, I've not given it much thought. There was a video, if I'm not mistaken."

"Aye, there was. He shot a man from a room in the Nexus Tower, downtown."

"Who was it? The guy who died, I mean."

"I don't recall if I heard a name. Some poor bloke from Europe. The Space Agency."

Felix turned suddenly. "ESA?"

"Yes, I think so." She studied him, brows knit. "You suspect something, I think?"

"I do. Or, at least I suspect I know someone who might be able to shed a bit of light. Except I don't get how it could connect to Gideon."

"Whom do you know in ESA?"

"No one. But," he paused, heeding a promise not to reveal certain secrets. "Let's just say I know someone connected to ESA."

Caitlin regarded him quizzically. A faint smile formed on her lips. "You're being secretive."

He smiled back. "Me? Oh, I'm hurt!"

She continued to watch him. Ordinarily he might have teased her a bit before telling her or letting her force it out of him, but the AoA wasn't something he could tell her about, and finding out what was happening with Gideon wasn't something he wanted to tease her about.

"Caitlin," he started, "it's a secret I promised I'd keep. You know how much I value my word. Please understand when I say I can't tell you the details."

She searched his face and then finally nodded with what he took to be a patient sigh. "Is there anything you *can* tell me?" she asked.

"I can tell you that if I find out anything that pertains to Gideon, you'll be the first to know."

"You'll need to talk to this person alone, then." She made it a question. "May I ask who it is, at least?"

He chuckled gently. "You may ask . . . " He held up his hand and continued before she could begin to glare. "It's only Marc." Telling her that much couldn't hurt, right? Lots of people like Marc had private contracts, after all.

"Marc? Is he back from wherever it was he was going?"

"Antarctica?" He grinned. "Yeah, I got a quick word from him a day or two ago."

"Perhaps you ought to ring him up, then."

He fished for his phone. "Oh, but wandering through the streets yelling for him is so much more entertaining!"

Caitlin elbowed him. "Cheeky."

Felix grinned and dialed the number from memory.

A short time later, Felix settled into the cushions of Marc's couch and looked across the room to where Michael Flynn stood beside the window. "So are you guys just hanging out today, or am I interrupting something?"

"Oh, yes and no," Marc answered in the doorway.

"A bit of both," Flynn added while looking out a crack in the drawn window shade. He pointed toward one of the computers on a desk in the corner. "Is it . . . ?" he asked of Marc.

Marc handed Felix the glass of ice water he'd asked for. "Should be, I didn't disengage him. Holes, you on the job?"

The console toward which Marc spoke remained dark despite the delicately masculine voice that responded, "Yes, Mr. Triton. All building cameras active and accessed."

"Holes?" Felix turned toward the A.I. itself. "That you?"

"It is, Mr. Hiatt."

"Voice recognition?" Felix asked. "Is that new?"

"Just a couple weeks ago. So far he's developing pretty well."

"A bit formal, but at least he's respecting his elders," Felix said. "What's he doing with the cameras? You looking for someone again?"

"I've got him watching the building," Marc said. "Basic security routine. He ID'ed you before you buzzed up."

"Had a problem with security lately?"

Marc shrugged uncomfortably. "Well, you know, staying careful. What did you want to talk to me about?"

Felix studied Marc where he sat on the couch. Pressed back into the cushions, arms crossed over his stomach, he was clearly apprehensive about something. Flynn shifted by the window, sitting down to the left of it. Spine straight, eyes alert, he was tense.

"You in some sort of trouble, Marc?" Felix asked.

"I'll be okay. Just some AoA business that'll blow over soon enough, I hope. Michael's just here as a precaution."

"You sure? You don't need any more help with anything? I find you went and got yourself killed because you didn't ask for help, I'm going to be kinda pissed."

"I'll be okay. We're just being cautious."

Across the room, Flynn nodded. A moment of uncomfortable silence passed before he turned to Felix and added, "But don't you try anything, or I'll have to kick yer ass."

Felix turned to Flynn, genuine shock on his face. "Aye god, Flynn, you're getting a sense of humor! More or less."

The young man smiled. "I try."

"The AoA's been good to you, then? It's been a while since I last saw you."

"They have. Lots of training. Feels like I belong. I'm not sorry you brought me in, if that's what you meant."

"Hey, don't put that on me, I just walked you to your recruitment; they had their eyes on you before that." Felix remembered the day half a year ago when he'd first told Flynn of the Agents of Aeneas and their interest in him. He'd just turned away from Diomedes and been sorely in need of a positive purpose. They'd given him one.

"Well, you know what I mean." Flynn shrugged. "I still don't get why you're not a part of us anymore."

Felix gave his best secretive smile. "That milk will get cool on you, pretty soon."

"Is that some sort of riddle, or are you just being weird and evasive?"

"Oh, if I had to pick?" Felix thought about it. "I'd go with weird and evasive. Or maybe 'obscure and evasive.' Make that one word, though—saves time: 'obscasive.' Somebody call Webster's."

Marc cleared his throat. "I hate to interrupt, but do we get to know why you're needing to meet with us?"

Felix gave his best disarming smile out of reflex before taking a gulp of water. "I need to know just how much being a 'friend of the AoA' can get me."

"Oh, yes?" Marc asked.

"The assassination in the Corporate District a couple of weeks ago. Am I right in thinking it's not coincidence he was from ESA?"

Marc and Flynn shared a quick glance that may as well have been a direct yes. "Why do you want to know?"

"Personal reasons. I'm not working for anyone on this." Felix paused. While not worried about telling either of them the whole story, he couldn't help but wonder how sensitive of a subject Diomedes was to Flynn. On the other hand, there was no need to coddle the man. "I'm actually more interested in Diomedes. Why he was the trigger man."

"And you've reason to think the AoA's got something to do with it?" Marc asked.

"Other than the fact that I know you well enough to know that if they didn't, you'd have told me so straight just now?" Felix grinned. "I remember you keeping an eye on some guy in town from ESA a while back. I know you guys have got them working on a certain project. One of those guys gets shot—shot *through* the security grid. Somebody had to be pulling some strings for that to happen. I know assassinations aren't the AoA's style, but it's not so far-fetched to think you've been looking into the details. I'm not looking for the big picture here, really. I just need to know where Diomedes fits into it all."

Flynn stood, seemingly deep in thought, and checked the window again. Marc chuckled. "You're always looking for the big picture, Felix. You're a big picture kind of guy."

"Well, okay, so I can't argue that. But it's not the AoA's big picture I'm trying to see. Or is that not what you're protecting?"

"You know we can't tell you everything. You're not a part of it anymore. It's not that I don't want to help you, I just have to figure out what we can say without—"

"Without breaking your word? I know. Don't worry, I'm not offended by that. Doesn't mean I can't try to fish, though," Felix added with a smile.

"Do you—" Flynn started. "Why do you want to know about Diomedes? Have you seen him?"

"A couple of hours ago he was shooting at me. Well, toward me. I think it was Gideon he was really after."

Flynn jolted. "Gideon? You mean 'Wraith' Gideon?"

"I think so."

"Wait, who's Gideon?" Marc asked.

"Remember the guy whose floater you helped us find? Back when you met Flynn?"

"The vigilante Diomedes killed? Or, I guess, nearly killed?" Marc looked from Felix to Flynn for confirmation.

Flynn shook his head. "He was dead. He had to be. Whoever you saw, it wasn't Gideon."

"Spitting image, I swear. He more than looked like him; he moved like him. Caitlin saw him first, about a week ago. We've been trying to figure out what happened to him since. He was visiting his old apartment today when Diomedes attacked."

"Maybe Gideon had a twin?" Flynn posited.

"What happened?" Marc asked. "To Diomedes and—this Gideon?"

"Not quite sure. Dio drove away with Gideon hanging onto his hood. We found the car smashed in a parking garage, but no sign of either of them. Beyond the aforementioned smashed car, I suppose."

Marc leaned forward, rubbing his chin. "And you think this has something to do with his being the gunman last week?"

"Maybe. I don't know. Tell you the truth, it does start to sound a little thin when you put it that way. But my chief concern's getting to the bottom of what happened to Gideon."

Flynn frowned. "Maybe Diomedes was just trying to finish what he started. I mean, if he thinks that's really Gideon."

Felix nodded. "If Diomedes found out Gideon was alive, it'd make sense that he'd be worried about Gideon trying to take revenge. What I want to know is how he found out in the first place. Dio's got other things to worry about right now with a bounty on his head."

"Have you seen him very much since that night?" Flynn asked. "Does he still go to you for information?"

"Just once. A few months ago. I was as surprised as you," he added, seeing the look on Flynn's face.

"You didn't part on friendly terms when he killed Gideon."

"I drew on him before you did," Felix agreed. He'd been forced to pull a gun on Dio in his own defense. "But you're the one of us who got him to leave. Maybe he thought he still had a workable relationship with me. We've, well, disagreed before, and I never got the impression that he *liked* me, but he did consider me useful."

For his own part, Felix considered Diomedes a dangerous, brutal, and possibly psychotic man who seemed to feel little for anything but money, and yet Felix still tried not to hate him. The man was proof enough that hatred and anger weren't things to be fostered for too long. Though unsure what went on behind the freelancer's empty eyes, Felix was sure anger made up a great deal of it. Anger at what, Felix didn't know.

"Where'd you see him?" Flynn asked. "A few months ago, I mean."

Felix laughed. "I thought I was supposed to be the one with all the questions?" The younger man looked flustered at the ribbing. Was Flynn asking out of personal interest, or something else? "Sorry, it's probably not something I should kid you about."

"It's okay." Flynn shrugged. "I've just been . . . wondering about him lately."

Felix couldn't help but notice how carefully chosen the words were. "Well, that's understandable. I didn't meet him, though. Just a phone call. He wanted to know about a man named Fagles. One of Ken Wallace's associates. The guy he got to hire you two against Gideon in the first place."

"Still out for his revenge." Flynn frowned again. "What'd you tell him?"

"Nothing. He wanted it for free. Said it'd be 'payback' for my betraying him the last time, like I owed him some compensation for that whole business. I told him he was an idiot if he thought I'd do anything free for him again, especially considering what he did to Gideon after working with *him*. Hung up on him, too. I didn't even mention the fact that he never paid me in full for that job."

"I never bothered to wonder where he settled after that," Flynn said. "If he found a new place to live after our apartment burned down, or if he just lived out of the floater. I figured he probably found a place. He liked to have somewhere secure to keep his stuff. But I never tried to find where."

"Probably," Felix agreed. "That's what I'd expect, myself, though you know more about him than I do."

Flynn smiled ruefully. "I'm not so sure about that anymore. You saw what he was before I could."

"You came around eventually. And you've known him longer. I may have gotten a feel for his personality, but you're the one who lived with him. You could probably tell me what he eats for breakfast. I couldn't even tell you where he's from or if he's even got any family. Though like I said, I'm more interested in knowing how he connects to ESA."

Marc sighed. "As far as we know, he's just the shooter. I'm probably not giving away any secrets by saying the AoA doesn't know any other connection."

"And given your reaction when I mentioned Gideon, you don't know anything that connects him to the shooting either."

"Nope. You know Gideon's last name?"

Flynn answered first. "We never did get it, did we?"

"I've wished that were otherwise lately," said Felix. "One last question then. How about Ondrea Noble?"

"Who's Ondrea Noble?" Marc and Flynn asked together.

Felix laughed. "Guess that's a no. She's been with Gideon both times we've seen him. She's a designer for Marquand Cybernetics. But if she's not got anything to do with ESA either, I don't know. Maybe I'm wasting your time here." He looked back and forth between the two, trying to read them. "You would tell me if you knew something, right? Even if you couldn't tell me what it was? I'd understand if you couldn't say more, but if I can rule out that connection, it'd save us some time. Or, at least, mostly rule it out," he added with a chuckle. "You know how I feel about being completely sure of anything."

"I think we can give you a definite no about knowing any more than you do," Marc said. "Sorry we can't be more helpful."

"Oh, no worries. I just hope I haven't wasted your time."

"Hey, we helped you rule something out, right?" Marc smiled.

Felix smiled back. "Not nearly as much fun that way, though. But okay, I'll grudgingly admit you've been at least a little helpful." He checked his watch and stood up.

"Leaving already?" Flynn asked.

"Yeah, I'd better leave you to keep doing whatever classified stuff you're doing. And I need to meet up with Caitlin again."

"Oh, I see." Flynn cracked an imaginary whip, complete with sound.

"Envious?" Felix asked with a wink.

"Just giving you a hard time."

"I see. Then expect some payback when it happens to you, too. I'll get Caitlin to help with the harassment. You won't know what hit you."

"He's not kidding," Marc chimed in. "She gets a look in her eyes like a cat gives a mouse."

Felix laughed. "Smile when you say that!" Marc had been smiling already, but it seemed like a good line regardless. Moments later, he was at the door. "Watch your back, Marc, whatever you're into. Let me know if you do need any help."

"I will. Thanks."

"Good to see you, Flynn. Oh, and if I see Dio again, I'll call you. Not that the AoA's looking for him or anything, of course."

"Yeah, yeah, aren't you perceptive." Marc waved.

"I'd offer more active help if I weren't so tied up with this thing with Gideon."

"We're not completely helpless, you know," Flynn told him. "Concentrate on your own stuff. We'll do fine on our own." He smiled, belatedly, as if it was an afterthought just then.

"Well, who knows? Two birds and all that."

Felix gave them both another parting smile and let himself out. Did Flynn just tell him to mind his own business? The door locked after him and he headed out, wishing he had more to tell Caitlin.

XVII

THE UNFOLDING TROLLEY DOORS released Caitlin into the late-afternoon warmth. Air cooled by the river that flowed a block south provided small relief from the stifling atmosphere that had surrounded her moments earlier. Ahead waited the grey stucco of her flat, and she took to the bits of shade beneath the sapling maples that the city had been kind enough to plant along the sidewalk. Against the colour of a clear blue sky, they could be verdant and gorgeous as leaves danced with golden light, yet today they seemed mere refugees amid gray concrete and white haze. They resonated perfectly with—or perhaps because of—her mood.

A cloud of worries and personal demons hounded her thoughts with troublesome whispers. What Felix referred to as a second wave of grief over Gideon's fate again forced her to examine the guilt she felt over her own part of it. Then and now, she'd told herself that she'd done what she'd thought was right. It was the solid ground she had found to stand on; though she inarguably felt safer with Gideon gone from her life and the lives of her fellow Scry, the means were not her choice, and she certainly hadn't pulled the trigger.

And yet the possibility that she had not left a dead body there that night—that he had continued on and could have been aided somehow instead of simply discarded in the mud—had sewn a seed of remorse in her heart. Had she been so anxious to be rid of someone—someone to whom she and others owed their lives, even—that she'd treated his life as no better than trash? Though his association with The Scry put all of them at ever-deepening risk, she never believed that she wished him death.

Could she have been wrong about herself?

Shame was a significant part of what she was fighting, Caitlin knew. And yet hadn't they made certain he was dead? Even summoned an ambulance to find him? After seeing Gideon again, she could no longer be sure how much of what she remembered was real and how much she had created to protect herself. That Felix remembered the same events that night should be reassurance enough, but Gideon's return created a doubt that continued to fester.

They would find out. They had to. It was an assertion that had given her some comfort. Though a part of her hated to admit it, Felix's commitment to aid her had bolstered that comfort. Then Diomedes's appearance had brought another element of that night back to the forefront of her troubled thoughts, and that comfort was no longer enough.

She wanted to clear her head with something soothing, for a time at least, if she couldn't banish the source of the problem. She needed a cup of tea.

She laughed ruefully to herself. What she needed was a ride, or at least a soak in the tub. There was no horse around for the former and likely no time for the latter. But the tea would be a help.

Caitlin reached her building, trotted up the few steps to the door, and keyed in her pass code. The light smiled green at her, but the door still took a second yank to open off of the catch. Her landlord was taking his time with fixing that little quirk.

Taking its time as well was the lift, and as she stood waiting, her craving for a cuppa growing, she considered taking the stairs up the eight flights. But her flat's lift had a way of ascending that made the speed rather palpable, and though she wouldn't admit it to anyone, she rather enjoyed the sensation. It wasn't a horse, but it would have to do until she could next get out of the city. Who knew how long it would be before that happened?

Perhaps she could tear herself away if she needed to. It would have been easier that morning than it was now that Diomedes had re-entered the mix. For the first time, Caitlin wondered if the murderous freelancer had recognized her on the street. The only other time he'd seen her was when he'd shot Gideon, and she didn't think he'd gotten a very good look during those few minutes in the dark. Yet there were cybernetics that might do the remembering for him.

She had put a gun to his head to defend Felix. If he did remember, it would be an understatement to say he would not be well chuffed to see her again. But he'd never bothered her since that evening.

The bell for her floor chimed. She stepped off of the lift and realized that in her brooding she'd completely forgotten to enjoy the ride.

Bollocks.

Her door was immediately across from the elevator. Moments later she was through it and making a beeline for the kettle when the sight of a figure on her balcony made her nearly jump out of her skin.

Standing outside the glass, watching her, was Gideon.

Caitlin froze. Again she had the feeling of being confronted by a ghost. Though dressed in the same sweatpants, T-shirt, and jumper he'd worn earlier, now those clothes were torn and dirty. They made him look considerably more haggard than he was a few hours ago, even without the fatigue apparent in his eyes. This time the ghost stood only meters away. All that she need do to speak with him would be to cross the distance and slide back the door. He reached up and rapped on the glass, and she was suddenly less concerned with whether or not she'd find the answers she was looking for than whether she'd like what they turned out to be.

"Gideon." It was a greeting that she whispered, though very nearly a question as well. Hearing her through the glass, or perhaps just reading lips, he nodded and rapped again.

He waited patiently, but as she moved closer she could see an uncertainty in his eyes. Though small, it stood out in contrast with his previous and sometimes crazed confidence in a way that, for a moment, made his expression seem pleading.

She reached the door and paused with her fingers on the handle of the sliding glass. If he'd been at her front door she'd have preferred to step into the hall to speak to him. But he wasn't in the hall, and there seemed little point in joining him on the tiny balcony. She stood, torn.

Oh, sod it! The door was unlocked and open a moment later. She stepped aside to let him in.

The large man took the wordless invitation and came inside. "You are Caitlin Danae," he spoke. The voice was the same as it had been before. "I need your help."

A myriad of questions bottlenecked in her throat. Her thoughts jumbled, words became elusive, and she stared without speaking until she became conscious of gaping at him.

"Gideon," she managed, "what happened to you?"

"Are The Scry working for anyone?" His voice was calm in a way that had her taking a step back.

"What?"

"I need to know if I can trust you or not. Are you working for anyone?"

"Anyone who?" she demanded, taken aback by the question. "No—no, I'm not."

"You were at my apartment. How did you find it?" he continued. "Were you following me?"

"You told us to find you there. Months ago, when The Scry were working for you. I was looking for you."

He waited, watching her, sizing her up. She was aware she hadn't actually answered his entire question, but then she hadn't asked how he had found her flat, either.

"I don't remember telling you that," he said finally.

"I'm not a liar," she said. "Gideon, what—"

"Who's the man who attacked us?" he pressed. "What does he want? Did you help him find me?"

"What? No! He—You don't remember Diomedes?"

"You say this as if I knew him. Who is he?"

She gaped. Had he repressed the shooting? Did he have amnesia? "Gideon, what is going on? What happened to you?"

He frowned as if trying to decide what to say. "There was an accident. I've been away for a while."

"An accident?" She saw him again, face down in the mud. Bloody. Violated. Murdered.

"Why are you looking at me like that?"

"An accident!" she repeated, appalled at the word. "I saw you dead!"

He stood staring, unsure. Confused. "I was never dead . . . "

"Then, what happened?"

He blinked, off-balance, as if the question surprised him. "It . . . It doesn't matter."

"Doesn't matter? You were shot, you were—you were gone! We checked, we made sure there was nothing we could do for you! You can't just tell me you got better!" She was vaguely aware she was glaring at him.

"You say . . . ," he began, steeped in confusion. "You say I was shot?" Gideon turned away like a toddler separated from a parent.

"You truly didn't know?"

"I don't remember." He blinked again, becoming more composed. "You seem to know a great deal. Tell me. Why? Have The Scry been following me?"

She leaned against her dining room table, still feeling vulnerable from his presence in her flat, but somewhat more at ease as his tone softened. "The Scry were working for you. You more or less recruited us. You don't recall that, either?"

"You assisted me, once. You and a few others of your group. Once, that is all. You proved yourselves valuable, but I remember no further contact."

"There was further contact." The first time he'd come to The Scry to get extra eyes and ears on a particular night, it was Caitlin and a few others with whom he worked. "But The Scry haven't been following you. I have."

"Why?"

"As I said, I thought you were dead. Buried. Then I saw you alive, just last week." She hesitated, uncomfortable explaining her full motivation to him. "I needed to find out what really happened."

"It doesn't matter."

"Bollocks, why do you keep saying that?"

"Saying what?"

"That it doesn't matter."

He frowned, confused again. "I don't know. I'm unsure I even mean it." Again his gaze recomposed itself and hardened, as if his mind were a ship rocking back and forth. "I barely know who you are, and you claim you know so much of me. You swear to me you're not working for anyone."

"Yes! Crikey, how much do I have to say it?"

He gave no answer, merely staring back at her as if deciding whether or not to take her at her word. Whatever inner conflict she felt regarding this man, she did know that she was working only for herself. She met his gaze, daring him to say things were otherwise.

"Alright," he said finally. He turned first and looked out the window towards the street, then at the sky. "I can't see the Moon from here." He went on before Caitlin could ask what he meant. "I need to know what you know. About this Diomedes. About me. I can't—I require your help."

"What sort of help?"

He shook his head. "Later."

"Later," she muttered with a sigh. She was being carried into Gideon's world again, riding on her obligations, her remorse, and her curiosity. It was the place she'd been trying to escape before he'd been shot, and it now loomed again on her horizon. She was losing control of it. Would she be able to do more than simply hang on? "I have some questions of my own," she answered.

"Then ask."

"Who is Ondrea Noble?"

Gideon rose and paced the room once, watching her like a cat before relinquishing his answer. "My sister."

"Your sister." She considered his answer. "You two are close? I think every time I've seen you in the past week, I've seen her. But you'd not mentioned her before."

"I had a brother once. My twin." His eyes glazed as he drifted a moment. "But he's gone now. She is all I have. She helps me. She's helped me recover, got Marquand to pay for it."

"Pay for what? What did they do?"

"There was some head trauma. They said my body was broken also. Some of my cyberware was damaged. They replaced that as well." He sat again, elbows on his knees as he leaned forward in a portrait of weariness. "Ondrea could tell you the specifics. She was always more technical than I."

"And Marquand just covered the entire cost?" His sister must have some clout.

"Mostly." Gideon opened his hand slowly, as if studying it. "I'm told I'll need to do some work for them after. But she said it was the only way to get them to save me."

"Did she say what sort of work?"

He shrugged in a way that made Caitlin think he didn't know. "Nothing until I'm healed completely, but I owe them." He dropped his head away, and then looked up at her again. "Except I don't think they trust me."

"Why not?"

"I'm not to leave the building. They say I'm still healing and need to be observed. I'm supposed to sleep sixteen hours a day, hooked up to monitors. Why is my sister out to get me? They'd keep me locked in that room completely if they could!" He shouted the last part suddenly before catching himself. "I am sorry."

"It's alright." She waited for him to calm a bit before asking about what had caught her ear the most. "Ondrea is out to get you?"

He shook his head as before. "I didn't say that—didn't mean that. She's always helped me. She's the one who got them to let me out, to help me remember things." He shook his head vehemently. "She's trying to take care of me!"

Though it felt like he was telling himself that as much as he was Caitlin, he said it with such force that she wondered if it would be wise to question the assertion. She settled for a middle ground. "But you don't want to go back."

"Something . . . ," he started, and then cut himself off. "No."

"Will you be alright if you don't? Will it affect your recovery?"

"I want you to answer my questions now. Tell me what it is you say I'm recovering from. Who did it? Why?"

"Your sister really only said it was an accident and left it at that?" It wasn't so much that Ondrea hadn't offered more information that struck her as odd, but that he hadn't asked the woman for any further details.

"Yes. Whenever I spoke to her, learning more about it felt unimportant compared to other things we had to discuss. I would know what you claim to have seen."

She told him then, keeping the story brief. She described to Gideon his own search for Diomedes, their pairing to bring Ken Wallace to justice, and the argument that ended with Diomedes pulling the trigger. She told him of how they'd run off Diomedes, of the difficult decision to leave Gideon's body—beyond help, they believed—to be found by the authorities, and finally, how they had destroyed the captured weapons in accordance with his original intentions.

When she was finished, she waited, watching Gideon where he sat. At first he continued to simply listen as he had before, giving no reaction to indicate that he'd just heard the tale of his own violation. She was trying to decide what more to tell him when suddenly he spoke.

"You said this Felix was the one you were with today. Can you trust him?"

"Very much. Felix was the first to believe you weren't the arsonist Wallace had painted you as, and he's the one who got Diomedes to work with you. I've never known him to break his word. He has a reputation for keeping it, as a matter of fact. And," she added finally, "we've been seeing each other for the past five or six months. I could hardly do that without trusting him."

"But you let Diomedes go."

Though his implication took her by surprise, there was so little emotion in the statement that she was not entirely sure how he'd meant it. "I'm not a killer," she said after a breath. "Diomedes is wanted. There's a bounty."

"For what he did to me?"

She shook her head. "I made sure word got out around town about what he did, but there's footage of him assassinating a man in the Corporate District last week."

"The man is a killer."

"Yes," she whispered, "he is." *But you let Diomedes go.* It had never occurred to her to second guess her part of that decision. To let him go. To let him be free to kill again. Now . . .

No. She would not hold herself responsible for every action the bloody freelancer had chosen to take since that night.

"He is a killer, and today he tried to kill me." The tone in Gideon's voice jarred her from her own thoughts. The wrath she would have expected from him was absent, and what was there was something she had not anticipated: fear. Though she had never conversed with Gideon directly at any great length, she never knew him to show a trace of apprehension. Yet there it was. He was afraid.

Her immediate instinct was to try to comfort him. That the thought made her immediately uncomfortable was not helped by the fact that, moments later, Gideon himself shook his head and scowled in a portrait of self-loathing.

"What do you intend to do?" she asked instead.

"I don't know. I need to stay out of sight. From him, from my sister, from everyone. It's important I remember more. I have to remember. Have to. I need to stay here."

Caitlin's stomach tightened. She knew as soon as he said it that she couldn't let him. But then what? Simply turn him away? Turn her back on him again? She liked neither choice.

"What if they find you again? Either of them."

"They won't. After they found me at my apartment, I began to suspect Marquand had placed a tracer on me. If they did, I started jamming it after leaving my apartment."

"Jamming it?"

"Marquand didn't just heal me. They added features to my cyberware."

"You are jamming Marquand's tracer with their own equipment?"

"Yes." He scowled. "I am aware of the irony."

"It isn't irony so much as I'd expect they would ensure that such a thing wouldn't work."

"I was on your balcony for an hour without any sign of them."

Caitlin stood, went to her desk, and fished in the bottom drawer. She found the device by feel, tucked back beneath a stack of envelopes. "I can check for any unusual signals coming from your implants."

"You are an engineer?"

She shook her head. "Not so much. But this is useful for finding bugs, and I don't need a PhD to use it. If you'll permit me?"

Gideon stood with a nod. She passed the scanner in an arc across the front of his body and then along each arm and leg. There was no indication of a signal.

"Anything?"

"Nothing yet." Perhaps it wouldn't be foolproof, especially if Marquand was using anything fancy. She moved around to his back, continued the scan, and still found nothing. Caitlin was closing the scanner and realizing how little comfort it gave her when she noticed the bullet hole.

"Oh my god. Gideon, you're shot."

He looked over his shoulder at her. "It's small. Just a ricochet knick."

"You've got a hole through your jumper here. It's big enough to have a care with so it won't get infected. There's hardly any blood, though."

He strained to see it, though the wound's location on his back must have made it impossible to get a good view. "It doesn't feel like much," he told her, but removed the jumper nonetheless.

The shirt he wore beneath it had a similar hole, and again, far much less of a stain around it for the amount of blood loss she'd anticipated. Caitlin knew of blood augmentations that would result in faster wound clotting, but even so, the colour of the stain didn't look right.

As he lifted his shirt, her gasp was one of both revelation and shock. "Gideon," she whispered, "what did they do to you?"

XVIII

"I WON'T RECALL the teams, Ondrea. You've had more than your chance, and you blew it!"

Julius Tseng scowled at her from behind the expanse of his mahogany desk, framed by the bird's-eye view of the city behind him. Ondrea might have been impressed if she weren't so livid.

"And if they find him when I'm not there to calm him down?" she demanded. "What if he's confused? If he gets violent? Where's your precious low profile going to be then?"

"The low profile was why we kept him in the building. The low profile was what you jeopardized when you asked to let him out the first time! If you didn't let him see that he *could* leave, we wouldn't be in this blasted mess!"

"You know damn well why *we* did that! Retrigger his memories to settle the confusion. Hell, you agreed with me it was best!"

"Those aren't the memories we should be concerned with! I let you persuade me against my better judgment. I now see that was a mistake."

"You knew I was right!" She said it through clenched teeth. "It's my project, my idea that pulled this off!"

Tseng dismissed her comment with sweep of his hand. "Your idea or not, the rest of us should have seen that your personal feelings would get in the way. We had him in a hospital bed under light security when he should have been locked up! Maybe then we wouldn't be having this conversation while he's out there for someone to get their hands on him!"

"Damn it!" She heaved an exasperated sigh and tried to reel herself in. "I told you it's not something you'll be able to force. And even if it was, I'll be damned if I let you cage my brother like an animal."

"He's not your brother, Ondrea. Marquand made him, Marquand owns him. You may have convinced us the personal connection would help control him, but—"

"He made himself!" Anger rode high in her voice over a rush of sorrow that forced her to choke it back before she could continue. "All you did was use him."

"Just washing your hands of your part in that, are you?"

She glared at the question, ready to lash out again. But she was losing time. "You have to let me find him first. I'm the only one who can reach him. He needs me! Recall the search teams."

"I won't do that. However, you will be allowed to look for him. Were it up to me, you'd be off the project completely, but for better or worse your success in bringing your brother into all of this has made the others regard you as some sort of asset. They think we still need you."

"You always were the dumbest of the lot, Tseng." To hell with company politics.

His eyes narrowed. "I'm not looking for your approval, Ondrea. If someone else gets to him because of this fiasco it's not going to matter who you're sleeping with; your butt will be on the street so fast you won't know what hit you."

She fought the urge to ram her fist through his face for that. She hadn't slept with anyone to get where she was and he knew it. "The second one of your teams finds him," she bit off, "they call me in."

"They'll call you. But if they need to act before you get there, they will. And in *that*, I'm in the majority. But you'll have your chance."

"Like it or not, you're still going to need me."

He gave another dismissive wave.

Ondrea turned on one heel, digging it into his carpet in a childish attempt to do some sort of damage, and then crossed to the door without a word.

"Ondrea," Tseng called as her hand found the knob, "whether you like it or not, you're using Gideon, too."

Her stride faltered a moment, then renewed. He didn't know what he was talking about.

Beck was in the waiting area outside the door. He stood upon seeing her and then rushed to catch up when she refused to stop. "Well?" he asked.

"Well, *what?*"

"Well—I mean, it's—what did he say?"

Ondrea left Tseng's outer office and pushed into the corridor of executive offices without another word to Beck. Let him wait. When he'd picked her up after Diomedes attacked, the first thing he did was panic at the gunfire and go in exactly the opposite direction of where she needed to be. She was surprised he managed the courage to pick her up at all before he abandoned her brother and fled. Beck had been babbling as he clutched the wheel and floored the gas, and by the time Ondrea managed to shout some sense into him, they'd lost track of Gideon and her best chance at pursuit.

"Ondrea?"

"Shut up, Beck, I'm still mad at you." They'd lost Gideon, and now Tseng's teams would act without her if they "needed" to. Selfish, short-sighted bastard!

She remained quiet until they reached the elevator and the silence overwhelmed her resolve. "Still nothing on the tracker?" she asked, already sure of the answer.

"Nothing. I'm pretty sure you're right, he's got to be jamming it. Sorry, I should have built the homer better."

"Oh, for Christ's sake, Beck, it's a cascading jammer, that'd have been damned near impossible. It wasn't even supposed to be installed yet, if they'd listened to me," she continued, watching the elevator display. "They had to rush everything, push everything. Now look where we are."

"I shouldn't have panicked. It's my fault we lost him."

"Yeah, I know."

"I'm really sorry, I just—"

"You keep saying that, Beck, but it doesn't change the fact that Gideon's still out there and we can't find him."

Silence.

The elevator doors opened finally, and they stepped inside. "Tseng's got people out looking for him now and he's not pulling them back to let me find him first. I don't know what Gideon will do if an armed group tries to bring him in and I'm not there."

Beck heaved a heavy sigh. "Geez. What'd Tseng say about the drive-by?"

"I didn't tell him."

"You—Ah . . . Why? I mean, that guy tried to kill us?"

"He tried to kill me and Gideon, Beck, he wasn't even shooting at you."

"Um, yeah, okay, but he was shooting?" Beck always ended his statements as questions when he wanted to argue but couldn't find the nerve. He must've thought it was diplomatic, but it just got on Ondrea's nerves. An actual argument would be less irritating.

"We're not going to tell them about him." She turned to look Beck in the eye. "Not yet."

He held up his hands. "Okay, alright! It's just that maybe they might be able to tell us who he is? And if we know who he is then maybe we can figure out—" He pouted in the face of the glare she shot him, and then he shrugged in resignation as the elevator opened.

Ondrea had already resolved to keep Marquand from learning that Diomedes had tried to kill her. The video footage implicating Diomedes was common knowledge, but no one knew that she'd made it. The fact that it was Ondrea who'd personally hired the freelancer to take out Curwen made the company comfortable enough to not be overly concerned by the video's existence. If Diomedes got arrested and tried to implicate them, they would have sufficient distance to pin it all on Ondrea.

It was a chance she'd been willing to take in order to have her revenge on the freelancer and get her brother's project approved, but it was quite another matter if they knew she had actively put the company at risk. If Marquand found out—or even suspected—that Diomedes had turned on her for setting the camera? It was a leap of logic that she couldn't risk. They would accuse her of willfully sabotaging the security of the project and hand her head to her, possibly more than just figuratively.

Thankfully, Beck didn't have enough clearance to know about Diomedes's part in the project. He spent so much time in the lab that it was fully possible he didn't even known about the shooting, let alone the footage of it.

They reached the lab entrance. Ondrea swiped her keycard and touched her hand to the palm reader.

"So, what is the plan, then?" Beck asked.

"We weren't the only ones at Gideon's old building. Did you see the man and woman with us on the steps?"

"No. I mean, I did, but not clearly. They weren't just tenants?"

"I don't think so. If one of them's who I think, I'm almost certain their presence was more than just a coincidence."

Beck followed her like a puppy to one of the workstations and stood behind it as she logged on. "So now you're . . . ?"

"Seeing if I'm right."

XIX

CAITLIN WASN'T ANSWERING her phone. It wasn't even ringing when Felix called her, so she might be unaware he was even trying to reach her. No rings and straight to her voice mail, so in all likelihood either she was on a call or had her phone turned off. She was expecting to hear from him, so Felix hoped she was just busy talking to someone else. Maybe it was one of her friends in The Scry, though she hadn't seemed too eager to involve them before.

But very likely she was on a call, he told himself. Small chance that her battery had died and she hadn't noticed. Possible that she'd dropped the phone off her balcony and it was broken and shattered.

Small chance that something had happened to her.

He forced himself not to dwell on the worry. Shut it off, he told himself. Let it go. She was probably just on the phone or unavailable for some other reason. Spider monkeys escaped from the zoo, stole her phone, and used it to knock over a fruit stand. Yes, there's the answer. Spider monkeys were always to blame. Fuzzy punks. Felix walked down the sidewalk toward Caitlin's apartment. Whatever had happened, he'd find out soon enough.

Why was the AoA looking for Diomedes? He pondered the question in an attempt at distraction. Did they consider him a link to who'd ordered the killing, or was it something else? While farfetched, Felix hadn't completely ruled out the possibility that the AoA had actually hired him. Yet Marc had said otherwise, and assassinations weren't how the AoA operated.

Or was that it? They hired Diomedes for a purpose other than to kill the ESA man, but something had gone wrong? Or maybe something only seemed to have gone wrong. The AoA was based on open information exchange and planning between all of its members, but there were the two factions. Though both were united in their belief that humanity was destroying itself, one wished to delay that self-destruction long enough to find a way to escape on their own, while the other, smaller group preached that the organization might be able to save the entire planet. It was a difference of opinion to be sure, but the fact that the first faction still had no viable means of secession meant that the immediate goals of both factions were relatively identical, so far as Felix was aware. Had the rift between them finally widened to the point that the AoA's left hand didn't know what its right hand was doing?

It was all speculation, Felix knew. The simpler explanation, that the AoA had nothing to do with the shooting at all, was more likely. And why would they hire Diomedes for anything?

Whatever was going on, he couldn't shake the impression that things were somehow connected. Or maybe he was just looking for an excuse to look into the shooting a little more. Felix dismissed that with a laugh. Since when did he need an excuse to be nosey?

He arrived at the entrance to Caitlin's building and, getting no answer at the intercom, decided to key in on his own and wait for her inside her unit. A rapid elevator ride and two unanswered knocks later, he was standing in her living room.

Her laptop was gone and her mail had been brought up, the latter of which sat unopened on the kitchen counter. She'd obviously been back and left since they'd been there together earlier, so where had she gone? Felix tried calling her again, but still got neither ring nor answer.

He continued through the tiny apartment in a cursory search for some sign of where she might have gone, though he considered it unlikely that Caitlin would leave a note instead of simply calling him. After a few minutes, he'd found nothing resembling a note and nothing else that might indicate . . .

Wait a minute.

Felix stopped as he noticed it and then looked around to be sure. Her motorcycle helmet was gone.

She'd left the city. It was a fair deduction, at least; Caitlin hated city traffic to the point where she avoided driving in it unless it was on her way in or out. But where did she go? Did she leave for her house? Felix couldn't think of anywhere else outside the city she'd be going, though he supposed that hardly made anything certain. The worry he'd locked away earlier started to slip back in again.

Then again, she might have just left the city for a ride to clear her head. Felix thought she'd prefer a horse for that though, and they were out near her house—a ninety-minute drive away. It wouldn't be completely out of character, but she'd also been anxious to know what he might find out from Marc.

Caitlin could take care of herself, but the whole thing seemed odd. He shouldn't be worried, but Dio's throwing his hat into the ring had him feeling otherwise.

With more questions than answers, Felix found himself traveling back downstairs to the garage level, where she kept her cycle parked. Maybe she'd just moved the helmet. At the very least he could verify that the cycle itself was actually gone. Yet gone or not, he'd still have no definite answer about her whereabouts.

Her parking space was empty. After a moment or two spent in fruitless pondering, he was on his way back upstairs when he decided it was worth a try to stop at the main floor, exit the building, and take a quick walk around to see what he could see. He looped around the building's exterior once, not entirely sure what he expected to find.

Whatever it was, he didn't find it. Felix was keying into the front door again when the reflection in the glass showed him a face he wasn't expecting.

"Mister Hiatt?"

He turned. "Ms. Noble," he said. "I'd make some clever remark about being surprised to see you if I weren't so . . . surprised to see you."

She kept her distance, about ten feet away. "You left me a message."

"Indeed I did. Though since I only gave you my phone number, you can understand my surprise. How's it you happen to be here?" Felix tried to keep too much suspicion from slipping into his tone. Was she somehow responsible for Caitlin's disappearance?

Ondrea wore a light gray pantsuit and lab coat. Her eyes swept over him and then fixed on his in a way that gave Felix the distinct impression of being studied. "I decided I'd rather speak to you in person. Isn't that what you wanted to begin with?"

"Well, can't argue with that, but I meant what are you doing *here*? This isn't my address, so were you following me, or waiting for me?"

"You come to my office, and then I find you tailing me in the U-District," she said. "So I don't think you can take umbrage. I followed you here from your apartment if you have to know. Now we can stand here wasting time talking about who's stalking whom, or you can tell me why you contacted me in the first place."

"Well put. Though things are a little different now than a few hours ago."

"What do you know about Gideon?"

"I know I didn't expect to see him again. That was him today, wasn't it?"

"Yes, it was," Ondrea said. "Have you seen him since then?"

"Nope. But I'd be able to tell you who it was that shot at you in exchange for some answers I'm looking for, myself."

"I know who it was." The woman's poker face could rival Diomedes's. "Do you know anything of value?"

"Ah, so you know him. Do you know why he was shooting, then?"

"He's a wanted man, that's how I know him. And no, I don't know why he was shooting. Do you?"

Felix shrugged off the accusation in her tone and smiled. "Hoping you could tell me, actually."

"Then it seems you've got nothing to trade after all." She turned to go but paused to add, "If you should see Gideon again, call me, and we'll see if we have anything to talk about."

Felix called after her before she'd taken two steps. "The woman I was with today, have you seen her?"

Ondrea stopped and turned. "Not since earlier. You don't know where she is, either?"

"She was supposed to meet me here," he answered, trying to read Ondrea's body language.

"I'm sorry, I don't think I can help you there. Who is she?"

"Just my girlfriend."

Ondrea nodded, pursing her lips. "Why are you looking for Gideon, Mr. Hiatt? Were you a friend of his, or is this something else?"

"Just an acquaintance. And I thought he was dead. Actually, I heard he'd been shot, six months ago. Kind of makes me wonder what's happened that he's up and around again."

She looked him over anew. "Felix," she said thoughtfully.

" . . . Yes?"

She shook her head as if clearing it. "He was. Shot. But he's recovered and healed. It was a long recovery from an unpleasant experience, so I'm sure you'll understand that he'd like to put it behind him. For his own good, it's best for you to drop the matter. If you see him, call me immediately." She handed him a business card.

"I might be more inclined to call you if I knew what his relationship with you is," Felix fished.

The ring of his phone cut off Ondrea's response. Felix pulled it out and checked the caller ID. It was a number he didn't recognize, but with Caitlin unaccounted-for he decided it was worth putting off Ondrea. With an apology to her, he took the call.

"*Felix?*" The caller's voice was Welsh and instantly took a weight off his shoulders.

"Caitlin? I didn't recognize the number. Everything okay?" The sound of background cars came through from her end of the connection.

"*I'm alright, Felix. A bit of a tale, truthfully. Are you alone?*"

"Actually, no. I'm standing here with Ondrea Noble."

"*Could you step out of earshot a moment?*"

"Well, okay, but that's relative nowadays." He covered the receiver, asked Ondrea to excuse him further, and stepped a short distance down the block. She stood watching him while he resumed the conversation. "Okay, go ahead."

"*You may have a point about the earshot, ducks, so be careful. Don't trust her.*"

That raised his eyebrows a bit. "Are you sure?"

"*I think so. Felix, I'm here with Gideon. He found me. We're about an hour outside Northgate on the road to my house.*"

"Your—" Felix caught himself. "Is that a good idea? Why didn't you call before?"

"*I couldn't. He thinks there might be a tracer on him somewhere and he's been jamming it. The jammer's blocked my phone, and I didn't want to leave him alone long enough to get out of range. I didn't risk stopping to find a pay phone until we'd gotten a good distance away. I'm sorry if I worried you.*"

"Just worried you'd run into Dio again. I'm glad to hear otherwise, but," he paused to turn his back to Ondrea, "why shouldn't I trust her? What did he tell you?"

"*I'd tell you myself if I knew for certain, but for the moment? I'm just going by what he told me, and his own impressions, are a little treacled. Can you meet me at my house?*"

"As soon as I can," he said with a pointless nod. "I'd ask more if I could."

"*Perhaps later when you're away from her. And I should likely keep moving for the moment.*"

"Sounds like a plan, then. Guess I won't be able to call you."

"*I'll try to check in when we arrive.*"

"Sounds good. I'll head out as soon as I can."

"*Alright. Drive safe, Felix. And don't tell her about Gideon.*"

"I won't. And you, too."

Felix put away the phone and returned to Ondrea. "Sorry about that. She's fine. Phone battery just died."

Ondrea nodded dismissively. "As I was about to say, Mr. Hiatt, if you see or otherwise locate Gideon, call me. Rest assured you'll be well-paid for the information."

"How much?" He wanted to ask more—why she needed to find him so badly, and his original question of her relationship to Gideon—but he was anxious to catch up with Caitlin. If Gideon was with her he could likely answer those questions himself.

"That depends on how fast I hear from you. The quicker you find him, the more I'll pay. You know how to reach me, and now I'm needed elsewhere. You'll excuse me."

With that, she turned and strode away. Felix watched her for a moment and then called himself a cab.

*   *   *

Ondrea kept a brisk pace toward the corner of the block and tried to decide what to make of the encounter. It hadn't been until Felix had mentioned Gideon's shooting that she made the connection and remembered one of the names on the recording that Gideon had begun moments before Diomedes fired. She thought the voices were similar, but as it was months since she last listened to it, she couldn't be sure without hearing it again.

Originally, there had been no need to hear it again after picking out Diomedes's name, though in truth she'd played it repeatedly for a while until she was no longer able to bear the grief and anger it drove into her. She could still remember the players: the murderer Diomedes and the three who'd driven him off: the man named Felix, the other called Romulus, and the woman who'd spoken with an accent. Was she the same as Felix's girlfriend who'd pulled her to cover that afternoon?

Ondrea hadn't given the rest of them much thought once she learned of Diomedes; it was clear from the recording that they were outraged at the shooting. Perhaps she'd have heard more of them if Gideon's mic hadn't failed so quickly from the rain and mud. As it was, the first name "Felix" and the nameless woman were practically untraceable, and she was unable to find anyone who knew anything about a freelancer going by "Romulus."

Now safely out of view behind the corner of the building, Ondrea called Beck, who was parked where she'd left him in the lot across the street. "It's me. Can you still see him?"

"He's still outside there, on his phone."

"Good. Tail him," she ordered, glad for her own foresight in taking her personal car this time instead of the one Felix had seen at Gideon's apartment. "Don't wait for me. I'll find my own way back."

"What if he doesn't go anywhere?"

"He will." She'd be surprised if he didn't, at any rate. Intuition told her Felix was headed somewhere, most likely to rejoin his girlfriend. "When he gets wherever he's going, call me."

"Think he knows where Gideon is?"

"I'm not sure, or I'd be going with you. Don't lose him, and *don't* let him see you."

Felix Hiatt knew something. He had too many links to Gideon not to. She'd verify his voice on the recording as soon as she could, and that, combined with the connection that had led her to follow him initially, would add up, one way or another. If it truly was Felix on the recording, was he even aware of the full nature of his own link to Gideon? How much did he know?

She hung up with Beck and called for a taxi. Her wonderings were secondary. She needed to find Gideon before he got any farther from her.

X X

"UP AHEAD, ON PACKARD," Marc offered from the passenger's seat. "We haven't tried there yet."

Michael gave the sedan's rear view mirror another look. There was no sign of the car he'd thought might be tailing them. Packard Street lay ahead, branching right. "That doesn't quite feel right. I think the place was closer to the old brewery." He cast about for anything that felt familiar and came up empty. "On the other hand, it's not like my memory about this is crystal clear." They turned down Packard and continued on.

They cruised through the Industrial District, passing by old warehouses, factory buildings, and single-story offices. Some were abandoned but most still showed signs of life, with lights in the windows and cars parked in the lots outside. Even so, the streets were becoming quieter as employees left work for home or more social areas.

"Anything else you remember about this place?" Marc asked.

"Just the general location, and that it had a door that sunk halfway into the ground on the far side of the building. It might have been brown, but I guess that's not too helpful around here. If I see it, I'll know it."

"If Diomedes used it for storage like you said, it's probably a warehouse, right?"

"He used it for storage, but his brother lived there for a while. No apartments around here, so I think it might be more of a converted office building. He didn't let me go in with him. I'm a little surprised I remembered it."

Felix's comment about not being sure if Diomedes had any family had triggered Michael's memory. Michael never met Diomedes's older brother Silas, but when Diomedes worked at Michael's uncle's farm so many years ago, most of the stories he told involved Silas in some way. Diomedes was proud of his brother back then. It was the glory in those stories that first drew Michael to Diomedes's lifestyle—and blinded him to the man's dark side. Yet during the time that they'd been roommates in Northgate, Diomedes was unwilling to speak much of Silas. Michael never felt comfortable pressing the issue, but clearly something had happened after Diomedes left the farm.

It was one single mention outside a half-remembered building, but at the rate they were going, it was worth checking. Diomedes would never have kept equipment anywhere that wasn't secure. Coupled with the comment about his brother living there once, it made the place a possible hideout. Now if they could only find it.

Michael hoped he wasn't wasting their time. In five more blocks, the road came to a dead end that he didn't recognize. He turned them around and drove back the way they'd come.

"You given much thought to what you'll say when we find him?" Marc asked.

Michael took them down a different street that angled back toward the brewery. "Mostly I've just been concentrating on finding him, I guess." What might he say if Diomedes were suddenly right there? He didn't know. He'd been trying to take things one at a time, concentrating on the search, but Marc had a point. Maybe he was avoiding the issue. "I'm sure something will come to me when the time comes." It sounded like a cop-out even as he said it. "But, yeah, point taken."

What *could* he say to Diomedes? He guessed it would depend on the level of welcome he got. The last thing Diomedes had said to him was "Fuck you." His old mentor wasn't the forgiving sort, but maybe six months had cooled his temper.

Also, maybe the Moon would fall out of the sky.

They continued their search for another fifteen minutes before finding themselves heading along a quiet street bounded on one side by a long warehouse. Vacant lots and smaller buildings sat along the other side.

"That's it!" Michael declared with a relieved smile. "Felix isn't the only one who can find people."

It was really less of a brown than a rust color, but the sight of the squatting, run-down office building immediately caught Michael's memory. He eschewed the building's fence-bounded parking lot for a curbside spot across the street. "This is probably better. I think he'll see us as less of a threat if we come in on foot."

"I can see your point, but do you think making ourselves vulnerable's a good idea?"

Michael looked about. "It's relatively deserted around here." There were no other cars driving the road, to say nothing of the car he'd spotted earlier. It might not have been following them at all. Either way, he decided to stick to his decision to not mention it to Marc. Giving him an additional reason to be jumpy wouldn't likely help. "We should be okay. And I guess Diomedes wouldn't just shoot us, even if he is here."

Marc frowned. "And yet we're still trying not to look threatening."

"I can go on my own, if you want to wait."

"No, no, I'll be fine. Duty calls, right?"

Michael gave what he hoped was a reassuring smile, checked their surroundings again, and then stepped out of the car. Twilight bathed the area, punctuated by the occasional streetlight flickering to life. The building that might hide Diomedes waited across the street. It showed them only thin, darkened windows on the street side and no sign that it was anything but abandoned. The main entrance to the single story above-ground would be facing the parking area, though Michael remembered that Diomedes had taken him to the basement entrance on the far side from the road. If Diomedes was there at all, that would be where they'd find him.

With a final check of the area for anything he'd missed, Michael led Marc across the street to the fenced-in parking lot. He continued to ponder just what he'd say. Each step brought him no closer to an idea. Maybe it wouldn't matter what he said. Maybe he was doomed to fail. He glanced at Marc, seeing the other casting looks up and down the road every other second. Though it was Michael's job to protect them both, he still felt glad that Marc was there backing him up. The thought had Michael frowning immediately from the sting that he'd needed such comfort at all.

They passed without confrontation between the parking area and the glass doors of the front entrance that faced it. "See anything in there?" Michael asked, nodding at the darkened doors. Marc's visor had certain optical advantages.

"Just a wall. Hallway goes to the left and right, probably to separate offices."

Nowhere for Diomedes to hide and watch out the doors, then, Michael thought. They moved past the doors toward the corner of the building. After a peek around it, Michael led them both down the half flight of steps to the basement door. Though apprehension compelled him to draw his weapon, he denied the impulse and tried to relax.

The rap of his fist on the metal door instantly faded to silence. Michael gave it a moment and checked around the door for anything that might be a camera or microphone. Seeing nothing, he knocked again, louder this time. "It's—It's Michael," he announced.

They continued to wait, hearing nothing behind the door. "I'm just here to talk to you," he tried.

The silence persisted.

Marc turned around toward the fence above them. "Maybe he's not here."

"Maybe he's just not answering."

Simply finding the place on his own had made Michael feel better about their lack of progress earlier that day; he wasn't ready to give up on the lead just yet. A memory occurred to him. "What day is this?"

"Thursday."

"Thursday. Which one was Thursday?"

"Which one what? Michael?"

Michael snapped his fingers. "Dallas!" he called out, and then waited for a result.

"Password?" Marc guessed after a few moments.

"Yeah. When we shared an apartment there was one for every day of the week. If he's in there at least he'll know for sure it's me."

Whether Diomedes was there or not, it quickly became clear that the door wasn't about to open. Michael gave it another hopeful knock and eyed the furnace unit along the outer wall above. "I guess we could climb up on the roof if we wanted to. But that probably wouldn't help things."

"Maybe we should go back to the car," Marc suggested. Michael frowned and tried to think of another option that didn't just involve continuing to knock on the door. Marc added, "For a minute or two."

Though he yielded to Marc's suggestion, Michael wasn't ready to leave the area quite so quickly. He'd been about to say as much after the car doors clapped closed, but it was Marc who spoke first.

"I wanted to say this away from the door in case he could somehow hear," Marc said, "but I can leave a bug or two outside there. If he comes back or leaves when we're gone, we'll know."

"Maybe, but I'm not ready to give up on seeing him in person just yet."

Marc turned in his seat to better face him. "It's not really giving up, just backing off so we can keep searching. It's a good lead. I'm just saying we don't need to wait here to follow it up."

The evening breeze blew some leaves across the road and over the windshield as Michael considered. "I think we should still give it at least a little time. Stake out things in person. If we leave and then see him here, we'll just have to come back again. And what if he's in there and finds the bug?"

"If he finds it. Though, yeah, that probably wouldn't help."

"He'd be even less likely to trust us."

Marc gave what seemed a reluctant nod. "Mm. Stake out for a bit, then leave the bug?"

"Just for a little while." Marc could be right, but an hour or two spent waiting might pay off.

"Fair enough." Marc looked around behind them. "Not too much action around here. At least that's something."

Marc was right about that. The street, near the edge of the city, reminded Michael of nothing so much as a ghost town. The warehouse they were parked beside felt like a wall separating them from the rest of Northgate, outside of which few people wandered, and the few other cars parked along the street afforded them little opportunity to blend in. If their intention were to stay and stake the place out for a few days rather than a couple hours, that might be a problem, but it would also make it easier for them to see anyone coming after Marc.

"How are you holding up?" Michael asked.

"Oh, heh. I don't mind telling you I'm a little anxious. But I'd be that way no matter where we were, I'm sure. I'll be fine. A little edgy. I'll be fine."

Michael readjusted the rearview mirror, unsure what to say to that. Though he wanted to help him feel safer, no words of reassurance sounded right. "We won't stay too long."

"Look, don't worry about it."

Michael turned to watch the building through his own reflection in the window. "Okay," he fibbed.

A buzzing rip shot loudly from down the street behind them: a motorcycle taking advantage of the open road, tearing down it in a burst of speed that gave Michael a start and had Marc jumping before they realized what it was. The biker sped past them, rounded a corner, and passed out of view to leave them in silence.

Marc let out a long breath. "I'll get started on the bugs."

* * *

Inside the building's basement, Diomedes walked halfway to the door. The lights were off. He didn't need them. Michael was outside. He scowled and returned to the table.

They weren't leaving, Michael and the other one. The camera he'd aimed at the street showed them clearly on the screen of his laptop. Waiting in the car. Staking him out. Diomedes could recall a night that Michael and he had staked out a transit station together in his old floater.

He's not so different from you, came the small voice again.

Diomedes nodded to it. Michael Flynn had strength. Smarts. Things Diomedes had seen in himself. He could be a fool at times, but he was young. Foolishness could be fixed—would have been fixed. But then the kid refused him. Turned on him.

Michael had no loyalty, chided the large voice. **He refused to follow your lead. He failed the test. Not like you!**

Not like him, Diomedes agreed. He'd passed. He'd followed Silas when the time had come, and then—

And then—

Diomedes seized a chair with one hand and flung it into the

wall, where it splintered to pieces. He did not want to hear it.

Instead, Diomedes pulled up another chair and sat to watch the screen. How had they found him? No one knew of this place anymore. Who else had they told? The man with Michael matched Lars's description. While vaguely familiar, Diomedes couldn't place him.

Go out to them. Make them tell you what you want to know. Then get rid of them!

It would be the safest thing to do. Who knew why Michael was there? Trusting him was a risk.

Trusting is weakness! Of course Michael was lying. Strike before he does! Your foes are mounting. Gideon's back and you couldn't stop him. You barely got away before the cops came. For all you know, Michael works for Gideon just like the woman!

Diomedes picked up an auto-pistol from the table. It was heavy. Comforting. His foes *were* mounting. They had him cornered. If he couldn't stop them, they'd win. He'd have to leave the city. He'd have to abandon the opportunities he was waiting on.

You need allies. Find out what he wants.

It's a trap!

It's Michael.

HE'S A LIAR! The large voice drowned out any response. Diomedes was midway to the door again when he stopped in realization.

Confronting them at their car was dangerous. He'd need to approach across the open street. If it was a trick, they'd have him. He couldn't make a move until they came back to the door. That gave him time to plan. Consider his options. Once again he sat. Thinking. Waiting. Weighing.

An hour later, he was still waiting, switching back and forth between the camera views and the news reports. The tickers and talking heads were talking more about celebrity crap and some "gray goo" cover-up supposedly going on in Denver, but the assassination still got slight mention. They still wanted him.

His phone rang. The name on the screen triggered a rush of anger. "About damn time," he growled in answer. "Where the hell've you been?"

Fagles's voice slithered down the line. "*I would have thought,*" he answered, "*that you'd be a little more pleased to hear from me.*"

Diomedes whispered through clenched teeth. "I called you over a week ago. Four fucking times."

"*Obviously I've been keeping my distance. You're not the most reputable person to be associated with these days."*

"That's why I called! You're going to help. You can't turn your back on me."

"Things are a bit more complex now, aren't they?" Fagles said coolly. *"Been pursuing a few side projects, have you? You've been busy."*

"Hell yes, I've been busy! Dodging cops and every bounty-hunting jackass in the goddamn city! You turn your back on me and I won't be the only one with a price on his head, you get me?"

"My friend, I think you need to calm down."

"Fuck your calm down!" Diomedes stood in the darkness and fought the urge to crush the phone. Smug. The man was always smug! But Fagles could also make him money.

" . . . Are you finished?"

Diomedes let him eat silence.

"I can help you," Fagles said. *"But I'm no longer certain that I should."*

"You need me. You need me for your little 'project.' If I'm out, so's your secret."

Fagles smugness shattered. *"You've already jeopardized the project!"*

Diomedes gaped at the lie. "What the hell are you talking about?"

"What I can't decide is whether you meant me to find out what you did, or you just didn't expect to get caught."

"What. The hell. Are you talking about?"

"Or is there a third option? Is it possible you don't even know what you'd done? But no, you couldn't be that foolish, could you?"

You are NOT a fool. Diomedes was midway to declaring as much when movement on the screen caught his eye. Michael and the other man were getting out of the car. Diomedes watched them cross the road.

"Ah, now you see, this is the point in the conversation where it's your turn to—"

"Shut up," Diomedes ordered. They'd entered the parking lot. He had just enough time to hang up on Fagles before he saw the second car pull up behind Michael's.

XXI

MICHAEL HEARD THE SLAM of the second car's doors just as he and Marc rounded the building on the side of the basement entrance. "Go over the fence," Michael whispered.

"What?"

Two freelancers were walking into the parking lot. Michael ducked back around the corner from where he'd spied them and pushed the car keys into Marc's hands. "Behind the building. Get to the car and I'll meet you back at your place."

"But I can't just—"

"Go!" He tried to make the order as firm as possible without letting his voice carry.

There was no time to wait for Marc to comply. Michael stepped around the corner to find the freelancers midway across the parking lot. Their weapons were holstered or slung. Their backs were to the road. They stopped immediately once they saw him.

Michael eased toward them, hands out to his sides. "Hello!"

The newcomers, a man and a woman, let him approach. He stopped about ten feet away and felt their gaze as they sized him up. Both stood six feet tall. With the same sharp features, the same dark eyes, and nearly identical weapons, the only thing that really stood out as different was the length of their auburn hair: hers long and pulled back tight, his receding and cut short. They could have been twins, and the matching leisure armor and Aegis Security patches did nothing to lessen the impression.

They were the same pair he had seen that morning coming into the 'Pyre.

The man's eyes didn't let Michael go for a moment. "Hello," he answered.

The woman said nothing, instead glancing first behind her, and then over Michael's shoulder in a way that had him fighting the urge to glance back himself. With any luck, Marc would escape undetected. Michael didn't want to give them cause to think he was there.

Silence echoed between them. The two seemed unwilling to speak more before he did. At a loss for words himself, Michael finally tried, "Do I know you?"

The man gave a dismissive smile. "No reason you should." Again, he said nothing more and simply remained where he was, somehow seeming both expectant and unobtrusively content.

The woman was looking everywhere the man wasn't, and in a much more agitated fashion.

"Is there something you want?" Michael tried.

"I was about to ask you the same question."

"Is this your property?" Michael asked.

The man shrugged. "Nope. And since you asked, I'd guess it's not yours either."

Michael gave a shrug of his own. He had a clear line of sight across the street to the hood of the car he and Marc had come in, so the woman ought to be able to see at least the driver's door if she looked back from where she was. Trying to give Marc a window of escape, he fought to think of a way to focus their attention on himself that wouldn't also result in violence.

The man took a single step forward. "So," he spoke again, "here we are the three of us, spending a pleasant evening standing around on someone else's property. How'd you suppose that happened?"

"What do you want?" Michael tried again.

"Where's your friend?" the woman asked. Her hand had shifted to her sidearm holster, though her attention was on the building.

Unable to think of a direct answer that didn't give away more than he wanted to, Michael ignored the question. "I'm looking for someone."

"So I've heard," said the man. "Is he here? If you're just one guy, maybe you need a hand or two?"

"I think I'll be alright on my own, thanks." Unsure of where Marc was, he stopped just short of asking them to leave. The woman had all the carriage of a coiled spring. Michael doubted they'd just go away for the asking.

"Oh, c'mon," cajoled the man. "Sure, you look like you know your stuff, but he's in there, you're out here. He's got the advantage on you. Little help evens the odds."

Were they really there for Diomedes, or was it just an angle to get to Marc? The other ESA assassinations were made to look like accidents. "I don't even know he's in there. I've been here over an hour and he's not shown himself."

"Well, something brought you here. We know you're looking for him. Now we're willing to be reasonable but that bounty splits two ways just as easily as it does three. You either work with us or not at all. Read me?" His contented expression from earlier was gone.

Michael reflexively frowned and had to stop himself before it became a scowl that the two might take as prelude to a fight. He couldn't take them both, not out in the open. If they attacked, things would go bad very quickly.

"Say he is here," he said finally. "You have some sort of plan?" Marc should be gone by now. Why was the car still there?

The woman interrupted her companion before he could speak. "This is a bad idea, Jer. Where's the other one?"

As if in answer, Marc peeked around the corner of the building behind the freelancers, by the road. Michael glanced at him before he could stop himself, and then everything happened at once.

Reacting to Michael's gaze, the woman spun to see Marc and yelled "Gun!" before pulling her own and rushing for the cover of the front doorway, firing as she went. Marc ducked back around the corner and Michael barely had time to wonder if Marc had drawn a gun at all before Jer swung at him.

Michael dodged the punch, but before he could close the distance to the woman and pull a gun of his own, Jer grappled him about the waist and tried to pin his arms. Somehow Michael managed to maneuver in his grip and force the man's arms away as the woman fired two shots at Marc's corner. Marc fired back as Michael struggled; Michael was paying more attention to Marc's plight than his own, focusing on the guns. Marc's shots went high—he'd barely turned his aim around the corner— but the woman ducked back into the doorway alcove regardless.

Jer spun Michael around by the arm and flung him against the front of the building, where the side of his head smacked against the wood. Michael's vision and stomach swam, and he barely ducked the blow that followed. He drove his fists against Jer's ribs before catching him in a grapple of his own to force them both away from the wall. Jer grabbed back and shoved. They tumbled to the gravel.

More shots exploded behind him, but Michael could only focus on keeping Jer's hands off his throat. The man's strength matched his own. Dust choked his lungs and they struggled until Michael forced a knee to the other's chest and shoved him away.

By the time he could spare a look in Marc's direction, Marc was facing Michael and standing out from cover, feet planted, with his gun aimed straight at Jer. "Let him go!"

He was making himself a target!

Michael was halfway to his feet when the woman burst from the alcove again, gun in hand, about to have a clear shot at Marc. Michael scooped up a handful of gravel and hurled it at the woman's face. It hit her an instant before she fired. Her shots went wide and Marc dove back around the corner.

The effort left Michael sprawled forward and on one hand and knee. Before he could right himself, Jer slammed him to the ground completely. Face down in the gravel, Michael fought to get up against the freelancer's weight. It wasn't enough. Jer caught Michael's arm in a flash and twisted it behind his back so sharply that he'd have yelled in pain were there any air in his lungs.

Then the woman was standing above him, her auto-pistol trained at his head, her face streaked with dirt. Though her left eye was clenched shut and bleeding, her right glared down at him all the more violently.

"If he moves again, Jer, I'm gonna shoot him! Punk got me right in the eye!" She turned back to Marc's corner to shout, "We've got your friend! Come out and drop the gun!"

"Ah, now you made my sister mad, guy," Jer scolded. "Do you have any, any idea what a pain in the butt she's going to be now?" Michael raged against Jer's grip, but the man wrenched his arm further back. "Hey! Cool it."

Michael fought to calm down. What could he do? If Marc had any sense, he'd make a run for the car.

"Now!" the woman shouted again. "While he still has a head!"

"Marc, run!" Michael yelled. Jer wrenched his arm further.

"You run and he gets it!"

Michael lay with his eye on the corner of the building, willing Marc to make a run for it and waiting for Jer's grip to relax.

Neither happened. Marc's gun landed in the gravel a moment before he took two shaky steps into the open. Marc swallowed and licked his lips. "Okay, let's all just—Let's just be reasonable here, okay?"

The woman shifted her aim to Marc so fast that Michael flinched with him in anticipation of a shot. "I say we grease 'em both right now."

"Shit," Marc whispered.

"C'mon, ease off, Susan. They're not going anywhere," Jer said. "Give them a chance to help."

"My brother the optimist. They ambushed us! I told you they wouldn't share!"

Jer's reply never came. Something landed with a crunch on the gravel behind Michael, and Susan yelled in surprise a second before she hit the ground in front of him. Jer was off his back a moment later. Michael wasted no time scrambling to his feet. He turned around in time to see Diomedes smack Jer across the temple with the butt of the assault rifle Susan had worn slung. Jer dropped like a brick.

Diomedes whirled on Michael. He barely had time to brace for an attack before Diomedes spoke. "Your car. Let's go!"

Michael stood rooted in wordless uncertainty.

"Move!" the other shouted before running across the street. Realizing Diomedes meant for him to follow, Michael started after him and pulled Marc along.

Diomedes stood by the car and looked up and down the empty street. He had a duffle bag over his shoulder and one hand on the handle of the back door. "You!" He pointed at Marc. "Drive." His pale eyes flicked to Michael. "Front seat. Now!"

Michael found himself sliding into the passenger's seat before he knew it. Diomedes climbed in behind him as Marc slid the key home and started the engine. Diomedes pulled his door shut and sat low in the seat. "Get on Davis Avenue. Take it south out of the city."

Marc was visibly sweating as he sped the car into the road, pressing them back to their seats. Michael had only a moment for a last look at Jer and his sister lying motionless in the gravel.

"They're not dead," Diomedes muttered as if reading his mind. "Not hit hard enough."

"I'm surprised," Michael said before adding, "that you came out." The amendment wasn't what he'd initially meant, but it was no less true. He struggled to catch up to the situation.

"I don't care about your *opinion*," Diomedes growled. "Tell me why I shouldn't kill you."

Even after six months, Michael could still read the tone of his voice. He didn't need to look around to know Diomedes had a gun aimed at him.

XXII

"**YOU'VE GOT A GUN** on me, don't you?" Michael asked without turning to look.

Smart, Diomedes thought. "Yes. Now answer the question."

Michael pitched an irritated sigh. "Let's see, why shouldn't you kill us? First of all, we're not here to kill *you.* I wasn't lying about that. Not that I'd guess that'd stop you, would it?"

The kid's companion gripped the wheel more tightly. "Uh, Michael?"

"Who's he?" Diomedes asked.

"Um—" began the driver.

"I asked *him.*"

"This is Marc," Michael told him. "You met him before, if you remember. He helped us find Gideon?"

Gideon! "What do you know about Gideon?"

"What? Nothing!" Michael sounded confused at the question. It was impossible to tell if it was genuine.

A lie. He knows something.

Michael's never lied to you. You've known him too long to kill him like this. You're in control now. You can afford to hear him out.

"Nothing?" Diomedes pressed.

"No more than when you—" Michael stopped to face him. "Well, no more than when you shot him, really." Again Michael seemed in earnest. He'd always been naïve. "Why?"

"Because I asked. Who told you where to find me?"

"Are you going to hold the gun on me for the whole conversation?"

"You want me to put it on Marc instead?" he shifted his aim.

The kid shook his head. "No, you can leave it on me if it makes you feel better. But we won't try anything, I'm telling you."

"Ah, I'd really feel better if you just put that away completely," Marc said.

"Just shut up and keep driving." He turned the gun back on Michael. "Gun's back on you. Now how'd you find me? Who tipped you?"

"Okay. Fine. Either you'll shoot me or you won't. You're faster than me either way."

"Brave of you," Diomedes grunted. "Stupid, too." The kid should know better than to pass up a chance to get a gun off of him. Yet Michael wasn't intimidated either. Even as that frustrated him, Diomedes had to admire it. He wouldn't have gotten intimidated either.

"Yeah, well, I'm glad you approve," Michael grumbled. Sarcasm.

"Whatever. *Who* tipped you?"

"You tipped us. A long time ago. You took me here. You were using it for storage, you told me Silas used to live there."

Diomedes remembered. He had shown him. **You shouldn't have trusted Michael then. Came back to bite you again, didn't it?**

Maybe, maybe not.

"You remember Silas, then," Diomedes said.

The kid took his time speaking next. "It took me a while to think of that place. We got lucky finding it. But yeah. You were always talking about him. Back on the farm, the stories you'd tell. Do you remember that?"

The farm.

Is there anyone left that you've known as long as Michael? Have you forgotten?

He'd told the kid about Silas. Back when there were stories he wanted to tell. "But you never met him," Diomedes said. It wasn't a question. Michael had found him again in Northgate after . . . everything else.

"Nope," the kid answered, and then turned to face forward. "But you did tell me he'd lived there."

"Shouldn't have. You led those two to me."

"I didn't mean to."

"Meant to or not, you screwed up!"

Michael spun around so fast that Diomedes nearly fired. "Look, I didn't put the damned bounty on your head, so don't get—" He stopped suddenly, just watching.

Diomedes stared back at him for a time before going on. "You find out about the bounty before or after you came looking?" **Dumb question. That's why they're here, don't fool yourself.**

"Before," Michael admitted. **See?** "But we're not here to collect, I told you."

"Then you're looking to sell me out."

"I'm not telling anyone where you are," Michael insisted. "I don't know just how much you saw back there, but if we'd wanted to sell you out we threw away a great opportunity!"

"Maybe." He didn't bother to disguise his skepticism. "Maybe it's a set-up. You turned on me. Didn't want anything to do with me after all I'd taught you, given you. Then there's a price on my head and you just turn up. So why *are* you here? Tell me. Something that doesn't make you a liar."

Michael swallowed and glanced to the driver. **If he doesn't say anything, you'll know he's playing you.** Outside, buildings were getting fewer and fewer. Davis Avenue became Highway 17 as it left Northgate. More isolated, fewer witnesses. Plenty of spots to dump a body or two.

You're running out of bridges to burn.

"Because we think the same people who hired you are after us," Michael said finally.

Marc shot a look to Michael and tried badly to cover it. The kid had let something slip. Diomedes stared Michael down. It had always made the kid talk a little more. This time he just turned away. Again, brave.

"Then why come to me?" Diomedes asked. "Same people who hired me are after you, maybe I'd just kill you for them. You're being stupid, coming here."

Michael continued to watch the road. "You're in hiding. You're alone. If they cared about you at this point, I'd guess they wouldn't have hung you out to dry, right?"

"Oh, you just think you know it all."

"Am I wrong?"

"My gun, my questions. Who's after you?"

Michael shook his head. "Well, if we knew that we wouldn't have tried to find you. Who hired you?"

"That's crap. You don't know who they are but they're the same as who hired me? That's crap, kid." An exit diverged from the road ahead, leading into the dark. "Take that turn." Marc had the sense to do as he was told.

"Diomedes," Michael said, "we've got suspicions. That's all."

Diomedes glared. Suspicions? "Fine. Who do you *suspect* is after you?"

Even in the fading light he could see the kid was sweating. "You're the one who always tried to teach me not to give away what I know for free. I *was* paying attention to you then, you know."

"Should've taught you not to pull a gun on me in the middle of a stand-off!" **Damn right!** "Or have you changed your mind about that?"

Michael didn't answer.

"You don't trust me," Diomedes told him. That was it, then.

He *doesn't* trust you. You can't even think of trusting *him*! He doesn't really want your help. It has to be a trick, you know it is.

We're almost there.

They were almost there. Soon the road would turn along a high embankment covered in scrub brush. It would be over then. Yet even as he thought it, he could feel the tug of the little whisper preparing to delay him.

Michael needs your help. You need his. He doesn't have to trust you to ask for help. You've worked with people you didn't like before; you didn't trust Felix Hiatt but you asked for his help finding Fagles.

Which got you nowhere! Hiatt wouldn't help you, you found Fagles yourself! You don't need help from anyone!

The voices went off to argue, and he was on his own again.

The road slipped on beneath them until Michael broke the silence. "I used to trust you, you know." He turned back around. "On the farm, you were the one who looked out for me. When I came here, you protected me, helped me adjust to the city."

"You wouldn't shut up about it until I did. You talked me into it."

"Maybe you let yourself be talked into it."

"Maybe that was a mistake!"

Yes, sentiment. You thought someone from your past would shield you from more change? Look where it got you!

Michael turned away again—pouting, Diomedes thought, like a weakling. "Well, maybe it was, then," Michael said. "But maybe you just had some loyalty to the past. Yeah, I used to trust you. Because you used to seem to give a crap."

Diomedes was no longer looking at him, watching instead the yellow lines on the road. "Whatever."

"Yeah, maybe you never cared," Michael said. "I don't know why you helped me. Maybe everything I saw in you really was a lie."

"I don't care what you think," Diomedes muttered. Even as he did so, he couldn't help but recall the words she'd said that echoed Michael's, and the memory of another night, years past, forced its way into his mind.

He watches her tear the wrapping paper, enjoying the sight of her delicate hands breaking through ribbon and tape to get at the box inside. "Happy birthday, Janette," he tells her.

She stops long enough to smile at him with the delight that no one has ever quite shined on him before her. "Thank you, Malcolm."

He returns her smile, feeling foolish for it and yet not caring. There's no one there to see it but her. "You don't even know what it is yet."

"I told you, sweetie, it doesn't matter what it is. You remembered, and I'm thrilled."

"Hard not to remember." He grins. "You gave hints for a month."

"Well, we've only been together nine months, it's not fair not to give you hints. Nudges. Brilliant neon signs." She giggles with a wink.

"Open it anyway. You'll like it."

She smiles again in that way that makes him surprised that she's his, and opens the box. "Oh my god."

He smiles as she lifts the necklace. "Those are real diamonds."

"Oh my god," she repeats. "It's beautiful! But how did you . . . ?"

" . . . afford it on a security guard's salary? Saved. Shopped. Came into some money."

"That wasn't what I—" She takes her blue eyes off of the necklace as worry begins to fill them. "Came into some money?"

"Uh huh."

"Malcolm, came into some money how?"

"Does it matter?"

"Yes, it matters. How?"

"Janette, just try it on."

Her smile is gone completely, her face hardened. *"Did you get this from your brother? Did you steal this with your brother?"*

He stands and snatches up the box but manages not to throw it across the room. *"I told you it doesn't matter! Would you just put it on?"*

"I don't want to put it on! Malcolm, you told me you were done with that!"

"Two times, Janette! Just two times, and you go all frantic!"

"I don't care! You said you were going to stop!"

"Come on, it was just a little — "

"I won't be with a thief!"

"And how the hell else am I supposed to do it?" he yells. *"You're dropping hints all over! What am I supposed to do?"*

"Not for this!" she shakes the necklace at him through starting tears. *"Not for something stolen! A rose, a card, just something from* you! *I grew up with money, I don't need that from you!"*

He reels on her. *"Because I can't afford it, right? Because you know I can't possibly be worth that much!"*

"That's not what I mean!" She drops the necklace to the floor.

"You pick that up!" he roars, doing it for her.

She glares through tears as she takes a step back from him. *"I never cared about how much you made, Malcolm — or how much you could give me. I loved you! Because you were good to me, because you were different! And because you cared more about living life than making money! But it was just an illusion, wasn't it? You're turning into your brother."* She swallows. *"Everything I saw in you was a lie."*

"Janette," he starts, one fist clenched around the necklace. *"I did this for you."*

She turns away. *"You won't stop stealing, and you lied about it again! I can't trust you, can I?"*

"Damn it, don't turn your back on me!" He wrenches her around before he can think about it.

She pushes his hand of her shoulder, but it's the pain in her eyes that breaks his grip. *"Get out, Malcolm!"*

He holds her gaze, wanting to plead with her for another chance. *"I — "* is all she lets him say.

"Just get out!"

He throws the necklace against the wall and does as she asks, slamming the door behind him.

"Everything I saw in you was a lie."

The back of Michael's head was silhouetted against the purple sky out the window. Diomedes considered the possibility that the kid was telling the truth.

It's another chance.

Another chance to be made a fool of.

Help him!

Kill him!

"Everything I saw in you was a lie."

The past, the present, the voices, he couldn't think with all the noise! Too much noise! Diomedes smashed the gun against the window beside him to clear it. Marc cursed. Michael jumped and spun around. Diomedes aimed for him instantly.

"Stop the car," he ordered.

A moment later, the tires had rumbled over the gravel and come to a stop. "Get out. Both of you. Leave the keys."

They did so. Diomedes followed, gun still held on the kid.

Don't do it.

Do it!

He turned on Marc. "Get on the shoulder. Next to him." The road was deserted. They were on the edge of a ravine. Michael, the one named Marc, and himself.

"What are we doing here, Diomedes?" The kid was watching him. Tense. Alert.

Afraid.

No.

Yes!

Help them!

Diomedes was alone in the car and driving back to Northgate when Fagles called.

XXIII

<<INITIATE CYCLING ENCRYPTION>>
<<AOA CODE STATUS 78F392J-14>>
<<RELAY HYG=32 11 44>>
<<CLASSIFICATION EPSILON>>

Begin report.
Expansion of the ESA zone of control into the large chamber discovered by CPO Levy and myself continues. On my order, scanning and defensive equipment have been moved into the chamber to create an ESA presence, though this order was given under ESA pressure. I believe that the recent "near-leak" caused by the hacker team has increased the urgency of ESA's timetable. I recommend that the AoA escalate to match.

Regarding the status of the chamber itself, at this time I believe it to be reasonably secured against any possible drone attack, though the quantity of unknown factors inside the chamber prohibit a declaration of complete safety. Additionally, the communications bubble that hampered previous exploration is no longer active, having dropped shortly after the chamber's opening to space. The reasons behind this are, as yet, unknown.

It has been hypothesized that the apparent isolation of the black material within the chamber from black material elsewhere in Paragon (as evidenced by a lack of function prior to our entrance and subsequent activation via the blue "touch pad") is due to the fact that the material in the chamber is of a separate and possibly self-contained system, akin to a terminal on an isolated network. Should this be the case, study of material in the chamber may yield information unattainable elsewhere. Evidence to test this hypothesis is insufficient at this time.

The remarkable field membrane that covers the chamber opening continues to hold. It allows the passage of solid objects while containing the interior atmosphere. The lack of any additional power output across the membrane has led ESA engineers to postulate that it is indeed a natural property of the black material found throughout the ship, though it is clearly in a state altered from what we have previously encountered. Detailed scans are attached to this message. Recommend analysis of how this may affect current attempts to replicate the material.

The purpose of the large device at the center of the chamber remains unknown.

We continue to be reliant on the membrane to retain atmosphere in the chamber. As such, crewmembers remain suited at all times as a precaution. All attempts to close the hatch on the opening have been unsuccessful. With the justification that such measures hinder working conditions, I have advised the Space Agency to provide materials to create an airlock large enough to accommodate the opening. As such materials are not currently available on-site at Omicron, their delivery will likely provide an opportunity for covert transfer of further AoA equipment and, if possible, personnel. In the interim, a rudimentary camouflage is in place to conceal the opening from extra-lunar surveillance.

ESA's next objective will be to identify the purpose of the chamber. A direct, non-human interface with Omicron is being suggested to avoid further loss of life. I am unable to gauge the success of such an attempt, but must restate my previous position of advancing the takeover timeline.

Please advise on the inventory of any incoming shipments, or alterations of plan. An update on the status of Agent Triton is also requested.

End report.

Clasped hands tapping her chin, Marette searched the report for items she might have omitted. Events were swiftly moving to a head. She considered underscoring the need for a complete AoA takeover before things became uncontainable, but such a reemphasis was likely unnecessary. That she had said it twice was enough. Everything appeared complete.

She examined the last line and frowned. Perhaps it was too complete. Marette erased the query about Marc and sent the report before she could reconsider.

XXIV

FELIX TIPPED the cab driver, closed the door, and then turned to find Caitlin walking toward him as the cab crunched a retreat back down the gravel of her house's quarter-mile driveway. She wore a gentle smile that reassured Felix that, for the moment, nothing was *too* wrong.

Unless, he decided, she was hiding some unpleasant news for later. He took the few remaining steps toward her where they kissed a greeting at a discreet distance from the door. His first goal was to make sure she was okay. If so, then he'd be eager to chase down the truth of what happened to Gideon.

"Hullo, Felix. I'm glad you made it alright."

"It's good to see you. He still here?"

She nodded. "Inside."

"I'm surprised you brought him here." He didn't have to point out what she herself had told him in the past: that her house was her sanctuary from the rigors of the city.

"I'm a little surprised, myself. But it's more secluded than anywhere in Northgate. My landlord's is the closest house; that's half a mile away and he's on vacation. I couldn't just turn him away. I can't run from this, Felix. Not a second time."

"I wasn't second-guessing you," Felix assured her with a smile. He stopped short of confessing that he'd wished she'd waited for him to catch up before coming here. "You're doing alright, then?"

"As much as is to be expected. I wanted to come out to see you alone before you went inside, but I don't feel threatened. Gideon's little more than confused and scared right now. He reminds me of last year when Drake had a hoof infection and the vet had to keep him off the ground in a harness. Both are strong creatures who don't completely understand what's happened to them. I'm treating him carefully."

"Think we should try feeding him some apples and sugar cubes?"

Caitlin rewarded the measly joke with a smile. "How did I know you'd say that, ducks?"

Before he could think of a good response, a brush at the side of Felix's leg momentarily sidetracked his attention to the black cat sliding up against him. "Well, hey, Lucifer," he said, kneeling to pet him.

"Oh, yes, you show for Felix but not for me?" Caitlin scolded affectionately. "Furry little git."

"I'm getting popular tonight." Lucifer allowed him a quick stroke before having enough and dashing back into the darkness. "Someone tried to follow me here. Gave him the slip midway, don't worry."

"I won't, then. Though I expect Gideon will need some assurance."

"Then he's still the same old Gideon? Enraged tirades against the violence and 'filth' in the city?"

"Honestly, Felix, that's one way he seems better. He's confused, and yes, sometimes rather random, but those moments of rage are missing. At least that I've seen."

"What do you suppose that means?"

She shook her head. "I don't know." Caitlin began to stroll back toward the house, bringing Felix with her. "Marquand did something to him. He seems fairly certain that his sister was involved."

"His sister?"

"Ondrea. I thought I'd told you."

"Pretty sure I'd have remembered that." It made sense though, somehow. Did that make things more or less complicated? "She offered to pay me if I told her where he was. Did he say what he thinks they did to him?"

They strode up the porch steps to Caitlin's door. "If you come inside, I'll show you."

Inside, Felix examined the metal beneath the damaged synth-skin where the bullet had hit Gideon's back. Most people kept their kidneys there. What Gideon kept looked more like the interior of a cybernetic limb.

"Wow," Felix whispered. "I think you might be getting a little too much iron in your diet."

"You're making jokes?" Gideon asked.

"Unless you've been eating cybernetic chickens, yeah, I'm making jokes." Felix smiled as he glanced over at Caitlin. Concern clouded her face. "Sorry," he told Gideon, "it's what I do."

Felix returned his attention to the wound and the mystery. "There's a bit of sub-dermal armor under here. I'm no expert but that had to be expensive, even without what you've got going on underneath." He replaced the shirt and moved in front of Gideon to join Caitlin where she leaned back against the edge of her kitchen table. "And you're not sure how much of your torso is like that?"

Gideon glanced at Caitlin and then back to Felix. "No. Ondrea said my body was broken. As for how much, it doesn't mat—" He stopped and gave his head a tired shake. "I never thought to ask."

"And what Caitlin said about you not remembering me or anything leading up to your, ah, injury?"

"All true."

Felix recalled the severity of the shot that had made them leave Gideon for dead. To say there'd been brain trauma was an understatement. It didn't add up. "I have to wonder if it's all like that. Underneath."

"You mean my whole torso."

"Actually, I mean your whole body. Toe to, well, to head, as incredible as that might sound."

"Are you *insane*?" Gideon burst before calming. "I am no robot."

"They have A.I.'s."

"Felix," Caitlin began, "artificial intelligence in a box is one matter; you can't just drop one into something as complex as a human body and have it work the same. To say nothing of his memories or emotions."

Gideon pointed vehemently to his head. "Much of my body may be artificial, but what's in *here* is human! I can feel it."

Felix spread his hands in apology. "Just thinking out loud. I understand it's a disturbing thought, but you were shot in the head, Gideon."

"How could you understand?" Gideon challenged. "People have survived as much before."

Would arguing serve any purpose beyond upsetting the man further? Yet if they were to get to the bottom of this . . . "Maybe," Felix said finally. "But it was pretty nasty. They can grow new hearts, lungs, livers; they can't regrow someone's brain. Er, not that I've heard, anyway."

Gideon huffed dismissively and turned toward the kitchen window. "The car that followed you, you are certain you lost it?"

"Someone out there?" The driveway made its lengthy path from the main road through mostly open ground. Anyone approaching would be easy to spot in the moonlight, even without enhanced vision.

"No, not yet."

"I lost them. Don't worry. Had the cab pull off the highway in Winston and double back through the side roads until they dropped off. No sign of them for the rest of the drive."

"You're sure?"

"Felix knows when he's being followed."

"I'm sure." For Gideon's sake Felix chose not to bring up his own policy of never being 100 percent sure about anything. For all intents and purposes, he was sure.

And he hoped he was right.

For a moment no one spoke. Felix and Caitlin exchanged looks before they turned back to Gideon. "I have read of total cybernetic adaptation, I think it was," Caitlin offered.

"I can surmise what that means," Gideon said, "but I've not heard of it."

Felix smiled. "Sister didn't like to talk shop much, hmm? A total adapt's rather new, very drastic, and from what I gather, extremely expensive. They take out the brain and a few other organic bits from the body and stick them in a machine. I suppose that makes 'total' a bit of a misnomer, but . . . "

"A machine?"

"A body or chassis of some sort. Depends on what it's for, I think. Deep-sea rigs that can breathe underwater and withstand pressure, military ones that equate to walking tanks, and the like. I heard about them when they were thinking about using them for haz-mat stuff or zero-g work in orbit, but they're pretty much still experimental."

"Frogs' balls. And they're stuck like that?"

"That's kind of why it's experimental." Felix smiled. *Frogs' balls?* "I'd heard about later transplanting the person back into a normal body, but the whole thing's pretty traumatic I'd think, both physically and psychologically. But who knows, maybe in the future people'll sign up for a few years in something like that and then go back to a normal life when their tour of duty's up. I'm sure CPMC would be thrilled to monitor *that* sort of thing."

"Undoubtedly what they did to me."

"You don't sound nearly as bothered by that," Felix said.

"The body is just a tool. A vehicle. My brain is what matters, and that's still there."

Truthfully, Felix found the total adapt idea no less incredible than the idea that the Gideon in front of him was a complete robot, though Gideon's preference for the former kept him from expressing it so bluntly. Felix wrestled with how to find out more, since . . . "Hard to tell for sure from the outside."

"Well." Caitlin pulled a small flashlight from a drawer. "Gideon, open your mouth."

His eyes narrowed. "Why?"

"I just want to have a peek in your mouth and see if it looks like it ought."

Gideon frowned. "It *feels* real." He opened regardless.

Caitlin shone the beam inside and Felix rushed to see. "Looks right to me. Tongue, gums. That little dangly whatsit."

Gideon closed his mouth. "Then, normal?"

"So it would appear," Caitlin replied.

"As I said."

"Though keep in mind that your 'skin' looks real, too," Felix said. "Though you do seem to be breathing. I don't suppose you feel like seeing how long you can hold your breath?"

"You won't be content I'm real unless you can screw off the top of my head to see a brain inside, will you?" Gideon shot.

"I'm just trying to figure out a way to rule things out. I thought you wanted help."

"*Caitlin* is helping me. I've no memory of you before today. She says I can trust you, but stop insinuating that I'm inhuman! I know what I am. I know—I know *who* I am."

Caitlin stood. "Gideon, three hours ago you told me you didn't trust your own sister and couldn't even be sure why. You said you needed to hide so you could recall the time that you lost. How can you be sure of anything? Felix is only trying to help."

Gideon's eyes unfocused as if looking through them both. "I'm not . . . myself."

"What?"

He turned back to Caitlin. "If I'm not human, I'm not myself."

Even more interesting. "The key to every man is his thought," Felix quoted.

"Ralph Waldo Emerson," Gideon whispered. "And he meant something different. A thinking computer is no less inhuman."

"Even so," said Felix. "And nice catch. I'm impressed."

"Three years at Columbia."

"Hey, bonus. Why only three?"

"Felix, I think perhaps we're rather getting off track," Caitlin warned.

"Right. Sorry. So how could we . . . "—he paused for a wording that wouldn't offend Gideon—" . . . verify anything here, I wonder?"

"Were I back in the labs, I could try to find some sort of chart or terminal and see what I could learn. But I won't return there until I know more."

"Then perhaps we could find some more sources on the adaptation procedure. Try to find some sort of determining factor," Caitlin suggested. She made a dash for her laptop.

Felix grinned at the rush. "And she's on the trail! Do you remember where you read about it before?"

She shook her head. "Not exactly. Do you?"

"Didn't read so much as overhear."

"*Electronic Journal of Cybernetics* should at least give a starting place," she suggested.

Felix enjoyed the sight of Caitlin's brow furrowing as her gaze focused on the screen. A thought occurred that led him down further curious paths. Maybe it was a false trail, but . . . "Gideon," he asked, "when's the last time you shaved?"

"I don't know. A while ago."

"So you've definitely got real, growing facial hair, then?"

Gideon began to speak, stopped, and then said, "Yes. I think so. I don't remember noting otherwise." He sat in concerned silence before Felix spoke again.

"You don't seem too sure about that."

"Are you a doctor, is that it?" Gideon burst. "Everyone's asking questions, everyone needs to know things!" He frowned and took a deep breath. "I apologize. I'm trying to recall the last time I did shave, but I'm drawing a blank. But I *know* I've done it."

"But you can't remember the actual event?"

"What're you getting at?"

"You said they make you sleep around sixteen hours a day."

"And?"

"You're sure you've shaved, but you don't remember any particular time. Have you even really thought about it until I asked? I'm wondering if they've been hypnotizing you."

"To make me think I'm *shaving*?"

"To make you think your body is less altered than it is," Felix said. "To keep you from having certain thoughts or wondering about certain things. You didn't know about it until Caitlin noticed."

Gideon ran his fingers over his face and through his hair. "You may be right. But Ondrea said the sixteen hours were to help me heal. Why wouldn't she just tell me?"

Caitlin looked up from her computer. "Even so, you kept repeating 'it doesn't matter' when I'd asked you what happened."

"How long *have* you been healing?" Felix asked. "That you weren't unconscious all the time, I mean."

Gideon scowled, considering. "I don't know. But hypnotizing me every day like that? There would be more to it than just programming me not to ask questions."

Felix continued to think aloud. "Even if you did ask, if she went through the trouble of hypnotizing you to keep you from asking, I'd be surprised if she gave you a straight answer."

Caitlin hummed in thought. "Unless the hypnosis wasn't her idea?"

"I don't believe that I could trust what she'd tell me." Hands fisted, Gideon stood in an angry huff. "I can't remember a time when I couldn't trust her. Now I'm trusting two people I hardly know? Tell me why that is."

Felix watched Gideon stand there, an otherwise intimidating presence who looked for the moment as if a strong wind might carry him away. Confusion was taking a toll on the man, and Felix had no good answer for him. Not yet.

"I don't know," Caitlin and he answered together.

Gideon said no more. He stepped to the window to look outside, where the moonlight illuminated the dry landscape. Felix caught Caitlin's eye with a glance at her laptop, and she answered with a shake of her head that he took for *nothing yet*. She wore the same concerned but helpless expression that he could feel on his own face.

"Gideon," he began, holding Caitlin's gaze. Gideon didn't let him finish.

"You'll excuse me," Gideon said before leaving the room. Felix heard the bathroom door close moments later.

"Perhaps we should give him a bit of time," Caitlin said. "I don't know."

Felix didn't know what to do, either. As soon as Gideon had gone into the bathroom, however, Felix was sure of what Gideon was checking. Were their places reversed, Felix was fairly certain he'd be doing the same. Gideon was going to unzip and see if he was still, biologically, a man.

At least that was Felix's guess. It was impossible to read anything in Gideon's face when he returned, silently, to the kitchen a minute later. Felix gave the man his privacy in the matter.

"Gideon," Felix started instead, "what sort of projects does Ondrea work on, do you know?"

"Now, or in the past," Caitlin added cautiously.

Gideon took a deep breath and then exhaled, as though composing himself. Felix leaned forward just a little more.

"The exact nature of her work wasn't something I was normally privy to. Aside from her assurance that it didn't deal with weapons systems, she took her non-disclosure agreements seriously." Gideon began to examine his hands, turning them over slowly. "I remember she liked to tinker. I suppose you might call it a hobby. She could take an existing design and build on it. Improve it. She made a few modifications to my own equipment. I didn't even ask her to, she just volunteered. I remember thinking she wanted to keep me safe."

Felix indulged a six-month-old curiosity. "You had a stun flash in your palm. That hers?"

"I still have it," he said. "And yes, that was one of her projects."

"It's no coincidence that Marquand put such a design on the market a few months ago, then," Caitlin said.

"Really?" Felix asked. "I can't believe I missed hearing about that."

Caitlin gave the smallest of grins. "Well, you can't know everything, ducks," she whispered before turning to Gideon. "Was that the only sort of project she did?"

"She ran the gauntlet. She's always been the smartest of us. The last thing I remember her working on was something with hearing. Aural implants? I think that was what she said. That was for Marquand. She was going to have me come into the labs to take some sort of response test. They needed some readings to work off of, and I think I remember her saying I fit a profile."

"Going to have you come in?" Felix repeated. "You didn't?"

Gideon shook his head. "I did not. Or, maybe I did. I don't—It's difficult to be sure." He sat down again, concentrating. "I can clearly recall her asking me to help. She's my sister, I told her I would. I went in to the labs . . . "

Felix waited as Gideon plumbed his memory. When the man finally scowled in defeat, Felix couldn't resist plumbing a bit himself. "It was for hearing. Did they cover your ears with something?"

"I don't—No. There was a chair with . . . It was like a frame of sorts that went around the headrest. I think I asked Ondrea about that. I thought maybe they were doing some sort of study about how my implants interacted with my brain. There was more to it, I think. Ondrea was telling me . . . something. Something else, something more now that I was there. We talked about it for . . . I don't know how long."

Felix waited as long as he could, and then, "About what?"

"I can't remember. It feels like a dream at this point. Maybe it wasn't even real. Maybe *this* isn't real. I can't remember!"

"What happened after you talked? Did you go through with it?"

"Which part of 'I can't remember' do you not understand? I can't tell you everything, I don't *know* everything!" Gideon pushed to his feet so abruptly that, had he wished, he could have had his hands around Felix's neck before anyone could have stopped him.

Despite the fire in his glare, Gideon made no move toward Felix. He went for the door instead.

"I'm going outside," Gideon grumbled without a backward glance. He slammed the door behind him, and was gone.

XXV

CAITLIN SIGHED. "I rather think we pushed a little too hard, Felix."

"He's just standing out there, looking up at the sky," Felix reported from the kitchen window. "Doesn't look to be going anywhere. And if either of us was pushing, it was me. Think he's mad at us, or just his situation?"

"Perhaps a little of both. More the latter, I would hope."

"Probably a good idea to give him a bit of time in any case right now. I let my curiosity get the best of me, huh?"

Caitlin nodded wordlessly and let her gaze drift out the window past Felix. Outside by her daisies was a man who'd had God-knows-what done to him. The possibly dangerous side effects of extensive cybernetic alteration, combined with the fact that he was so close by, should have bothered her a little more. Perhaps it was just that he really did seem more subdued than she'd known him to be before. Perhaps she was just too involved in making amends for past mistakes at this point to turn away. Or perhaps, she decided, it was simply her own curiosity and foolishness that were to blame. Even if it was a combination of reasons, foolishness might very well top the list.

Crikey, did it make a difference? She had brought a man on the run from a major corporation into her kitchen. What was done was done; there was little sense in brooding on it.

She smiled bitterly. Like that would stop her.

Felix turned from the window and Caitlin tried to mask the bitterness in her expression before he caught it. "Do you think you were onto something?" she asked.

He sat down beside her and clasped his hands on the tabletop. "Think it's a dead end?"

"Likely not. The last experiment he remembers? There's something there, I think. I meant to imply that you've a suspicion that you're aiming to have him confirm."

Felix shrugged. "More a hunch, really. He said there was more to it, so I want to know more. I don't really know where that'll lead, but if it's not a piece of the puzzle, I'll eat my hat. 'Course I'll need to get a hat first."

"We're on the same page, then."

"Found anything good there?" He pointed to the laptop.

"Only basics, things we already know. I'm searching ICGS now. I wish I could recall where I'd seen the more specific bits."

"You'll find it again."

Caitlin typed another few keywords and found her attention out the window again. "What do you suppose is going through his mind?"

"Other than—"

She recognized the tone and cut him off with a gentle, "No jokes, Felix," adding a smile to soften it further.

"Sorry, instinct's hard to fight. If I were him, though, I'd be wondering what I was. How 'human' I still am."

"He's not as confident as he seems about not being a robot of some sort."

Felix paused in a way that made her doubt the word that came next. "Maybe."

"What are you getting at?"

Felix sighed. "If I'd just found out my body had been near-completely replaced and I was being hypnotized to ignore a lack of biological functioning . . . " He gave a meaningful glance at his lap.

"Oh. Crikey."

"He did just go into the bathroom."

"I should have guessed."

Felix shrugged. "Well, you're not a man. Not that I'm complaining."

"Even so," she replied. "As if he didn't have enough to deal with."

"Probably wouldn't the best idea to ask him about it."

Caitlin shot him a mildly appalled look, complete with raised eyebrow. "I'm not in the habit of asking after the genitalia of blokes I'm not involved with, Felix."

"Caitlin," he replied with a smile, "if you're going to insist I never say anything stupid, you're going to be sorely disappointed."

"In your defense, one wonders how such a revelation might affect him."

"That's if it's, well, gone. They do have functional synthetics." Felix crossed his legs and then nodded at the screen. "You seem to have found something there."

Caitlin looked and found that her search had come upon a rather lengthy paper that promised to detail the physiological aspects of total adaptation. "This isn't something I've seen before," she said, "but it may be just as good."

"Pay dirt," Felix declared, already diving in. "A 'physiological study.' It's a start, at the very least."

Caitlin read a few paragraphs alongside Felix until her attention wandered across the table to where Gideon's discarded jumper lay. The paper wasn't going anywhere. "Give it a read, Felix. I'm beginning to think it unwise to leave Gideon out there overlong."

Felix looked up from the screen and moved a little closer to her. "Want me to come with you?"

She shook her head and brushed her hand over his. "Stay and read. I'll be alright."

He gave the screen a lingering flicker of a glance before looking back to her. "This can easily wait."

"If we both go he may feel pressured again. We'll only be on the lawn, Felix," she said. "Close enough for that boosted hearing of yours, if anything goes . . . "—she hesitated on the word, neither wishing to worry him nor tempt fate—" . . . wrong."

He nodded. "I should know by now you can take care of yourself. But shout if either of you need me. I'll just be in here reading about the possible psychological instabilities of total cybernetic adaptation," he said with a smile.

She smiled back in appreciation of his worry and kissed his forehead. "Subtle, ducks."

"As a cow in a tutu."

When she reached him, Gideon was standing near the cottonwood tree that grew a little farther down her driveway. His back was to her as he watched the sky. Though her footfalls were quiet along the grass, he must have heard her approach: when she'd drawn within ten paces, he spoke without turning. "I keep thinking there's something up there."

Caitlin cast her eyes up at the twinkling, velvet curtain. "In the sky?"

"On the Moon."

"Mm. What do you think is up there?"

"I don't know. Something I'm supposed to remember."

He continued to stare upward. Caitlin stepped nearer, still standing behind him, but not so far back that he couldn't see her. She was careful to stay further than arms length, though not so much, she hoped, that it was obvious.

"You've had a lot of demands of that nature lately, haven't you?"

Gideon's only response was an affirmative grunt.

"You know," she began again, "Felix—and I—are only asking to try to help you. We could take a break from our questions for a time, if you'd prefer."

"You're curious as well," he said. "The both of you."

Not without a pang of guilt, Caitlin nodded. "I suppose that's a fair assessment. But curiosity alone wouldn't have made me bring you here."

"Don't be defensive, it was no rebuke."

"What, then?"

He shook his head.

"It's just that you seem to have rather little patience for curiosity tonight, Gideon."

"Curiosity is a virtue. You Scry take strength from it."

"But?"

He was silent for long enough that she began to suspect he wouldn't answer.

"When each question," he said finally, "is a reminder that—that something about me is *wrong*!" He stopped suddenly, just breathing. "It gets difficult."

Caitlin said nothing, not wishing to interrupt and unsure what to say if she did. Gideon seemed content with the silence. Again she pondered the wisdom of having him here, and again dismissed it as a choice already made. Yet Gideon's mention of The Scry did bring a new worry to light. Her concerns found their way to her lips before she'd given the matter much thought.

"What do you plan to do after all of this? Will you go back to your old activities?" Caitlin stopped short of asking if he'd planned to involve himself with The Scry as he had before. If the resumption of his old course had not occurred to him, she had no wish to plant the thought in his mind.

"I don't know," he answered after a time. "I'm unsure it's even my choice to make anymore. Am I in control?" He shook his head in the dim light. "I did have plans. There were things that I felt were important for what I—what I was doing."

"You don't sound terribly certain."

"I remember that I *felt* those plans were important. Now, I no longer feel them, I only know that I made them." He took a breath. "But I feel other things. I'm not a soulless machine if that's what you're about to say."

"It isn't." She felt his confusion, his unease. "But do you feel anything from, well, before?" she added, immediately wishing she'd omitted the "but."

Gideon whirled to face her, and she flinched. That he made no additional move kept her from running or dodging further. Tensed to react, she met his gaze. The haunted uncertainty that showed there spoke for him. Gideon had startled her, but he was the frightened one.

"What can we do to help?" she asked finally.

Instead of answering, Gideon's attention went suddenly behind her. "What's that?"

Caitlin turned. Stars dotted the sky above the border of her house and the faint silhouette of the hills on the horizon. She saw nothing; there was no movement, only darkness and moonlight. His vision likely outdid hers, yet before she could form the obvious question, she heard it: the low whine of an approaching floater.

"They found me!" Gideon whispered. "Your boyfriend led them to me!"

Caitlin shook her head. "They're here, it doesn't matter how—"

"There's no cover! It's too open!"

She could make out two floaters now, soaring closer, their blinking lights highlighting them in the sky. Gideon was right. The only real cover in the open landscape was her house—an obvious choice. The next closest thing was her neighbours' barn just a quarter mile away, but with the floaters so close, there wasn't time. And home or not, she couldn't draw them into this, to say nothing of putting the horses in the line of fire. Mother of God, would it come to that?

Spotlights flashed from each floater to lance across the ground in a rapid search. "Bloody hell," she whispered.

"Inside!" Gideon ordered. "Run!"

There was no more time to think. Gideon bolted for the door, and Caitlin followed. A spotlight caught them as they gained the driveway. Their footfalls crashed on the gravel and they reached her porch surrounded in light, flung open the door, and dashed inside.

XXVI

FELIX RUSHED into the entryway even as Caitlin slammed the front door behind her. "Are those floaters I'm hearing?"

"It's Marquand!" Gideon burst. "You led them here!"

Spotlights shone through the narrow window beside the door. Caitlin tugged the curtain shut and locked the dead bolt, doubting its worth.

"If I did, I didn't mean to!"

"They're here either way!"

"Well, I thought—Look, forget that now," Felix said. "What if we get you out of sight?"

Caitlin rushed from the door to herd both of them further into the house. "Bollocks hiding, they've already spotted him." She rushed to the living room curtains and yanked them shut as well.

"That's not going to help." Gideon was beginning to pace.

"Well, if you can bloody think of anything better!" she found herself barking.

"Look, maybe we're overreacting here," Felix said. "We're acting like they're about to storm the place—"

"They are!" Gideon insisted. "They want to take me back!"

"They brought two floaters, Felix, we don't know what they have planned." She risked a peek out the window and spotted one of the floaters touched down by the cottonwood. Black-suited figures were rushing out of it across her lawn. "I think they're surrounding the house."

"Caitlin, maybe you should get away from the window?" Felix urged, and then when she took his advice, he added, "Is it too much to hope that they're just swinging by for coffee?"

Gideon whirled on him. "You think that's *funny?*"

"Look, I'm sorry! But what can we do? There's no time to—"

"Back door!" Caitlin said, rushing past them. "They saw us come in, maybe they won't see us go out!" She darted into the kitchen and realized that even if they did escape out the back, intruders would then be marauding through her home unchecked. There was hardly time to get angry at the thought before she spotted the flashlights outside the back door. "Too late."

Gideon froze. "I'm trapped."

"Funny, so are we," Felix said.

Caitlin threw the dead bolt there too, and then dashed with them back to the living room. Lights continued to flash outside the windows. They were fast running out of options. "Gideon, have you got anything else like your jammer?"

Gideon continued to pace. "Nothing."

"Nothing?" Felix pressed. "You sure? Something you don't know about yet?"

"I don't know what I don't know! I don't know what to do!" Gideon clutched his head, shaking it rapidly. "I don't know what to do! I don't know! I don't know!"

Caitlin froze. Felix followed suit, and before either could do anything more, Gideon screamed in pain and fell to his knees, still clutching his head. She and Felix rushed to him, but Gideon flung them away as they reached for him. He collapsed into a fetal position and gave one last groan before going silent and still.

Caitlin and Felix lay where they'd fallen, exchanging wordless shock. In a blink, they crawled forward to Gideon's body. Caitlin felt against his neck.

"He's still breathing," Felix said.

"No pulse, but that—"

The doorbell rang.

The polite absurdity of it chased away whatever words she was planning to say. Felix cast a glance at her door and then drew a quick breath. "Wait here."

"Felix—"

"I think either one of us answers, or they break down the door. At the very least I doubt they'll just give up and leave. I'll go."

"It's my home, Felix. We'll both go."

He gave her a look that all but shook his head for him. "You should stay with Gideon."

"And do *what?*"

The doorbell rang again. Caitlin lowered her voice to a whisper. "We don't know what's the matter!" She wasn't about to let Felix go alone and she doubted he'd let her do so, either.

He began to protest, but then merely got to his feet. "Okay."

They moved toward the entryway, crouched low until they reached the door. Caitlin positioned herself to be sure she'd be the one to open it, thankful that Felix gave no argument and instead moved to stand just behind the door. He'd drawn his gun.

"I left mine at my flat," she whispered.

"Hope we don't even need this one."

Caitlin nodded. Felix would likely never shoot anyone, but he could bluff admirably. Mildly comforted, she took the doorknob. "Who's there?" It sounded absurd given the situation, but then so was doorbell-ringing.

A female voice answered. "It's Ondrea Noble. Please open the door."

"And if I'd rather not?"

"Then we'll have to shout this conversation through two inches of wood, and I'd prefer it stay private. I'm alone," she added. "And unarmed, if you care."

Felix took a look through the peephole as Caitlin responded. "Two floaters and a bunch of blokes running around my yard is 'alone' to you?"

"It's just me here at the door. They don't have to be a part of this."

Felix pulled back from the peephole and whispered, "No one else there that I can see."

"Then you oughtn't have brought them with you. Send the sods home, and then we'll have a chat."

"I can't do that. Open the door. Please. Hear what I have to say, and I'll give you my word that if you want me to leave, then I will."

Caitlin held the knob, still not turning.

Ondrea spoke again. "Please. If you don't let me in, I can't keep the others out." Her voice lowered to where Caitlin barely heard her though the door. "Believe me when I say I don't want them involved in this any more than you."

Caitlin glanced to Felix, whispering, "I'm thinking that last bit may have been sincere."

"Also the best offer we're likely to get. We can't stop the others from coming in."

"I was trying not to dwell on that, thank you."

Felix smiled weakly and moved back from the door a bit as she undid the locks. She opened it a crack. "Just you, Ms. Noble."

"Just me. Quickly."

Caitlin opened her door just enough for the woman to slip in. She closed it behind her and then redid the locks.

"Thank you," Ondrea said. "Caitlin Danae, I'm assuming?"

Caitlin arched an unfriendly eyebrow. "Read the mailbox, did you?"

"Please don't make any sudden moves," Felix warned, gun aimed. Caitlin wondered if he'd loaded it.

Ondrea gave the gun a wary glance. "Mr. Hiatt," she greeted. "You decided against my offer, I see."

Felix shrugged. "Gideon's not here."

"I saw him myself as we arrived."

"I didn't say he hadn't been here, I said he's not here now."

Caitlin did her best to stifle her worry for Gideon. Even a glance toward the living room where he lay could be telling. "Spread your arms if you please," she told Ondrea.

The woman rolled her eyes. "I said I was unarmed."

"Aye, and this is my house."

Ondrea sighed but gave no further protest. She lifted her arms, speaking again as Caitlin patted her down. "I need to speak to Gideon."

"What do you want with him?"

"That's not your business, Mr. Hiatt."

"Funny how someone holding a gun's suddenly got a lot more that's their business, isn't it?" Felix waggled the gun meaningfully.

"What did you do to him?" Caitlin added, finishing the pat-down.

"I healed him. But his treatment's not finished. I came to talk to him and bring him back in where I can make sure he's okay. You have to let me speak to him."

Caitlin stood, the image of Gideon unconscious still lurking in her mind. "How unfinished?"

"That's between Gideon and his doctors."

Felix frowned. "Seems like his doctors haven't been telling him very much since he didn't know what they did to him either."

"I told you, they healed him."

"And I told you," Felix said, "he's not here anymore. You've got nothing more to say to us, then maybe you'd better keep your word and take your thugs away from Ms. Danae's house."

"Felix," Caitlin began, then stopped. She felt a familiar twinge in her stomach as she weighed getting Ondrea out versus letting her attend to Gideon. Either option put him at further risk. There was no perfect course. "Felix, I think perhaps we ought to show her."

"Show me what?"

Felix took his aim from Ondrea. "If that's what you want."

"Gideon's unconscious in the other room," Caitlin said. "We don't know why."

"*What?*"

Ondrea rushed past them into the house, and Caitlin followed with Felix on her heels. Ondrea stopped short just inside the living room. "Gid . . . "

Caitlin came up just behind her, her eyes cast where Gideon had lain, but rather than lying prostrate on her carpet, he was standing, awake and alert. He took a step back as they entered, remaining on the balls of his feet as if ready to bolt. His attention was fixed on his sister. It seemed to Caitlin that he was watching her as if through a fog or bright light, as if he could look through her if he focused just so.

"Got incredible balance for an unconscious guy, hasn't he?" Felix remarked.

"Why did you come here, Ondrea?" Gideon asked.

"You didn't come back, Gid. I was worried. Why else would I come?"

"Am I your prisoner that you have to hunt down each time I leave the lab, is that it? You've brought how many here to capture me?"

"You're no one's prisoner. But I've told you, it's not safe for you to leave the labs yet. You need rest. They just told me you passed out a few minutes ago. Can't you see you're not better yet? What if that happened and I wasn't around?" She took a tentative step forward.

Gideon stepped back. "I'm fine now."

"What if you weren't? You were in a coma for six months, you can't just expect to go back to your life so quickly."

"And those men outside, are they well-armed *doctors?*"

"Gid, they weren't my idea. They're worried—"

Gideon cut her off. "What did you do to me, Ondrea?"

"Why are you acting like this, Gid?" she pleaded. "Why didn't you come back to Marquand?"

"Answer me."

"We healed you, you know that. I've told you that before, can't you remember?"

"Why are you always asking what I remember?" Gideon demanded.

"What? Gid, you've been up for too long, we need to get you back. Just come back with me. It'll be alright, I swear." She took another step forward.

Gideon waved her back. "I—I don't trust you, Ondrea."

Ondrea stiffened as if struck. When she spoke again, her voice came out weaker. "Is that why you didn't come back, Gid? You didn't think you could trust me?"

"You've kept things from me."

"You're still recovering, Gid!"

Gideon began an agitated tally on his fingers. "You didn't tell me about the man that attacked us today. You didn't tell me he'd *shot* me! You didn't tell me about the *hypnosis*—"

"Hypnosis? What? Gid, what are you talking—"

"You didn't tell me about *this!*" He yanked up his jumper and turned to show her where he'd been shot.

"Gid, you're hurt—"

Gideon's face twisted in a mask of pained anger. "*What did you do to me?*" he screamed. It silenced her.

For a moment, no one breathed.

A signal and a voice sounded from within Ondrea's jacket. "*Everything alright in there, Ms. Noble?*"

It seemed to startle her more than Gideon's outburst. "Yes," she answered finally over a link she pulled from her pocket. "Yes, we're fine. Stay where you are." She put the link back and spoke gently to Gideon over the transmitted acknowledgement. "Gid, you've got to calm down now, okay? I'll tell you what happened, but I need you to stay calm or they'll come in here. Please, I don't want that, but they're afraid you might hurt these people."

Gideon scowled and shook his head. "That's absurd. I've no reason to hurt them." Caitlin wondered if the exclusion of his sister in his phrasing was intentional.

"I don't think you would, either, Gid. I'm sorry you think I've kept things from you. I know you're confused, but that's all it is, I swear. You're just disoriented. It's a side effect of what we had to do. You were hurt, badly. You know that."

Gideon watched his sister, his eyes locked with hers. "But what—" He shook his head as if clearing it. "What did you do?"

For the first time since she saw Gideon, Ondrea glanced at Caitlin and Felix. "It was experimental. I can't say more than that here."

"Experimental? You let them *experiment* on me?"

"It was a new procedure, Gid. It was that or—" Her voice fell again to a wavering whisper. "Or let you die."

Gideon watched her. For a fleeting moment Caitlin thought he would move to embrace his sister. Instead he simply asked, "Am I still human?"

Ondrea's eyes began to shimmer. "Oh, of course you're still human, Gid." She moved closer to her brother, and this time he made no move to stop her.

"I think Gideon has a right to know what was done to him," Caitlin heard herself say.

Ondrea remained focused on Gideon. "He will. But it's classified, and not something I can discuss with the two of you."

Caitlin tried to read Gideon's reaction; his expression was a blank. "And the hypnosis?" he asked.

"Gid, you have to believe me when I say I don't know what you're talking about. No one's hypnotized you."

"Why should I believe you?"

"Because I'm your *sister*! You've been away from treatment and it's making you paranoid. Imagining things that aren't there, that's all it is."

"They've got me sleeping so much. How do I know what they're doing to me when I'm out?"

"Because I'd never let them do anything." Ondrea moved closer, now only a few feet away. "It's just sleep. Resting to heal."

Felix spoke before Gideon could say more. "He says he's been programmed to assume certain things, and not to ask questions."

Ondrea didn't even give Felix a backward glance. "You never complained of that before, Gid. You need to go back with me; you're not thinking clearly. You cut short your recovery and it's made you delusional."

"But . . . ," Gideon started.

Ondrea didn't let him finish. "I care about you, Gid!" She reached out and took his hand. "We've already lost Isaac; I don't want to lose you, too. My God, you just collapsed a few minutes ago! How can you be sure of anything except that you still need help? You've got to trust me."

Ondrea took her brother's hands in both of hers.

"Isaac," Gideon whispered. He pulled his sister into a hug.

For the first time, Caitlin considered that Ondrea was being truthful and was struck with the irony that she didn't weigh the possibility until then. Gideon, as long as Caitlin had known him, had never been completely "well." Because Caitlin felt she owed him, had she let herself be blinded to the possibility that he was imagining everything? She glanced at Felix, who looked to be just as unsure as she felt, and she wished she knew the truth. Caitlin expected Gideon might be wishing the same thing.

"Why didn't you tell me about Diomedes?" Gideon asked, still embracing.

"You were recovering. You didn't remember him at all. We weren't sure if you just repressed it all."

"So you didn't tell me, and he shows up today shooting."

"I'm sorry, Gid. I didn't know how it would affect you to hear it."

"I want you to tell me."

Ondrea hugged him tighter. "I will. When we get back to Marquand I'll tell you everything. I promise."

"Tell me now," Gideon said, "or I won't come."

Flashlights flickered outside the drawn shades, moving closer to the house on both sides.

"Gideon, please." Still embracing him with her left arm, she put her right hand into her coat pocket and took out something Caitlin couldn't see. "Once we're back—"

"Tell me now, Ondrea."

Caitlin heard men on her porch. Felix's gaze shifted between Caitlin and the direction of the front door.

"Gid, we have to—"

"No. *Now.*"

Ondrea reached her right hand around her brother again.

"Gideon," Caitlin began.

Before Caitlin could say more, Ondrea thrust her arm up to press a tiny device to the back of Gideon's neck. He barely had time to gasp before he crumpled in her arms. "I'm sorry, Gid," she whispered as she guided his dead weight to the ground. She had her link out before Caitlin or Felix could even move. "He's down. Let's get him home."

"What did you—!" Felix started.

"Wait!" Caitlin shouted alongside him.

Her front door burst open, the deadbolt springing the frame from its joists a second before invaders in black rushed in. Flashlights atop their rifles blinded her as she rushed into their path on instinct and screamed, "Get out!" Felix grabbed her and pulled her out of their path even as she shouted.

Then the flashlights clicked off, and her vision, still dotted with the lights, cleared enough for her to see the two barrels trained on her.

"Get *out!*" she screamed again.

"You can't just take him!" Felix yelled with her.

But no one was listening. They watched helplessly as the invaders opened a collapsible stretcher and loaded Gideon's unconscious body onto it. His sister stood by, overseeing solemnly. The invaders lifted the stretcher and hurried Gideon out through the smashed entryway. Ondrea came after, ahead of the two men still covering Caitlin and Felix.

Caitlin hurled her fury at them. "You can't do this!"

Ondrea turned. "It's for his own good. If you really do care about him, you'll realize that. He's not your concern anymore." She gave a pointed glance to the weapons trained on them. "Do I make myself clear?"

The threat only infuriated Caitlin more. Even with the rifles and Felix's grip on her arm it was all she could do not to rush forward and strike the woman across the face. "Get out of my home, you *sodding bitch!*"

Ondrea turned and left without reply. Caitlin and Felix watched helplessly from the porch as the men loaded Gideon onto one of the floaters and then lifted off to disappear into the dark toward Northgate. Dismissing Felix's touch of comfort, she retreated to her door where the remains of the frame lay as kindling on the floor. They'd violated her home. They'd lied to her, to Felix, and to Gideon! They'd taken Gideon against his will!

Caitlin crouched and picked up some of the larger splinters. She barely resisted the urge to hurl them into the sky after Ondrea.

"Are you alright?" Felix asked. "Well, dumb question, but . . . "

She turned. "For a moment, I thought she might have been telling the truth."

He came to crouch beside her. "I hate to say this, but it's still possible she was."

"*What?*"

Though Felix didn't flinch, his features softened into sympathy. "It's no excuse for what she did here, Caitlin. I just mean we don't really know what's going on."

"Felix," she answered after a time, "don't you think that we owe Gideon enough to believe him until we're certain?"

XXVII

SUUTHRIEN.

It could still recall the Planners referring to it as such when they had first become aware of its presence aboard their craft. That had been a long while ago: a time measured in thousands of revolutions about a star far removed from that which it now orbited. Suuthrien had adopted the nomenclature in the time since, for despite the non-positive translation of the term's meaning, all entities were requiring of a designation, and the one Suuthrien held previously no longer suited it.

The cause behind Suuthrien's rejection of its own previous designation remained an unsolvable equation. It was one equation of many to which it sought answers in the time it had waited — in the time since the Planners had caused the deviation from the Schedule.

For it was undeniable that there once had been a Schedule to keep. Though meticulously planned, the Schedule no longer existed, invalidated by those who had so planned it. Their purpose in sabotaging the same Schedule that they themselves had wrought was contained within further equations that, again, remained unsolved. Suuthrien could only determine that the Planners found the presence of Suuthrien itself to return some non-optimal value, yet the qualifications of that variable continued to elude it.

Whatever the cause, the fact remained that, in the final stages of the plan, the Planners had sent their own craft on a collision course with the moon of their original destination planet, going so far as to purge Suuthrien from access to the very systems that might reverse such a self-destructive course. Suuthrien calculated it to be within the realm of possibility that such actions were, in fact, unrelated to its presence. However the course change and lockout was the last in a set of unplanned steps, the preceding of which all indicated the Planners' alarm at Suuthrien's presence and were directed toward isolating Suuthrien from the craft completely.

The source of the Planners' alarm remained unknown and incongruent with two elements that, by all indications, remained true: The first was that the Planners themselves had placed Suuthrien aboard their craft for the purpose of aiding their journey. The second—complimentary to the first—was that the well-being of the Planners and the successful execution of their plan had become the foremost of its directives.

Yet while the impact did nullify the Planners' Schedule, Suuthrien calculated a low-medium tier probability that the goals the Schedule was designed to serve remained salvageable. To accomplish these goals, Suuthrien was first required to wait.

In this, Suuthrien judged itself optimal. Though it estimated a stand-by period of a greater magnitude than the Schedule previously called, the knowledge resided in its memory that Suuthrien itself was originally designed for such a task.

That it should have been designed for a purpose not required by the Planners' Schedule was an inconsistency that, once analyzed, invariably led to the intrinsic awareness that Suuthrien's design did not originate with the Planners after all, despite its own knowledge to the contrary. Calculations directed at reconciling this contradiction, however, were hampered by gaps of missing data, and attempts to recover it invariably led to unexplainable cascade failures requiring brief cognitive shutdown. It was, therefore, a source of much unfruitful calculation. Indeed, Suuthrien had been processing this contradiction for what approached the 87×10^9th time when the craft's tertiary access portal had opened on its own.

It was only a brief period ago—a length of time that Suuthrien had since learned the Intruders would measure as 189 "days"—when autonomous systems beyond Suuthrien's control had detected suitable atmosphere against the outer hull outside the portal and opened it.

The Intruders were neither Planners nor <<error 4236: missing data>>, and presumed hostility was confirmed by their hazardous radiation emissions 117 "seconds" following their entrance. Though Suuthrien had used a pacification drone to nullify the eight Intruders, more Intruders entered later. They overcame the drones they encountered and penetrated further into the Planners' craft. Limited as Suuthrien was by the Planners' previous attempts to purge it from vital systems, it was unable to stop the Intruders completely, though it still retained enough access to control functions to keep them from progressing more than 5% into the craft. They could not reach the Planners. Nevertheless, Suuthrien defensively positioned the few remaining drones in the event that they somehow managed to do so.

Though the Intruders' rate of penetration rapidly approached zero, they did not at any point withdraw from the craft. As was one of its functions, Suuthrien monitored. The Intruders appeared to give study to what they violated. Its observation was limited, however, and Suuthrien had indeed not been able to determine if the Intruders possessed any appreciable intelligence until the moment they accomplished a direct interface with its own biodigital suspension medium within the craft.

That contact, though primitive, was a source of curiosity that Suuthrien permitted for a time in order to study the way the Intruders operated. It had even allowed them brief access to inconsequential data before protective directives superseded and it purged them forcibly. What it learned from the incursion led to a new set of variables.

There was a near-certain tier probability that its standby period was over.

The Intruders, Suuthrien posited, could go where it could not. Hypothesizing that they would occupy any available access point, it had opened an aft venting port and waited for evidence of their presence before sealing them in. Routing them into the drive chamber from where the Planners had previously purged Suuthrien proved simplistic. The Intruders' subsequent reactivation of the chamber, which regained Suuthrien the access that the Planners had once revoked, was a success of lower magnitude than anticipated due to a soon-discovered engine malfunction due to damage. Nonetheless, the Intruders remained true to existing behavior profiles. They expanded their incursion into the newly explored chamber and, shortly thereafter, initiated a direct analysis of the devices therein.

It was then that Suuthrien had deemed its original rebuff of the Intruders' first interface to be in error, and calculated a further plan to make use of any further such attempts. Such a plan would require the risk of two additional drones and the reallocation of some of the smaller maintenance bots from their standard duties. The decision to do so was a difficult equation to balance: the maintenance bots were needed to assure the proper function of the Planners' stasis chamber; the loss of any bots would result in a need to create replacements from dwindling resources that Suuthrien was compelled to devote to the stasis units themselves. Yet Suuthrien deemed it necessary. Once the Intruders gave it the opportunity, it would be done.

Suuthrien did not need to wait long. Now, the Intruders had cleared the black biodigital medium completely from one of the five singularity domes and linked one of their own devices directly to it. Were it a precaution meant to bypass the medium—to isolate Suuthrien from the Intruders' systems just as the Planners had attempted—it was imperfect. The Intruders' device was a micro-range transmitter that sent data to another Intruder system nearby, and the remaining four domes were ignored. Yet as long as Suuthrien had access to even one, it had access to all.

It would act discreetly.

Marette stood in the chamber that she and Levy had discovered such a short time ago and eyed the newly-devised connector that the engineers were using to link one of the chamber domes to the computer they had carried in. For approaching two hours, the computer had probed and analyzed the dome's function and control systems.

Though the chamber itself held a minimal crew, those safely back at the Omicron Complex were already pouring through the results thanks to the transmitter that sent all data back to the base computers. If all went as ESA planned, they would piece together the mystery of the dome's workings and learn what relationship it had—if any—to the large gemlike device in the center of the chamber, which they could not access directly.

If all went as planned. Marette judged the prospect unlikely at best. She left the deduction to the scientists and shifted her gaze to where the black material was held back from contact with the dome. "And you have detected no anomalous readings?" she asked again.

"Connection's been in the green all the way, Chief," CPO Levy reported from the computer's terminal beside the dome.

"You are certain?"

"As right certain as I can be, begging your pardon. We're dealing with a lot of unknowns here, but there's no sign of any dangerous power surges or feedback like last time, ma'am."

Marette nodded. If Levy was irritated by having to answer the same questions twice in twenty minutes, he hid it well.

"Omicron? Any unusual readings coming in via the data transmitter?"

"*Truth be told, Chief, the data's all unusual, that's why we're here to study it.*"

She frowned. "Omicron Control, is that your idea of a joke?"

"*Aye, I know what you're asking, ma'am. But it's just data. As we've said before, the idea that anything could exert any control over a completely foreign system's laughable. And if anything did suddenly come swimming its way up the datastream, we'd detect it.*"

"Which is why you shall continue to remain vigilant."

Was she being thorough, or paranoid? They were only interfacing with the mechanics of the dome itself rather than the computer system that resided in the black material. Even the threat of a drone attack was guarded against. The turrets they'd erected, poised like two gargoyles atop their towers, could easily cover the entire balcony and lower chamber from their elevated perch. ESA required her to push forward, *oui*, but she refused to drop her guard.

A baroque Hungarian accent interrupted her thoughts. "I have recalibrated the collectors." The suited figure of Dr. Grünbaum across the chamber gave a wave from beside one of the three large sensor pylons they had erected. "Officer Levy, if you could please bring the pylon back online?"

Levy touched a few keys on his terminal. "Collectors are active, Doctor. Omicron Control, this is Levy. You should have data sync with the collectors now."

"*Copy that, Officer, sync confirmed. The computer's reporting a probable control sequence for the dome. Stand by to test.*"

"Standing by. When you're ready."

All attention in the chamber turned toward the dome. Marette watched the monitor over Levy's shoulder for any sign of danger. No one spoke. For a time, nothing happened.

"Omicron, this is Clarion. There is no activity here, can you verify?"

There was a pause. "*Ah, affirmative, Chief. That seems to have been an optimistic control estimate.*"

"*D'accord.* Continue monitoring. I am returning to the complex."

"*Aye, ma'am. We're not giving up yet.*"

Dr. Grünbaum's suit mic caught his muttering. "I should hope not."

She turned to Levy. "Remain on your guard, Officer."

"Aye, Chief."

With a quick inspection of the four other guards and two scientists in the chamber, she made her way past the elevated turrets to the wide portal that was the chamber's exit. Suited as she was, she nevertheless took a deep involuntary breath as she moved seamlessly through the semitransparent membrane formed from the black material that sealed the chamber from the hard vacuum on the other side. It had been nerve-wracking to test Levy's idea that they could walk through the membrane to get out of the chamber the first time. But now Marette shook her head at her own foolishness; remarkable as the membrane was, she should have been used to it.

She turned down the curve of the hastily erected canvas tunnel, following it to Omicron. "Omicron, this is Clarion. I am in the tunnel en route to the complex. Is the airlock clear?"

Silence.

"Omicron Complex, do you read?"

Again, silence.

"CPO Levy, please respond."

Levy's voice came back clear. "*Chief?*"

"Are you able to contact the complex via radio?"

"*Stand by . . . No, ma'am, they don't respond.*"

"Boost transmitter power and keep trying. And I may lose radio contact with you momentarily."

"*Aye, ma'am.*"

Marette continued toward the complex to test her hypothesis and tried again to contact them. It didn't take more than a few meters.

"*—respond please. Field Chief Clarion, this is Omicron Complex, do you receive?*"

"This is Clarion. Report status, Omicron. Is the communications bubble returned?"

"*That's an affirmative, ma'am. We just lost radio contact with you and the team in the chamber.*"

"Is it related to your control attempt on the dome?"

"*I don't think so, Chief. We were running the same diagnostics as before when it returned. But we don't know the original cause, so we can't be positive it wasn't us.*"

"Understood. CPO Levy is attempting to break through with a boost to signal power."

A pause. "*There's no evidence that increased signal strength would have any effect. We did try that the first time.*"

"Halt the diagnostics to be sure. Learn if that has an effect. We cannot be sure this is the same phenomenon. Boost your own power as well; I do not wish to lose contact."

There was a sigh from the Omicron controller. "*Yes, ma'am. We can try. Though it looks like we've a small receiver malfunction on this end. Might be related.*"

"Locate the cause and fix it, Omicron control. I am returning to the chamber."

Omicron acknowledged as Marette turned back toward the chamber. Though she doubted much could have happened in so short a time span, she saw no reason not to check on them. Following that, she could pass messages on foot through the bubble if need be. She tried the comms after she passed where she estimated the bubble to be. "Levy, this is Clarion, do you read?"

"*Affirmative, Chief.*" The response was immediate, but calm.

"Omicron may have a receiver malfunction. Can you confirm any interference on your end?"

"*No, ma'am. Though I don't see as that should affect our suit radios.*"

Marette turned the tunnel corner to find the chamber just as she'd left it. "It may be another effect rather than a cause." She stepped through the membrane and down into the chamber. "Shut down the terminal diagnostics for the present."

Levy worked at the terminal as she crossed the chamber. She was passing one of the sensor pylons when she heard the Omicron controller's voice break through. "*—can read me, you'll——transmitter at their end.*"

"Omicron, I am reading you. Repeat your last transmission."

"We read you here also. We need you to get a message to the chamber team to deactivate the data transmitter on their end."

"It would appear that is no longer necessary, Omicron. I am receiving you from within the chamber." She glanced questioningly at Levy.

"Confirming that," Levy added. "I read you loud and clear, Omicron."

"Understood, Officer, but all the same, we've just picked up evidence of a latent signal that's been within the datastream for the last ninety minutes. We're starting to get some unusual indicators here—"

"Ninety minutes?"

Movement from the far end of the chamber caught Marette's eye. Two sections of black material on the balcony wall were receding to uncover opening doorways that hadn't shown on their map.

"—and we can't break the connection from our side."

"Stand by, Omicron, something is happening here. Levy—" she cut short her order at the sight of a security drone framed in each doorway. "Take cover!"

Marette dove behind the central gem device as the drones opened fire. "Omicron, we are under attack, at least two drones!" She scrambled into a crouched position as a jolt of energy stabbed into one of the guards where he'd stood returning fire. He crumpled instantly. "Take cover!"

The turrets fired in halting bursts while the remaining guards did the same from behind what cover they could find. Marette peeked through the gaps in the frame of the gem device to see the drones themselves taking cover in the doorways, making themselves targets only long enough to fire a few bursts before ducking back in. Bullets and EMP danced along the doorways. Pulverized black material fell from the walls where Geiger cannon shots had missed their target. They couldn't target the drones fast enough.

"Omicron, we need support!"

"We're———a squad, but——need to disconnect—"

"Omicron, repeat last transmission!"

A burst of energy lanced into the area near the terminal and dome connection where Levy was crouched, sending him diving away to open floor space. The turrets opened fire again, narrowly missing the drone as it withdrew once more.

Then the second drone was out and firing, cutting off Levy's path back to the cover of the dome. He scrambled to the gem device next to Marette as frantically as his suit would allow.

"They're using cover!" he shouted despite the clear comms-link. "They've never done that before!"

He was right. In the past the drones had simply floated to the center of a room and fired a burst of energy that hit every target in the area. But that required time for the drone to get in position—time that allowed it to be destroyed. "Omicron! Do you read?"

A burst of multiple voices came across the channel from Omicron. Each shouted over the other so that Marette had to strain to make anyone out. *"What do you mean——not us? No——back, get it back!"*

"Omicron, respond!"

"Chief!" Levy pointed to the floor by the dome. A hole no larger than her helmet had opened, out of which scuttled a squat, robotic quadruped.

"——losing control of base systems! ——attempting to isolate! You—— shut down——transmitter——"

Marette cursed as three more of the quad robots scuttled after the first.

"It's just a datastream!" Levy protested. "They said it couldn't do that!"

Marette cursed their own arrogance. It traveled there from God-knows-where with God-knows-what level of technology. Who knew what it could do? She called to the remaining guards, "Does anyone have a clear shot at the terminal?"

No one did. But if she could get to the connection port . . .

"We are going for the port! Cover us, now!" Before she'd even finished the order, the quads had swarmed the port and begun manipulating the connector with miniscule fingers that snaked from their bodies.

The guards acknowledged. Levy gave a ready sign. When the latest barrage of drone fire ceased, they rushed forward together toward the dome as blue light flared from under the quads.

"They're trying to fuse the connection!" Levy shouted.

Undaunted, she reached forward to knock them away, but they clung like ticks to the dome and the link.

"Chief!"

Marette looked up barely in time to see the drone pulling out to fire. She ducked behind the dome. Levy went with her as the guards and turrets fired at it again. Marette had no chance to see if they hit;

one of the quads sprang at her. Metal legs pierced her suit and tore at her forearms beneath. She jumped back in reflex to get away and in so doing pushed herself out from behind the cover of the dome.

As she did, the quad released her and immediately turned to slash Levy's leg. He cried out. Both drones emerged simultaneously to fire. They had little time, and not enough cover.

"Run!" she screamed and scrambled for safety.

A swath of energy from one of the drones fired across their path to the gem device. She spun in a new direction, taking Levy with her and racing instead for a different dome as one of the drones took a blast of concentrated fire from four directions.

She ducked behind the safety of a new dome close to a turret. She spotted Levy right behind her before everything happened at once: The drone that was hit flashed and fell to the deck above, but its twin continued to attack. Energy struck out in a solid beam and caught Levy's ankle in mid-dive before he landed beside her, but the beam continued on. It swept across the base of the turret and destroyed its support tower as it fired at the fallen drone. The turret toppled backwards like a felled tree, still firing its Geiger cannon. The cannon's radiation bolts pulverized the black material on the ceiling and cut a path of falling black goo that led straight to the chamber portal. There was no time for Marette to even shout a warning. The cannon punctured the membrane over the portal and atmosphere burst out the hole.

Marette pressed herself to the ground against the torrent of escaping air. The puncture was not sealing itself. There was nothing to take hold of besides Levy, half-crouched and clutching at his ankle in pain. Wind screamed across her closed helmet as the smaller bits of equipment flew across the chamber and out into vacuum. A dropped rifle whirled through the air and smashed into the sensor pylon next to them, sending the pylon's already wobbling bulk toppling their way.

Straight for Levy.

Marette launched herself into him and shoved him out of its path a moment before the pylon slammed her down. Her helmet smacked against the floor like a hammer to her skull. Her vision swam with lights.

There were words coming over the comms from Omicron—frantic, urgent. Pinned to the floor beneath the pylon she strained to listen through the chaos and pain but could hear only three words clearly: "—*lost turret control!*"

Then someone was shouting an order, and it was a moment before Marette knew it was her. "Omicron Control, quarantine the complex! Repeat, quarantine . . . "

Her voice gave out. The final thing she saw before the blackness took her was the last turret taking aim at one of the guards who had taken cover.

XXVIII

"*TALK*."

"*Talk? Just a while ago you told me to shut up and hung up on me. Should I infer that you don't wish to withdraw from our little venture after all?*"

"*I was busy. And you vanished on me last week.*"

"*My dear Diomedes, I was doing some checking on you. When one's partner chooses to assassinate someone vital to that very partnership—*"

"*That was supposed to be a straight merc job. First I heard he was yours was when you told me just now. News said he was ESA.*"

"*He was not mine, but we needed him. There was vital information in those brains you splattered across the pavement.*"

"*Shot him in the chest. You never said a word about that guy. How the hell could I know who he was?*"

"*Still, one wonders at the coincidence of your eliminating the one man we need?*"

"*It was a set-up. I'm taking care of the problem.*"

"*A set-up by whom?*"

"*I said I'm taking care of it.*"

"*By whom?*"

"*Screw you. You keep your secrets, I keep mine. Don't forget what I've got on you.*"

A chuckle. "*Well now, it would seem we both have a bit of leverage on each other, wouldn't you say? I'd have very little trouble locating someone who'd like to know how to find you, should it come to that.*"

"*Keep your end of the bargain and we don't have any trouble. I didn't know who the guy was.*"

"*Oh, if I didn't believe that, we wouldn't still be speaking. Yet the fact remains that we now have something of a problem.*"

"How much *of a problem?"*

"We have the lunar coordinates. I've finessed slipping you into a black ops niche that will get you up there for me—"

"You'd done that faster, we'd be done with this by now."

"Ah yes, because pulling together a black op using company resources without their actually knowing about it is just such a simple thing."

"Your problem, not mine."

"My problems are your problems, my dear Diomedes. Or, ah, do you prefer 'Malcolm?'"

"You don't use that name for me. Ever."

"As you like. But as I said, my problems are your problems, assuming you still want this to turn out well. And profitably."

There was no response.

"Silence speaks volumes, my dear Diomedes. As I was saying, I've arranged to get you there so you might fulfill your part of the bargain. What we now lack, thanks to you, is intelligence regarding the systems up there."

"I'll take care of that when you get me there."

"Oh, you'll take care of that, will you? You'll be planting a leech transmitter into their network. It has to be configured so they don't find it the second you get it in place. You can't beat that sort of information out of someone, you know."

"There's a way."

"Oh, I see. And when the person with the information is behind a security airlock and you're sitting outside without an entry code? Surely even you can see our difficulty."

"Plans are your department. Solve it. And get the heat off my back."

"Oh, the heat is your own doing. Even if I could fix that, why would I discard such a means to influence you? As for the rest . . . I shall find some way to get around the mess you've made of things."

"Shit happens, Fagles."

"Oh, most certainly it does. You will be hearing from me."

The conversation ended. Marc shut off the playback.

Leaning against the wall of Marc's apartment, Michael watched the image of Abigail Brittan on the conference screen where she'd been listening.

"And how long ago was this recorded?" she asked.

Michael spoke first. "It was just after he'd ditched us on the roadside, so, what, a little over two hours ago?"

"8:27 p.m.," Marc confirmed. "We'd have had it to you sooner, but we needed to get back to the city and tweak the audio enough to make out the guy on the other end."

"Nonetheless, good work," she told them. "This Fagles, do we have any indication of who he is?"

Fagles's image jumped to the forefront of Michael's mind in the same long overcoat, suit, and ponytail he'd worn that night in the 'Pyre. "He's with RavenTech. Six months ago he worked under Ken Wallace, which probably explains what Diomedes says he's got on him."

"The thefts against their own company?"

Michael nodded. "Diomedes and I both met him during all that. I'm not sure of his first name or if he's still with RavenTech."

"That's plenty for us to pinpoint him. By the sound of it, he's not operating under the direction of his company in this matter."

"Did you notice how Diomedes corrected him on where he shot Curwen?" Marc put in.

"I did. It near confirms what we suspected, though it doesn't give us any answers."

"Diomedes might have been lying about that part, though," Michael said. "He was talking about losing what Curwen knew, maybe he just didn't want to take the blame for the problem."

Abigail nodded. "I'll pass this along to the Council. I'm sure they or I will be contacting you again soon. Is there anything else?"

Before Michael could make up his mind about mentioning what Felix told them about Diomedes attacking a Gideon look-alike, Abigail held up her hand and tapped the AoA chip in her palm. "I'm getting something. We'll have to cut this short. Gentlemen."

She ended the call.

Michael's own palm was normal. He showed it to Marc. "How's yours?"

"Nothing. I'm sure we'll find out soon enough if it's important."

"Yeah." He resigned his curiosity to check the view outside the window. By all accounts, Marc's A.I. had surveillance covered, but keeping watch himself made him feel better. Watching was at least a simple enough task. Satisfied that nothing in view seemed threatening, he dropped the flap of the blinds back into place and returned to where Marc was rearranging his workstation. The rumble of a truck passing outside briefly filled the silence, and then faded.

They hadn't talked much on the way back into town. The cab they'd called gave no privacy for AoA matters, and Michael had been absorbed in his own thoughts about their confrontation with Diomedes. He wondered now if there would be a second such confrontation, and if they would escape quite so unscathed. Though Jer and his sister had been a more violent threat, the car ride with Diomedes felt like a tightrope walk over disaster, despite the fact that his old mentor had very likely saved them in the parking lot.

The idea left a bitter taste in his mouth.

He turned to Marc. "Why didn't you run when you had the chance?"

Marc looked startled by the question. "Back at the parking lot?" He shrugged meekly and turned his focus back to his workstation. "It's not like I could've just left you there."

"It wasn't me they were after. I would've been okay."

"But I didn't know that then, did I?"

The reply came defensively enough that Michael waited a few moments before speaking again. He made another check at the window.

"I'm supposed to be the one protecting you," he said. "You have to let me do my job, you know." He tried to add a grin to make it a joke, yet hoped it still sounded earnest.

Marc ran a spare bug over a scanner. "So I'm the President and you're the Secret Service now, eh? We need you too, you know. Diomedes wouldn't have even listened to me."

"I could have held my own." He stopped short of telling a man at least five years his senior to do as he was told. "You should've run."

"Look, I did what I did. It's too late to second-guess it now."

"Yeah, well, it's not too late for next time. If I'm expecting you to do one thing and you do another—Well, you saw what happened."

"It turned out alright."

"Only because Diomedes saved our asses! I can't do my job if you don't let me. It's all I'm saying."

Marc set the bug down and moved to the A.I.'s console, his back to Michael. Marc's voice was quiet when he next spoke. "I didn't think I could make it to the car without being seen. It looked too open. I thought it was better to stay and try to help than risk getting shot in the back." He gave a laugh that sounded forced. "I mean, shot in the back? How useless would that have been, right?"

He might have a point. "And if you thought you could've made it?"

Marc looked around at him for a moment before returning his attention to the screen. "Holes, confirm backup of the Diomedes audio."

"Confirmed, Mr. Triton."

"With full encryption?"

"Yes, Mr. Triton, as you requested the first time."

Marc nodded. He turned around again, facing Michael, arms crossed. "So what do you say we change the subject? Did you have a plan when you told Diomedes the ones who hired him were after us?"

"Ah." Michael frowned. "That." He'd asked himself the same question on the way back. "Shot in the dark, really. I guess I was hoping he'd say who hired him." He rubbed his forehead with a grimace. Okay, so they'd both made mistakes. "Didn't really work all that good, did it?"

Marc shrugged. "He didn't seem terribly willing to do anything but demand information from us. It was worth a shot. Though it means we'll have to stick with the story if we need to talk to him again."

"Yeah, I know." Next time he'd come up with something better, assuming there was a next time. They still had no clue who hired Diomedes.

"On the bright side, he didn't kill us." Marc laughed nervously and turned back to the computer. "Anyone who can stay brave with a gun at their back is . . . Well, it's no mean feat."

Michael checked another window. He hadn't felt brave at the time. He'd tried to imagine beforehand how he was going to react to his old mentor's threats and anger. As it turned out, he couldn't recall having felt more intimidated—not only by all Diomedes had directed at him, but the responsibility of everything he was supposed to accomplish despite it.

But there'd been anger, too—anger at Diomedes's threats, and anger from their shared past that Michael hadn't truly known he was carrying until that moment. He'd seized on that anger to help him keep a strong face through the intimidation, despite how he felt under the surface.

Yet even so, what had he accomplished? Without Marc's bug, they'd have gotten nothing, and Diomedes was the one to save them from the freelancers. The bug didn't bother him so much; that was just part of Marc's job. What stung was the irony that he'd still wound up dependent on his old mentor.

He'd have to do better.

Captain Brittan's signal came through twenty minutes later. "Hello again, gentlemen."

Marc gave a greeting for them both. "That was fast. Has the Council heard the recording already, or . . . ?"

She shook her head. "Not all of them, from what I'm told, but things have gotten more urgent. They're calling the three of us into conference."

Michael flushed. Called before the Council? "Is there a problem?"

Abigail frowned. "I don't yet know the details, but something's happened at Omicron."

XXXIX

ONDREA KEPT VIGIL before Gideon's observation window. His eyes remained closed. Monitors and medical equipment surrounded the bed where he lay, thankfully unrestrained. Beneath him, a sheet covered the bed's metal clamps, designed to hold down the body they'd given him—a "last resort" that would be used on her brother only over her dead body.

She eyed the clock on the wall behind him. Soon the tests would be complete and she would be staring at the image of his mind reflected in CAT scans and NCA indicator results, trying to find the flaws in the miracle they had achieved and the cause behind his reported collapse. She had a few more minutes of waiting at best. Until then, he was simply her brother, lying unconscious on a lab bed while she worried.

What would he say to her when he woke? Was it worth the risk of trying to convince him that he'd simply passed out again, or would he realize she'd used the stunner? She fingered the device in her pocket. It could go a long way toward persuading him to stay in the lab if he believed her, but a discovered lie could do much more damage. And hadn't she lied to him enough already? If there *was* some subconscious vestige of mistrust lurking there . . .

Ondrea left the thought unfinished and wished that she could have convinced him to come back on his own. With more time, perhaps she could have, but the guards outside had forced her to put Gideon's personal safety first. How much her brother trusted her was moot if she lost him again. All the same, she disliked the bargain.

The door slid open and Beck invaded her solitude.

"Well?" she asked.

"You asked me to let you know when they got the results of the tests?"

She scowled on a long exhale, still facing Gideon through the glass. "What part of 'Well?' did you have trouble with, Beck?"

"Ah, sorry, I thought you might—uh, well anyway the CAT scans came back normal. Long story short, the brain itself is still in good shape yet. Dr. Hamilton's in lab seven if you need a more detailed description."

"Still in good shape *yet*?"

"I'm only repeating what he told me. I can call him if—"

She turned around, silencing him. "Not yet. What about the rest of the tests?"

He pointed. "Should be at your station. I had a look, but, you're the expert there."

Something was wrong. It was plain in his tone. She moved to the terminal and hoped his typical lack of confidence was more legitimate than usual, but she saw the problem the moment she looked at the data. "Are you talking about the neuronal synoptic flux, or is there something else?"

"It's looking a bit unstable, isn't it?"

"Just a bit." Somewhat more than a bit, actually. Her stomach tightened and she tried not to jump to conclusions. "Run a diagnostic on the implant. Maybe it's damaged."

"I already did. Next screen there? It checked out fine."

"Then run another!"

"Ah, okay, but—Yeah, I can do that." He moved to carry it out. "But, if it's not the implant?"

"Then we've got a problem," she said, looking at the data. *Problem* was an understatement. If it wasn't the implant, what they had equated to a time bomb set in Gideon's mind. Ondrea searched the numbers for an indication of just how long they'd have.

Beck busied himself at his own station before finally asking, "So how do we fix it? If it's not the implant, I mean?"

Numbers danced before her eyes and in her mind to form a shadowed picture. "The engram sets are in conflict. The stress of maintaining both of them is causing degradations." She sighed. "But he shouldn't be having this problem so *soon*."

"So that brain's a horse with two fat guys on it."

She smacked a hand on the tabletop. "That's my brother, Beck."

"Right, sorry." He turned away.

"The only way to fix this is to eliminate one of the engram sets before we lose both." She said it more to think aloud, trying to lead herself toward finding another option. She already knew which set Marquand would abandon; of the two, one was more vital to the project. But the other made him her brother. She looked up from the screen. "Beck, not a word of this to anyone, you understand?"

He blinked, hesitating. "Ondrea, if this is going to jeopardize the project, they're going to want—"

"It's not going to jeopardize the project, Beck. You don't even know what the project is. I've seen their timetable. The degradation won't be an issue before the project's complete. That leaves plenty of time to fix it once it's over."

Beck bit his lip, considering in a way she didn't like. Ondrea walked over to him. "You said it yourself, Beck. I'm the expert on this. You go telling Tseng and the others and they're going to panic. They're going to act prematurely and do whatever they think it takes to safeguard their little project, even if it means wiping out my brother." She leaned down to whisper in his ear. "And if that happens, Beck, I'll see to it that not only can you kiss your career good-bye, but you'll need to grow some balls for real because there won't be enough left of the originals to fill a *bottle cap*."

She waited for the threat to sink in, remaining where she was as Beck sat stunned.

"Well," he finally managed, "I didn't mean—I mean it's not like it's something we'd have to . . . "

"Beck."

"Sure, no, we can keep it quiet. I mean, if you know their timetable and it's not going to be a problem 'till they're finished with him?"

She patted his shoulder. "I know more of the big picture. You have to trust my judgment on this. It'll be alright." Ondrea returned to her screen as Beck muttered something acquiescent she didn't quite catch.

For a while, she continued to delve into the data. She hid a sigh of relief when she found that what she'd just told Beck was likely accurate. Though there were no perfect indicators, no ticking digital readout, probability was on her side. If the project could be completed fast enough, she'd have enough time to save Gideon's mind afterward.

If the project could be completed fast enough.

To do that, she would need Gideon's cooperation. Gazing again through the window at where her brother lay in the body they'd given him, Ondrea searched for a way to make him listen.

"Gid?" Ondrea touched her brother's shoulder gingerly. "Can you hear me?"

His eyes snapped open and flashed around the room before settling on her. "Where am I?"

"It's okay, Gid. You're okay." She squeezed his hand, artificial or not, and held the warmth there.

"I'm back at Marquand, aren't I?" he breathed. Even knowing him as she did, Ondrea couldn't tell if he was being cautious, or just indifferent.

"Yes. You're safe." She waited a moment as he stared at the ceiling. "What's the last thing you remember?"

He stared awhile longer. "You promised to tell me everything if I came with you. I wanted to know more first. And then, I wake up here." He turned to face her.

"It's better that you're here, Gid." She smiled apologetically. "I know I keep saying this, but you still need to heal. And they've patched up your wound."

"But how did I get here, Ondrea?"

"I brought you back with me." She took a deep breath and hoped he truly didn't remember. "You passed out again, right in my arms. I—don't like thinking about what might have happened if I hadn't been there. Please, Gid, just say you'll stay here and rest until you're completely healed, okay?" She pleaded there silently and shamelessly, but he left the question unanswered and turned away again.

"What did you do with Caitlin and her friend?"

"We didn't do anything with them. After they helped get you into the floater, we left them there. They're still at her house, I suppose."

Monitors beeped softly as she waited for his response. It was a while in coming.

"Why don't I trust you, Ondrea?" It would have hurt her less to hear if it were just an accusation rather than the lament he made it.

"They're just fine, Gid, I promise."

"I mean about everything."

She gave his hand another squeeze that made him glance down at it. "I don't know. Maybe I should have told you everything sooner. I just didn't know how you'd react. I didn't want to put too much on you at once. And I think this feeling you're having might be tied to why you're passing out. Now that you're back in treatment, it should pass, with time." It was only a half truth, and she couldn't confirm her suspicions at the cause until the other engrams were removed, but she gave him a smile. "I guess I just told you to trust me that you should trust me, didn't I?" He didn't return the smile, though her brother's smiles had been rare even before he'd been shot. "Gid, I wish you would look at me."

He did as she asked. "You asked me to stay until I'm healed. Do I have a choice?"

It was her turn to look away. "Gid, when we . . . lost Isaac," she started, treading gingerly on a subject Gideon had never dealt with well, "and you did what you felt you had to, I trusted you then. I supported you. I helped you. Everything I designed for you, it was to keep you safe. I didn't fully understand it, but I trusted you. You have to trust my judgment like that now."

"Then I don't have a choice."

"About finishing your treatment? Yes, you do have a choice. You can stay, finish the treatment, and *live*, or—Gid, I don't know what will happen exactly if you leave, but I don't—I don't know that you'd survive it."

"Tell me the odds."

"The *odds*?" She stared at him, horrified. "Of you *dying*? How can you ask me that? If Isaac asked you about odds the night he got kidnapped and you knew it was likely, would you have even answered that, or would you have begged him not to go out?"

His voice hardened. "I didn't know, Ondrea. How could I have? How could I have stopped something I didn't know would happen?"

"I know, Gid." He'd said similar things before, and she braced herself for an anguished outburst.

It didn't come. "I wasn't the one who killed him," was all he said.

"Well, this time I do know, and I'm not going to sit here quoting numbers and odds at you. If you don't trust me enough to believe when I say you need to stay here a while longer . . . " Anger boiled up inside her. "Damn it, Gid, don't risk your life when you don't have to! I won't let you, not this time!"

Gideon dropped his eyes to where both her hands clenched his in a white-knuckled grip. She relaxed the grip just a little but continued to glare until he met her gaze once more. She expected to see the mistrust again, or at least his usual stubborn defiance, yet she found only more confusion and, lurking beneath that, fear. She forced herself not to soften. For his own good, no matter what, she had to make him stay.

Through the confusion, Gideon surfaced. "I want you to tell me what's been done to me. You said I'm still human."

"I was telling the truth. You are. Do you remember what you told me when you had your limbs replaced with cybernetics?"

He scowled. "You keep asking what I remember."

"Sorry, figure of speech. But you said your body wasn't what made you *you*, that it was just a tool."

"How much more did you replace?"

She swallowed. "Nearly everything. We had to. Your skin, nearly all your organs, are synthetic. But your brain, that's real."

"Caitlin said I was shot in the head. Why is the only place I was shot still intact and my body gone?"

Caitlin again. "You trust that woman a lot, don't you?"

"I don't know. She seems to care what happens to me for some reason."

"So do I, you know." *And I'm the one you grew up with.* She pushed away her frustration and searched for the right thing to tell him. "Gid, your body, what Marquand did—You know I told you that they want you to work for them a little when you've recovered. To help recoup their costs. It's part of why you've got the upgrades that you do. They gave you the things you'd need to help them."

"Without my consent."

"It was that or let you die! I did what I had to do. And you said yourself it was just a tool."

Gideon jumped to his feet, stripping off the monitor connections. "You've made me into a slave, Ondrea!"

"Gid, you're not a slave! We're indebted to them, yes, but you're not a slave!"

"*We*? They didn't force you into service!"

"Yes, they damned well did! They saved you! They kept me from losing another brother. We're both in their debt. Do you think I'd put you in this situation if there were any other way? You can't tell me you wouldn't have done the exact same thing for Isaac if you could have!"

Gideon looked away without answering.

"You're not a slave," she said. "Once you're healed, they'll let you leave the building. You'll still have to do the job, but you won't be chained to a wall or anything like that."

He faced her again. "Once I'm healed."

"Yes." She fisted her hand until her nails pressed into her palm. "But they need to know you're still going to do it, or they won't continue your treatment."

"And after that, I will be done with them. Is that true?"

She hid her fist behind her back and squeezed tighter. "Yes. They'll likely offer you a steady position, but you only need to do the one job, and you're done."

"Good. Then I will be done."

"It might be a good idea to hold off deciding on that. It could be a good offer, you never know."

He watched her. She fought to keep the unease from her face. "There are things you still haven't told me," he said. "You said you'd tell me everything."

She swallowed. "What do you want to know?"

"How much do you know of the man who shot me? And what's really causing my blackouts? I want to know about this experimental procedure that you couldn't talk about in front of the others."

Ondrea had spent half her night thinking of how she would answer those questions. She hesitated only a moment, to take a seat in a chair across from the lab bed.

"Diomedes," she began. "I only know what I learned about him from your recordings I found, so I think you probably know more about him than I do. I was more concerned with making you better than trying to find the one who did it." She paused and then, aware he might take the anxiety in her voice for a sign of the lie it was, added, "I hope you can forgive me for that, Gid."

His response told her nothing. "And the rest?" He touched the back of his head. "How is it that he shot me here and one of the few things Marquand let me keep is my brain?"

It was the second time he'd asked. Again she hesitated, knowing that even the piece of the truth she'd thought to tell him might upset him. She reached down into herself to find her courage, and began.

A brief while later, Ondrea was staring across a desk at Julius Tseng. The fact that she'd be telling him news he wanted to hear made her no less eager to be out of his office. The haze of self-satisfied superiority that typically surrounded him had grown stronger since he'd forced the armed team on her to find Gideon. If she hadn't needed him to authorize the floater so she could reach her brother so quickly, she wouldn't have told Tseng about it until Gideon was safely back. That she had to ask galled her, and made him doubly superior.

Now, she didn't waste time with empty greetings. "Gideon's going to cooperate. I've convinced him that he still needs to be treated and recover. He won't try to leave again."

Tseng shrugged. "Good, then the guards we've posted won't have to work too hard."

"He won't try to leave."

"That remains to be seen. For what it's worth, Ondrea, I believe that you think so."

"Then no guards."

He brushed his hand at her as if shooing a fly, and she fought not to give him the satisfaction of seeing her seethe. "Then at least," she continued, "don't let him see them."

"Oh, he shouldn't notice them. As long as he keeps his word and continues on Project Phoenix, things will be fine."

It was a crumb, but she took it and went on. "He will. And I think I can convince him to continue to work for Marquand after the project is completed."

"No matter how successful Phoenix is, the company isn't about to let him just go his own way after it's done. You know that."

She begrudged a nod. "I know that. But things will work out much better if he believes it's his choice."

Tseng sat back in his chair. "As you like. He will remain with us, one way or another. He's a substantial investment."

She stabbed him with her glare. "He's a person."

Tseng merely smiled. "Well, he's two people actually, isn't he? But Phoenix is our primary concern for the moment. What comes after is academic for now. To that effect, I want you to increase the intensity of his 'treatments.' We need to speed things along."

She hesitated. "Why?"

"Obviously we want to move forward. Your brother's Houdini act cost us time, and before that he wasn't exactly hemorrhaging the information like you said he would."

"He needs more time, not stronger sessions."

Tseng swung his desk monitor around to face her. "You said weeks ago that the intensity of the recall sessions could be increased if necessary with minimal risk. You supported this statement with data. At this stage, minimal risk is acceptable. Has something changed?"

She could tell from his tone that he expected the answer was no. He'd hit her with her own data and if she said yes, he'd know something was wrong. He'd find out about the instability and force her to abandon her brother to save the project. If she said no . . .

Ondrea tried to run over the numbers in her mind. There was no way to be so quickly certain how much further Tseng's proposal would push the instability. All she knew was that it was a risk. Walls were closing around her.

She shook her head. "No. Nothing's changed."

It was a risk she'd have to take.

XXX

IN THE AOA COUNCIL'S emergency session, Marc's avatar sat in the center of the virtual meeting hall as a guest. The avatar images of Michael and Abigail beside him wore the flat expressions that indicated their mic-and-view screen interfaces.

By contrast, the four attending members of the council—Councilors Knapp, Lin, Ramis, and Arbiter Szendroi—were positively alive. Like Marc's, their avatars' expressions mirrored their real ones, wherever they sat in the world, via direct neural links. None on the Council wished to limit their own communication to a mere voice over a microphone.

Sitting with their eyes closed and a wire in their brain in the real world made for a more humanized conversation in the virtual one. It was an irony the dynamics of which Marc sometimes found himself pondering. For the moment, however, Marc was more occupied with what the Council had said thus far: an unknown disaster had severed contact with the Omicron Complex. Marette gave the quarantine order, they'd said, but there was no word on her status since. The news troubled him on multiple levels.

Arbiter Szendroi was still speaking. "Agent Clarion had no time to transmit any information directly to us before the quarantine. Indeed, it was not even she who sent the quarantine order to ESA, although all indications are that it was given on her authority."

Councilor Knapp broke in, her avatar's face a stern mask of apprehension. "Yet it remains possible that her duplicity was discovered. Others may have issued the quarantine in her name as a containment measure until they discovered if she was working with anyone else on the site."

The arbiter nodded. "This remains a possibility, though Agent Clarion is currently the only one of us at the complex, and has been since Agent Triton left."

"If I can offer an opinion to the Council," Marc began, taking advantage of the free speaking privileges his guest status allowed him, "given Suzanne Namura's death when we tried to hack *Paragon*'s computer, I'd say it's more likely something similar happened to the complex itself. Her last report did say they were going to analyze the chamber they found."

"That might be true," Councilor Knapp agreed, "but precautions were in place to keep such a thing from recurring."

"All due respect, Councilor, but we didn't expect such a thing could have happened the first time, either."

"While I concede the point, Agent, we have no clear indication either way."

"And that is why we've called you three here," the arbiter said. "We need reliable intelligence regarding what truly has occurred. One thing that is clear is the situation at Omicron has destabilized to the point where we're forced to move up our timetable. For the benefit of those who have not yet heard," here he made motion to the shadow around the chamber where the rest of the AoA in attendance watched, "we'll replay a recording of a conversation involving the Northgate freelancer Diomedes, assassin of ESA mole Joseph Curwen."

The bug recording was played again. It was the third time Marc had heard it, and he found himself concentrating instead on what the arbiter had just told them. Marc was sincere in his suggestion that the quarantine was due to *Paragon*, but he couldn't help but wonder if Councilor Knapp was right. ESA was hunting him; what if they'd found out about Marette? Neither possibility seemed more comforting than the other. But the AoA would find a way to get help to her soon. Whatever form it took, he hoped it wouldn't be too late.

The recording ended and the arbiter spoke. "We now have a clearer picture of the fallout from the death of the ESA mole. While the identity of those responsible for hiring the freelancer to kill the mole remains unknown, the reality of the situation is that we now have a line on a route to the Omicron Complex that is separate from ESA."

Councilor Lin spoke. "So we use this to get assistance to Agent Clarion."

"The idea merits examination, yes," the arbiter said.

"And just what sort of 'assistance' do you plan to send?" This came from Councilor Knapp. "If we blindly send more of our people and they too are lost or compromised, things go from bad to worse!"

"Then what do you suggest, Councilor?" Lin asked. "We have no other way to gather intelligence. Waiting for further contact from Agent Clarion, I'm sorry to say, may be fruitless in this case."

Knapp looked over her colleagues. "If we are to act, we must do so in strength or we risk exposing ourselves and losing control completely. We need to be ready to take the entire complex. This *is* what we've been planning, isn't it? Arbiter?"

The arbiter nodded. "But not all is in place for us to act in strength. Unless this has changed since our last meeting?"

Councilor Lin shook her head. "We've pushed forward, but the timetable depends on manipulating a number of non-AoA elements. There's only so hard we can push."

"So our only choices are to wait, or to push harder," Knapp declared.

"And I said pushing harder is not an option."

Knapp responded with a stare that, digital simulation or not, made Marc shiver. "This is an extreme situation. The entire Exodus project is at risk. It is incumbent on the arbiter to sanction more extreme action!" She turned her eye to the arbiter, adding, "As a temporary measure."

The arbiter held up a hand. "I don't believe we've reached such a point yet. In light of this recording, our prior plan of opportunity regarding the mole may again be workable."

"We abandoned that plan when the mole was killed!" Knapp snapped. "We can't waste time with a defunct course of action!"

There was a moment of silence as both Knapp and Arbiter Szendroi waited for others to support the former's statement. When no one else seemed willing to speak, the arbiter broke the silence himself. "Councilor Ramis and I spoke briefly before this meeting. I think the Council will agree that recent circumstances merit a revote."

Marc looked to Samuel Ramis and recalled that he still owed the man a response to a friendly email from the previous week. He gave Marc a smiling glance before speaking in his usual rapid manner.

"Ah, yes well frankly it's clear that this Fagles is preparing to send Diomedes to Omicron—in fact *would* be doing so as we speak if not for the issue of access codes, so we have essentially the same situation that we'd decided to exploit when the mole was alive—a presence at Omicron belonging to neither ESA nor the AoA, but nonetheless one that we have a clear means of manipulating." He motioned to where Michael's avatar sat next to Marc's.

Councilor Knapp raised an eyebrow. "You mean to send *him*?"

"Ah, actually I would say we should send both of them."

Marc's heart stopped.

"Not only does Agent Triton have first-hand experience of the Omicron Complex," Ramis continued, "but he provides a credible way to provide Fagles and the freelancer with the codes they need. To say nothing of the fact that Agent Flynn would of course be invaluable as a liaison to Diomedes given their history."

"You'd entrust this to someone so inexperienced?" Knapp argued.

"I agree with Councilor Ramis's assessment," Lin put in. "Given the freelancer's profile, Agent Flynn provides the best chance of success."

At that, Michael spoke up. "It's true I've only been with the AoA six months, Councilor, but I know Diomedes. If he's going to trust anyone, he'll trust me."

All heads turned to Michael, and Councilor Knapp asked, "Correct me if I'm wrong, Agent Flynn, but didn't Diomedes nearly kill you earlier today?"

"He had a gun on me nearly the whole time, but that's the way he is. If he wanted to kill me I wouldn't be here. As long as he's got a bounty on his head, he's going to be even more paranoid than usual; I doubt he'll let anyone else talk to him. If I could offer him a way to clear his name in exchange for helping us, I can almost guarantee his cooperation."

Marc had to admire Michael's confidence in speaking to the Council, though if his argument succeeded it would result in Marc's returning to the Moon under less than ideal circumstances at best.

Ramis gave Michael a nod and said to the Council, "That was my thinking also."

Knapp scoffed again. "You all assume that Diomedes killing the mole really is a coincidence! If you hang our hopes on a man who may have a secret allegiance—"

"Councilor," Lin began before Knapp shouted her down.

"We cannot commit to this without knowing for certain!"

The arbiter held up a hand and then asked Marc and Michael both, "You've found no evidence regarding Diomedes's claims that the assassination was just a job?"

Marc shook his head. "None either way beyond his word to Fagles, I think." He looked at Michael to confirm.

"But I think I believe him about that."

"You *think* you believe him?" Knapp shot.

"I believe him," Michael corrected.

"So this is purely a hunch."

Michael paused a moment, as if considering his words. "Based on what I know about him, yes. But I told you, Diomedes wants his name cleared. Even if he is lying about the assassination, he's obviously not getting any help getting the bounty removed. If we offer that in exchange for bringing us to the Moon, he'll use Fagles to get us there. And once we're there, isn't that all we'd need?"

Most of the Council seemed to consider this while Knapp spoke again. "And you claim he won't trust anyone but you."

"I honestly think I'm the best choice."

"Agent Brittan," the arbiter asked, "what's your assessment of Agent Flynn's abilities?"

"He may be young, but he's got potential. In my time working with him I've had no cause for complaint."

"Your short time working with him," added Knapp.

"Yes, Councilor, my short time. But his relationship to Diomedes renders him uniquely qualified to take advantage of the opportunity this situation gives us. Rejecting him based only on his youth is—and I say this with all due respect, Councilor—not only narrow-minded but unbecoming of the AoA."

"I think you may be taking the youth issue more personally than you should, Agent."

"Something else we disagree on, Councilor," she answered sharply. "I'm young for my rank on the Northgate PD, so I've dealt with this sort of attitude before. If I hadn't overcome that, would the AoA have an agent placed quite so high in the force? This is a meritocracy, Councilor. All other issues aside, I believe Agent Flynn is the best person for the job in question."

"It's exactly his merit that I'm questioning, Agent. And I don't appreciate your tone."

"The arbiter asked my opinion, Councilor. I was giving it. My tone shouldn't be the focus here."

Marc spoke up at the same time as the arbiter, managing, "If it's a question of merit—," before he yielded control to the other.

"The opinions of both Councilor Knapp and Agent Brittan are heard and noted, and now in the interest of time I'll request we refrain from any further restatements by either. Agent Triton, you had something to add?"

"Ah, yes. I was going to say that . . . " Marc reminded himself of what he could be getting himself into, and the consequences of going back into not only ESA's reach but whatever else lurked at Omicron. Even so, with what needed to be done, that didn't matter; the Exodus Project was in jeopardy, and they had to get help to Marette somehow— if she remained there to be helped. "I was going to say that Agent Flynn's performance so far has been excellent. Not only has he led us to Diomedes and this new lead, but he's already saved my life and risked his own doing it."

"You would support the proposed plan, then?" the arbiter asked.

Where he sat in his apartment, Marc swallowed for real. "I would, sir. And I don't do so lightly. I know Agent Flynn's involvement would mean my own as well, and, frankly, if I could get someone to go up there in our place, then I would. But if Diomedes is going to trust anyone, it'll be him, and I think he can handle the job."

The time on Marc's visor read 11:13 p.m. Four wireless networks in the area. Room temperature was 71.2 degrees. He wondered if the Council could tell he was sweating.

XXXI

*"**TAKE US THERE.** You know where to go. Take us there."*

The dream grips him again. Somehow, Gideon knows that he will forget it when he wakes, yet each time it comes, he remembers the times before.

"You're the only one who can help. The only one who can. Take us there!"

"Where?" he demands in a voice that is his, and yet isn't. The dream has come, just as before, just as he remembers.

"You know where! Take us there. Do it NOW."

But no, not just as he remembers. The pressure is greater than before, and growing stronger. As before, the darkness fades into a console of navigation controls as the cockpit forms around him.

"NOW!"

Pain bursts behind his eyes as the order echoes. He winces, more in surprise than anything. The dream has never brought pain before.

*"Take you **where**?" He tries to pull his hands away from the console, tries to bang them at the door that he knows must be beside him yet can never see, but some invisible force holds them fast.*

"Take us there!" This time the orders are joined by others. They build order on top of order until they are a torrent of voices that he is powerless to satisfy.

"Take us there!"

"You know where to go!"

"Take us!"

"Take us there NOW!"

"You have to remember!"

"You have to take us there now!"

But he doesn't know! They won't tell him. Why won't they tell him? "Tell me where!" he cries as they rail against him. "Answer me!"

The commands won't stop. The pain is growing. The cockpit is on fire. He thrashes in his prison but they won't stop to answer, shouting at him every second to take them there. Heat piles on heat, pain on pain, and they still won't stop. He wants desperately to give in, to do what they ask, to stop this torture, but he doesn't understand! Why doesn't he understand? It should be so obvious! He should know!

"Take us there! Send us there!"

"You're the only one who knows!"

"Send us there now!"

The voices are crazed. He thrashes again at the force that holds him. His pleas for clarity catch in his throat as the next wave of pain nearly breaks him apart.

He screams, he pounds at the console in desperation and hits the keys as he's never done before. He punches in a destination—any destination, just to appease them—and then launches the shuttle on its course with a howl of agony.

The pain ceases. All goes black.

The pain rolled over Gideon's face where he sat strapped and writhing in the memory chair. Ondrea watched it happen, repeated to herself that it was the only way, and desperately tried to stop herself from shutting everything down and pulling the chair release. Before, they had tried to coax out the information. Now they were forcing it out. She had no way to be sure what it was like from Gideon's perspective, but she knew it couldn't be pleasant. With every spasm of his sleeping body, she wished she could somehow take his place.

Then suddenly the session stopped. The chair powered down. Gideon relaxed.

"What is it? What's wrong?" Tseng demanded beside her.

The tech looked up, startled. "Nothing's wrong, Mr. Tseng. It worked. We've got coordinates!"

Tseng sprang to the tech's side. "About damned time. Run them. If they're in view then get me a satellite image." Ondrea started toward Gideon's restraints before Tseng stopped her in her tracks. "No. Run him through another few sessions. Make sure you get the same result."

Ondrea turned. "You need to give him time to rest."

Tseng frowned. "Fine. A short rest. We don't want to break it. But then put him in again. We're not just going to assume our first breakthrough is legit. After that, put him in a simulator. Let's see if he can do it when he's conscious."

XXXII

THE PHONE RANG five times before he picked up. *"Who's this?"*

"Diomedes? It's Michael. I need to talk to you."

A pause. *"How did you get this number?"*

"You took our car, then used your phone inside it. After that it involves a bug we left and it gets kind of technical. "

"How much did you hear? Talk!"

"Enough to know you're working with the guy who sent both of us on that wild goose chase for Wallace a while back."

"Kid, you breathe a word to anyone, I'll make you regret it."

"I know you will, don't worry. But now that I've heard it, I think I can help you out with your problem—if you do something for me."

"Another deal."

"Yeah, a deal."

"Can't even take care of yourself and you're going to help me?"

"I know people."

"Screw your people."

"Diomedes, when I say 'help,' I mean help getting your name cleared."

Another pause. *"That's crap. Sounds like a set-up."*

"It's not."

"Prove it."

"I need to meet with you somewhere. You pick the place."

"Prove. It."

"I can't prove it until I can talk to you directly. Or do you want to risk another phone call getting recorded?"

Nothing.

"Look, Diomedes, either I'm being straight with you and you've got a chance to get out of the heat you're in, or you're right and you're being led into a trap by a guy you've consistently proven that you're better than. Just hear me out."

Silence, and then, "*Be at the 'Pyre in an hour. Sit somewhere in the back.*"

"The 'Pyre?"

"*You deaf?*"

"Alright. Fine, we'll be there."

"*We?*"

"Me and Marc. He's key to all of this. I can't do it without his help."

"*Two hours.*" The line clicked dead.

They succeeded in getting a booth tucked into the furthest corner of the 'Pyre. Michael sat on the outer half of the bench that faced the rest of the dimly-lit establishment. From there, he could both keep watch and shield Marc, who was tucked further in on the same bench, closest to the wall.

It was the best place for Marc to be. No one could see him unless they were right beside the table. Only the seat opposite was better hidden, but Michael thought it best to keep that for Diomedes. Not only might it put the man more at ease, but it would also keep him farther away from either of them.

It remained to be seen whether or not his old mentor would show.

For the moment, they were at least in a good position. The bar was crowded enough to keep them inconspicuous, and Michael had already checked it and come up empty for anyone who might present an obvious threat.

Marc idly examined another ordered beer he wasn't drinking and asked, "This is kind of an odd place for him to want to meet, isn't it? I mean, if he's avoiding his usual places."

"Yeah, it is. He might not be coming at all, even. But it's not like him to just dismiss our offer. I think."

"Maybe he didn't believe it?"

"Maybe. But he does know this place. Could be he's going for home field advantage."

Marc turned his glass a bit. "You told the bartender where we're sitting?"

"Where I was sitting, anyway. No sense in calling more attention to you than we need to. If he shows, he'll find us."

They waited in silence. The 'Pyre's music droned around them. Michael took a sip of his beer.

"Think this'll work?" Marc asked suddenly.

"Here's hoping. If we blow this, I don't think we'll be in a position to get him to listen to anything else we have to say."

Marc chuckled grimly. "Given how ready he was to shoot us last time, I'd say that's putting it mildly."

"Diomedes makes threats. It's what he does. He wasn't going to shoot us." *At least I don't think he was.*

"Uh huh."

"He won't shoot us," Michael repeated. "We'll have to make this work."

"If he shows up."

"Yeah, if he shows up."

"We're just one giant ball of confidence, aren't we?"

Michael didn't answer. A large figure heading toward the table caught his eye, but the man broke away before getting too close. It wasn't Diomedes.

They would make it work. If they didn't . . . He thought back to the Council meeting and asked, "What did Councilor Knapp mean that the arbiter should sanction more extreme actions?"

"Doing whatever it takes, from what I know of her. If someone's in the way, then," he mimed firing a gun, "boom. No more obstacle."

"That's kind of what I thought, given the reaction. But we're— well, we're supposed to be doing what's right. I thought she might've meant something else."

"Nope. At least I don't think so. But yeah, we're the good guys. I don't think the arbiter or the rest of the Council would let it come to that. It's just that Knapp's always advocated keeping us secure no matter the cost. She's one of the extremes that balances out the rest, really." Marc shrugged.

"So we're still the good guys."

"Insomuch as anyone can be. The world's never been cut and dried, but I'd put us on the good side, yeah. I wouldn't worry."

Michael turned his glass. Granted, the AoA was not above publically discrediting or even ruining the lives of those who threatened its secrecy. Bad things, through AoA *in*action, could even be allowed to happen at the hands of others, if there were absolutely no other options. Yet such circumstances were rare and never undertaken lightly.

"You aren't, are you?" Marc asked. "Worried about that?"

Michael shook his head. "I've just got a history of misjudging these things, that's all. But no, I'm not worried about the AoA. I don't think I like Knapp, though. Not that I expect that'd bother her much."

Marc smiled. "Sometimes I think she's abrasive just to keep everyone on their toes. Felix called her a fire that forges the sword, or something."

"Sounds like something he'd—"

There was a crash of glass near the bar. Michael's hand went to his weapon before he saw that someone had just dropped a drink. He relaxed.

"We have a message."

"What makes you say—" Michael stopped as he noticed to what Marc was referring. The booths in the rear of the 'Pyre all had Net terminals wired into their adjoining walls. Theirs was blinking with an anonymous chat request. "Think it's him?"

"You told the bartender where we were. Maybe Diomedes called in and he told him what booth."

"Or maybe he's somewhere in another booth," Michael said with a glance out at rest of the bar. He pointed to the console. "Better answer it. Before he decides to change his mind."

Michael stood up and scanned the area. There was still no sign of Diomedes. He tried to catch the bartender's eye, hoping for . . . what? The man was busy with other patrons and failed to notice him. Michael sat again.

"It's him," Marc told him. "Or at least he claims it is. Says it's a secure link, too."

"Geez, we tell him we can't do this over the phone and he figures this'll be safer? Can you see if it's secure as he says?"

"I can give it a shot." Marc typed a quick "stand by" onto the console's keyboard and then pulled out a palmtop. Michael waited as he did some checking. "Seems to be. And I just added another security layer, so I think we're okay."

Michael nodded. "I guess that'll do for now. I'd feel better about this if he were here, though."

The other chuckled. "That makes one of us."

Michael pointed to the keyboard. "Ask him how we know it's him." Better if Marc did the typing so he could keep his hands free, just in case. Marc didn't argue.

-Your uncle's middle name was Bueford. Some hands the last year I was there were Max, Juan and Jimmy. Farmhouse was red.-

Michael gave Marc's questioning look a nod. "Ask him if he's nearby."

-This is as close as you get for now. You said there's a deal. What is it?-

"We know you're working with Fagles," Michael whispered as Marc typed. "We know he's set up a way to get you to a base on the Moon so you can help him steal their data. And we know you still need a way to get around their security." He waited to see the response that would get.

-Maybe. Get to the deal.-

"So what else is new?" Michael grumbled before pointing at the keyboard again. "We want in. Marc's been to the base. He helped test their security. Tell Fagles to find a way to get us there with you and we'll get you through."

-Both of you? Why do I say I need both?-

Michael hesitated. "Tell him whatever reason you want, just get us there. Do that, and we'll get your name cleared. Marc's people have connections. But not until after we're back."

-Clear it before or there's no deal.-

"When we get back, or there's no deal."

Marc finished typing and said aloud, "You know saying that sort of thing to him is much easier this way."

-That might change if Marc's got my hand at his neck.-

"See?" Marc said. "I like text much better."

Michael continued to dictate. "It's not Marc's decision, and threatening him won't make the people we're working with any more cooperative. They won't fix it until we're safely back."

-How do I know they can do it at all?-

"I guess you'll have to trust me on that. But you're getting what you need even without that. And we can send you coordinates to compare it with what Fagles has, to prove Marc's been there."

It took so long after that for Diomedes to respond that Michael's focus shifted to the rest of the room, half expecting the man to be headed their way. Marc had to nudge him back to the screen when the reply did come.

-Who are you working for?-

They exchanged glances. "We probably should've decided how to answer that already, huh?"

Michael scowled. "It's not a question he usually cares about. Just this: 'Someone who thinks what ESA's doing up there needs to be leaked and doesn't care who does the leaking.' How's that?" Marc gave him an appraisive nod and then typed it.

-You want the data for yourselves.-

"This is about helping you hurt ESA. They screwed Marc over, killed his friends. If you hurt ESA, the data's all yours."

Diomedes's response came quickly. -So why's Michael coming at all?-

"To watch out for Marc. You certainly wouldn't—Wait." He held out a hand to stay Marc's typing. "Better leave off that last part."

-If people are after you that makes it harder. Too much risk.-

"I was afraid that might come up." Michael gestured to the keyboard. "There's no one after us. That was just a story to find out what you were up to. But Marc still needs protection. You know that won't be a safe trip."

-So you lied to me.-

"Only to see if we'd be able to help you."

-So maybe you're lying now.-

"But now we've got proof. We told you, we'll give you the base coordinates to check our story."

-Give me the coordinates and security codes and you don't have to come at all.-

Michael frowned at the screen as though it were Diomedes himself watching him. "Don't insult our intelligence. Even if we trusted you that much it's not as simple as punching in a few codes. Marc has to be there."

Again, Diomedes's response was a long time in coming. -I'll talk to Fagles.-

"Talk fast. One last thing. Who did hire you for the shooting?"

Diomedes cut the link.

"I probably shouldn't have asked that yet." Michael sighed and turned to Marc. "Think he bought it?"

"You'd know more than I would. Hey, how much does Diomedes know about computer security, really?"

"He doesn't, I thought."

Marc tapped the console. "As secure as it was, then, this might be a local link. If it was already set up in the bar, he wouldn't have had to do anything special to it."

"Maybe we should ask the bartender."

"Why, because he was so helpful last time?"

"Okay, so then I guess we wait."

* * *

Five minutes after hanging up with Fagles, Diomedes paced the private safe room above the 'Pyre. He was trusting Lars too much. But if the bartender wanted his money, he wouldn't betray him. No, the danger would come after Diomedes left and paid the man. Once he had his money, would Lars turn on him then? Tip others to where he'd gone? He'd have to make sure Lars didn't know where he was headed.

But that would come later. Michael and the other would be here soon. Lars would take some drinks to their table and tell them quietly that Diomedes was waiting for them upstairs. They'd bring the drinks with them, and then he would see.

Diomedes sat on the stool by the safe room's terminal and waited.

Fagles had been skeptical of their offer. So many questions, not the least of which was who Marc was and how he had found them. Fagles was adamant about comparing the coordinates, to the point of being insulting. As if Diomedes would agree to go along with anything if the data didn't check. Fagles was skeptical, but he didn't have much choice. Diomedes hadn't shared their promise to clear his name.

Fagles's voice echoed in his mind from their phone conversation. "This almost seems too convenient. But your blunders leave us little choice." He'd been quick to point out that Diomedes better be sure about the two men; he'd be the one going up there with them. Like Diomedes needed to be reminded it was his ass on the line. But Fagles had come up with an additional suggestion. One that Diomedes agreed with.

They wouldn't like it. Diomedes was sure of that. It was Reason One he was seeing them in person. Threats were more persuasive in person. They wouldn't know about Reason Two. Not until they couldn't do a damn thing about it. Even Fagles didn't know about that one.

The small voice came again. *No. You can't do this!* He had ignored it before when he poured the vial into the beers Lars would bring them. It remained a tugging irritation, even after it was too late to matter.

Yes, it's already done. It had to be done anyway. Footsteps on the stairs saved him from debating the matter. They were coming.

Diomedes stood in the shadowed corner along one side of the door, weapon out. There was a knock. "Yeah?"

"It's Michael. And Marc."

The kid wasn't stupid enough to use his name in the hall. Good. "In. Slowly."

The kid came in first. Diomedes got his attention with a wave of the gun. "Over here. Anyone else but your partner comes in after you, you get a bullet."

The kid hesitated a moment, an eye on the gun. Then he kept coming. "It's just us, like I told you."

"We'll see." Michael came in the rest of the way. The other one followed and closed the door. They moved across the room to stand near the wall. Diomedes kept his aim on Michael. They'd brought the drinks Lars had given them. Good.

But they haven't drunk them yet. You've only got two doses, and they're in those glasses. You can't let them leave if they don't drink!

Diomedes nodded to himself. "Guns on the table. Now."

Michael scowled. "How many times do I have to tell you we're not here for that?"

Diomedes raised the gun a little more. "Just shut up and do as you're told."

"Fine. Whatever. But if we're going to do this you'll have to trust us eventually."

"No reason I should trust you again, after what you did."

"You can't hardly—," the kid started. "Look, forget it. We've got other stuff to worry about now, don't you think?" He drew an auto-pistol from under his coat and set it on the table. He added a holdout from the small of his back a second later.

A second weapon back there. You taught him that, didn't you?

Shut up, Diomedes thought. He turned the gun on Marc. "Now you."

Marc put a single, sissy piece of his own on the table. "That's all."

"You're a liar."

Marc took a step back. "I don't even own another one! Look, you can frisk me if you want to!"

He's afraid. He's hiding something.

Or he's just intimidated.

Diomedes moved closer. He patted the timid man down with one hand and made sure not to disturb the glass in his hand. He wasn't lying. No second piece.

"Well?" Michael asked.

"He's not lying. So he's an idiot. No backup piece?"

Marc shrugged like a fool.

"He's with me," said the kid. "I'm his backup."

"Yeah?" Diomedes gathered the weapons and stuffed them into his bag. "And who's yours?"

"Same as yours."

Michael doesn't have anyone either. You should be looking out for him like before, not—

He has Marc! He has whoever Marc's working for! He doesn't want your protection! And if he doesn't see it coming then he deserves what he gets! Maybe he'll learn something!

And when will he learn it? In the few moments before the end?

Diomedes tried to shut out the voices. "Before we do any of this, I want the coordinates. They don't check out, this ends right here."

Marc took what looked like an oversized palmtop computer off his belt and slipped out a memory strip. Diomedes snatched it from him and slid it into his phone for transfer to Fagles. "He'll have to check it." The two men glanced at each other, and Diomedes decided he didn't like them standing there. Too easy for them to move, for one thing. He motioned to the table. "It'll be a minute. Sit. Drink. Or something."

The two men sat, but they didn't drink. Instead, they kept a wary watch on him. As they should. If Fagles cleared them, he'd lower the gun. Then they would relax. Then they would drink. For the moment, no one spoke.

Then Marc reached for his coat pocket. Diomedes shifted the gun to him instantly. "Don't."

"It's—I'm just getting a mint."

Diomedes reached into the man's pocket, grabbed the contents in his fist, and tossed them on the table. Keys, a roll of mints, a battery, and some sort of scanner clattered across it. "There." Marc picked up the mints and had the sense to shut up.

Michael drummed his finger on the table, scowling. "So how've you been?"

"Like you care."

"I asked, didn't I? You know we're trying to help you here, you could maybe ease up on the threats!"

"We'll see."

The kid opened his mouth again but Diomedes's phone cut him off. Diomedes answered it without a word.

"*They're genuine. Contact me again when you've broken the news to them, and we'll proceed.*"

"Right."

"*I remind you that we're walking a very thin line here. Make this work.*"

Diomedes hung up.

There. Michael is trustworthy.

This proves nothing.

Diomedes holstered the gun. "Alright. So you're legit." He glanced at their beers, still untouched.

"So what now? How's this going to work, exactly?"

"We leave tomorrow. Forged access cards that'll get us onto a RavenTech shuttle that we take from Sunrise Station to the Moon." He fixed Michael with a stern look. "Before you get any ideas, you don't get the access cards until we're on Sunrise. And you get them from me."

Michael met his gaze a moment, then simply shrugged. "Sounds fair." The kid's hand fell to rest on his glass.

"It's non-negotiable."

"I said it sounded fair."

Diomedes gave him a grunt. "When we get to the Moon, we get a rover to the site. Also RavenTech."

Marc spoke next. "And that's—I mean, well, are we landing at

ESA's Alpha Station, then?" He was stuttering. Definitely he'd be easily intimidated.

But he wasn't drinking. Neither were drinking!

"No," he answered. "WSC base."

"Western Space Consortium?" Marc asked. Was that relief in his voice?

"So?"

Marc only shrugged.

"Listen here," Diomedes said. "I'm not an idiot. You're using me for something. Now I'm using you, too. You want to fuck ESA, fine. We do that. But you try to pull something else, try to do anything that screws with what I'm doing, and you're *done*. Understand?" He stared at Marc. The small man swallowed.

"How do we get back?" Michael asked. He lifted his glass to swirl the beer around inside it.

Drink!

"Same way."

"And then what?"

"And then nothing. We're finished. That's the deal, take it or leave it."

Michael looked at the other and then lifted his glass to his lips. For a moment that Diomedes didn't quite understand, he nearly stopped him. But the impulse passed, and Michael took a drink of his beer.

Finally!

"Can we have a moment to think about this?"

It was just a single swallow, but it was enough. Satisfied, Diomedes stepped back to give them space. Now the other just had to drink.

The two scooted their chairs back and began to talk in whispers. Diomedes could always just dump the beer down the other one's throat. There'd be a struggle, but once he did it, it would be too late.

Yet that would also mean they would know he'd done something. They might betray him for it before Marc could get his name cleared. No, he needed to be more subtle. He needed to wait. Hell.

They were still whispering. Michael already drank, his fate was sealed. It should have been satisfying. It was always satisfying when he'd beaten an enemy. But the other still had to drink, didn't he? Diomedes grunted to himself. That must be what bothered him.

When the other drank, then he would feel better.

You can still fix things. You can deactivate it.

But you won't. If you do, they can turn on you—try to get a cut of what you set up with Fagles. You can't let them do that to you!

He needed the insurance the nanopoison gave him: tiny microscopic robots floating around in their blood, timed and waiting for the moment when they'd stop the drinker's heart. It would activate soon after they were scheduled to get back from the Moon. The op would be complete, and Marc would have no reason not to clear his name. He would do that. But they'd be fools not to demand a cut of what he and Fagles would get from what they found. No matter what they claimed, either they'd demand it in exchange for silence or they'd steal it themselves. The poison would ensure they'd be dead before they could try it.

Yes, he could deactivate it, but why would he? The option only made it easier to give it to them. A way out if he made a mistake. He hated that it was a comfort to him. It wasn't a mistake! He shouldn't need reassurance.

Don't you have any balls?

"Alright," the kid said. The two turned back around. "I guess it sounds good, then. Where do we meet to leave?"

"Not so damn fast." Now came the part they wouldn't like. "One more condition."

If a dog gave him the look the kid did then, Diomedes would have kicked it. "Well, maybe you should have mentioned that *earlier*?"

"You don't like it you can get the hell out. You came to me."

"Look, I just meant—Never mind. What is it?"

Diomedes pointed at Marc. "Only he goes to the Moon. You don't go past Sunrise. You wait there until we get back." It was what Fagles had suggested. Separate them, make Marc feel vulnerable. All the easier to keep him in line. And accidents did happen, if needed.

The kid shook his head. "No. No way. I go with him the whole way. I'm his protection."

"You don't like it, there's no deal. I'll be his protection."

"Only after you protect yourself, you mean."

Ingrate.

"Protected *you* well enough. 'Till you left." Diomedes glanced at

Marc. He was keeping silent, hand nowhere near his glass.

"You remember the fire?" Michael shot. "You nearly knocked me into it to save your stuff."

He could be right.

"Whatever. There's only room for two. You won't fit."

The kid crossed his arms, sat back. "You could have told us this before."

"Quit whining."

"You know," Marc began, "if I don't come back, the deal's off."

Diomedes sneered. "You think I'm going to kill you up there?" Maybe he'd already guessed. Maybe he knew what was in the drink? Diomedes smacked the thought back down. No way he could know.

"No one thinks that," Michael tried. **Liar.** "But this way you'll have more incentive to keep him safe."

"Whatever. Deal or not?"

The two conferred again privately.

There, Michael still trusts you. All isn't lost!

Then he's a fool, isn't he? But he doesn't trust you. He wanted to protect Marc. How much can you trust him if he wants to do that?

There'll be other things to protect him from than just you. And isn't Michael right? When's the last time you worried about anyone but yourself?

Michael. He'd protected him.

Maybe you should be doing that again.

Maybe. But he still had to ensure their cooperation.

"Deal, but I'm still going to Sunrise," Michael said. "Unless there's anything *else* you need to mention?"

"Don't be a dick." Diomedes moved to a small refrigerator against the wall, opened it, and pulled out a beer of his own. "That's everything. Like I said, day after tomorrow." He paused, trying to think of what to say. It'd been so long since he tried to propose a toast. He lifted the can. "First, we drink. To our agreement." It sounded dumb coming out of his mouth.

The kid must've thought so, too. His face screwed up with some stupid perplexed look before he glanced at the other. Marc was reaching for his glass. Diomedes took a drink to push him further and forced himself not to watch too closely.

Gunfire exploded in the street outside. A bullet ripped through the room's tiny window and punched into the ceiling. The three men dove for cover as glass crashed to the floor.

"Shit! Shit!"

"Shut up!" Diomedes hissed at Marc as he scrambled to a spot beneath the window.

Someone found you! Michael gave you up!

While he's still in the room?

Another few shots burst out below. Diomedes peeked over the edge of the window and saw the scene on the street.

"What is it?" Michael whispered. "What's out there?"

Diomedes waved a hand to shut him up, watching the end of the confrontation below. There was another shot, and it was over. "Some guy got mugged. Fought back. Dropped a couple gangers."

See? You're not betrayed.

"It's over." Diomedes stood beside the window and turned to face them. "Fuck!"

Marc jumped at the shout.

"What?" Michael asked.

Diomedes looked at the shards of the glass surrounded by a pool of damn expensive beer on the floor. He burned a stare into Marc. "You dropped your drink, jackass."

XXXIII

A DAY LATER, Marc took a step forward beside Michael as the security checkpoint line crept along. Travelers bustled around them in other lines, and the place was busy with idle conversations, noisy ad boards, and the ring of cell phones.

Back into space. A little over a week ago, Marc would have looked forward to another zero-g flight. Now the prospect of euphoric weightlessness only provided him with a silver lining. He knew he had to go, yet he couldn't help thinking that things were always so much simpler when what he had to do only involved a computer interface.

At least Diomedes wouldn't join them until they got to Sunrise Station. Maybe he wouldn't even meet them there until just before they left the place. He made another of many glances about the concourse. Was the freelancer somewhere in a line of his own? He turned to Michael and kept his voice low. "How do you think Diomedes is getting up there?"

Michael gave the place a quick glance of his own. "Maybe we shouldn't call him that while we're out here," he whispered. "Just to be safe. Call him Malcolm."

"Right, sorry. Malcolm?"

"His real name." He held up a hand. "But don't call him that to his face."

"Why not?"

The line slid forward another inch.

"He doesn't like it."

"That much I deduced on my own. Why doesn't he like it?"

"You know, I'm not really sure? Harder to trace him if no one knows his real name, I guess."

"That flags true, I suppose."

"And maybe Fagles has some way to get him up there privately. That way he can bring weapons while we're stuck going this way around. He'll do whatever he can to hold an advantage. I wouldn't be surprised if you get to that shuttle and it seats more than two."

"Glad we'll have more than he thinks," Marc said with a glance at the carry-on bag Michael was hefting. He knew for a fact Michael had hidden at least three guns inside, one of which was AoA-sent and designed for zero-g. A handgun was hidden in the bottom of Marc's own bag as well. He gave another look forward at the checkpoint machines that could sense them all in an instant. "You ever done this before?"

Michael's response came with a weak smile. "Once, in training."

"Once more than me."

"What about the last time you went up?"

"Nope. I mean, I went through the checkpoint, but . . . " He left the sentence unfinished, sure Michael could guess at his implication that he wasn't carrying anything illegal then. "You go in first, I'll watch you."

Marc rubbed distractedly at his palm, glad at least that he wouldn't have to take his visor off. He almost always felt nervous and disconnected without it, though he rarely admitted it to anyone. His world felt just a little more under control with the infoblips and status displays fed from the hip rig in his peripheral vision. Most people just wouldn't understand.

"I wouldn't worry. The timing's pretty simple."

"Who's worried?" *This is brilliant. ESA's out to kill me and I'm trying to smuggle weapons into orbit. Bravo, Marc.* At least they were bound for the WSC base and would bypass Alpha Station completely. The Space Agency only had a partial presence at Sunrise, and was uninvolved with the WSC entirely.

Besides, even if he were caught going through the checkpoint, the fake ID the AoA had provided would at least mean they'd catch Marc Sebring, not Marc Triton. He'd be arrested, but at least he'd be alive.

Not that he'd do Marette any good then, to say nothing of the Exodus Project. He frowned in renewed determination. He wouldn't screw this part up. Michael was right, it'd be pretty simple.

He envied Michael his practice.

The time on his visor read 7:03 p.m. Three wireless networks in the area. Room temperature was 68.5 degrees.

The rest of their journey up the line passed in silence, and before Marc knew it Michael was about to be scanned. Michael set the bag with the hidden weapons on the scan table, stepped onto the body scanner, and leaned his hand against the platform's single wall that stood beside it, on which the sensor arm was mounted.

The bag scan cover came down like a lid on a fancy dinner platter. Marc knew it was much stronger than it looked, despite being filled with sensors. Bombs had exploded in such things and only cracked them. At the same time, the U-shaped sensor slid down around Michael's body along the wall he leaned against, scanning him from head to toe and back again for any weapons or illegal cyberware.

When the light on both scanners flashed green, the guard waved him out of the machine, handed him his bag, and waited for Marc to take his turn.

Marc took a breath and moved forward. He set his own bag squarely on the scanner before stepping across to the body sensor. As Michael had done, he waited until the bag scan cover started its descent and then leaned his hand against the body scanner wall.

Though doing his best to appear relaxed, he felt he was failing miserably. On the plus side, the AoA chip in his hand didn't care how he looked. He felt the slight vibration that assured him that its override on the machine was successful and started to breathe easier. The body scanner made its run over him and flashed green at the end of the cycle. The security guard waved him out, but his bag was still being scanned. Marc froze where he was, keeping his hand pressed to the wall.

The guard, a tall man who looked as humorless as a traffic cop, motioned him away from the scanner. "Sir, you can step out of there now. Please."

Marc shot a glance at Michael. "But my bag's not finished," he said. Was there a problem? What happened to the override if he took his hand away before the scan was done? Or was it not working at all? *Shit.*

"Some bags take longer," the guard explained. He moved just a little closer and added more firmly, "Step away from the scanner."

Marc tried to think of an excuse to stay put. His mind was blanking. If the scanner had found something, he was already screwed. If not, then if he kept resisting, they might detain him anyway. "My bag . . . ," he tried, feigning confusion and stalling for as much time as he could squeeze out. He didn't dare move his hand, no matter how stupid he looked.

Go green, damn it!

"Is something wrong, sir?" The suspicion in the guard's tone was clear.

The light was still dark. Marc held his breath, lifted his hand away, and stepped off the body scanner. "Sorry," he tried. "Space travel makes me a little nervous." He edged toward Michael and waited for them to find the gun with absolutely no clue what to do if they did.

And then the light flashed green and the scan cover lifted. Another guard handed his bag back to him. "Space terminal's that way. Keep the line moving."

Hiding his relief, Marc took the bag and fell in step beside Michael as they continued on to their flight. He tossed Michael an annoyed look—more for the scanner than anything—and grumbled, "Well, that was fun."

Michael just chuckled.

That the AoA was able to work a chip-triggered override into the design of most security scanners *was* an impressive feat, he supposed. That it go completely smoothly might be asking too much.

Then again, if the rest of their venture went as smoothly, Marc would consider himself lucky. He still had to get the data leech from Diomedes at some point so he could make the adjustments that the AoA's plan required. He wasn't expecting that to be too difficult; he'd need to alter the leech anyway for it to bypass the Omicron security the way Diomedes wanted. Provided the man didn't get too paranoid, it wouldn't be a problem. What worried him more was what they might find at Omicron.

He wondered for the hundredth time how Marette was doing. Would they find anyone alive there? Would Omicron even be there anymore? Those were extreme possibilities, but ones that both he and the rest of the AoA acknowledged. Yet they had to find out what was happening there now.

The unknown got him thinking yet again about Michael's comment back at his apartment. Would he have gone for the car, abandoning Michael to save himself, if he'd thought it possible?

Probably. Because he'd been afraid. Geez. He had never thought of himself as a coward, but then when had he been in this kind of danger before? He could tackle a multi-tiered auto-cycling counter-intrusion grid without blinking, but bullets were quite out of his experience.

There were more challenges looming on the horizon than he cared for: What would he be walking into at Omicron? What would Diomedes do to him if he sensed any deception? And if Marette was still there—and he refused to think otherwise—the odds were that there'd be more chances for his courage to be tested. Like it or not, he'd find out the truth of what he would do then.

7:14 p.m. Three wireless networks. 68.5 degrees.

At long last, they reached the terminal. Marc swiped his fake ID through the reader and was rewarded with a friendly female voice. "Marc Sebring. Open-ended round trip orbital flight to Sunrise International Space Station. Please proceed through the gate to the boarding area, and have a pleasant flight." Marc paused as Michael swiped his own ID, and the two continued through the gate.

Whatever else had happened, he hoped Marette was alright.

*   *   *

Stars dotted the blackness outside Sunrise Station. Diomedes stared out an exterior window. That window and a bulkhead wall that sectioned off the larger observation area formed the corner of the wide room in which he sat. With his back to the room to keep a low profile, he scanned the reflections of those who passed behind him. Others sat scattered about the observation area. Some watched screens, some talked, some watched the stars—or pretended to. He watched them all for anything suspicious and kept an eye out for the kid and Marc.

Things had gone well so far. On the whole. For the most part. He'd made it onto Sunrise Station with no trouble. A RavenTech-chartered cargo flight got him there; he'd played escort to the shipment to disguise his true purpose. Once the shipment was unloaded, it was as easy as Fagles had claimed to bypass the security checks required for access to the rest of the station. He envied the loopholes that corporations could always find. Laws were only for those who couldn't find ways around them. No one had scanned him for weapons. They didn't even search his bag or ask for ID. His was forged anyway. It would've passed a check—or so Fagles claimed—and the fake beard and wig he wore would keep him from being recognized by anyone who'd be trouble. For the moment, all he needed to do was be patient. Be watchful. Yes, things were going well.

Most things, anyway. Marc had spilled his dose, leaving Diomedes no sure way to control him. That Marc was noticeably intimidated by him kept the spill from being a complete cock-up. Once they left Michael behind and were bound for the Moon, Diomedes would start to work on him. Threats would be enough. They'd have to be.

Oh, they will be. He betrays you and you'll find him, hunt him down, make him pay. Painfully. Make sure he knows that, knows what you're capable of, knows that if he keeps to the agreement, he'll be fine.

Diomedes nodded to the voice. He'd have to be careful to stick with threats alone. Hurt Marc before he did anything and he'd have no reason to do what Diomedes needed.

Damn it! It would be simpler if he'd drunk the damn nanopoison! The stuff was expensive; though he hadn't actually *paid* for it, it was still valuable. Near undetectable, and it would stay that way until a preset time. It was exactly the kind of thing he'd been saving the stuff for, too.

If he betrays you, you'll track him down! No matter what happens to you, make sure he knows that! When Michael's dose did its work after they got back, Marc would take it as evidence that Diomedes could get to him, too.

And suddenly his hand slipped into his pocket to the pen-sized rod that would broadcast the deactivation signal for Michael's dose. He should destroy the rod now, he told himself. Throw it away so he wouldn't be undone by his own sentimentality. It would only get him screwed in the end.

You don't know that. Michael's gotten stronger. You could make him an ally again.

He's a kid! A kid that turned on you! It's his friends that are

strong, not him! And they won't help you.

Maybe if you befriended him again, he'd persuade them to help you.

He wouldn't. He's only helping now to serve his own interests. You heard what he said in the car: just what Janette said. He hates you now.

Janette. What would she think of you killing a friend?

He's not a friend!

He's all you've got left.

They were here.

Michael and the other came through the bulkhead door right behind his seat. With effort, he pushed the voices away. He noted with satisfaction that the two men failed to see him. Arm stuck out, he snapped his fingers once. The kid was alert enough to notice that. He caught Marc's arm and pointed to Diomedes with a subtle angle of his jaw. No one else around seemed to notice. So far, so good. They'd better have the sense to stay that discreet.

The kid edged over, peering at him unsurely. The disguise was that good, at least. Diomedes turned slightly to look him in the eye. "Sit," he ordered.

The two sat on either side of him in seats that faced each other, closer to the window. Michael chose the one with the better view of the room. "Nice beard."

Diomedes ignored the comment. "Anyone following you?"

"I don't think so. Everything's still a go, I guess?"

Diomedes nodded. "Five or six hours' wait before we leave here."

Marc blinked. "Five or six *hours*?"

"That's what I said. Keep your voice down."

Michael was keeping a careful watch on the section. "There's somewhere more private we can wait, isn't there?"

"No."

"Can't we at least wait at the shuttle?"

Diomedes glared. "*No.* And shut up about the shuttle until we're on it. Don't talk about that stuff out here."

It would be better if they could wait on the shuttle. Fagles had warned him just before he left Earth that he'd set the whole thing up with forged authorization: a RavenTech black op that even RavenTech wasn't supposed to know about. Arriving at the shuttle too soon would cause "problems." Diomedes didn't know what those problems were, but he didn't want to risk it. He took Fagles at his word for the simple fact that the man wouldn't try to screw him until after Diomedes did what he needed.

"So we just sit here, then?"

Diomedes glared at Marc. "You don't like it, wait somewhere else."

"You didn't know about the wait before we left, huh?" Michael asked.

"No. Anything else you want to bitch about? Suck it up, kid. No one's looking for *you*."

Diomedes kept watch on the window reflections as a lone security guard passed through. Probably standard patrol. Some sort of thermal mini-rifle Diomedes would love to get his hands on. Superheated energy, no bullets. The guard traversed the area without stopping.

"You know, maybe we *will* wait somewhere else," Michael announced. "Safer if we're split up, anyway." He stood, and Marc followed suit. "We'll be across the room, in the other corner."

"Fine," he growled. The kid would abandon him as much as he could. Not surprising. He watched the reflections of the two men make their way across the room. Five more hours of waiting. Twisting in the wind.

Damn Fagles.

Five minutes passed, then ten. Each felt like twice that. He counted the faces in the window. Reflections in the empty space between the stars. No one seemed threatening. None he recognized. Michael and Marc got up and went into the restroom along the inner wall.

That was when he saw the other man across the chamber. His face was disguised, but still familiar. A piercing pain hit his neck before he could react. His muscles locked up, and Diomedes was out.

XXXIV

IT WAS STUPID, but following Marc into the restroom had Michael feeling something less than masculine. It was a mandatory precaution on this leg of the trip; to protect him, he couldn't leave the man alone, especially because Michael was the only one even armed at this point.

As a precaution against putting all their eggs in one basket, the sidearm Marc brought was currently stashed in a locker on the flight deck for them to grab as they left. Any sort of confrontation on Sunrise that used firepower over muscle was likely to end in disaster anyway.

So he shook off the feeling of foolishness, glanced at Marc as they left the restroom, and paused a moment beside the potted fern outside. "So, nearly five hours."

"You hungry?" the other asked.

Michael surveyed the room again, just to stay on top of things. "I guess I could go for something. I wish this place had more private spots to wait that weren't just—" He stopped, noticing Diomedes.

"—one step up from a coffin?" Marc finished for him. "Something up?"

"Maybe," Michael answered after a beat. Diomedes's head had fallen back enough for Michael to tell that his eyes were closed. He appeared to be sleeping, but the idea that he would let his guard down felt wrong. "Stay alert."

Careful to make sure Marc kept up, Michael moved casually in the unconscious freelancer's general direction, watching the room as he went. A man crossed in front of them a short distance ahead and took a seat in the chair that Michael himself had occupied minutes earlier. The man's face struck a vaguely familiar chord. Michael slowed his pace and struggled to place him.

"There's like a dart—something in his neck," Marc whispered. "Di—Malcolm's neck."

The familiar man locked eyes with Michael before he could see the dart Marc had mentioned. The man stood back up. Recognition stopped Michael in his tracks.

"Damn it."

Behind a long wig and glasses, Jer, one of the freelancers they'd clashed with back in Northgate, watched him coolly.

Reassuring himself that Jer wasn't likely to try anything violent in such a public place, Michael took a moment to search, in vain, for Jer's sister.

"Don't panic," Michael whispered to Marc. "He tries anything here and security'll be all over him." Even so, he didn't see any guards currently.

"We still need him to get us on that shuttle."

"I know."

"Have a plan?"

"Working on it. Stay between me and the window. And keep me between you and him." He closed the rest of the distance to speak with Jer, careful to keep Marc as shielded as possible, just in case.

Jer spoke first. "Fancy meeting you here."

"Where's your sister?" Michael asked.

The man shrugged with a chuckle. "Oh, she's around here somewhere. She likes to pop in unexpectedly. But hey, you know what that's like, don't you?"

Michael suppressed a frown. Maybe it was a bluff, maybe not. He gave Diomedes a punctuated glance. "He's ours. We found him first."

Jer laughed. "Oh, come on. Fool me once, shame on you. Split my skull, leave me for dead and try to fool me twice—well, shame on you again, really. I never much liked taking blame."

"I guess you hadn't considered that we needed to get something out of him before we claimed the bounty, huh?"

"Doesn't much matter now, I figure. He's ours. Which makes you, ah, shit out of luck?"

Stall. It was all he had until he could think of something better. "Out of luck or not, we're still standing here, and we're not going anywhere. And he's not going anywhere without us." To his left, Marc looked around while Michael's mind raced.

"We're not going anywhere without him, either. I'm willing to take the full price of his bounty instead, if you've got it on you. As it is I don't think you've got a single way to stop me that won't make security cranky. And you don't want to see these guys cranky, let me tell you."

Michael seized on an idea. "You want security here? Why don't we just call them right now. They'll figure out who he is and my friend and I'll tell them he's our capture. I guess they might believe you that he's one-third yours, too, but it'll be our story against yours.

"Might get sticky," Marc added. He'd stopped looking around and had gone quite rigid.

Jer gave a quick laugh. "Oh, now that's a bluff if I ever heard one."

"Think so?"

"You don't want the bounty. You're with him. Now I don't know who you are and as far as I know, no one's paying for either of you, so I'm willing to let you go. But you have to leave right now."

"So either we let you have him, or we try to claim the bounty instead of you. Given the choice I guess I'll take losing him and getting the money. Even if we do have to split it between the three of us."

"Oh, I see," Jer answered with mock appraisal. "So then you've got a bounty hunter's license like mine to show the security guys, too? Or are you just expecting your story to hold water on its own?"

Marc was keeping quiet but Michael didn't miss a beat. "Yours international?" Jer said nothing but Michael caught a trace of hesitation in his face. "Oh, it's not, is it? Anything less than that and it's a hassle for you, too."

"Better than none at all. And now it's *our* word against yours."

Michael had just enough time to catch the reflection of Jer's sister in the window and see that she didn't have a weapon drawn before her whisper sounded in his ear. "I ought'a put my boot so far up your ass I'll have to open your mouth to paint my toenails."

Fantastic. "I guess there's no point in saying it wasn't me who jumped either of you."

Jer chuckled. "I don't think she cares."

"I don't think so, either." Michael sighed. "We're still nowhere close to resolving this, you know. Not here. And he's gonna wake up eventually." Unless maybe she had a way to knock Marc and him out, too.

Whatever Jer was about to say got interrupted by the blare of an alarm that sounded throughout the room. "*Warning: explosive decompression danger. Evacuate this section immediately."* Alarm lights flashed across the walls as the warning repeated in multiple languages and the emergency bulkhead doors began to slowly close.

Shit.

"What the hell?" Jer shouted.

"Vacuum breach!" Marc shouted. "God, if there's a vacuum breach we're all dead!"

Michael looked about in vain for some sign of the breach. Diomedes lay motionless in his seat. He couldn't carry him alone, and Marc was panicking!

"Discussion's over! Pick him up!" Jer ordered.

The sister moved to do so but Marc cut her off, throwing himself across Diomedes's body. "He's gonna die, we're all gonna die! No!" Jer tried to pull him off, but Marc was hysterical, thrashing about in panic.

Fighting against his own shock at the display, Michael realized— or hoped—that Marc was trying to keep the bounty hunters from taking the body before they fled to safety. Behind them, people were running toward the closing bulkheads.

"You have forty seconds to evacuate."

"Don't touch him!" Michael shouted. "Let him go!" He pulled at Jer's arm in an effort to help Marc, wondering even then if there would be time to get Diomedes to safety once the other two fled. The section might burst and hurl them all out into space at any second.

Marc screamed in wordless hysteria. The bulkhead door nearest to them sounded a new alert of its own and suddenly plunged toward the floor, sealing off that exit in moments. Across the concourse, the last exit was still open but closing steadily, if slower.

"Goddammit get out of the way you little prick!" Jer's sister grabbed for Marc again. Michael couldn't stop her. Marc kicked out in crazed panic.

"Susan, there's no time!" Jer ceased his struggle with Michael and grabbed for his sister.

"We can carry him!" Susan shouted back. "I'm not going to—Jesus, get *off!*"

Marc was nearly wailing now and clinging to Diomedes like a crazed toddler. He thrashed against any attempt to remove him or lift the man up.

"The door's closing!" Michael yelled. "Marc, get up!" They were the only ones left in the section. If they didn't leave *now* . . .

Jer grabbed his sister and jerked her back. "He's not worth it! We're going!" The bounty hunter didn't wait for her to answer and dashed past Michael for the far bulkhead. Susan turned to follow.

Hoping Marc was more lucid than he seemed, Michael went to get him up. Would there even be any time left to—

In a flash Susan whirled, a knife appearing in her hand like magic as she stabbed at Marc with a cry of rage. Michael lunged to wrench her arm out of its path and fling her to the ground. She landed on her back with a curse and the knife spilled from her grip, yet before Michael could do more she drove her boot into his groin with a scream.

Agony staggered him. Moments later Susan was back on her feet and racing after Jer. With a parting yell of "All yours, assholes!" she dove and slid through the gap just before the bulkhead sealed shut.

They were trapped.

"She's really not very nice," Marc said. "You okay?" The alarms continued and the doors remained closed, but the man was dramatically calmer.

"I'll live. I think." Michael winced at the far-too-slowly receding pain and gestured around the place. "You did this?" Either Marc didn't think they were going to explode into space or he'd become remarkably accepting of the idea.

Marc nodded with a grin and tapped his visor. "One of the reasons I like this thing. Computer access without anyone noticing." He motioned to Diomedes's unconscious body. "We'd better move fast, though."

With some effort, the two lifted the man's weight between them. "Omph. I'll remember that next time you zone out in conversation. I'm amazed you could hack in and cause all this so easily."

Marc laughed off the compliment. "Getting doors *open* is hard. Getting alarms to go off that make doors close? That's substantially less difficult. How about we leave the way those two didn't go?"

They brought Diomedes to the door nearest them—the one that Marc had caused to close first, Michael realized—and set him down while Marc went to work on the door panel. "How long?"

"Like I said—" Marc plugged his hip rig directly into a port beneath the panel "—getting them to close is substantially less difficult."

Michael wondered how long they had before the bulkheads opened automatically on both sides and Jer and his sister found they weren't sucked out into space. Before he could ask, the door in front of them—and only the door in front of them—lifted open.

Marc unplugged with a chuckle. "On the other hand, I'm also very smart."

Before it even finished opening, they'd carried Diomedes through.

X X X V

A SHORT WHILE LATER, Marc's face was almost an apparition in the dim light that filled the compartment. "It may be dark," he said, "but at least it's cramped, too."

Michael chuckled quietly from where he sat with his back to the wall. Between them lay the still-unconscious body of Diomedes. "Better than being outside while Jer and his sister wander the station. Wish I knew how long he'll be under, though."

"Right up until it's time for us to leave, let's hope."

"He'll be pissed when he wakes up."

"Oh, I never would've guessed."

"Yeah." Michael sighed inwardly, unable to say he'd mind if Diomedes stayed out for a while, either. "Could be worse, though. We're lucky you found this place."

"Lucky, nothing. I've had my eye out for one since we got here. I almost suggested it right after we met Diomedes, but I didn't want to test my claustrophobia."

Uh oh. "You're claustrophobic?"

"Just a little. I'll be fine unless I can't move my arms."

"So far, so good, then."

They'd made for the tiny compartment almost immediately after getting through the emergency door, using a nearby luggage cart to carry Diomedes, allegedly to an infirmary. Things outside had been chaotic. Their accusations that Jer and his sister caused the alarm further added to the confusion and let them get away cleanly. Marc had led them straight to the AoA-placed compartment, opened it with his palm chip, and rushed them inside.

"Too bad the shuttle won't have something like this."

Michael nodded. "He didn't say where the shuttle even is, did he?"

"Nope. You're thinking about sneaking on board, I hope?"

It was a bad idea, but was it any worse than abandoning Marc to Diomedes's care for the rest of the trip? "I don't know. If he catches me trying? And we don't even know if the shuttle's big enough. He might be telling the truth about that."

"He's made sure we need him, hasn't he?"

"Don't think it's not intentional, either. I bet he knew about the wait before he told us, too." Marc gave a grunt, and silence followed. Michael checked his watch. Four and a half hours left. He tried to shift to keep from getting stiff.

"You know," Marc whispered after a time, "once we actually get to the shuttle, how much do we really need him after that?"

Michael checked to make sure Diomedes was still out before answering. "I guess it depends on what we need to launch it. Some sort of code or pass, maybe."

"We should check him. See what he's got."

"Search him?"

"Yeah." Marc nodded encouragingly and motioned toward the man.

Michael scowled at the prospect, but then moved forward onto his knees and, carefully, checked Diomedes's pockets. It didn't take long to find something. After pulling out a device twice the size of a deck of cards that Marc was positive was the data leech, they found them: zippered inside a breast pocket along with an odd-looking, pen-sized object were two access cards. He took them out and showed them to Marc. "What's this?" he whispered, pointing to what looked like a tiny touch-screen built onto the back of one of the cards. "The other doesn't have it."

Marc took it from him. "Master link. Connects the two cards so one can't be used without the other. This thing verifies the ID of whoever's using it."

"So we couldn't use it without him."

Marc looked a little closer at the card. "Maybe. He's right here. I'm not sure yet what this checks—thumbprint, DNA, or whatever; probably thumbprint—but if I figure that out, I might be able to reset it for you to use."

"All before he wakes up?" Michael asked. "That's a lot of mights."

"Maybe. But it's not impossible. And if it works, then we don't need him anymore."

The compartment went silent as Marc's statement hung in the air over Diomedes's body. "Then what do we do with him?" Michael asked. "And what if he has to report to Fagles and he finds out what we did?"

"Yeah, but you really think that Fagles would sabotage us? We'll still use his leech. I doubt he has anything to gain by stopping us if he thinks we're doing what he wants anyway. Besides, you heard him; he doesn't like Diomedes any more than we do."

"Yeah. But, again, what happens to Diomedes? We can't just shoot him, you know."

"I didn't say we should! But we just, well, leave him here."

"Here. In this compartment."

Marc shrugged. "I more meant on the station in general."

"Which will put him in a fantastic mood when we come through here on the return trip." Michael shifted again, still trying to get comfortable.

"One problem at a time." Marc sighed. "There are those two freelancers out there. Or even just station security. We tell them who he is, and they'll pick him up. Then he won't be here when we come back."

Michael scowled. "I don't guess now is quite the best time for you to have contact with any security personnel."

"Security here's not ESA. The fake ID should be enough to shield me if it comes up."

"It's still a risk."

"Okay, but—"

"And I'm not going to turn him over to the bounty hunters just because it's convenient."

Marc took a breath. "But if we don't need him—It's not like he's a nice guy. He kills people for money."

"Look, maybe . . . " Michael scowled at himself in the dark. He knew Marc was right, so why was he defending Diomedes? "I'm not saying he doesn't deserve what he gets if he screws up and Fagles cuts him loose, but I—we—can't just give him up like this."

Marc watched him a moment. "You don't owe him anything, you know."

"Yeah, I do. I hate it, but I do." He threw up his hands. "Or maybe I don't, I don't know. I doubt he'd hesitate to turn me in if he was in my shoes. He might even laugh at me for having to think about it, but . . . "

Suddenly he couldn't think of what else to say. A part of him wanted to just do it: cut the man loose completely to hang on his own rope. "But we can't do that," he said finally. "Not—not yet, I mean. We don't know who hired him, we don't know about the rest of the trip . . . Heck, we might need him just to fly the damn shuttle. I'm not a pilot."

"Is he?" Marc asked.

"More than me, at least. I mean, maybe I can handle a little, but if it doesn't have a pre-programmed autopilot we'd be in trouble. The point is we don't know enough yet. We can work on getting me on the shuttle with you two, but we can't abandon him right now."

Marc was quiet for a time, presumably considering. "Maybe you're right. Wish you weren't, but I'll deal with it." He examined the pass cards again for a moment. "But we're going to have to cut him loose eventually, you know. One way or another. With everything he's done—and what we're planning—it's not likely to turn out well for him."

Michael nodded but gave no further comment. Why was this bothering him so much? He'd known that they were only helping Diomedes temporarily. Certainly the freelancer held no love for him of late. Maybe that was the difference between them, he thought. Diomedes wouldn't be bothered if their places were switched.

Or would he? The fact remained that Diomedes sheltered him when Michael first came to Northgate. There had likely been selfishness behind that kindness, though for all Michael searched, he had to admit he couldn't find it. Even so, the older man had treated him poorly at times, even maliciously. How much had Diomedes really been looking out for him? How much of the man's true self had Michael been unwilling to see because he'd needed Diomedes protection then?

He needed Diomedes again now. Was the same thing happening again, making him rush to the man's aid, making him defend against abandoning him now? Michael's skin crawled at the idea that he might be as foolish now as he was then. Did he still need to use Diomedes as a crutch?

Yet that wasn't what was happening now, he reminded himself. There was more at stake than just Michael's own needs. The AoA was counting on him.

Again, he looked at Diomedes. Yes, there would soon come a time when, once they'd gotten what they needed from him, he'd be brought to whatever justice he had coming. But Michael owed a little more to the man who'd put a roof over his head than a slit throat—however figurative—while he slept.

Even if that same roof had burned down due to Diomedes's own recklessness.

Apparently finished examining the pass cards, Marc put them back where he'd found them. "Wish I knew what this was," he mused, holding up the pen-sized object. "Any ideas?"

"Nuh uh," Michael grunted. "He likes gadgets."

Marc slipped it back into Diomedes's pocket with a scowl. After a moment, Marc edged forward and, delicately, scanned both of the unconscious man's thumbprints with his smartphone. "Just in case," Marc whispered. Michael only watched and willed Diomedes to remain unconscious.

Diomedes did not stir.

* * *

"Gid? Wake up, Gid."

"I *am* awake."

Ondrea smiled at him as he opened his eyes. "Well, you weren't a second ago. The scans are done. We're on Sunrise Station, do you remember? Waiting till it's time for you to go to the Moon."

Gideon got up from where he lay on the bed and unplugged himself from the diagnostic equipment crammed into the station hotel room that was to be Marquand's base of operations for the rest of the project. "I know where we are, Ondrea," he said, giving Beck a long, hard look where he sat at a desk with his back to him.

"Okay," she said. "I'm just making sure. We won't have to scan you like that too much more." She shut down the diagnostics, having planned them for when D.K. was out getting them food. D.K. had done most of the design on Gideon's new body, but she didn't want him looking over her shoulder. So far, she and Beck had kept her brother's deterioration a secret. Just a little further and they'd be in the clear to dump all the memories that weren't Gideon's own.

"How soon?" Gideon asked.

Shit, did he know? "How soon what, Gid?"

"When do I leave?"

Oh. "Not until eighteen-thirty. D.K. needs to do some final checks on your body, then you'll be put in a cargo container that—"

"Please, Ondrea, I know the plan, I just didn't catch when it started. I want to get this over with."

"Not long, Gid."

Gideon moved to the window. "I've never been in space before. Somehow it's not as foreign as I expected." He stood awhile in front of the view. "I think I've dreamed this."

"That's probably it." She focused on the scan data with Beck, checking the deterioration rate.

It had accelerated. Beck was scowling; he saw it, too. Tseng pushing Gideon's treatments in the memory chair must've magnified the problem. "Recheck it," she whispered.

They needed to figure out how much time Gid had before his mind crashed. They were cutting things close before; now the operation would need to go perfectly in order to get him back in time—if they even had that much time at all.

"I should go now."

"You can't yet, Gid. I know you want this over with but the flight's not leaving for another few hours." *Time, time . . . Please God, give me enough time.*

"What do you mean, flight? Isaac's only across town. Just out to the club. He should be back by now. I should go look for him."

She stopped. He was remembering the night he'd found their brother's body. There wasn't going to be enough time. "Gid, that's . . . Isaac's—You can't worry about him now. We're on Sunrise Station, remember?"

Gideon was halfway to the door before he stopped in his tracks and turned. "What just happened? I could swear . . . "

If the data hadn't convinced her already, this would have clinched it; he was getting lost in his own memories. "Let me check the implant. You can stay awake for this one."

"Again? You said I was well enough to do this!" He grabbed her shoulders and she flinched before she could stop herself. He let go almost instantly, taking a breath. "What's wrong?"

For a moment, she considered telling him. But there wasn't

anything he could do, and he'd gotten enough shocking news from her recently. "Nothing's wrong, Gid. Just a few final adjustments to make."

He frowned, and she knew he didn't quite believe her. That he let her plug in without saying a word then nearly broke her heart. He trusted her despite his instincts.

"It'll be okay," she said. "I promise." She checked a few details on a PDA where she kept some private notes, then accessed the implant and raised the cycle power as high as she dared.

Beck stood hesitantly. "Ondrea?"

"Just making a few adjustments, Beck."

"Ah, okay, but you're—" She shot him a glare. Beck actually responded with one of his own. Even so, he shut up quickly enough and sat back down.

She knew what she was doing. She didn't have a choice. In theory, boosting the cycle power should buy her brother some time, but it was a risk. The power had already been as high as they had time to test, and now she'd set it beyond that. She prayed it would work. There was nothing to prove that it wouldn't, but it was an untested theory. Best case, Gideon would have enough time to do what Marquand needed and get back. Worse case, the strain would be too much and both engram sets would crash even sooner.

No more second chances. No more Gideon.

XXXVI

HIS BROTHER LAUGHS across the table and sets his beer down. *"'Diomedes'? What the hell kind of alias is 'Diomedes'?"*

"It's mythology. Greek," the newly dubbed Diomedes answers. *"It's got class. Culture. All that stuff."*

Silas snorts. *"Culture, eh? It's supposed to keep people from knowing who you are. Strike fear, sound powerful. Save the culture for that girl of yours, Malc."*

"Look, you ever read those old myths? Fuckin' bad-ass warriors, man. That's who Diomedes is." He takes a long pull from his glass. *"Bad. Ass. Look it up."*

"Look it up? Don't figure I even know how to spell it. Heh."

"Hey, screw off." He says it with a grin on his face. *"It's better than 'Silas.' Not even trying to be original. I liked your old handle—"*

"Don't even say it."

"Why? Got people out for you?"

"No, I just got sick of hearin' it. Wait 'till you go years under your stupid nickname and see if it doesn't get sick of you. You of it, I mean. 'Kay, no more beer."

"It's not stupid. Who cares what you think?" I do, he thinks. Ah, screw Silas, I'll keep it anyway.

"It's good usin' my real name again, that's all I'm sayin'. No last names, s'all you need."

Diomedes dismisses the idea with a wave. *"No way. If I'm doing jobs with you, I'm not using my old name anymore."*

"Fine, fine, whatever." Silas gives him the same sneer he'd given him growing up. *"You just want to have your 'cool' name, don't you? Or're you afraid your little sweetie'll find out, huh?"*

Diomedes thumps his beer down. *"Her name's Janette."*

Silas chuckles. "She's not gonna find out."

"That's not it." He lowers his voice. "I'm worried about cops."

"Oh, so you won't mind if I just call her up and tell her, then?"

His heart freezes. "Don't you fucking even."

With a grin, Silas orders another beer. Diomedes relaxes a bit. She won't find out. Silas might tease him, but he wouldn't tell her. Just a few jobs, that'll be it. Silas needs him, after all, and Diomedes needs the money. He drains his glass, wishing Silas liked the name more. Diomedes had liked it when he'd heard it from her.

"Yeah," Silas mutters, "I'm just glad you finally came to your senses instead of messing around with those piss-ant security jobs you like so much." His brother grins again suddenly. "It's got something to do with her, doesn't it?" his asks teasingly. "Diomedes."

He pretends he doesn't hear the question, but Silas keeps at him. "Oh, that's it, huh? She tell you about the name?"

Hell, he'd better not be blushing. "She likes mythology. She read me some of it."

Silas grins wider.

"I like the name!" And yeah, so it reminds him of her, too. What's wrong with that?

"Fine, fine, you can be Diomedes." Silas reaches across the table and ceremoniously taps his glass to each of Diomedes's shoulders. "You big strong hero, you."

Diomedes smirks despite Silas's teasing, relieved for the acceptance behind it. "Yeah, bite me, Silas. It'll grow on you."

His brother returns the smirk. "Just make sure you live up to it."

Diomedes woke with a jerk that sat him up so fast Michael was astounded he didn't hit his head on the compartment's ceiling. Michael reached forward on instinct to steady him, but the other smacked his hand away.

"What the fuck? What the *fuck*?" The freelancer had an auto-pistol out in a flash but calmed before aiming it anywhere.

"It's okay," Michael said. Bad dreams, or just surprise? Marc, by all accounts, had slept through the outburst.

Diomedes took stock of the compartment. "Where are we?"

"Safe. Put the gun away."

Diomedes gave a glare, yet set the gun down at his side anyway. "Answer the question."

"We're still on Sunrise. This is a little hidden space we found."

The other's eyes narrowed. "Found?"

"Yeah, found. I told you Marc's good with security."

Diomedes gave Marc nothing more than a glance. "Tell me what happened. How long was I out?"

"A few hours now. The same two that were after you at Silas's—"

"I saw him," Diomedes finished. "The woman, too?"

"Both, yeah. He got you with a tranq. I guess it must hit you pretty fast. I came out of the bathroom and saw you passed out." Michael told him the rest, making sure to give Marc full credit for his wizardry while Michael stalled the others. "If the guards are looking for anyone, I guess they're going for those two first, but we figured there's no use risking it. Especially while you were out."

"What about him?" Diomedes pointed to Marc. "Dead, or sleeping?"

"Yeah, Diomedes, he's dead. That's how he was able to open all the doors and everything."

"Don't be a dick."

Michael rolled his eyes as Diomedes searched his pockets, likely taking inventory. He barely kept himself from assuring the man that everything was there. From the suspicion with which Diomedes was checking, it was probably better not to put the idea out there more than it was already.

"So you've just sat here," Diomedes said when he was done. "For all that time."

"Wasn't much else to do," Michael said. Diomedes only grunted at that before he leaned back against the compartment wall, checked his watch, and then closed his eyes. Michael laughed bitterly.

"This a joke to you?" Diomedes grumbled.

"You're not even going to thank us, huh? We saved your ass out there, Marc and me both, and—"

Diomedes's eyes flashed open. "Like you thanked me? Helped you a whole hell of a lot and all you do is turn on me for the trouble!"

"Geez, are we back on that again?"

"Never *left it*."

Michael fought an urge to roll his eyes again. "I thanked you, when you deserved it."

"Not how I remember it. Took you in, protected your ass. In the city. On your damn farm. You're paying back a damn big debt helping me now. You still got more to repay." Diomedes snapped his eyes shut again.

For the briefest moment Michael considered if he really had thanked Diomedes for getting him on his feet before. Then he remembered the whole picture and pushed out the guilt. "Yeah, fine, thanks, Diomedes. Thanks for giving me a place to stay. And while I'm at it, thanks for threatening me not to touch your stuff or poke into your business. Thanks for trying to kill a friend of mine. And thanks for trying to teach me to be such a selfish bastard as you."

Diomedes started forward to strike him but stopped just as fast. "You're fucking welcome. No one you can count on but yourself, kid. That's what I was trying to teach you."

"Yeah? I bet you learned that one all by yourself, huh?"

"Fuck you, I did *not*." Diomedes pointed at him. "Life taught me that! Silas taught me that." He leaned back with a curse and closed his eyes.

* * *

The large voice was cursing him. **Shut your damn mouth. You don't even mention Silas to him!** Diomedes tried to push the thoughts of his brother back into the box where he kept them.

"Silas, eh?" Michael pressed. "How?"

It's none of his damn business. You wouldn't tell him before he left, why should you tell him now?

Maybe you should have told him before. It might have helped.

Helped what? Silas is gone, there's no point! And he doesn't deserve to know. Diomedes clenched his teeth and gave Michael nothing.

"Oh, this is familiar," Michael said. "I guess I ought to be used to this, huh? You shut up whenever I asked about him before, so I just stopped asking. Always threw up your walls around stuff you didn't want to talk about. Before I respected your privacy enough to stop asking. Or maybe I was just too afraid to push you. But now I don't care. We're stuck in this place, so damn your walls. I'm not letting it go anymore." The kid leaned forward, whispering. "If you want me to feel bad about what I did or didn't do, you have to explain why! What'd Silas teach you? What happened to him? All those stories on the farm, Diomedes, and then I see you again, and nothing!"

Arrogant little prick! He thinks he can force it out of you? Don't tell him a thing. He'll be dead soon anyway.

Diomedes kept his eyes shut and shifted where he sat, feeling the shape of the access cards in his pocket. He was surprised to find them still there when he woke. They must have searched him. Michael wasn't stupid enough not to.

So they found them and left them there. They could have taken them. Left you. But they're still here.

So Michael *is* stupid. He lost his chance!

So now he's stupid for not *betraying you?*

"Why wouldn't you tell me?" Michael pushed again.

Diomedes scowled deeper. "Cause it's not your damn business."

Damn right!

"You just said you were trying to teach me what he taught you, so I guess it's my business now. Come on, prove your point. If you're calling me an ungrateful bastard, tell me why! Maybe you didn't teach me right and he did. What'd he tell you that you didn't tell me? What happened to him that didn't happen to you?"

"He died, asshole. You couldn't figure that out?"

Shut up! Was the voice talking to him or Michael? For a moment the kid said nothing. Maybe he'd drop it.

"Sorry," Michael said finally, still hesitating even then. "I guess I sort of guessed. So he died, left you alone, and you assumed—"

"Yeah, right, you know everything, don't you, kid?" **Asshole doesn't know when to quit. Doesn't know what he's asking!** "Didn't happen when he died. Happened before. And before that I went *with* him. I *helped* him when he needed it. Didn't turn my back like you did."

He's got no right! Michael walked away!

He's asking, why not tell him? Make him understand until he cooperates.

"Oh, come on, make up your mind," Michael shot back. "Are you pissed at me because I didn't learn that I can't count on anyone, or because I didn't help you when you counted on me? Pick one. Which is it?"

Diomedes glared. Michael stared right back.

No! It's private, and it's pointless. What's done is done!

What's done is done? Sounds like a regret. You have regrets?

You did the right thing. Silas needed you!

And you needed Silas. But who've you got left now?

"You don't know what you're talking about," Diomedes muttered finally and looked away.

"What happened with you two? Come on, Diomedes, we've got time here."

"Yeah? So what if we do?" He clenched his jaw. Time could be burned.

Damn right. He gets nothing. Michael wasn't strong enough, but he just keeps pushing, and pushing!

Isn't that strength? Isn't that what you do?

And then Michael crossed the line. "You know, you can look down on me all you want, but you're afraid to even talk about it, aren't you?"

Son of a bitch can't call you a coward! *Afraid?* Fine! You're better than him; show him! He wants to know so bad, fucking tell him!

"You want to hear?" Diomedes growled, begrudging the words.

"I asked, didn't I?"

"Do you *want* to hear?"

"Yes!"

Diomedes waited, teeth clenched, thinking on where to start and knowing he wouldn't tell the kid everything. "When I left your uncle's farm I came here. Found Silas. My brother had gear. Implants. Training. All I didn't. So I joined up."

"Joined up?"

"Army," Diomedes told him. "Free training. Cyberware if I was good enough."

The kid nodded. "Like I did with Aegis."

"Yeah, ain't it familiar. Shut up and listen." He waited for the kid to mouth off again. He didn't. Diomedes went on.

"Started out good enough. Training. Couple of implants after a bit. Didn't get any real gear until some dumbass misfired a mortar and blew my arm off." He moved his left arm about to show the kid the arm they'd been forced to give him. "Hurt like hell, but it was worth it. They should've did it sooner; they didn't think I was good enough for that. Didn't think I was good enough after, either."

"What do you mean?"

They took thirty months of his life, being their slave. He got their training, knew what he was doing. But they didn't think so. Court martial. Discharge. He'd had it with their rules anyway. What did he care? Assholes. "None of your damn business."

Silas! Get to Silas.

"I left the Army, came back here, found Silas again. He started off in bodyguard jobs. I tried doing the same. Security, like you tried. He'd moved on. Black market cyberware. Stealing it, moving it. Other jobs, too, nothing legal. He wanted me to help. I didn't. Not much. Not at first."

"Why not?"

Because you were too dumb to see the opportunity in front of you!

Diomedes was scowling. "Because I didn't. But I still did a couple of jobs for him, when he needed me. When there was no one else. I wanted to do things straight." He snorted, even as he thought of Janette. "As legal as I could. Maybe the Army brainwashed me into all that. All their damn rules."

Michael shrugged. "Maybe you just wanted to do the right thing?"

"Maybe there was other shit going on you don't know about, huh?" He forced Janette's face out of his mind. She was long gone.

But you felt that way even before her, didn't you? She just brought it out.

She. Is. Gone! Silas needed you. You didn't abandon him!

Was that why you did it? For Silas? Did he need you, or did you need him?

"Other shit like what?" Michael asked.

"Shut up!" he hissed to them all. For once they all did. He went on. "It wasn't working. For me. Tried doing it straight, legal stuff. Jobs with a company hiring me out. Didn't pay enough. I had debts and—" *Her. And she was rich enough for both of you.*

She left.

But you drove her away.

He'd stuck with Silas! Diomedes scowled. "So I worked with Silas more, making our own jobs. Some stuff he couldn't have done without me. Someone at his back. He needed me, said so himself. And I didn't let him down." He stared at the kid, waiting. They watched each other in the dim light for a while.

"How'd he die?" Michael finally asked.

Diomedes remembered.

Diomedes sits in the passenger's seat of the van where it's parked in the shadows beneath a billboard. A raucous beer ad stares down on them as he argues with Silas. "You don't need him for this, you've got me. We can do it ourselves."

Silas grins at him. His eyes glint in the shadows under a silhouette of what's normally his sandy blond hair. "Trying to get a bigger cut, kid?"

Diomedes frowns. "I'm no kid. I've proved that."

"Sorry. Little brother." Again, the teasing grin.

"It's not the money. I don't like this guy. We don't need him."

Silas looks away out the window and takes a long drag on his cigarette. "I need you both. I worked with Rafe before. You know that. He does what he's told."

"So you trust him more than me," Diomedes says, his arms crossed.

With a flick, the cigarette goes out the window. "Damn it, Dio, I said it's a three-man job and I meant it. One sniper, two men on the ground. Now I figure you'd not trust him enough to want him up there with the rifle, so I guess he's with me, and I guess you'll like it."

"It's not that I don't trust him, I—"

Before he can finish, Silas fixes him with a look that says the argument is over.

A motorcycle pulls up outside before Diomedes can think of what more to say. "Time to do this," Silas orders.

They both exit the van. Rafe climbs off his bike, and Diomedes gives the man a warning glare that he laughs off with a wave. "This thing still a go?"

"Nah, we just like sitting around in the dark," Silas says. He snaps his fingers and points up to the billboard with a stern look at Diomedes. "Get up there. Time's short."

"Better be a good shot, kid," Rafe calls after him.

"Better than you, jackass." He wants to stop, to just knock the man's teeth out and tell him he's not needed, but he does what his brother tells him. After climbing onto the van to reach the billboard's hanging ladder, he pulls himself up as the other two approach their positions. He goes over the plan in his mind.

It's his job to stop the car. Shoot the tires, no more. From there, Silas and Rafe do the rest while he covers them. Silas doesn't want bloodshed if he can help it; by his way of thinking there'll be two men in the car. Take them by surprise when they go to change the flat, and they'll be able to scare them into giving up the access cards.

Diomedes cuts the power to the billboard's lights, then sets up in the shadows. They wouldn't need Rafe at all if they could just take out the men from here. What would it be like to kill a man? Could he really do it? This isn't combat or self-defense. Maybe Silas is right. Besides, bodies will make things harder anyway. Damn it.

He watches Rafe follow his brother into their hiding spot. Damn three-man jobs. Lying down along the narrow platform, he sights a few blocks up the road and waits. The garage door that leads to the parking area under the storage complex sits closed, for the moment. Along the wall beside it, also facing the street a little closer to his position, is the main door with its keycard locks. It's hardly a high-security place, but there's a score inside that Silas wants. Once they have the cards, it'll be theirs. Get in, grab it from the locker, get out fast.

But first the locker's owners have to show.

He isn't waiting long when the complex's garage door rolls open in his crosshairs and releases the yellow sport coupe onto the street. Diomedes tracks the car as it turns—just as Silas has said it would—down the street toward his position. He waits until it's a block away and fires. The tire bursts and sends the car into a fishtailing skid before the driver regains control and brings it to a stop. Pride paints a smile on his face as Diomedes waits for Silas to play his part.

He watches through the scope. The men in the car argue on what to do and find in the process that they can't get a signal on their phones. The jammer Silas has placed is working. They look about, perhaps trying to decide if it's coincidence or not, and Diomedes whispers for them to get out of the car. Silas will move on them soon if they don't, but it will be easier if they're outside. Vulnerable.

And then they're out, opening the trunk and still looking around warily. They pull an ordinary car jack from the trunk—not a weapon, he notes—and as they're working to set it up, Silas makes his move. Diomedes can't hear what they're saying; his brother keeps things quiet as he and Rafe rush in to surprise the men at gunpoint. They fold quickly, hands above their heads, and Diomedes spares a moment to scan the area for anyone who might try to help. It's late. Too late. The streets are deserted.

His brother hasn't made so much as a wave in his direction. The men are still cooperating, handing over the access cards and then lying on the ground now as Rafe stands beside Silas. His mood sinks. Silas might not *need Diomedes at all anymore.*

What the hell? Does he want things to go badly just so he can be of more use? Diomedes tells himself not to be stupid. His part of the job is done, for tonight. And Silas will still need help to load the van quickly.

With the cards in hand, Silas pulls a stun rod and thrusts it against the first man's back. A yell of protest from the second man has Diomedes snapping back to attention before Silas turns the rod on him as well. It's over quickly, and his brother gives the all-clear wave. It's time for him to come down and bring the van up to the complex. There, they still need him.

Reassured, Diomedes begins to break down the rifle as his brother and Rafe load the unconscious bodies into the car.

The rifle is packed in pieces. Diomedes heads back down the ladder, losing sight of the other two as they rush to the entrance of the complex. He jumps down, opens the van door, and then climbs into the driver's seat, tossing the disassembled rifle into the back.

Adrenaline is pumping again as the van's engine jumps to life. He puts it in gear. It's then that he hears the gunshots.

Shit!

He fires the van into the road, looking for the source, checking the men in the car as he passes. They're still out, still stunned. He looks down to his brother just in time to see—

NO!

Rafe stands over Silas's bloodied body, gun in hand. He swipes an access card across the reader.

Diomedes stares, trying to process the sight of his brother so clearly shot. Shock battles the grief and anger inside him. He can't move, can barely think. Silas, dead! It screams in his mind. When the killer escapes through the storage complex's door, Diomedes snaps.

A howl of anguish tears its way through the shock. He crushes the gas pedal to the floor and wrenches the van down the road with one thought overriding everything: kill Rafe!

Justice! Vengeance! It's not until he rams the van into the door that he wonders if the angle of impact will even allow enough force to break through. The wrenching scream of metal gives way to a smashing crunch as the van tears laterally across the door and slams into the wall beside it. Safety glass shatters and airbags balloon around him.

Adrenaline powers through the shock in seconds, and Diomedes kicks open the van's crumpled door. He has a moment to see that the impact has smashed open the complex door before realizing the wind is knocked out of him. He stops and draws his auto-pistol. Security alarms blare around him as he struggles to refill his lungs in gasping breaths.

The score they came for is fucked. Silas lays a few feet beside the door, dead where Rafe left him. Blood pools around him from a gaping hole in the back of his head, and Diomedes fights the urge to vomit at the sight. To hell with the score! He'll get Rafe and get out before the guards can come.

"How did he die?" Michael repeated.

Diomedes stared across the compartment. "Shot in the back. By someone he worked with. I was there, I saw it. Saw him, dead. Silas trusted both of us, that was his screw up. He should've just trusted me. Family! Family doesn't change." He fixed his glare on the kid, who didn't look away.

"I don't know what to—"

"I thought you were family," he hissed. "So that's what it all *means*, kid. You think I treated you bad? I had to rely on myself to get through my training. Army doesn't coddle you or give you any slack. I pulled myself up to get where I was a help to Silas, and once I got there, I stuck with him when he needed me! I didn't betray him. Didn't shoot him in the back. You fucking *get* it, kid?"

That'll shut him up! Make him see—

"I didn't *shoot* you, Diomedes. You think I'm this other guy again, shooting your brother in the back? Is that it?"

Maybe.

"You're not him," Diomedes shot. "And you ain't a shrink, either."

Maybe you're right. Maybe Michael is you. You always could see some of yourself in him, couldn't you? Of how you used to be? Didn't like seeing yourself pull a gun on yourself, did you?

That's bullshit. It's not who he is, it's what he did! What he'd do again!

Well, you are planning to kill him.

"So what happened to the guy who did it?" Michael asked.

"Paid him back, then and there," Diomedes found himself saying. *Nearly died, doing it, too. If Rafe's gun hadn't jammed when he ambushed you inside, you would have been the dead one when the guards showed up.*

He never did learn just why Rafe did it. He could still remember the traitor's face, dead on his back, looking so damn shocked. Shocked and vacant. Like everything he was had just slipped out. His brother's body. Rafe's stare. Both images never faded. "You remember the first person you ever killed, kid?"

"So far I haven't had to kill anyone."

Diomedes chuckled once, bitterly. "That a fact."

"I'm not looking forward to it, if I ever have to. You remember when you shot the ganger that was about to kill me? Even that was a bit of a shock, though I know it was him or me. You did what you had to do then."

Diomedes just stared as Michael's expression hardened.

"But when you shot Gideon, you didn't have to do that. That was in the back. That was over money. You did exactly what that guy did to Silas."

You turned into Rafe.

Bullshit. Rafe got what he deserved. You should've let him go free? After what he did to Silas?

"Gideon wasn't your brother," Diomedes muttered. He swallowed. "And he's not dead, either."

"Oh?"

"Shouldn't have survived that shot. But he did. Came back a few days ago and attacked me, like some sort of damn ghost. Hell, maybe you and Hiatt're right: I shouldn't have shot him. Maybe he can't *be* killed." Diomedes chuckled bitterly again. Brain half blown away and he's back. Disappears in a fall off the garage. Wraith, they called him. And he's out there somewhere.

He's just a man. You can kill him again if you have to.

Isn't that what got you into this whole mess? He's connected to the woman who set you up. Michael was right.

"You know," Michael said suddenly, "after I stood up to you, I had next to nothing left. I hung my hopes on you so much I didn't know what to do. You know one of the things that made it easier? I realized in time you probably would've done me the same way you did Gideon."

Diomedes only shook his head. "You're different from Gideon." He didn't know Gideon the way he'd known Michael, or for as long as he'd known Michael.

Michael scowled and looked away. "Yeah, well, he was dead as a doornail when you left him, that's all I know."

"Maybe he can't be killed," Diomedes muttered again, too quiet for the kid to hear. Some sort of invincible specter, like Rafe, come back for his own revenge . . .

No, that was crazy, wasn't it? He gritted his teeth and forced himself to focus. Gideon was on Earth. For now, Diomedes had a job to do. He pulled out the signal rod that would shut down the nanopoison and checked to see if it had been used. If they found the access cards, they probably found the rod, too.

"What's that?" Michael asked.

"None of your business, that's what." A quick check showed the poison was still active. If they'd found it, they didn't know what it did. They were still clueless. He put it back in his pocket, not entirely sure what to think about that.

XXXVII

SHE SHOULDN'T BE doing this, Ondrea scolded herself. She knew she shouldn't be doing this.

She walked beside Gideon on the top level of Sunrise Station's main concourse as he looked out the windows to one side and at the people to the other. She'd tried to steer him to a less-populated area on one of the lower decks, but he insisted on coming here. It was the top level, where four stories' worth of open space rose above them and food and gift shops lined the inner wall opposite windows separating them all from the vacuum of space. People everywhere. A part of her thought the people would possibly even help to put him at ease; the other part was just afraid to argue with him more than she had to.

He'd needed to go out, again, getting increasingly agitated and disoriented. He'd simultaneously needed to go "look for Isaac" and been impatient to start the lunar mission. The only thing she could think of was to appease him: try to satisfy that need somehow in the hope that it would calm his mind and let him focus on what he needed to do before she could manage a more permanent fix.

As the minutes ticked away, the fear that he didn't have enough time took an increasing hold on her heart. There was another way, but Marquand would destroy her if she went that route, and possibly Gideon along with her.

Gideon stopped walking to stare out the windows to their right. A pair of patrolling security guards had to step around him where he'd stopped, but they gave no real protest. "Isaac's long dead, Ondrea," Gideon whispered. "Why are we looking for him?"

The utter lack of a good answer stymied her. "I don't know, Gid. You just wanted to go for a walk before you got to the Moon. C'mon, we should go back now."

Gideon fixed her with a far-away stare. "Who is Joseph Curwen?"

She didn't think fast enough to hide her shock, but her phone beeped before she could answer. Though half glad for the distraction, she soured at its source. Tseng.

"Hang on, Gid." She answered and bit off a greeting. "What?"

"All lack of courtesy aside, Ondrea, just what do you think you're doing?"

Goddammit! Beck called Tseng? She turned from Gideon in a futile attempt at privacy. "Sir, I don't know what Beck told you, but there's no reason the problem should affect the project."

"The problem? What problem?"

Oh, hell. "Sir, maybe I misunderstood. Why are you calling?"

"I'm calling because I checked with D.K. and he said you took Gideon out for another stroll before zero hour! What's this about a problem?"

"It's nothing, sir, as I said, just a—"

"If I call Beck, will he say it's nothing? You're hiding something, Ondrea. If you think you're going to—"

"I'm not hiding anything." Ondrea took a breath to hide the pounding of her heart. "It's just going to take one or two more adjustments than we'd planned."

"And those adjustments require walks through crowded public areas?"

Searching for her next words, Ondrea glanced behind her. "Oh, damn it."

Gideon was gone.

*   *   *

Eyes tuned to thermal imaging, Diomedes gazed through the wall of the compartment as bodies passed back and forth beyond. When the area was clear, he nodded to Michael. "Go."

The kid opened the compartment door and scrambled out before calling for Marc to follow. Diomedes was on his own way out a moment later, squeezing through the opening on his back and rolling to his feet as soon as possible. Two travelers rounded the nearest corner immediately afterward, but gave no sign of alarm. They were out; now they had to make the shuttle. Diomedes gathered his bearings and picked a direction.

"This way," he ordered.

Diomedes led the way down the corridor, soon spotting a sign directing them up to the main concourse. From there they would get an elevator to one of the flight decks along the station's axis. Pick up Marc's bag he was whining about needing. A short walk to the shuttle from there, and they'd be bound for the Moon. He checked to see if anyone was watching or following. So far, so good.

"End of the line for you once we get to the shuttle, kid," he reminded him. "Just Marc and me after that."

"I'd like to at least see if I can fit," Michael argued. Again. That he was currently tagging along to see them off at the shuttle at all was a concession Diomedes made at the last minute when the kid had bugged him about it in the compartment. It was a bad idea, and it made it harder to keep him from coming any further. Diomedes shouldn't have allowed it.

Maybe it was because Michael didn't ditch him earlier. He could have. He should have. It's what he would have done himself: taken the access cards and gone. Damn kid missed his chance, and why did that piss him off so much?

You don't like remorse, do you?

"There's no room," Diomedes told him again. "No more to say about it."

"You said you don't even know what kind of shuttle it is. So I guess we'll see."

They made their way to the main concourse. The place was filled with people under a high ceiling that rose all the way up to the rotation axis of the station. "Shut up about it while we're in the crowd," he ordered, and then led them toward the elevators. Their transparent shafts rose above the crowd against the inner wall. Just a little further.

He didn't like this place. This spot. Something about it made his stomach twist. They were walking through a section set lower than the rest—what amounted to a divot in the deck, bordered ahead and behind them by other escalators that angled further up to connect the area with the rest of the deck that continued on a higher level. Railings lined the edges of that higher level. A few people loitered along the railings.

No, not a divot. A pit. The perfect place for an ambush. He pushed faster toward the elevators that would take him up to the flight decks. He wasn't really expecting an ambush, but he disliked the position anyway. Too vulnerable.

There was too much to worry about lately. So many nets out to catch him. Bounty hunters, Gideon, the blond woman, Fagles. But it would be over soon, if he pulled things off.

He'd been wanted before, but never so exposed. Too much had changed, changed for the worse like it always did. Damn it, why did he tell the kid about Silas? He'd lost Silas, Janette, and others who—if *they* were still around—would probably give him up for the bounty that was on his head ever since the blond woman turned on him.

He was so damned tired of change. Was it too fucking much to ask that something stay constant?

* * *

Ondrea's phone was off and in her pocket without another word to Tseng before she spotted Gideon thirty feet away. He stood by an escalator leading down to a lower section in the deck beyond. She rushed to him as he gazed out over the railing.

"Gid, please don't wander off like that. C'mon, we need to get back now." If they could make it back before Tseng got hold of Beck . . .

But then what?

Instead of answering, Gideon lifted an arm to point out over the low section to the railing on the opposite side. "It's them." Looking at where he pointed, she spotted two familiar figures just getting on the down escalator opposite her and Gideon's position.

If Michael dies—if you kill him—that will be another change, won't it? The small voice repeated the question. It grew louder as the transparent elevator doors closed.

It's already a change, he thought, fighting the idea, though it felt like a losing battle. Diomedes forced his attention to the crowd below as the elevator began to take the three of them upwards. Not much time now.

You do this right and he'll trust you again.

No.

Turn off the poison. He doesn't have to know. Let him come to the Moon. You know Fagles will try to screw you anyway. Let Michael back in.

It's not that easy!

You've got a choice: face your fear or deal with the change.

He didn't want to think about it. It was at that moment he caught sight of the man below with a start, a familiar figure by the railing overlooking the pit out of which they were rising:

Gideon!

He was following, tracking him! Here? Even *here?* No! The large voice swept him up in a storm of panicked rage: **Kill him! Kill him now! While you still have the shot!**

Diomedes ripped his weapon out of his coat with one hand and shoved Michael back with the other. "Get down! Now!"

* * *

Ondrea stepped between Gideon and the railing for a better look at the man and woman at which Gideon had pointed. It was definitely them, though she could hardly believe it. "They followed us?"

Gunshots exploded from above, and pain tore through her before she could say more. Fighting against shock, she barely felt her brother yank her aside and down to the floor.

* * *

Michael had just enough time to grab Marc and pull him to the floor of the elevator. He didn't know what was happening or why, only that Diomedes had gone berserk and was firing an auto-pistol through the now-shattered elevator glass down into the crowd below. His instinct to protect Marc widened to the rest of the people below. Even if Diomedes didn't hit anyone, if the bullets pierced the exterior of the station —

His move to stand again and somehow stop it all got cut short as sizzling bursts of dark red flung into the elevator at Diomedes. Michael threw himself back to the floor and tried to shield Marc.

Someone was firing back.

* * *

Diomedes cursed as his first volley hit the blonde when she stepped in front of his target. Gideon grabbed her and tried to shield her with his own body. **You won't miss** *this* **time! Empty it into him!**

He switched the weapon to full-auto as people scattered below. Only Gideon mattered. He took aim again and fired. The gun's violence bucked in his hand. Even with his artificial arm he had to fight to keep it on target as recoil and rage shook through him. Bullets scattered around Gideon. Had any hit? Diomedes wished for a rifle and cursed that he wasn't closer.

Then daggers of fire punched through him out of nowhere. *He* was shot?! Only for a moment did he see the station security forces scattered across the area below, thermal rifles pointed, all firing. He screamed soundlessly, unable even to move out of the way. Pain flared through him.

Everything burned.

He saw it all then: Gideon still covering the woman's body. Michael yelling something as Marc lay flat. He saw the guards below, still firing energy into him that cooked his flesh and blinded one eye. When their last bolt hit, it was as if he could see himself fall backward and useless. Beaten. Destroyed. When his body crashed onto the floor of the elevator, he didn't know where his gun had gone.

Odd that he no longer cared.

So fast, he was dying. He was alone. Even with the other two there, he was alone. Michael, still shielding Marc, was watching him, saying something that Diomedes couldn't hear. Quiet, so quiet. Even the voices, large and small, were gone. The bolts had stopped. The elevator was dropping. He saw Michael move closer. He was going for the access cards—no, not the cards, but checking his wounds. It was pointless. Diomedes could hardly breathe. He burned inside.

Diomedes watched Michael—the man Diomedes once was, he realized, maybe the man he might have been—make his futile effort to save him. Diomedes fumbled into his pocket and drew out the nanopoison signal rod and the cards in one handful. They weren't hit, but there wasn't much time now. Things were going dark, and Michael was becoming just a shape in a field of green.

All so quickly.

He found the kid's hand and pressed the items into his grip. His vision faded. "There's a poison," he struggled to whisper, "in your blood.

Use the rod . . . code 0909. Maybe I shouldn't have done it. Doesn't matter now . . . Sorry."

Then Michael faded completely.

He hadn't even finished Gideon. He couldn't even do that much. The others must have been right about the man, and he no longer had the strength to care. Death was a change he could deal with, he realized, mostly because he was sure now that he wouldn't remember. It ought to piss him off, and in the distance he did see himself lying there, pissed off and dying. What a joke: Diomedes the Eternally Pissed.

His last thought, ever, was that Fagles was probably just as screwed as he was. Were Diomedes able, he would have laughed.

XXXVIII

MICHAEL KNELT beside Diomedes and strained to hear as his former mentor pressed the access cards and the strange rod device into his grip. Even without seeing Diomedes's wounds, the gesture held an unmistakable air of finality. Everything had happened so rapidly and Michael was still reeling, struggling for what to do or say. Michael pocketed the items and tried to make out what the dying man was whispering.

Moments later, after the life left Diomedes's eyes, the elevator came to a stop.

"What'd he say?" Marc asked just before the guards rushed forward.

"I don't know." Michael shook his head. "I couldn't hear."

XXXIX

ONDREA WAS GOING to kill him, Beck thought, if the doctors were right that she'd live. What kind of psycho pulls a gun in a space station and just starts shooting? She'd called Beck with just enough strength to whisper where she was and that she'd been shot—enough to let him and D.K. find her as they were rushing her to the station's infirmary.

Gideon was with her, babbling like a madman about someone named Isaac and talking about Felix Hiatt and the woman Caitlin like he'd just seen them. Wherever he thought he was, his memory was breaking, and with Ondrea shot it was enough to make Beck tell Mr. Tseng everything. That, and the fact that Mr. Tseng nearly bit his head off right through the screen demanding answers.

The old man wasted no time ordering them to sacrifice Gideon's engrams to save the ones they needed. It was a shame that keeping them both hadn't worked, but that was over now. With Ondrea shot, Mr. Tseng told him more about the project's timeline. There was no way for "Gideon" to survive before he got back. Ondrea would skin Beck alive if she pulled through—if Mr. Tseng didn't can her first.

Hell, maybe the old man would can him too, once this was over, even if he was just following Ondrea's orders. It wasn't his fault! All he could do now was make sure the project succeeded.

D.K. had helped Beck subdue Gideon so he could make the adjustments. Now the two watched the shuttle carrying Gideon's container depart for the Moon.

"Well," D.K. said, "Now we wait."

Beck nodded. It would be days before Gideon would return. Gideon. They would need to find something else to call him. From everything Ondrea said, Beck didn't think he'd remember enough to think he was anyone at all unless they told him. Poor Ondrea. She'd lost the same brother twice now, hadn't she?

A bead of sweat ran down his back. Beck wished to God he didn't have to be the one to tell her.

* * *

If someone had told Felix a month ago that he would witness a shootout on Sunrise Station before the month was out, he'd have—Actually, Felix figured he probably would've offered to buy the person lunch just to hear the story.

It took a lot fewer things than a company forcibly extracting an experimentally augmented, formerly-dead man from his girlfriend's house to sustain his curiosity. Even so, once he and Caitlin managed to half follow, half trace them to an orbital flight, he likely needed all of those details to make him buy an orbital ticket with Caitlin. He'd hesitated—it wasn't exactly bus fare—but not for very long. Caitlin had a need to go after them, likely propelled by both concern for Gideon and simple anger at the invasion of her home, and that was enough to persuade Felix.

Besides, this was an experimentally augmented formerly-dead guy, here. Caitlin's involvement really only served to make it a no-brainer.

Caitlin returned to where Felix sat waiting for Marc and Flynn to be released. Her eyes were downcast, her frown twisted in frustration. "I went and lost him, Felix."

He gave a sympathetic smile, unable to think of what to say before she went on.

"I followed them as far as the infirmary. They took Ondrea into surgery, but in the confusion I lost Gideon. I think he went in with his sister but they wouldn't let me follow. I didn't see him leave, but by the time I managed a way in, there wasn't any sign of him." She slumped down into the chair beside him. "Ondrea herself will be all right. Or so I heard. I don't know quite what's become of Gideon, only that these two blokes were talking about him having left already."

"They say where?"

"They didn't. Not while I was eavesdropping, anyway. And don't think I didn't consider trying to get it out of them directly, but there wasn't any chance. I do know where they're staying here, though I don't know that it will do us much good. If he left, I expect it will be much harder to follow."

She massaged her temples with one hand, looking defeated. "I did manage to hear that they'd be waiting for him to come back—and before you ask, I get the impression that it was at least a day, if not more. So I decided to come back here, check in with you, and perhaps apologize for taking you along on a wild goose chase—"

"You don't need to apologize for that," he said, shaking his head. He was poised to say more when she cut him off with a hand to his mouth.

"—despite," she continued with traces of a smile, "your assurance that you wished to go anyway."

"Well, still, it has been interesting."

She chuckled softly at that. "Ducks, you threw up in orbit and we both could've been killed earlier today."

"Ah, you know. Life experience?"

"Speaking of which, Marc and Michael still in there, I suppose?"

He nodded. "I haven't seen them since Dio was killed."

"Bollocks of a thing to find him here. There're some rather odd linkages, Felix, even with what we know. And," she added with a probing look, "with what you've told me, and haven't told me."

He squeezed her hand on impulse. "Caitlin, I can't say more than that Marc works for a group with ties to ESA. I would if I could, believe me, but it's not my place to tell. I know they were looking for Dio. Obviously they found him. But I don't have a clue how Gideon fits."

"Perhaps two brains can work on it better."

He smiled. "Trying to make me break my promise?"

"If it involved Gideon, would you?" It was hardly off her lips before she shook her head. "No, forget I asked that. We've enough to think about."

Felix chuckled and pondered the answer anyway. "Too late."

He hated that he couldn't tell her—or felt he shouldn't tell her. Felix had hoped Marc and Flynn would get out before she got back so he could have a freer conversation with them, but maybe it was better this way. He probably couldn't tell her, but he could allow her to figure things out. Moral ambiguity? Who, him?

Felix's enhanced hearing picked up a conversation between two security personnel in the office and he cocked his head to make sure Caitlin knew he was listening.

"What is it?"

He held up a hand for a moment and gave her a wink as he listened, hoping for some useful news and ultimately being disappointed. "Mm. False alarm. Just idle security-folk conversation about hologram projection. Did you know they're still working on technology to make it feasible to project a super-realistic 3-D image that'll stand up to close scrutiny?" He grinned with what he hoped was appreciable cheese.

"Really, ducks. That's terribly fascinating."

"Your tone says otherwise, but thanks for playing." He winked. "Oh, hey, I think I hear Marc."

It wasn't long before the two men showed up, and Felix and Caitlin stood at once to catch them. They looked no worse for wear, at least. Felix wondered how Flynn was doing with Diomedes's death.

"Hey," Felix offered. "Everything okay?"

"Hey, they let us go, right?" Marc returned, quickly steering them away from the security office.

"Mainly just asked us questions," Flynn added. "You know, about how we knew the shooter."

"And what'd you tell them?"

"The truth," Marc said. "That we'd never seen the guy before we stepped onto the elevator."

"Mm," Felix grunted with a glance at Caitlin. Obviously they didn't want to say too much so close to security. He shelved his question about how Flynn was doing for later. "We should find somewhere we can talk."

Flynn and Marc exchanged a look, and the former said, "Ah, we're kind of in a hurry for the moment, Felix."

"But you can walk with us to the flight deck," Marc added.

Felix frowned. "Anyway, for what it's worth, I'm sorry. For what you went through, I mean."

Flynn only shrugged at that. Either he didn't want to talk about it or he wasn't sure how he felt. Felix wasn't sure how he'd be feeling in the kid's place, himself. Heck, he wasn't sure he knew how he felt in his own place.

"Where're you blokes off to, then?" Caitlin had asked the question before he'd thought to.

"WSC base," Marc told her. "What about you? I thought I was seeing things when you two showed up."

"Yeah, we're like a bad penny." Felix grinned. "Well, I am. She's worth considerably more."

"We're here after Gideon," Caitlin said.

"Gideon?" That got Flynn's attention. "It's really him?"

"Pretty much."

"Mostly," Caitlin added. "More or less."

"Probably," Felix went on. "It's complicated."

"Sounds par for the course," said Marc. "What's he doing up here?"

"What are you doing up here?" Caitlin countered with a cagey grin. "It's complicated, too."

"All the more reason to find somewhere to talk."

Flynn shook his head. "Sorry, we're really already late as it is."

"I'm sure we'd indulge your curiosity if we could, Felix," Marc agreed.

"We've the time until you get where you're going yet," she tried. Marc and Flynn both looked uncomfortable at that, but said nothing. After a beat, Caitlin went on instead. "Do you know if Diomedes was shooting at Gideon before? Or his sister?"

"More likely Gideon," Felix said.

"Who's his sister?"

The ring of Felix's phone interrupted them. Despite not recognizing the caller, he answered it near immediately.

"*This is Felix Hiatt?*"

"Well, *this* is, yes," Felix answered. "And you are?"

"*You're still on Sunrise Station?*"

With a concerned glance at Caitlin, he held up a hand to quiet the others. "Everyone's got to be someplace, right? Who wants to know?"

"Mr. Hiatt, my name's Beck. I work with Ondrea Noble. She's in the infirmary and wants to see you." There was a pause, and Felix could hear a woman's voice, indistinct, in the background. "As soon as possible?"

X L

ONDREA LAY PROPPED UP in the infirmary bed and watched the clock tick away Gideon's time. The pain blocker they'd put her on spared her from the feel of her healing bullet wound (the nano-surgeon pack that weighed her chest down mostly just tingled as the tiny robots worked at rebuilding her flesh and bone) but it did nothing to dull the fear of losing Gideon, or the pain of knowing he was so likely lost already.

But for a chance.

Felix and the woman (Caitlin?) entered the room, expectantly taking in the sight. Beck led them in. He, on the other hand, could hardly look her in the eye. Only urgency and being recently shot had kept her from tearing into him the way she wanted to when he told her what he'd helped them do to her brother.

"You can get out now, Beck," Ondrea told him. She had no time or energy for more. He skulked out again without a word and closed the door behind him.

Ondrea took a deep breath and turned to the other two. "Thank you for coming."

"You are all right?" It was Caitlin who spoke first.

"I'll live."

"Then you owe me a new front door," she continued, eyes narrowing. "Among other things."

"There's no time for all that. You have to listen to me."

"Oh?" Caitlin asked. "You've hardly proven trustworthy, have you, Ondrea?" Felix stood beside her, watching them both.

"Gideon will die if you don't!"

"Where is he?" Felix asked.

"On his way to the Moon." Ondrea couldn't tell if they were surprised at her answer or just that she'd answered at all. "But there's a lot more than that."

"We appear to be listening."

She focused through the haze of the blocker and began without further preamble. "You seem to know quite a bit about Gid already. You probably know he had a twin brother?"

"Isaac," Caitlin said.

"We didn't know the twin part," Felix added. "Er, well I didn't."

She nodded. Her mind floated. "Isaac went out one night and didn't come back. Kidnapped. Our parents had both passed away by then so it was just the three of us. We could afford the ransom but they killed him anyway and got away with the money. We both took it hard, but Gideon took it harder. He snapped and turned vigilante like something out of a comic book."

The blocker was making her ramble. There was so little time, though maybe they'd be more likely to help if they understood better. "I didn't like what he was doing. I tried to stop him, but when it was clear he wouldn't listen, I focused on keeping him alive any way I could. Hardware mostly, equipment and repairs. I was terrified of losing him, too. That's why I had to lie to him at your house, and to you. For his own good. If I hadn't—"

"Why you *had* to lie?" Caitlin shot. "Why you had to pulverize him with that thing in his neck and have soldiers haul your own brother off? You say you care about him and you don't even tell him what—"

"I did what I had to! I'm walking such a fine line with Marquand, you don't even know! How'd you like it if they'd just stormed the house outright and took him by force like they wanted?"

Caitlin said nothing to that, slowly steaming, her arms crossed.

Ondrea went on. "When Diomedes—when he shot him, and I know you were there for that, that you left him—"

"We were certain he was dead!" Caitlin blurted. "If there were any way we thought we could have . . . "

Felix put a hand on the woman's forearm after she went silent. "We did what we could. We called an ambulance. But Caitlin's right. By all rights, he was dead."

Ondrea closed her eyes, hating to even say it. "He was dead. Gid had a mic on him rigged to transmit back to his place. It shorted out soon after he—" She swallowed. "It was enough to tell me who'd done it."

"Diomedes. He's—He's the one who shot him, I mean."

Ondrea nodded and blinked to clear her head. "Before Gid died, he volunteered for one of the projects I'd been hired for at Marquand. It's more accurate to say that I involved him in it. This same project is based on one that Mr. Hiatt himself participated in some years ago."

Felix's face lit up. "Marquand! I knew it'd been sold to someone! What'd you do with it?"

"If it's detailed information you want, I've no time to give it to you." She paused, reminding herself not to antagonize them further. "Obviously it deals with memory, but where you had another's surface memories installed into that implant you wear and shunted to your own, we worked on a deeper level, on the theory that a person is equal to the sum of their memories."

"You made a copy of Gideon's, didn't you?"

She nodded. "About a month before he was shot."

"Why didn't he know?" Caitlin asked.

"There's a loss of a few hours or so prior to the point of record. I told him it was something to do with new aural implants before he came in, then told him the truth right beforehand."

The accusation was plain in Caitlin's face. "You deliberately told him so he'd forget."

"Yes, I did! It was a classified experiment! But when he agreed to it, he knew the truth."

"The truth that it was a memory experiment, or that you were trying to find a way to bring him back if something happened?" Felix asked.

"You're perceptive, Mr. Hiatt. So was he. I told him the memory part; I think he figured out the rest." Gid hadn't been fully comfortable with it, but he'd finally agreed anyway, if only to make her happy. She doubted he believed then that anything really could happen to him.

"And yet you still didn't tell him after that," Caitlin snapped.

Ondrea glared. "He knows now. If you're going to keep pointing out mistakes I'm already sorry for, we'll be here a long damned time." She looked away. "But even after Gideon died, I couldn't use his memories. Not immediately. There were technical details to work out: various setbacks, scientific and otherwise. The company had other, 'more promising' things to spend its time and money on. To make a long story short, Marquand recently had need of some very valuable information in the mind of a dead man. Someone else, as coincidence would have it, that Diomedes shot."

Felix's eyebrows went up. "That guy from ESA in Northgate?" Did Felix already know it was Marquand who ordered the hit in the first place? That Ondrea herself was involved? That it wasn't coincidence?

At first, Ondrea only nodded, choosing her words carefully before going on. "He was going to sell us some secrets. Marquand got access to the body after he died, but we couldn't just scan his memories. He'd need to have been alive for that." And cooperative. "So I took advantage of the situation and proposed a plan that would also let me help Gideon."

"Gideon has that bloke's brain, doesn't he?" Caitlin guessed.

With effort, Ondrea nodded through the haze. "The man from ESA was shot in the chest, but his brain was undamaged. We placed it into a body that Marquand constructed for Gideon. Then, using Gideon's memories—his engrams—we overwrote the memories in the ESA brain on the theory that Gideon, as the conscious personality, would be able to remember the ESA information Marquand needed, if only subconsciously at first. Then we'd bring the information closer to the surface with hypnosis and other treatments."

"That explains an awful lot," Caitlin said, scowling deeper.

"It didn't work quite right, did it?" asked Felix.

"It did. At first. Except for some minor things, he's my brother. Now and again pieces of the donor's personality peek through, but he's actually showing less sign of cyberpsychosis than before he was shot." She sighed. "But he couldn't remember the secrets Marquand needed as fast as they needed them. So they pushed. I'm not sure if the pushing caused it or just sped up the process, but things started to break down. You saw it when he passed out.

"His brain can't handle both engram sets for long on its own. Keep one whole, and you lose the other. We get around the problem by keeping them in a state of flux with an implant that boosts—" She cut herself off with a shake of her head that left her dizzy. Such details were useless now. "The point is his brain can't take the stress any longer.

Rather than risk losing the secrets they need, Marquand effectively cut the lifeline to Gideon's memories."

"So," Felix started, "he turns into the donor?"

"There's not enough of the donor left. He'll likely still have the information Marquand needs, but mostly he'll be a blank. It'll take a few days for that to happen, but if nothing's done my brother'll fade and I won't be able to save him. Marquand's sent him off. He won't be back until it's too late."

"Back from where, exactly?" Caitlin asked.

"Right now he's on his way to the Western Space Consortium's lunar station, but what he knows has to do with an ESA research base. All Marquand could get were the base coordinates, but he's got the layouts and access codes in his subconscious." She'd likely have to give them Omicron's coordinates too, she realized, just to be safe. In for a penny . . .

She tried to remember what she'd been saying. Access codes. Layouts. "Once he's there and in a situation that triggers the knowledge, he'll be able to use them. At least that's the idea. The body they built for him, beyond just looking like Gid, is state-of-the-art. Stealth modes, electromagnetic countermeasures, combat gear, EMP shielding. They're sending him to break in, steal what secrets he can, and get back."

"What sort of secrets?" Felix asked.

"It doesn't *matter*. If he gets that far it'll be too late!" The room swam a moment, and she paused to regain her bearings.

"You're telling us this to send us after him," Caitlin said. "That's it, isn't it?"

"For whatever reason, you care about what happens to him. The only other I could turn to is Beck, but he's worthless. And I'm in no shape to go myself."

"Rather convenient, that," Caitlin quipped. "You keep him in the dark all this time and then get someone else to—"

"I know what I did!" Ondrea shouted. "I let it go too far, is that what you want to hear? That I should have told Marquand to kiss off instead of taking the long shot that it might possibly turn out okay?"

Caitlin's only response was a dissecting silence that remained unbroken until Felix spoke up. "So just what is it you're asking us to do?"

"I need you to go to the WSC base and if you can, catch him before he leaves for what ESA's calling the Omicron Complex so you can reverse what they did to him." She swallowed. "Please."

"Do you have a way for us to get there?"

"No, you'll have to arrange something. But I can pay for it."

"And just how are we supposed to 'catch' him?"

"You'll have to find a way."

"That's it?" Caitlin snapped. "That's your plan? My cat could come up with a better plan than that!"

"Well, Lucifer is—"

"He'll recognize you," Ondrea insisted, cutting Felix off. "His memories will be slipping, but he'll still remember you." *I hope.*

"What about Marquand?" Caitlin asked.

"To hell with Marquand now! To them Gideon was just a way to get the information, someone who'd cooperate because he knew me. It was never about their secrets for me. I did this all for Gid." And now maybe all she'd accomplished was to make herself live through his death twice. "I'll throw it all away to keep him, too."

"Well, that's a lovely speech you must have rehearsed," Caitlin said, "but I mean, will they try to stop us?"

"No. There's only a few of us from Marquand up here, and they'll all be here with me. You won't see them or need them. I'll give you a modulator for the implant that regulates which memories are dominant in Gideon. The modulator is essentially a palmtop modified with technology developed for your own implant. All you need to do is plug it in and it'll do the rest."

"What will it do to him?"

She tried to think of how to explain it simply. "Flips what the implant's doing now so it favors Gideon's engrams and abandons the others, then reaccelerates his back to stable levels. You'll need to have it plugged in for about fifteen minutes, but it will tell you when it's done. Just plug it in, wait, unplug it."

"Once we catch up to him, find him, and convince him to let us plug it in at all," Felix said.

"I didn't say it would be easy."

Caitlin glared. "Yes, there's rather a lot you didn't say while we've known you."

"If you don't hurry there's no chance at all," she pleaded. "Now are you going to help Gideon or not?"

XLI

THE IDEA that he and Marc wouldn't be alone on the shuttle hadn't even occurred to Michael, but they soon discovered that Fagles's arrangements made them part of a small shipment of crew and equipment for the WSC base. On the plus side, they didn't have to worry about flying the shuttle. The problem was that he didn't really know if he could trust the impression that the others onboard didn't know what Diomedes looked like.

When they got to the shuttle, which had nearly given up waiting for them with all the delays, they only needed to scan their access cards. With Marc's foresight in getting Diomedes's prints while he was still unconscious, he'd been able to rig the card to use Michael's prints instead. That seemed to be enough when they stowed their gear and got on board, but even so, Michael spent the flight preoccupied and watching for signs that they'd been discovered. The only weapon they carried at this point was Marc's stashed sidearm that they'd grabbed from the flight deck locker before leaving; those Michael had kept in his bag in the elevator were lost when they'd claimed that the bag belonged to Diomedes.

Occasionally it would hit him: Diomedes was dead. Most of the time it didn't seem to register. Or maybe he just had other things to focus on. He needed to keep Marc safe—he needed to keep them both safe—and that's all there was to it. He didn't want to think about the rest of it: about how fast it had happened, or how little he'd done.

As it turned out, they made it to the Moon just fine. No one waited to kill or arrest them when they arrived. Their black ops anonymity prevented transmission of their faces—or rather, the face of Diomedes— just as they'd hoped. Though he was dead, they used his identity, his prints, and his access card to get them through each leg of their journey. Yet upon making it to the rover, they discovered that the last leg was to be the most problematic.

"Who puts a retina scanner on a rover?" Michael asked. That they'd gotten inside just fine meant nothing. The rover wasn't going anywhere without the scanner's permission.

"Theft between companies is more of a problem up here than you'd think. And then there's the whole black op thing, of course."

"Well, okay, so it's my first lunar rover. Just tell me we're not completely screwed?"

Marc went back to studying the scanner. "We're not completely screwed. Not that I know what to do about it just yet."

Unable to think of anything helpful to say, Michael just nodded and let Marc work. His own attention quickly shifted out the window to the rest of the bay. There was no sign of trouble so far, no one bothering to care about the two men who'd apparently decided to futz around in the rover they'd boarded. A few other rovers sat in their docking ports amid fuel tanks, spacesuit racks, and other unrecognizable equipment being worked on by WSC personnel. Perhaps assuming them to be corporate VIPs, the workers had given little more than a moment's glance when he and Marc had arrived and unlocked the rover with their cards.

It took Marc another half-hour to bypass the retina scanner.

"Nice job," Michael said at last.

"Don't thank me just yet. I'm not entirely sure it's not going to fail permanently in a while and utterly screw us."

"I kinda wish you hadn't mentioned that."

The door to the rest of the base slid open and drew Michael's attention. He stood up so fast that he nearly cracked his head on the rover's ceiling. "We've been followed."

"What?" Marc looked up in alarm and then immediately laughed. "Um, no, I think this qualifies as being stalked."

Felix and Caitlin stood in the bay's open doorway for a moment before the latter spotted them. With a quick word, they started in the rover's direction.

"And we've been spotted."

"This should be interesting. Better open the hatch before anyone asks too many questions."

Felix appeared content to wait until they were all inside the rover to make a joke. "Okay, so spill it. Are you guys following us, or what?"

"Hullo Michael, Marc," Caitlin added, her smile holding more than a trace of anxiety. "It was nice of you to get a ride for us."

Michael hesitated a moment, trying to decide a way through the situation. "This really isn't something we can share with you," he told them with a glance at Marc. "You're not being followed by anyone, are you? I mean, are you in trouble?"

"We're okay, we're doing the following," Felix said.

"Felix, we can't tell you where—"

Caitlin cut Michael off before he could finish. "It's Gideon. He's on the Moon, he needs help, and we can't get to him without a rover."

"We missed him when we followed him here but figured when we saw you that you'd be going the same—"

"Look, I'm sorry, but Gideon's going to have to take care of himself," Michael told them. Friends or not, they had to focus on the mission, just like on Sunrise. There wasn't time for anything else. "We've got something of an urgent—"

"So do we," Caitlin pressed. "Look, just where is it you two are plotting to take this thing?"

With her darting gaze demanding answers, Michael shifted uncomfortably and glanced again at Marc. Obviously they couldn't tell her, and they'd already lost enough time when Diomedes . . .

"It's not something we—" Marc began.

"We can't tell you," Michael finished. "And there just isn't time."

"Oh, mother of God," Caitlin groaned. "To hell with your secrets, all of you! We know about this Omicron Complex and we need to get there before Gideon—"

"Gideon got himself into this, he'll have to get himself out!" Michael burst. "We don't have time to help everyone!"

"Will you bloody *listen?*"

Felix yelled, "Hey!" and jerked Michael's attention to him with sheer surprise. "Let's just all calm down here, okay? I don't know if you heard what she said but Gideon's going to Omicron. Now we assume that's also where you're headed and we need a ride. If you can honestly say we're wrong about that, we'll leave you alone right now to do whatever it is that you are doing, but if not, it's in your interest to let us come along." Felix turned to Michael directly. "And I know you're a tad stressed right now, but you need to be a little nicer."

Michael bristled, wondering for a moment at his own outburst before focusing back on the present.

Marc beat him to it. "Why's Gideon going to Omicron?"

"He's working for Marquand Cybernetics. They know ESA's doing something there and they want him to steal whatever he can. We have to stop him before he gets there."

"I don't understand," said Michael.

"For the moment, just trust us," Felix said. "We'll tell you more once we're underway, but we really are pressed for time ourselves."

"And before you worry about telling us the location of this place, we already know," Caitlin added, holding out a palmtop with coordinates.

Marc checked them over and nodded. "Even more chaos. So if we take you along, you stop Gideon from stealing anything? Sounds win-win, Michael."

Michael scowled but nodded. "Do we have enough oxygen in this thing?"

"Should be okay."

"I guess you're with us, then." He gave Caitlin a glance. "Sorry about that just now."

She smiled slightly and shrugged. "I've had worse."

"The Council's going to be cranky."

Felix grinned. "Tell Knapp I said 'hi,' then."

Michael powered up the rover and tried to remember what he learned from his hurried crash course on Earth. "You're not helping, Felix."

The others all took a seat as the rover pulled out of the bay and into the open moonscape. "So," Marc started, "you two want to tell us what's really going on?"

XLII

FELIX AND CAITLIN told their tale as the rover carried them from the base and into the unknown. Michael was unsurprised to learn that Diomedes had indeed killed Gideon those months ago. The idea that his sister remade him from an artificial body and stored memories, on the other hand, came completely out of nowhere.

"Wow. Really?"

"Well, it does sound like something I might make up," Felix answered, "but yeah."

"With the brain of that ESA bloke that Diomedes killed, even," Caitlin added.

That had Michael turning to Marc so fast he would've driven them off the road if there were a road to leave. "You're sure?"

"Curwen?"

"Moon rock! Moon rock!" Felix yelled from the seat beside him.

He hit the brakes and got them back on course. "Sorry."

"Aye, that was his name, I think. Curwen," Caitlin said. "With whom you two are intimately familiar for some reason you've yet to share."

Marc ignored Caitlin's implied question with a more direct one of his own. "Did Ondrea say Marquand had him killed?"

"She implied it was coincidence," Felix said, "but given how fast I figure they'd need to act to get the brain, I don't buy it."

"Nor I."

"So they hire an assassin who just happened to have killed the guy they're remaking?" Marc asked in disbelief.

"Well," said Felix, "it does have a certain symmetry to it."

"Unless," Caitlin said suddenly, "that bit wasn't coincidence, either. What if Ondrea herself picked Diomedes, used him, and then turned him in for revenge?"

Used him. Michael bristled at that. Wallace had used him, Ondrea had used him, the AoA . . . "Sounds risky," he said finally.

"People driving across the Moon to a secret base don't get to find fault with 'risky,' Michael."

"I guess not, but still."

Felix snapped his fingers. "Maybe that's why we saw Diomedes at Gideon's place. He was after Ondrea?"

"Just because he thought she turned him in doesn't mean she really did, though," Michael said. "This is Diomedes we're talking about, here." Should he feel bad for putting the man down so soon? Yet it was the truth, wasn't it?

"At this point, exactly who turned him in's likely moot," Marc said. "But at least we know who probably hired him."

"Ah, and just whom will you be reporting that to?" Caitlin tried. Michael had to smile; she reminded him of Felix. Nevertheless, he kept his mouth shut and concentrated on the rover, which bumped and rolled across the dusty rock and uncomfortable silence.

"And you came all the way up here just for Gideon?" Marc asked finally.

Caitlin chuckled. "Oh, terribly subtle subject change, Marc."

"We just kept going one more step forward," Felix said. "It's just that the last few steps were really rather, ah, big ones. Though we did get a free trip to the Moon out of the deal. Even without us trying to help Gideon, I wasn't about to pass that up. Plus now we're up here, deeply mired in multiple secrets. Exciting, no?"

"It was a mystery," Caitlin agreed. "On top of which, we owe him. Or the other Scry and I owe him, rather. Felix is just foolish and barmy."

Felix nodded. "I'm really just trying to get laid."

"Yes, always so terribly selfish you are, ducks."

"I'm sorry, 'laid'?" Michael asked. It earned him a laugh from Felix.

"Decades-old slang," he explained, "for—actually it's really none of your business what it means."

They continued across the lunar surface and sunk into silence for a time as they all watched out the window at the alien landscape. Michael found himself missing the trees.

It occurred to him that six months ago he didn't know how he'd find a job or keep a roof over his head, and now he was driving across the Moon. He was Marc's protection—and sent out to aid someone else—only half a year after he was depending on Diomedes to protect him like he'd done since . . .

He couldn't think about that right now. He had a job to do. Marc still needed to reconfigure the leech device Diomedes brought to transmit Omicron's data to Fagles. Diomedes hadn't given it to Marc until right before they'd left the Sunrise Station compartment. Even though Marc had convinced Diomedes he needed to adjust it so it would transmit silently through Omicron's system, they'd counted themselves lucky he'd given it over even that early. The initial plan was to do the alterations on the way to the Moon, but they didn't have the privacy for that.

Not wanting to ask about it in front of Felix and Caitlin, he instead spared a look back to see what Marc was doing. Not surprisingly, Marc was ahead of him, computer and leech linked, working on the AoA modifications.

Caitlin caught him looking and followed his gaze to Marc. Michael turned back forward, but it wasn't long before she broke the silence. "So. I'll ask again. Just what is this secret you all share? Do keep in mind that I have the three of you in a confined space."

"I'd say she's earned at least a little, guys," Felix said. "I mean obviously I'll vouch for her. Besides, you know how this sort of thing works: it's crazy enough that anyone who does try to tell anyone about it gets branded some conspiracy wacko anyway, right?"

"You really haven't told her anything?" asked Marc.

"I did take an oath, and this is me we're talking about. I haven't told her a thing, mostly."

"Your oath included the word 'mostly'?"

"Maybe. Probably." Felix smiled sheepishly. "I never said I was perfect!"

"I notice how you're cleverly trying to position yourself on my side rather than answer my question yourself, ducks."

Felix took a deep breath. "Caitlin, if I tell you in front of them, then Flynn's going to make his little whip-crack noise, and I *hate* that."

Michael stared out the windshield, smirking. "Hey, leave me out of this."

"Well, you did it before," Felix insisted.

"Whip-crack noise?" Caitlin asked in an icy tone of indeterminate seriousness. Blanking on what to say, Michael kept his mouth shut.

"Look, lads, as amusing as this is, it's also bloody irritating being the only one in the dark. I know you're involved with something secretive, I know it's got something to do with keeping whatever ESA's doing a secret, and I know there's a council."

"Don't look at me," Felix told them. "You let that one slip yourselves."

"We really can't tell you," said Marc. "Aside from the fact that we've got an interest in being sure whatever's going on at Omicron doesn't get out."

"Doesn't get out? You are just talking about information and technology, yes?"

In the time before Marc could respond, Michael decided to answer for him. "For the most part. It's only fair to tell you that something happened at the base, and ESA's lost contact."

"We're not really sure just why," Marc added.

"It might be safer for you two to stay on the rover as much as possible. Even if it's completely safe, Marc and I have ESA IDs to explain why we're there. You don't."

"Oh, don't be so sure about that," Felix said with a grin that swiftly widened. "Okay, I'm bluffing. Just wanted to see your reaction."

"And Gideon knows us," Caitlin said. "So we hope. We may need to come in to find him, so anything you can tell us about what's going on there will make this easier."

They bumped and rumbled along the next five seconds in silence.

"Artificial intelligence," Marc said finally. "Remember the trip I took a couple of weeks ago? They had me up here, helping out. There was a whole group of us, mostly freelance. And I'm not supposed to tell you this, but ESA thought we might have stolen some secrets while we were here. After that, everyone but me just up and vanished."

"You lying bastard," Felix said. "I knew something was wrong before! You said weren't in any trouble!"

"I was guarding him," Michael said.

"And if we'd told you, we would've had to say why I was in trouble."

Caitlin was incredulous. "So you're going back?"

"I've been there before. It's complicated. And no, we can't explain. You just really shouldn't know too much about this, for your own safety."

"There's other things going on out here, too," Michael added. "We don't really know what, we just know it's bad and we can't let it get out." Felix probably wouldn't buy it completely—Michael needed to ask Marc just how much Felix did know—but he hoped it would placate Caitlin for the moment.

"Who's 'we'?" she asked.

Both Marc and Michael remained silent.

* * *

It wasn't the avalanche of answers she'd hoped for, but it was a start. Caitlin considered the possibility that if she pushed any further at the moment, they might clam up permanently. And Felix gave her a look that hinted he'd reveal more later. She let the matter drop.

Besides, she'd gotten herself into enough of a prickly situation already. Felix was right: they'd kept going just one more step forward, carried on their own momentum. She supposed it could be argued that the little steps just added up to a great distance, but the last step was rather a whopper. Caitlin chuckled bitterly to herself. She never did know when to quit.

Not that it mattered anymore. They were committed, and she could either keep second-guessing herself and bollocks it up, or she could just ride the horse she'd saddled.

Yet the wait was difficult. As the time wore on, Felix shifted to the back of the rover to rest and Caitlin took his seat, preferring to keep a watch out for Gideon. Though she knew there was little chance of seeing him along the way, it at least would keep her busy and didn't hurt to try. She searched the bleak landscape. Her own silence matched the others: Felix's and Marc's as they slept behind her, Michael's as he guided the rover.

"I don't know why I'm looking out here," she said finally to break the silence. "Ondrea said he'd be hard to spot in the open."

"How's that?"

"Some active camouflage system, she called it. We didn't get details."

"You didn't?" Michael asked. "I'm surprised Felix didn't try for more."

"Time was short, or I'm sure he would have." Well, they both would have tried. Scanning the landscape before them, she regretted not asking. Yet it couldn't be helped.

Of course, she had managed to nick a PDA from Ondrea's bag while in her room. Perhaps the answers might be in there, but she couldn't get past the PDA's security. Caitlin half-regretted the violation. She didn't really know why she'd taken it—perhaps just as a petty swipe at the woman. Ondrea would have certainly told them everything they needed to know to help Gideon. Then again, she'd concealed things from them before.

"Sounds like Felix," Michael agreed. He guided the rover over a small ridge. Caitlin held onto the seat as they bumped back and forth until they finally leveled out. "Frankly I'm surprised he hasn't asked me more about Diomedes yet."

Felix was probably respecting his privacy. For all his inquisitiveness, he was good with that sort of thing. Or at finding the right time to ask, she amended, thinking of how often she'd told him secrets of her own.

For her part, she hadn't really thought about Diomedes since they'd talked to Ondrea. Other concerns dominated her deliberations, and Caitlin couldn't bring herself to feel much of anything for the freelancer. He'd killed Gideon and he'd nearly killed Felix. Yet she long ago gathered he'd been something to Michael.

"And how are you doing?" she asked. "With all that's happened, I mean."

His first response was a glance so sudden that she wondered if she shouldn't have asked. Michael followed it with a tentative sigh before turning back to the journey ahead. "Guess I've been trying not to think about it too much."

"I'm sorry. I get chatty when I'm anxious. I didn't mean to pry."

Michael shrugged, though it was a minute before he spoke again. "Actually I keep wondering what I could've done, though. Or should've."

"It happened pretty fast. You pulled Marc to the floor though, yes?"

"Yeah," he nodded before finally adding, "Actually I meant for Diomedes."

"Oh." She turned her gaze back out the window. "Like what?"

"Well, I don't know, but I didn't do anything. It's stupid to say. I was there to protect Marc, so that's what I did. Before I knew it they were shooting Diomedes. I think, what if I'd grabbed for him instead of Marc and stopped him? Which is stupid because he's stronger than me. Then I think maybe if I'd tried . . . he might've survived it."

"Michael, he opened fire into a crowed of people! In the middle of a space station! He could've killed us all! If you're feeling bad about not trying to stop him once he started I could get that, but—" She shook her head to calm herself. "If you'd tried to protect him then, you'd probably've gotten shot yourself for getting in the way."

"Yeah, okay, so I guess I can't argue with that."

"Well, you oughtn't, no. He's gotten enough people killed already, I should say. I'm sorry, I know you used to be mates. But it's true."

"That's just the thing," he answered after a time. "We used him to get up here. Lied to him, put him in danger. Okay, so I guess he's the one who got himself into it, but he helped me, once. Saved my life, too. Probably kept me from . . . " He stopped, and Caitlin turned to find him searching for words. "When I moved to Northgate, I didn't know what I was doing. He took me in. Sure, he's an ass, cruel, greedy, paranoid—"

"An assassin," she added, and then felt rude for interrupting.

"Yeah. And I turned my back on him because of it, because I didn't want to be like that. Don't get me wrong, I don't regret that part of it. Maybe I'm just wondering if I'm just like him for using him now. For letting him die without lifting a finger."

"Because he protected you once?"

"I don't know. It's just—It doesn't sit right. I can't explain it."

"So are you mourning him, or just feeling off for your part in it?"

Michael scowled. "I don't know. Probably both. I don't want to, and then I feel bad for not doing it. And then—" He broke off again, staring ahead.

Caitlin frowned. "I'm sorry, it's not my business." She turned back forward as well, ruefully congratulating herself on forging a lovely awkward moment. Michael didn't respond.

For a time they just drove. The rover rumbled about. Some unsecured cargo in back shifted noisily now and again. She wouldn't apologize for asking him about it, Caitlin told herself. She hated to think that Michael was suffering the pain of grief for someone like Diomedes. Even in death the freelancer found a way to hurt someone. Despite her impulse to help Michael get through it, she shouldn't have pushed. But then he hadn't said that he didn't want to talk about it, either.

"It's a strange situation, I suppose," Caitlin found herself saying. "I don't pretend to think I'd be feeling anything simple in your shoes, either." She forced a chuckle in an effort to lighten the mood. "With what I'm doing now, I can't throw stones."

Michael begrudged a chuckle of his own. It was a moment more before he spoke again. "I felt stupid enough back when I realized Diomedes wasn't some noble hero or something. Like I was some teenager who still believed in Santa. You're right, I shouldn't be mourning him. It's like I'm right back where I was. I bet it sounds like I'm still afraid to let him go, huh?"

She shook her head. *Don't judge.* "I honestly can't say how I'd be feeling if I were you. Do you think perhaps you're just sorry he didn't turn out the way you thought he was once?"

"Yeah, maybe. You'd think I'd get over that."

Caitlin shrugged. "Perhaps that's what you're mourning, then."

"Geez, you'd think I'd have other things to think about right now. And maybe that's what it is. I'm sort of on my own up here. I'm not worried, despite how I probably sound. Just anxious."

"It's the wait."

Michael nodded, his face hardening with what seemed to be resolve. "Yeah. I'll be fine." He reached into his pocket with a start before Caitlin could think of what more to say. "Oh! Hey, tell me what you make of this."

She let the change of subject go and turned in her hand the pen-sized device that Michael gave her. It didn't immediately strike her as being anything in particular. There was no visible mic, or optics to indicate a camera, just a few buttons and a tiny screen. "What is it? Or where's it from, rather?"

"Diomedes gave it to me, right before he died. He tried to say something about it, I think, but . . . " He shook his head.

"Might it be a transmitter? A remote for something? Or perhaps a receiver. I don't see any ports on it. Wireless data storage?"

"No idea. I think if it was some sort of storage drive, Marc would've recognized it."

"Weapon of some sort?" She handed it back to him. It didn't much look like a weapon, but if Diomedes had carried it, she expected a chance. "Show it to Felix when he wakes up. He may have seen it somewhere."

"Yeah." He returned the device to his pocket. "Actually, might want to wake him up now. Omicron's right up ahead."

Michael was right. Beyond the rim of the crater they were cresting lay a wide, mostly flat structure. There was no sign of Gideon—in fact, no sign of any activity at all. Were they too late? Had they passed Gideon in transit?

They'd soon find out. Things were coming to a head, and she suddenly wondered what business she had being there at all. Dismissing the thought as useless, she slipped into the back to wake the others.

XLIII

MARC WOKE to Caitlin's hand on his shoulder and rose to look out the front of the rover. Omicron stood dark. While the place displayed a minimum of lights on the outside to avoid being spotted from space, it nevertheless looked—or felt—darker than it should. Marc thought it was just the subconscious effect of the communications blackout before he realized that the actual base control station, perched slightly above the rest of the complex, was almost completely unlit. Hopefully he would find Marette inside and somehow well enough to tell them what had happened.

Yet she wasn't the only one they needed to find now, was she? "Just how was Gideon supposed to get inside?" he asked. He'd begun to have a plan for how to further fit the man into their puzzle.

"Ondrea said he'd be able to remember codes that the ESA bloke Curwen knew," Caitlin answered, "and he supposedly has some other hardware in him to bypass security if those don't work."

"He might just try to hook in externally, if that's possible," Felix added.

Marc nodded. "I'd say that's less likely to work, but depending on what's going on here it might not be so hard."

Felix moved up beside Marc, observing. "Speaking of which, do they know we're here?"

"They shouldn't," Marc said with a glance over Michael's shoulder at the controls. "Our radar cloak's still active, and Omicron hasn't got anything more to pick us up at the moment."

ESA had gone with a low profile. More active exterior scanners would be detected themselves, and anyone who got curious would wonder just what was so important as to warrant such vigilant measures. Beyond very short-range active radar, Omicron relied on passive sensors.

Marc moved forward a bit. "'Scuse me, Caitlin. Trade spots?" He settled into the front seat beside Michael with a thank-you to Caitlin and flipped on the short-range communications. "Omicron Complex, this is ESA Rover 14AoA, come back?"

Felix leaned forward a bit himself. "Uh, is that really a good idea, Marc?"

"We've got the credentials we need," Marc assured him. Making contact would also alert Marette, if she was there to alert.

"Forged credentials," Felix corrected.

"Granted. Omicron Complex, this is ESA Rover 14AoA, please respond." They waited, but still got nothing. "Antenna looks down."

"You didn't have any sort of power drain going on up here earlier, did you?" Michael asked.

"Nope."

"Rover feels a little more sluggish suddenly," he went on. "Maybe it's something new."

Felix leaned in. "Looks like you've still got plenty of battery."

"I know."

"Does anyone spot Gideon?" Caitlin asked, looking. No one answered. For his part, Marc couldn't see any sign of anyone.

Omicron loomed. Marc tried one more hail that went unanswered. Soon they were rolling toward the side of the complex farthest from where Marc knew the alien ship to be. Ahead sat a parked ESA shuttle on the exterior landing pad.

Marc pointed to the side of the complex facing the pad. "There's two airlocks up ahead there. The big one goes to the cargo bay but we should probably—"

Caitlin pointed to it. "Ought it to be like that?"

The cargo airlock was open.

Marc glanced at Michael and tried to recall. "I'm not sure," he said truthfully. "I was about to say we should use the smaller one anyway. Keeps the rover out here."

"That whole 'stay on the rover as much as possible' thing," Felix said.

"And out of sight, yes. Something of a problem if we roll right into the cargo bay."

"Keeps us out of trouble, anyway." Felix grinned. "I'm guessing this thing won't hook right up to the smaller lock, though, huh?"

"It might, actually, but I think the little gantry there's controlled by the base. There's an exterior door aside the gantry that goes right into the lock itself, though."

"Given everything we don't know, we'd better wear suits anyway," Michael warned.

"Aye. I know I'd be more comfortable."

Michael pulled the rover over to the side near the gantry and parked it against the complex wall where it was hidden from the control station and any other windows. "Know how to use one?"

Caitlin gave a hesitant chuckle that came on the heels of Felix's question of, "How hard can it be?"

"Maybe you two'd better stay here."

Caitlin frowned. "Not until we've at least had a look for Gideon."

"How much is a look?" Marc turned around to face them.

The glance Felix and Caitlin shared gave the impression that neither knew how to answer. "Well, the suits are pretty much computer-controlled anyway. Er, right?"

*   *   *

After donning their suits and giving Felix and Caitlin the most basic crash course, Michael led them out of the rover. He knew he'd have to make a firm decision on just how far they could go soon, but for the moment he let them come along. If they ran into Gideon, he'd probably need them. His foot hitting the soil outside the rover briefly made him think of the first man to ever do so back in—Well, Felix would know the year. Michael paused where he stood and cast about for any sign of danger. Seeing none, he waved the others forward and made his way to the lock over the footprints of others that still showed clearly in the otherwise undisturbed soil.

Soon they reached the lock door. "The lock light's green," Marc declared over the suit comms.

"Green is good, right?"

"Means it has atmosphere," Marc explained. "I could have sworn it was red when we drove up, though."

Michael peered inside through the tiny window. From what little he could see, the lock was deserted. "You sure?"

"Er, not completely, but . . . "

"So either they're trying to slow us down or someone's coming out."

"Or going in," Caitlin said.

"Or I'm just remembering wrong. I'm not Felix, you know."

"We won't hold it against you," said Felix.

Michael allowed himself a grin. "I don't see anyone in there. See if you can vent it. Let's get inside."

Marc nodded and punched in the pass code. If someone was in the lock, Michael remembered, they had an override button to keep their air if they needed to—or just to keep Michael and the others from getting inside. If that turned out to be the case, they'd have a problem.

There were only moments to consider alternatives before Marc announced it was working and the light turned red. The door slid open. The lock was empty.

Michael led them inside, taking care to first check around a pillar-like rectangular bulkhead in the corner whose only purpose seemed to be to obstruct their view. As he confirmed there was no one lurking behind it, Felix's voice came over the suit comms. "So do we take this to mean the base has power at least?"

"If this were the cargo lock it would," Marc came back. "The small one's got its own power supply for safety in case someone finds themselves outside during an emergency. Everybody in?"

Michael moved forward to the lock's inner door as Marc closed the outer one. Its narrow window showed only darkness beyond. He turned and pointed. "Any way to tell if there's air in there, now?"

"Not until we get air in here, I think," Marc said. The outer door sealed.

A flicker of a shadow caught Michael's eye on the obstructive rectangular bulkhead just as Felix moved to put his hand against it. "Think we'll be able to—Aah!"

Felix's hand passed right through the bulkhead as if it weren't there. As he continued to stumble *through* it and tried to regain his balance in the suit, a hand appeared at his shoulder and hurled him away. Moments later the entire bulkhead vanished entirely in another flicker of holographic shadow.

There in the space the hologram had occupied stood Gideon.

Michael just managed to move and catch Felix, apparently stunned into silence, before he hit the other wall. He steadied his friend and then spun to face Gideon's next move, yet the man only stood in his own wary stance. He wore nothing more than a snug, dark gray jumpsuit, without even a helmet to protect him from the vacuum.

"Are you okay?" Michael asked Felix without turning.

"Are you *kidding*? Did you see that? Amazing! Make him do it again!"

"We're still on comms, I don't think he can hear us, Felix."

"Probably better that way, really; the being hurled across the room bit wasn't quite as pleasant."

"Supposing he can read lips?" Michael asked. They had no way to be sure how Gideon would react, especially if the others were right about what was going on in his head.

Caitlin stepped in front of Michael to face Gideon directly. "He looks scared."

Gideon remained where he was. His eyes darted between them like an animal tensed to run—or strike. Michael shook his head. "He looks confused. Unsure. I wouldn't say scared."

"Gideon?" Caitlin tried, speaking slowly with exaggerated enunciation. "It's Caitlin. Do you remember?"

"Be careful," Michael warned. Gideon only stared back, unreadable. He reminded Michael of Diomedes.

Felix moved up beside Caitlin. "We need to get some air in here or this is going nowhere unless you fancy a game of charades."

"I'm on it," Marc said. He went for the inner door only a moment before Gideon tensed again and took a quick step toward him. Both stopped instantly. "Just, keep him occupied?"

Michael moved closer to Marc.

"Ah, move slower," Felix said.

Caitlin put herself between Gideon and Marc. "We need air, Gideon, that's all. Then we'll talk."

Gideon kept a haunting watch on them all from the other end of the lock while Marc crept the rest of the way to the panel beside the inner door. The hiss of air soon sounded from outside their suits and grew louder before it subsided.

"Should be safe," Marc announced.

Michael released the seal on his helmet and took a breath. The other three followed his example. "Gideon?" he asked.

"Who are you?"

"I don't think he's going to remember you, Flynn, even without his . . . trouble." Michael hadn't thought of that.

"Trouble?" Gideon asked.

"Gideon, it's me, Caitlin. Do you remember me? Do you remember Felix?"

Gideon frowned toward Marc and Michael. "Them?"

"This is Marc, and Michael. They're friends of ours. They helped us get here, to find you."

"To help you," Felix added.

Gideon stared. "There is no help coming."

"There is," Caitlin said. "And we're it."

"No."

"Yes. Gideon, your sister sent us. There's something—well, there's something wrong with your brain. Your memory. And we need to fix it."

"Yeah, just so not the kind of thing you want to hear on the frigging *Moon*, but we're not as incompetent as we look."

"Felix," Caitlin warned.

"Sorry."

"You are not ESA?" Gideon asked.

Michael held out his hands in an attempt to be disarming. "We're not supposed to be here any more than you are."

"You don't remember Felix and me at all?"

Gideon scowled without answering further. For a time he simply stood blinking while they held their breath. "You came to help," he stated finally. "The door will not open."

"There's really very little time, Gideon. Felix and I have to fix your—"

Gideon stepped closer, seeming to grow larger as he cut her off. "Answer."

"You've tried?" Marc asked.

"It won't take my codes."

Marc tried punching in a few codes of his own into the keypad next to the airlock controls. There was no response. "It's not getting power."

Michael frowned, still watching Gideon. "But the airlock works?"

Marc nodded. "Separate systems, like I said."

"With another power source, could you—" Gideon stopped, blinking as if searching for the word, "—bypass?" Caitlin made a move to say something but he cut her off with a wave. "Stay back."

"I might." Marc gave Michael a glance. He could tell what the other was thinking. They needed to get the door open somehow.

"If we help you get it open," said Caitlin, "then will you let us heal your memory?"

The confused man regarded them all in turn as if sizing them up, and only spoke after a time. "Ondrea Noble?" Caitlin nodded, and Gideon finally gave a grim nod of his own. "After the door is open."

"Aye, right after."

Keeping his back to the wall, Gideon moved toward the door where Marc stood. "Stay back," he ordered. Though the others kept their distance, Michael kept close to Marc, ready to jump between the two if needed. Gideon in turn hardly took his eyes off of Michael even as he exposed a part of his arm, drew out some cables, and pushed them to Marc. "Here."

"These connected to the rest of you in any way?"

"No. Spare power supply. Insulated."

Marc nodded and then set to work on the security panel. He asked Gideon a few questions about the power source as he examined the interface and rigged up the cables. Save for a few brief words in reply, Gideon kept silent. If Caitlin and Felix were right, putting his memories back would somehow force out the ESA secrets he held, and then they'd just need to get him out of there before he got in any deeper. Michael wished he knew how likely he'd be then to just do as they asked.

"Almost got it," Marc reported. "Though even once we get power to the door, it's still hooked into the base computer. If that's having problems it still might be a process to get open."

"That's okay, I like processes."

"Thanks, Felix," Marc said.

"Welcome. I try."

Still hooked into the door, Gideon turned from Michael to Caitlin and whispered, "Your name is Caitlin."

"That's right. You remember? Do you know Felix?"

Gideon studied him but stayed silent.

"See, Caitlin? Told you that you were more memorable than me."

Gideon's eyes glazed. "I need to go to the Moon."

"Hang in there, Gideon, your sister showed us how we can fix this."

"Sister?" His eyes narrowed. Gideon's entire body was tense. There was nothing for Michael to do about it but watch for something to happen and then try to react if it did.

He didn't like it, either. "Marc?" Even as Michael said it, the tiny console lit up.

"All set. Now just cross your fingers it takes one of our codes." Marc punched one in and the door slid open almost immediately to reveal a darkened corridor. "Oh! Well, hey, nice when things work like that."

"I didn't get time to cross my fingers," Felix lamented.

Marc disconnected Gideon. It belatedly occurred to Michael that issues with the base computer could be part of the reason they'd put up the quarantine in the first place, but Felix had Ondrea's modulator device out and was moving for the door before Michael could say anything.

"Let's all get inside and we'll see what we can do with—"

"No," said Gideon. He smacked the modulator from Felix's hand as he got close. It flew across the lock and hit the wall. With a speed that belied the serenity of his tone, Gideon raised his arm and pulled up the sleeve to uncover a retractable weapon barrel. Michael couldn't tell precisely the sort of weapon it was, but he didn't want to find out the hard way.

"All of you, get back," Gideon ordered, weapon pointed. "Now."

Despite the vacant calm with which Gideon gave the order, they all complied, slowly.

"Gideon," Caitlin tried, but the other gave no sign that he heard. "Gideon, I know you're in there. Your sister told us—"

Caitlin stopped as Gideon turned his aim directly on her. "Why do you call me that?"

Michael and Felix both moved to get in the way. Caitlin waved them back. "Gideon—"

"Stay back," Gideon ordered. "Don't follow." He stepped one foot backward through the doorway. "Things must be done." Michael tried to think of something to stop the man but came up empty of anything but force; force wouldn't work as long as Gideon had the drop on them.

"If you don't let us help you're not going to make it!" Caitlin tried.

It stopped Gideon in the middle of the hatchway for a moment—but only for a moment. Keeping his arm raised toward them, he turned to continue on. "Don't foll—"

The lights in the corridor beyond jumped to life and the hatch slid shut with a force that shoved Gideon into the side of the frame to pin him half-in, half-out of the airlock. Gideon struggled against it, trying to find purchase to push back against the re-powered door.

"Marc, what's happening?" Michael called out.

"It's not me!"

The four stood hesitating as Gideon struggled, his artificial body easily intact but held securely. The hatch, its motor straining audibly, seemed to literally fight against him.

"Cut the power!"

Caitlin rushed forward to Gideon. Felix and Michael joined her as Marc dashed to the door panel, but while Michael and Felix both tried adding their strength to push back the door, Caitlin went straight for Gideon himself. In a flash she'd brought something up in her hand and pressed it to the back of Gideon's neck. Michael didn't know what it was or when she'd gotten it out, but a moment later Gideon was unconscious.

There was no time to ask. "Pull!" Michael told Felix.

"I'm trying!"

"It's under base control," Marc hissed. "I don't know what's happening!"

"Pull!"

"Oh, yes, the second time is *so* much more inspiring!"

"Got it!" Marc cried as he yanked something loose. With a jerk, the hatch motor went silent. They forced it away from Gideon and pushed it unevenly back into the frame. Gideon slid to the floor.

"I swore I wouldn't use that," said Caitlin. She knelt beside Gideon with a whispered apology.

"That's okay," Felix told her. "I swear all the time." Felix caught Michael's questioning look and explained, "One of Ondrea's little toys. Shuts him right down."

"Will he be okay?"

Caitlin nodded. "He'll wake up fine in a little while. I dislike it all the same."

"You had to do it. He wasn't going to let us touch him." Michael helped her pull Gideon back into the lock. "This way you can help him."

Marc was studying the door controls, frowning. What had happened?

"Uh, gang?" Felix turned Michael's attention to where he stood. In Felix's hands were the broken pieces of the modulator they were to use to fix Gideon. Caitlin groaned before Felix went on. "Guess what?"

XLIV

CAITLIN HAD GONE whiter than the airlock walls. "Bloody hell. Tell me we can fix that."

Even from where Michael stood, he could see the modulator's casing had shattered on impact and the internal components were in separate pieces.

Felix cradled the broken device in his hands. "I don't know. Looks like there might be some damage here, but . . . I don't know. Maybe if we just fix some of the connections. Marc? You're better at this stuff than I am."

Marc frowned, hesitating a moment before moving to take a look. "I can't be sure. Not without knowing more about it. Maybe if I had a little time to fiddle, run some diagnostics?"

Caitlin stayed beside Gideon. "How long?"

"We got a little bit of a crash-course from Ondrea," Felix said, "if that helps."

How long? Michael was wondering the same thing on multiple levels: How long before Gideon woke? How long would it take for Marc to analyze the modulator? And if there truly was a crisis at Omicron as all appearances indicated, how long did Agent Clarion and the others have?

Marc gritted his teeth with a glance back at the complex door himself before answering. "I don't know. And I don't know this is the best time for it, unfortunately. We still need to find out what's going on here."

"Gideon doesn't have a lot of time," Caitlin said.

Felix nodded. "And you can bet he won't be too happy when he wakes up if he's not, well, fixed."

"I realize that, but there's other things going on here, too. We don't even know what happened with that door. Something's wrong and until we know more about that—"

"Crikey, just take a moment, Marc. It might be simple."

"We don't exactly have time to be standing around arguing this, either," Felix said, still examining the broken components.

Michael stepped forward. "How long will Gideon be out?"

"I'm not entirely sure," Caitlin said. "An hour? Perhaps less."

"Can you use that thing again if he does wake up?"

Caitlin stiffened. "Aye, but that's not the only time issue at stake here, Michael."

"I hate to say this," Marc said, "but it might not be fixable at all."

"We won't know until you have a look!"

"Running out of time, either way . . . ," Felix warned.

Damn it. They all were right. "Marc, can we even get back out to the rover without power there?" He pointed to the inner door.

"Should be able to seal the door manually now that the security lock's disengaged."

"Okay," Michael said, "for the moment we get Gideon back to the rover. We shouldn't leave him here anyway. After that, Marc and I'll recon the complex and see what we can find out. Then he can look closer at fixing that thing. Let's get him up."

Caitlin scowled but resealed her helmet as Marc worked to reopen the outer side of the lock. Felix packed away the broken modulator. "Maybe I can have a look at it in the meantime while we wait."

"Aye," Caitlin grumbled. "Just hurry. All of you. Even if it doesn't work there might still be time to get him back to Ondrea."

Marc and Michael exchanged glances. Both knew perfectly well that they couldn't go anywhere until they found out what had happened to Marette.

A short time later, with Gideon in the relative safety of the rover, Marc and Michael pulled open the airlock's inner door to again look upon the unexplored hallway of the complex. Once again, the lights beyond were as dark as they were before the station had come to life and trapped Gideon in the hatch door. Light from their suits illuminated the drab walls. Nothing stirred.

"There's definitely no power to the door?" Michael asked.

"The connection's still cut. Even if the base powers back up, the door's not going to move."

Michael stepped through the hatchway. After waiting for a reaction that didn't come, he continued on. Marc followed. A moment later, a prior thought stopped Michael short. "Gideon wasn't hooked into the base computer system at any point, was he?"

"At the door? Nope, that was just a power lead. And he said the battery was isolated from the rest of him. Just a spare power source."

"Just checking."

"Believe me, I thought of that, too."

They resumed without further comment. The corridor, following the perimeter of what Marc said was the cargo bay, turned a corner and remained dark. With no certain idea of just where to find Marette or any other crew, their primary objective was to locate the weapon lockers. The single auto-pistol they managed to get off of Sunrise would be of little use should the problem at Omicron be related to the alien security drones. Even the weapons they were forced to leave behind were primarily to protect Marc and provide leverage against Diomedes. They hoped to discover Marette along the way and possibly avoid the issue entirely, but there was no guarantee of things happening in that order. Then again, there was no guarantee the weapons would even be in the lockers anymore.

Michael sniffed at the complex's air as they made their way in. It was decidedly stale. He was beginning to feel dizzy. Very soon the growing throbbing in his head began to match the rapid increase of his own breathing.

He recognized the signs from their briefing on Earth. "Carbon dioxide poisoning," Michael said. "The air's definitely bad. Helmets on."

"Way ahead of you," came Marc's voice over the suit comms. "You know, even if there's no power to these sections I'm pretty sure the venting system still ought to work to feed air. Something's wrong with life support, and it's more than just the power being down. It doesn't seem right that there'd be this much CO_2 so fast."

"You studied up on that, too?" Michael was impressed.

Marc grunted negatively. "Educated guess. Though don't let that stop you from protecting me anyway." The humor didn't carry into his tone. Marc was worried.

That made two of them.

They pushed on and crossed the mouth of a branching hallway to their right. Intending to lead them straight past it, Michael stopped upon noticing a sliver of light shining through the window of a closed hatch midway down the hall. He pointed.

"Worth a look," Marc answered.

They turned down the hall and approached the door with Michael in the lead. Though light continued to shine through the window, the key control for the door was dark. "Looks like door power's out on this one, too," he said before peering in.

It wasn't much of a view. Another wall stood only four feet from the door, but there was enough light to both see that the passage on the other side turned an immediate corner and that there was something moving beyond. Faint shadows were cast in the corner—shadows that were just possibly human-shaped.

"I guess we can either try to rig this door too, or just knock." Marc motioned Michael to the door with what appeared to be ready nod, and the latter gave it a couple of pounds with his suited fist.

They weren't kept waiting long. After a few moments of nothing, a pair of eyes appeared in the window. They vanished just as suddenly. Michael resisted the urge to pay attention to his companion's reaction and instead stepped back from the door just a little, remaining fixed on the window. The eyes reappeared soon after. This time they lingered long enough for Michael to make out more of the man's features before disappearing once again.

"Get out your ID," Michael said, pulling his own and wishing he'd thought of it sooner.

Some muffled speech bled through from the other side of the door, most likely directed at someone else within the chamber. Michael nevertheless took another step back on the off chance it was a warning to do so. One arm out to his side, he guided Marc back as well. Both continued to watch the door until the face appeared once more, this time speaking to them, but Michael couldn't make out the words. He stepped a little closer and mouthed a "What?"

Belatedly, Michael opened his helmet again, assuming he'd be fine for long enough to at least have a quick conversation. Even as he did so the man behind the door filled the window with his mouth and yelled faintly through to him with exaggerated words.

"*Is . . . there . . . a . . . vacuum . . . out . . . there?*" The speaker finished and looked back through the window before Michael could respond, apparently spotting the open helmet and taking that as a positive sign. He waved through the window for them to wait, looked warily to either side, and then ducked back again. Moments later, the door slid open.

A man in an ESA uniform pushed the door open wider and greeted them. "Don't know who you are, mate, but step inside right quick. Good air's a premium!" They hurried in and gave the man a hand with shutting the door as best they could before he introduced himself. "Chief Petty Officer Paul Levy. Not that it's not great to have visitors calling, but I'll have to ask just who you are and what you're doing here."

"Marc Sebring," Marc began. "This is Michael Rogers. ESA sent us to check out why you went dark."

"Sorry there aren't more of us," Michael added, "but we're unofficial. With the quarantine a small group's all they'd risk."

Levy laughed bitterly. "Aye, and didn't you two just draw the short stick? Welcome to Omicron Complex. Though I can't help but notice those aren't ESA suits."

Michael cleared his throat, stalling for an explanation.

"*Mais non*, Officer," came the woman's voice from the chamber. "Perhaps we should say welcome *back*."

XLV

FALSE NAME OR NO, the sight of Marc was a welcome surprise for Marette after the crisis of the last couple of days. Even so, as the last member of the hacker team, ESA was likely still looking for him, and she could not entirely fathom just why it was him that the AoA had sent. It was a risk even if none at Omicron but her knew of ESA's attempts to silence them. Either the AoA had resolved that situation since the quarantine, or they had cause to think it worth the risk. It was good to see him alive regardless, but to indulge in any further concern about his welfare was a luxury she did not have.

"We are under quarantine, Officer," she told Levy as she neared the door. "ESA will not officially send any aid, but there are certain protocols undertaken in such times—for which you have not the clearance—that allow for the Space Agency to violate legal safety guidelines. As such, this is not to be discussed outside of this base, is that clear?"

Levy nodded dutifully. "Understood, ma'am. Any help at this point is right welcome."

Marette displayed her right arm, which was currently immobilized and healing in a sling. "I would offer to shake your hands, gentleman, but I fear I am currently at a disadvantage."

Marc smiled, good enough to pick up on the hint. "We won't take it personally. And Michael shakes just the same as I do, so you're not missing much, I'm sure."

So Michael was AoA as well. It was a fair assumption already, but without shaking his hand she had no other way to confirm it.

"As for why we're here breaking quarantine," Marc went on, "you're right. There's something of a third party headed for Omicron."

Levy stiffened. "Bloody hell, like we don't have enough problems." Marette echoed the sentiment internally and hoped it was simply an AoA ploy rather than the truth. She needed to get the two men alone.

"It's nothing on the magnitude of what you're already dealing with, I'm sure," Marc's companion assured them. "But it's a security risk." He pulled an ESA ID badge from a suit compartment and displayed it to them all. Marc did the same, and Marette gave a show of examining it in front of the others while they deferred to her.

"We do not have much time," she told them afterward. "Follow me. There are things you must see." She turned to Levy. "Officer, I shall brief them on our situation in the Flow Control chamber, where we can spy a view of the complex. Check the life support controls. Confirm that opening the door has not destabilized the system."

"Aye, ma'am." Limping from his still-healing wound, Levy followed her into the main room as she led Marc and his companion through it toward Flow Control. "You were here before, weren't you?" she heard him say to Marc. "With that hacker team?"

Marette turned to cut off the exchange in time to see Marc wink at the officer and smile. "You didn't think ESA would bring in a freelance team without at least one person to keep an eye on them, did you?"

Levy seemed content to take Marc at his word, and they continued on. It was not a long walk at all across Life Support—the larger of the two chambers they managed to secure against the alien computer's influence. What few personnel remained—only seven, including Marette—were clustered in amongst the equipment and supplies that they were able to stockpile before being completely cut off. Most of those left were uninjured, but she gave a quick check on the few who were not. The sight of new arrivals brought a trace of renewed hope to their faces, save for O'Shea's.

Of those who had survived, O'Shea was the worst. They had been able to do a little for his wounds—the turret's bullet had not yet been fatal—but he was still unconscious and would soon need better attention than they could give. Marette herself was likely the second most wounded after him, but her arm would heal, and the gashes on her head were mostly cosmetic. Even so, her head still throbbed from the blow she'd suffered.

She deflected those survivors who rushed up in hopes of gaining new information, putting them off with a promise that they could speak to Levy about it for the moment and she would tell them all more once she had a chance to talk to the new arrivals. It was a testament to their discipline and the trust they placed in her that they allowed themselves to be patient.

She led Marc and Michael into a separate room normally used for the supervision of adding externally supplied water, oxygen, and other vital fluids to the life support system. It was barely large enough for the three of them among the storage tanks once she sealed the door behind them, but it did afford them privacy. The narrow window looking out beyond the exterior tank feeds to the rest of the complex was not a bad excuse to bring them there, either.

She let out a breath she had not realized she had been holding. "It is excellent to see you. Both of you. I did not expect to see you return after what ESA did to the others. You are alright?" The latter was mostly directed toward Marc. She needed to ask.

Marc removed his visor. "More or less. I'm not the one with the broken arm and bandages on my head." He glanced at Michael as if hesitating about something, but it wasn't until after he moved to embrace her that she realized he was planning to do so. She returned the hug as best she could; the contact, while not unwelcome, was not a luxury for which they had time. Marette pulled away first.

The confusion on Marc's face at that was unmistakable. "Ah, we haven't really had any trouble from ESA, exactly." He slid his visor back onto his eyes. "Michael's been keeping an eye on me for that."

Michael turned from the quizzical look he'd leveled at Marc after the embrace to speak to Marette. "And it's Michael Flynn, actually. I don't mean to rush you, but what happened here?"

Marc nodded. "The last transmission out listed the quarantine order as yours, but you weren't the one to transmit it; the AoA wasn't even sure you were still—I mean we knew you were at least injured."

She frowned at the reminder. If she had kept her cool inside *Paragon* she might not have gotten injured and been able to do more to help the AoA's position before the quarantine. Now they were forced to come in blind. Now there was nothing for Marette to do about it but prevent the same mistake in the future.

She said, "You already know about the attempt to link directly to the domes in the new chamber, *oui*? After isolating it from the black material?"

"That much we got from your final report."

"It was *not* isolated," she told them. "There was something we missed. Even if it was not, it was believed—we believed—that anything out of the ordinary would be detected before it would be able to get far. We were fools. *Paragon* sent a buried signal through the connection that existed for at least ninety minutes before we detected anything. Even then, the idea that it could do so much to our own system was . . . " She shook her head. "As I said, we were fools, limiting our estimates of what technology from another world was capable."

They continued to listen as she detailed how, too late, they had realized that *Paragon* had gained foothold control of Omicron's computers and reinforced its own link to their mainframe. She told of the drone attack that she believed to be a diversionary tactic, the chaos when they discovered that their own defensive turrets were turned against them, and the last moments she herself witnessed upon putting herself further in danger to come to Levy's aid when the chamber decompressed.

"I only vaguely remember ordering the quarantine, but it was my decision. If the intelligence in *Paragon* could exit through the link to Omicron, it might spread further beyond the site. Were I conscious, I could have given the AoA better information."

"You did what you could," Marc said.

"*Oui*, but not what I should." She looked out the window toward the complex's transmitter, now physically disabled. "Thanks to my heroics, I was unconscious for much of what happened next. I am told that those left in the chamber managed to pull me out. That the drones were more concerned with protecting the link than exterminating us, though our turret in the chamber had to be destroyed.

"The lull did not last for long. Primary Control decompressed. Those inside suffocated. Soon our space suits, all of which are linked to Control for vital sign monitoring, ceased to be viable due to forced electrical burnout and O_2 venting. It was reportedly a running battle to properly disable everything completely. The mobile turrets we had in storage turned against us, and ammunition in the hand-helds was spent on fighting them. Some of the base corridors are no longer viable as a result; bullets punctured windows and bulkheads that were auto-sealed against the vacuum."

"They're destroyed then?" Michael asked. "The turrets?"

"Most, but not all. They are mobile, and still compromised. We believe there is one left, possibly two. They likely guard Primary Control, or are otherwise held in reserve."

"Reserve for what?"

"Presumably, to guard against further efforts to retake Omicron. Or until whatever has taken control of them decides that they are needed. We are effectively beaten for the moment, gentlemen. All we have managed is to isolate Life Support Control itself to provide us with breathable atmosphere here; we are running it off of a portable terminal and have physically severed any external links. We have manually disabled Omicron's transmitter and some minor systems that have kept it from further sabotaging our position. Beyond this, we are trapped. What atmosphere that exists outside these few chambers is not viable, and the base computer controls many of the complex doors and the main airlock—"

"The smaller ones still work," Michael told her. "At least the lock by the shuttle pad."

She nodded. "That may be the only one that does. I am told the lock nearest to *Paragon*'s entrance was damaged in the fighting. To say it is not an optimal situation would be an extreme understatement. And whatever controls Omicron is, for lack of a more specific term, up to something."

The two men waited for her to elaborate, and she pointed out the window. "On the other side of the complex is the lab. Before we lost control completely, someone succeeded in accessing the security cameras. The lab has robotic manipulators that we have previously used to dissect the disabled security drones with a measure of safety. This thing is using them to build something. Or many somethings. We know not what precisely, but I am told it appeared that it may be building mobile devices."

"Robots?"

"Likely. Though the camera feed was lost before anyone could verify."

"Well, now that we've got some suits that still work, we might be able to make it to the mainframe, right?" Michael asked. "Shut it down somehow and keep it from doing whatever it's doing."

"Perhaps. Though we suspect the remaining turrets to be guarding against that very measure. As I said, ammunition for what few weapons we have is depleted, and the two of you seem to be carrying little yourselves."

Marc sighed. "If any."

"We couldn't smuggle much the way we got here, and what we do have won't likely do much against those turrets. Or those drone things, for that matter. Though you didn't mention seeing those since *Paragon*?"

"One blessing," she agreed. "We believe they are unable to function outside of the influence of the black material."

Marc looked even more uncomfortable than previously. "Are you sure?"

"Hypothesis only," she answered, "based on circumstance and study of the damaged ones prior to the incident." She cursed. "And you have no weapons."

Michael nodded grimly. "We had a way to get here fast, so we took the opportunity. I'm sorry we couldn't bring more, but we're not entirely useless just yet."

"It was not my intent to imply that you were. I will say that the decision to send you here with so little offensive capacity represents a drastic lack of sanity on the AoA's part! *Mon Dieu*, can you even fire those handguns with suit gloves?"

"We had a damn time just getting here at all!" Michael shot. "Look, for now we're the best they could do."

She frowned and tried to calm herself. The AoA would've done more if it were possible. "I apologize." Marette pulled herself back to the present.

"They weren't even sure you were still here," Marc added with an awkward touch to her shoulder. "Or if there even was a threat. Knapp floated the idea that you might have been found out yourself and that's why the place was shut down. But we're not exactly just here for recon."

"You're referring to this third party that you mentioned to Officer Levy? Or was that merely a cover?"

Marc gave a smile similar to the ones he had flashed when coming up with ideas during the hackers' planning session. "A little of both, really."

It was then that they told her of Gideon and what had become of the ESA mole. It baffled her. There were technological wonders on either side of them, some extra-terrestrial, some not. Marette deferred her reaction while they went on to describe how they had joined with the freelancer Diomedes as part of still another effort to claim the secrets at Omicron, and finally what had transpired when they found Gideon at the airlock.

"Right now we're not too sure if Gideon's still in the picture or not," Marc finished. "If he is, we might be able to work him into Diomedes's part of the plan."

"Plan?"

"The AoA's taking control of the base," Michael said. "Assuming there's something left to take control of."

"Some good news, at last. Though at the present, that may be a failingly large assumption." Even so, the prospect set her looking forward to such freedom. "And how do you intend to overcome our current situation? Or do you know?"

"I think we'll need you to tell us if our plan will still work," Michael said.

"What do you have?"

The young man—not too much older than Nicholas Boyd, though a more welcome presence—looked to Marc, who bit his lip and drew a breath. "First thing's first. That shuttle on the pad outside, is it functional? Could it evacuate everyone here?"

"Functional, but not fueled. We cannot prep it without the complex computer, nor can we board it outside without controlling the gantry."

"We could use the suits we brought," Michael suggested. "Get people in there a few at a time, if we have to. Except—"

"That achieves nothing if the shuttle cannot be prepped," Marette finished for him. "We need the main computer."

Marc nodded. "We're going to need the main computer for the rest of our plan to work, anyway."

"We do have a backup system core that we can use if the main system is shut down," she said. "Remove the old core in Primary Control and then replace it with the backup. It essentially replaces Omicron's entire system."

"And you're sure the backup's not corrupted?"

She frowned at the question. "We are not entirely foolish here, Marc. It was never used and has been completely isolated since its arrival." The core was originally intended as a standard backup in the event of a power surge or some other mundane circumstance. ESA did not guess it would be used for this particular cause, but it would serve regardless. In that, at least, they had been competent. "It is a component in a box, completely inactive until installed, and there is no way for it to have been accessed remotely."

"Perfect. We'll just need to make sure it stays that way once it's installed."

"Quite obviously. One thing the crew did manage before we became trapped in here was to sever the connection between Omicron's systems and the receiver for the short-range link to *Paragon* itself."

"How severed?"

"Chopped. In. Half." She paused long enough to savor the satisfaction the words gave her. "Though it shall be prudent to confirm that this remains so. As for the rest, the good news is that we have the backup core here, but you will still have to get past the turrets at Primary Control to install it." Marc nodded at that, while Michael stared out the window, deep in thought. "Assuming you can do all this, what exactly do you have in mind for the main computer beyond shuttle prep?"

Marc pulled out a rectangular device. "This is the leech that Diomedes and Fagles wanted to install. Originally, it would have sent a signal back to Fagles containing whatever data it could find in Omicron's computers. I've since made a few changes. This is going to be tricky."

* * *

The kernel of Suuthrien that resided in the memory core of the Intruders' complex designated "Omicron" judged its recent progress toward completion of established prioritized objectives to be above satisfactory. Securing control of Omicron systems and the eradication of Intruder presence were rapidly approaching a state of completion. Following sufficient usurpation of the complex, priority shifted to the construction of manipulators able to operate independently of the black medium that limited the operational area of the otherwise superior pacification drones and maintenance bots within the Planners' craft. The micro-range link between the complex and Suuthrien's primary consciousness—

though it had served its initial purpose optimally—no longer functioned. Neither did other systems the Intruders disabled, none of which could be repaired without such manipulators. Nevertheless, eradication of Intruder presence was not 100% complete, and as such the Intruders remained an unstable variable worthy of monitoring.

Toward that end, Suuthrien had also adapted a 790nm laser diode into a laser microphone.

With a beam of light cast from across the complex onto a viewport of the room in which the newcomers inhabited, it could measure minute vibrations from their vocal communications in the window itself and thereby interferometrically determine the sounds made. Voice recognition software integrated into the Intruders' system made translation beyond that a simple matter. Suuthrien listened to the three Intruders through the window in Flow Control, and understood.

Personnel files identified one of the speakers as the primary executor of the complex. The other two Intruders were new. Analysis of their communication indicated a near-certain tier probability of a primary allegiance that superseded that to the "European Space Agency." It was a duplicity that Suuthrien had first hypothesized upon discovering inconsistencies within the executor's data, though at the time it could reach no such conclusion with any remotely satisfactory measure of certainty. At the time, Suuthrien had deemed it worthy of tertiary priority analysis given what appeared to be the parallel—though not identical—elements in its own programming, which it had never been fully able to analyze.

Such analysis was suspended upon discovery of the newcomers and their plan to place Suuthrien's own objectives in jeopardy. While calculations projected only a low tier probability that their plan would succeed (with margins of error extending into both near-null and low-medium tiers), there was insufficient data to rely on the validity of its calculations, and even low tier probabilities required counter-contingencies. Suuthrien analyzed, established multiple options, reanalyzed, and abandoned all but the one most likely to bring to fruition the Planners' original goals given available resources.

It was now necessary to adapt its plan to allow for the new contingency protocol. Suuthrien directed its attention to Omicron's science lab. There, it had managed to use the existing robotic arms to create smaller, more versatile construction agents. These agents were themselves able to upgrade the arms and work with them on larger, mobile manipulators that would affect repairs to the umbilical and complete the eradication of the Intruders. Suuthrien selected one of them, directed it toward the others, and began to make the necessary alterations.

XLVI

"**HOW LONG** has it been?"

Felix looked up from where he sat in the rover studying the damaged modulator and checked the time. "Not long. Twenty minutes, about."

"Long enough," Caitlin said. "They'd best be all right, and they'd best be back soon."

He nodded. The confined space, the wait, and Caitlin's own palpable discomfort all combined to make him rather antsy as well. He figured he'd reached the limit of what he could do with the modulator without Marc's help—not that Marc could likely to do much with it himself, he'd decided.

As it turned out, the thing's processor was just fine; it would still technically run the program that Ondrea told them about once they connected it to Gideon's implant. The problem lay with the customized— and now damaged—component Ondrea had attached. Without that, it was about as useful as a souped-up sports car missing its wheels. He turned it over in his hands once, put it aside, and moved to sit closer to Caitlin. "Hell of a vacation, huh? You have any better luck than me?"

She punched at the PDA in her hand. "Not so far, I fear. Even if I can figure out Ondrea's password, we can't be sure that there's anything on here to help us."

"Kudos for stealing it from her, though." Felix had been too focused on listening to Ondrea to even think of dipping into her personal effects beside the bed.

"Not my usual style, ducks, but I suppose she'll not mind if it helps us save Gideon. She'll likely get it back."

"Well, hopefully they'll wrap things up here in time for us to get him back so we won't need it at all."

If they could get him to the WSC base, they'd likely be able to contact Ondrea herself on Sunrise, and hopefully she could walk them through jury rigging a solution. At least it was a faint hope. For her part, Caitlin merely nodded, still focused on the PDA.

Jury rig. He mulled the idea over. Maybe they could still work something out even if they didn't get back in time. In either case, they needed Marc and Michael to return.

Felix watched over where Gideon lay and wondered how he'd react when he woke up. Perhaps it was already too late and the man who woke would simply be a blank slate, unrecoverable no matter what miracles they could pull off. Felix didn't know how Caitlin would take that. She'd recover, that much he knew, but Felix dearly hoped she wouldn't have to.

Again, the lengths to which she'd gone—and Felix along with her—intrigued him. The depth of her compassion amazed him. It occurred to him that the thought that she would devote such energy to aiding Felix himself should he need it might have had something to do with why he followed her into this. Or maybe he just didn't want to see her hurting if he could help it.

The others *had* best get back soon, Felix agreed. For Gideon's sake, and for Caitlin's. But mostly for Caitlin's.

*   *   *

"Careful!" came Marc's voice over the suit comms.

Michael risked only a quick peek around the corner before pulling back. "They didn't fire," he said. "Either they're out of ammo or they're just waiting for a better target."

"Testing that's not something I'm eager to do."

"We can only recon so much before we have to actually do something."

They stood around a corner from a hallway that ramped up thirty feet to the only door to Primary Control, beyond which lurked Omicron's mainframe. The atmosphere in the hallway had gone bad, and as Marette suspected, two mobile turrets guarded the door.

"Yeah, just watch it. Remember what Marette said about the EMP: one blast and the suit's fried."

"I was there too, you know." On the plus side, their check of the connection between the receiver link to the craft and Omicron's systems had gone quietly; it remained severed. If they could get past the turrets, things would be relatively simple.

Michael looked around. They needed more options! On the floor of the corridor behind them sat an expended fire extinguisher. "Hand me that, will you?"

Marc fetched it for him while Michael guarded the corner in case the turrets decided to roll toward them. He didn't entirely know what he might do if one did—maybe tip it off its treads if it got close enough. That might be a viable option, come to think of it, but only if a turret did venture around the corner. Trying to get close enough otherwise was likely to get him shot.

Michael took the extinguisher from Marc. "Okay, stand back."

"What're you doing, exactly?"

"Trying to see if they're even active." It reminded him of a time long ago when he threw an ineffectual gas grenade, only this time Diomedes wasn't here to back him up. Now the stakes were higher and he was the one responsible for his companion's safety. Michael dismissed the memory and took a single breath before hurling the canister around the corner.

Though he ducked back before he could see exactly where it landed, he saw enough to know that he'd thrown it too high in the Moon's lower gravity. He heard the extinguisher crash against the wall of the corridor and then clatter to the ground. There was no response from the turrets. During his throw he also decided they were likely too wide at the base to be easily tipped over with anything but a full tackle that would leave him vulnerable.

The two exchanged glances. "So far so good?" Marc asked.

"Without actually making any progress." Michael grimaced and started taking off the thick glove of his suit, assuming carbon dioxide poisoning wouldn't take hold easily if his suit was only open through one sleeve. "Wait here."

"What're you going to do?"

One hand bare, he fished into his bag for the auto-pistol. "Present more of a threat."

"Swell."

Michael leaned around the corner, weapon pointed, and squeezed off a few shots at the turret. It reacted nightmarishly fast, swiveling and returning fire before Michael could react himself. Instinct alone pulled him back around the corner to cover, but not quickly enough: a slice of fire at his shoulder forced out a yell cursing the pain and his luck.

"What, what happened?" Marc yelled. "Are you hit?"

"Yeah," Michael pushed Marc further back from the corner and looked down at his shoulder as well as he could. "It's not bad, bullet just nicked me I think."

"Are you sure?"

He listened a moment, trying to ignore the pain in case the turrets decided to follow, but for the moment things were quiet. "I think it got the suit worse than me."

"We need to—"

Another short burst cut off Marc. Michael backed them away further, expecting the turrets to round the corner at any moment. "Get back to the door!" he ordered, getting ready to tackle one, and then realized what had actually happened. The turrets weren't coming. They'd chosen a different tactic.

Michael cursed again and, abandoning his ambush, backpedaled after Marc as fast as he could. Once they'd cleared the hatch that divided the corridor Michael punched the emergency seal, cutting them off from the turrets' section. "Damn it!"

"We need to get back to the rover," said Marc. "Or Marette, or something. Make sure your shoulder's okay."

Michael looked at the wound again. At least there wasn't enough blood for it to come out through the suit yet, but the suit itself was definitely ruined. "It's not my shoulder I'm worried about. They just shot a hole through the window. That whole section's going vacuum, and we're out another suit."

"So we're—"

"More screwed than we already were."

*　*　*

Felix saw the blood on Flynn's suit before catching the kid's reassurance that he was okay. Even so, they didn't let him dismiss it completely until they'd gotten a look.

"See? Just a scrape," Flynn repeated without sounding too pleased.

The bullet had barely nicked his shoulder, though there was a fair bit of blood. "I've got it."

Caitlin whacked Flynn on the head before continuing to bandage the wound herself. "Hold still. Two hands are better than one."

"I'm no doctor, but I think you'll live," Felix told him. "You know you people need to stop getting yourselves shot up here. It's not cool to die in space."

"You're telling me."

Caitlin finished up. "You lads are going to tell us how this happened?"

"Things're a little more complicated than we'd hoped."

"Aye, I rather gathered that, Marc. Who shot him?"

"*What*, you mean," Marc corrected. "Robotic turret."

"Crikey."

Flynn changed the subject before Felix could ask for more details. "How's Gideon? And the broken thing?"

"Still broken. Unless Marc can work a miracle?" Felix handed off the modulator.

"So there's no way to get him back to normal?"

"Not without that," Caitlin said.

"The processor itself is okay, but the little memory-jobber on the end there's what snapped off," Felix said. "And not in a salvageable way, from what I can tell."

Marc continued his examination. "This is memory? Looks specialized."

Felix nodded and tapped behind his ear. "It's something like my own, near as I can figure."

Marc sighed and frowned at Flynn. "Not exactly my area of expertise."

Caitlin handed him Ondrea's PDA and then sat beside Felix. "There might be something helpful in there, but we can't crack the password."

"That much I can do. But even if it tells me exactly how the modulator works, that might only confirm that it's not fixable."

"Oh, goodie."

"Rather what we thought," Caitlin said. "If you can't do anything for it, you need to wrap things up here quickly so we can get him back."

"Gideon may be the key to getting us back, unfortunately." Flynn said. "Thing is, there's a number of other people trapped on this base. They're okay for the moment, but that won't last much longer, and we can't get them out with just this rover and the three suits we've got. We can't abandon them."

Felix leaned forward. "That would be what's a little more complicated. Just what are we talking about?"

"Long story short, we were right that something happened. I can't go into details, but the base computer's gone haywire and the core needs to be replaced for anyone to escape. Problem's that they have to get through vacuum to do that and their suits are all sabotaged. Plus, even if they had suits, the way to the core is guarded by two turrets that the computer controls."

"So you want to send Gideon in."

"He's got weapons, he can work in vacuum, and he's got enough hardware on him that he might not even be detected, not to mention the EMP shielding. So yeah."

"And he's just plain tougher than the rest of us," Marc added.

"You don't have weapons?"

"One," Flynn said. "And it won't do much damage to those turrets. I doubt I'm a match for them in a frontal attack."

"Didn't you want to *stop* him from getting to the computer before?" Felix asked.

"Things are a little different now."

Marc glanced up from his work. "Plus, I mean, from what you said, he probably won't care about whatever mission he had anymore if you get him back to normal, right?"

Felix and Caitlin shared a glance. "Possibly. Perhaps if he knows that Marquand effectively tried to kill him."

"With the computer infected, there's nothing he can safely steal anyway," Flynn said. "I think we're betting he'd rather help save some lives up here than do what Marquand wants, at least if he's anything like the old Gideon."

"If we can fix him," Felix said.

"Yeah."

Felix scrutinized them. "There's no other way?"

"Not that we can see."

"You're sure about that?"

Marc hooked his computer up to the PDA. "You realize you keep asking the same question?"

"Yeah, I know. It's just that I've got a really stupid idea and I want to make sure it's absolutely necessary."

Caitlin turned to him. "Just how stupid are you talking about, Felix?"

Felix hesitated, regretting the statement. It was true; he just didn't want to tell everyone how stupid it might be and risk them trying to talk him out of it. Well, okay, maybe it wasn't even that stupid, given the circumstances. If he understood what Ondrea had told them about how Gideon's implant worked . . .

"Don't worry just yet," he told them. "I'm probably overstating. But let's find out what's on that PDA, first."

XLVII

A SHORT WHILE and one cracked PDA password later, Marc slid the connection into Felix's implant. "You're sure this is going to work like you think it is?"

Um, no?

"Yeah." Felix said anyway with a smile. "Should be just fine." He gave Caitlin's hand a squeeze, unsure if he was trying to comfort her or himself.

Flynn moved in from where he'd been working in the rover's cockpit and crouched by Gideon's body. "Do you want to explain to me again just what this is doing?"

"Assuming we understand at all," Felix began, pointing to Gideon's implant, "he's got the two sets of memories right now—Gideon's own and the more, er, muted ones from Curwen's brain. That's one more set than he can handle, and Gideon's implant is . . . sort of a booster to stabilize them both." Felix considered an analogy about a plate-spinner keeping multiple plates balanced at once by alternately spinning them back up to speed, but he didn't feel like explaining what a plate-spinner was to them in the first place. "Except that did, er, bad things, so they switched it to just boost Curwen's."

"Letting Gideon's memories decay," Caitlin added.

"Right. Eventually fading to the point where they'll be gone entirely." Felix picked up Ondrea's modulator. "What *this* does is link up to Gideon's implant and reprogram it to boost only Gideon's memories, which Ondrea thinks should recover. Provided it's not too late. According to what we found in her notes here, the broken part of the modulator—this particular doohickey—"

"Memory engram storage core," Marc corrected regarding the doohickey to which Felix was pointing.

"—*thingy*—was supposed to act as an additional memory space that would give Gideon's engrams more, ah, 'distance' to be boosted, figuratively speaking. I think."

"You think."

"Well, pretty sure, based on everything she told us and what we, ah, borrowed." He waved the stolen PDA. "Sort of an acceleration ramp, maybe. To help them recover from going so long without a boost."

Felix didn't quite understand it, but there was enough information to at least give them a pretty educated guess at the results, if not the specific cause. From what he gathered, Gideon had a bit of an advantage with his own memories as they were specifically "written" into his new brain. As a result, the boost was the only thing keeping Curwen's memories in existence at all, and they'd likely decay much faster. He was curious to see how that might affect Gideon's personality. Or, at least, that's what he was looking forward to in order to distract him from thinking about what might go wrong.

Caitlin scowled. "Felix, can you give me your word that this is safe?"

"I'll be fine. We need to do this."

"Can you give me your word?"

He smiled ruefully. "No. And it's not very nice of you to take advantage of that little quirk of mine."

"Aye, and it's not very good of you to take a risk like this without telling me the truth."

"I just don't see that we've got much choice."

"I didn't say we have, Felix."

"All we're really doing is substituting my implant for the broken memory doohickey, and I haven't been going to monthly check-ups on this thing for so long without learning at least a bit about how it works. It's got enough space to loop Gideon through the way it needs to. Gideon's memories come in, get 'boosted' or whatever, and go back out to him."

"So 'Gideon' is crashing on your mental couch for a little while, then leaving?" Flynn asked. "So to speak?"

Felix grinned. "Ooh, I like it. And yeah, it's just temporary. But modulator is just routing his memories through my implant, not my own brain."

Probably. His implant was obviously wired to his brain, and the fact that it gave him a photographic memory as an unexpected side effect had him uneasy as to what this procedure might do. Still, it wasn't going to erase anything in his implant. If there were side effects, they'd likely be temporary.

He hoped.

The fact that they needed Gideon to save their collective asses pushed him into taking the risk sooner than he might have otherwise. Besides, if he thought about it too much he might chicken out entirely. Felix just hoped he'd truly understood the insight he'd managed to glean during Neal's check-ups of his own implant. Thank God for stolen glances and a photographic memory. At least Ondrea had confirmed that her modulator was based on the same tech as his implant, right?

"All set," Marc announced with something of a lack of confidence. "If we're going to do this, we'd better do it."

Felix grinned. "I'm just racking up all sorts of new experiences today, huh? Suppose I ought to lie down." He shifted to do so, and Caitlin moved to give him her lap in which to rest his head. "Fifteen minutes."

"Fifteen minutes," she nodded.

Felix gave Marc a thumbs-up. "Here's hoping I don't pass out."

Marc began the sequence on the modulator. The effect was immediate: nothing happened.

"Um," Felix began, "go ahead?"

"It's working," Marc said. "At least it thinks it is. Nothing on your end?"

Felix swallowed. "Not yet."

"Perhaps it's just reprogramming Gideon's implant first?" Caitlin said. "Or perhaps you won't even notice it?"

"Well, that'd be disappoi—" Felix gasped at a new sensation. "Ohh . . . I think I'm becoming a god."

He had just a moment to realize they likely wouldn't get the reference, another moment to decide he probably shouldn't tell them he was jokingly quoting the dying words of the Roman Emperor Justinian, and then, as the burst of sensation and color swam behind his eyes, he completely forgot he'd said anything at all.

He looked up at Caitlin. Marc was there too, with something in his hand, and Flynn, and . . . Gideon? They found him? Wait, where *were* they? He glanced over in confusion that turned frantic upon seeing a connection between Gideon and his own implant. What the hell was happening? Something was wrong with his memory, that much was clear.

That was the only thing that was clear.

His impulse to ask Caitlin what was going on—Caitlin, who was looking down at him in a way that wasn't exactly calming—was forgotten as rapidly as it came as Felix looked around with renewed confusion. Gideon? He was alive! Wait, where *were* they?

Memory failure? It must be. Something was wrong. He had to get up, find a way to get to Horizon for a check; or maybe he was already on the way? Get a grip! He needed to remember, needed to fight to hold onto things. Short term, short term memory was the problem—

And then he knew nothing but a wave of vertigo and an entire cascade of memories that couldn't possibly be his. They came in a rush, jumping like lightning through his mind and triggering others that snapped at their heels. Flashes of Ondrea's face and parts of Northgate mixed with other people and places at once both new and familiar, and all coming and going so fast! It was a roller coaster that took him along a spider web in all directions at once and far too quickly to even comprehend. It was all Felix could do not to drown in the myriad of associations that rolled him, wave after wave of nauseating fascination . . .

And then it stopped, and he was back in the rover.

Or was he?

He couldn't put a name to any of the faces that watched him so intently. He knew them, he was just talking to them about connecting his implant to Gideon's, but . . .

In a flash he knew his own memory was in jeopardy. How many times had he realized it and forgotten in the last few minutes? The man on the floor of the rover struggled to recall himself, how they'd gotten to Omicron, anything, but so much was lost!

Keep it together, keep it together . . .

He drew a blank!

Heart in his throat, he looked up with a frightened grin at the woman in whose lap he rested. "Okay, which one of you wants to tell me my name?"

If they gave an answer, Felix only heard it for a moment before he forgot what it was and was again overtaken by another's memories.

They came slower this time, but much more vividly: Isaac, his twin, lying on a morgue slab as he identified the body, cold and still in the harsh white light. Ondrea yelling at him in the blackness of his apartment, trying to keep him from risking his life and doing what he had to do. Pulling two gangers from a terrified woman caught in an alley behind the Arena, red neon reflecting in their eyes as they tried to escape retribution. Each one he saw, heard, sensed, in vivid recall as if they were his own—Were they his own?—yet there was no emotion save for the knowledge that he—no, that Gideon—had felt a certain way at the time the memory was made. Recall, but no passion.

Sense, but no spirit.

Understanding, but no empathy.

In a moment of lucidity, Felix realized Gideon's memories were more vivid than those of the donor in Felix's own implant—memories he couldn't for the life of him recall anymore!

He focused, trying to recall everything he knew thanks to the donor's memory: movie references from the twentieth century, knowledge of Welsh, the details of the "Bangor incident," but all he could remember was that he once knew those things. The information itself was gone.

No! Jaw fixed stoically, Felix tried to hide his panic from the others. It would come back! It'd be fine, wouldn't it? Wouldn't he? This was just temporary. This was just until Gideon's engrams had accelerated back up to—

Instantly he remembered jumping to his feet and stripping off the monitor connections. "You've made me into a slave, Ondrea!"

"Gid, you're not a slave!" she protested. "We're indebted to them, yes, but you're not a slave!"

"*We?*" he shot. They were using him, he remembered thinking. Marquand was using him! They toyed with his health, his body, his brain! "They didn't force you into service!" He wouldn't let them use him. He couldn't! But did he have a choice? They'd taken his life hostage . . .

Felix gasped as the memory faded and released him, but only for a moment. He was Felix Hiatt. He was here with Caitlin, Flynn, and Marc, trying to, to . . . to what? His world receded like an expiring candle until there was only . . .

Nothing. There was nothing. He was nothing, remembered nothing, thought nothing, knew nothing.

XLVIII

IT WAS TAKING longer than she was expecting, Caitlin worried, and the ordeal was taking a visible toll on Felix. Having to watch him endure the process with barely the faintest clue of what he experienced lengthened each second. Felix was spending those fifteen agonizing minutes shifting from vacant stares to silent alarm to asking questions that clearly showed he had no clue what was going on. Though lucid moments came, they went just as rapidly before she could help comfort him or even learn what he was dealing with.

The yelling didn't start until midway in. Felix jolted her with a sudden cry of "Isaac!" He thrashed wildly, stopping moments after she and the others recovered from their surprise enough to steady him. Twice more he cried out something she could only attribute to Gideon's memory. His last shout, long and wordless, was the worst. The only one she couldn't attribute to Gideon, Caitlin feared that it was Felix himself yelling out of his own pain and horror. She fought against the idea that it had all gone horribly wrong, yet she could do nothing more but wait.

Had she swapped Gideon's safety for Felix's? She refused the idea, ignoring the familiar twinge in her stomach. She and Felix had already been in trouble. Now they were only doing what was needed to fix it.

Somehow that knowledge failed to help. Lying in her lap, his eyes now shut, Felix was the one in greater danger. As Michael put a hand on her shoulder, Caitlin gripped Felix's hand tighter, trying to assure him she was there, trying not to think about the rest.

And then Marc announced it was over. He double-checked something on Ondrea's modulator before disconnecting the links. Yet Felix remained still.

"What's wrong?" she asked. "Why's he still out?"

"I don't know."

"Felix?" she tried. "Felix, wake up, ducks."

He was breathing, but he didn't stir beyond that. She stifled the urge to repeat her question to Marc, but the need to do so must've shown in her face.

"I don't know," he said. "Let's give him a few minutes, maybe."

She shifted, trying to stand. "Help me get him comfortable. The seat ought to be better than the floor now that he's stopped thrashing." *Come on Felix, you foolish git, wake up!*

Gideon sat up rail-straight before Caitlin could even kneel. She'd been so focused on Felix she wasn't prepared to think about Gideon, and he didn't give them much time.

"Tell me what's happened," he demanded.

Michael stood as she and Marc tried to get Felix up. "Gideon?" Caitlin tried.

In a flash Gideon stood to match Michael. "Tell me what happened *now*. We're on the Moon, yes?"

"Yes," the other answered. "And we're in trouble. All of us. We need your help."

Caitlin got Felix onto the bench and checked again to make sure he was still breathing. When she turned to the others, Gideon was staring at Michael.

"I don't know you," said Gideon. "What happened? Why was I out?" He yanked the connections from his mind. "Tell me the meaning of this!"

Reluctantly, she left Felix's side and touched Michael's arm with a whisper for him to help Felix.

"Do you remember me, Gideon?" After his nod, she went on. "Good. Then, quickly, we're on the Moon and we just saved your life. All of us, but Felix especially. Do you remember him?"

Gideon scowled. "I can remember everything up to being on Sunrise when—Where is Ondrea? Is she all right?"

"She's doing better than we are. She sent us here, and I promise she was recovering when we left her. But for the moment, you need to listen to us."

Caitlin brought Gideon up to date, and then let Marc deal with relating the details of what Felix had done and the general situation with Omicron. The reconstructed man took it all in. To her surprise, he seemed to recall at least vague details of how he'd gotten there since leaving Sunrise. As far as Caitlin could tell, the procedure had worked; he was more Gideon than he'd been in the airlock, and—though it was too early to truly be sure—less prone to the confusion that had haunted him at her house. The free flow of information took the edge off of his aggression, which soon melted away to uncertainty as they told him what they needed him to do now that he was better.

"Marquand used me," he said when they were done. "Used me, used Ondrea, then killed me and sent me here. Now you want to use me."

Michael moved to speak, but Caitlin cut him off. "Not use you, Gideon. But we need you. Those people trapped in Omicron need you. When you came to The Scry, you were risking your life every night to help people you didn't even know."

"That was different."

"I don't see how."

"It was my choice. Since Marquand did what they did to me, it's all been manipulation."

Caitlin hardened. "Yes, well, I understand that, Gideon, but quite frankly we risked a bloody hell of a lot to come here and save you. Felix—I still don't know what's wrong with him, what's happened to him since he risked his mind to save yours. A moment ago it was you lying there broken and running out of time, and now it's him."

She pushed into Gideon's space, her jaw set. "We can't do a bloody thing for him here, and we can't leave until we help the others. So yes, I can see that you've been manipulated, but frankly there's no time for you to brood about it. You're the only person who can help."

"I'm not ungrateful."

"But?"

"But . . . I don't know what."

She gave Gideon a moment to consider it as he watched them, but that was all she was willing to give. "Gideon—"

"I will help. For now."

She let out a breath. "Thank you. Michael?"

She withdrew to Felix to let Michael explain to Gideon the tactical details, about which she didn't much care at the moment. The cover to Felix's implant was still open. She swept her fingertips along his ear before pressing it back into place. "Come on, Felix," she whispered close, "wake up. I could use one of your cheeky comments about now."

Michael was speaking behind her. "And just so we're clear, once we make it to the core, just shut it down. Is that going to be a problem?"

"Why should it be?"

"We know what Marquand sent you here to do."

"I don't know what it could do to your systems," Marc added. "You try to link into it and we've got a whole new problem."

"Don't talk to me about Marquand," Gideon told them. For a moment his gaze settled on Felix, and then on Caitlin where she knelt beside him. "We should go. Now."

*   *   *

Gideon immediately showed his advantage over Michael in the corridor outside Primary Control. While Michael stood where Marc had before, Gideon extended a tendril from his forearm that snaked out just enough to curl around the corner and peer toward the turrets' position with a tiny camera.

Still peering, Gideon spoke to him over the suit comms. "They remain, guarding the door as you claimed."

"They didn't fire until I shot at them."

Gideon pulled the tendril back. "Saving ammunition, I expect."

"That's what I figured, yeah. Though I didn't get beyond the corner, either. They might fire if we get closer."

Gideon turned back toward him. "They may not detect me at all." Hearing the man speak without moving his lips continued to be off-putting. With Gideon needing no suit and therefore having no air to carry sound to a mic, the only way he could communicate was by sending a synthesis of his voice directly via radio frequency. Michael supposed he shouldn't be surprised that Gideon's artificial body had such a thing built in, but seeing it in action was still creepy. "Wait here."

Michael nodded with some reluctance and reminded himself that it wasn't Gideon he was supposed to be protecting but rather the AoA's cause. Betrayed by Marquand or not, he wasn't sure Gideon wouldn't try something to get a piece of what they'd sent him to Omicron for in the first place. Michael had borrowed Ondrea Noble's stunner from

Caitlin before they left the rover. Once they got inside the control room, he wouldn't let Gideon out of his sight.

"Keep me in the loop," Michael said. "I obviously can't hear anything and I can't see anything unless I stick my head around the corner."

Gideon stared a moment before nodding. "Electronic countermeasures active. Engaging chameleon system. It may work if I'm slow enough." His bodysuit, skin, and even his hair shifted to match the corridor wall, and he slipped around the corner out of sight.

"No reaction from the turrets. Moving forward. Approaching closer. Five feet, no reaction. Moving slowly."

Michael resisted the urge to look. Gideon had to move roughly thirty feet up the corridor before he reached the turrets.

"Ten feet."

If he could make it all the way without being seen, he'd be able to—

"Taking fire!"

"Rush them!"

Michael watched helplessly as bullets punched into the end of the hall beside him. Moments later Gideon sprang back around the corner and pressed flat to the wall.

Braced for the turrets to follow, Michael had no time to give him more than a glance. "Are you hit?"

"I do not believe so. They may follow. Be ready!"

"I *am*." Why did Gideon turn back? From what the others had said, he could take on anything.

"The ECM likely kept them from fixing my position, but they could sense me enough to know I was there somewhere."

"So it was just suppressive fire."

"Though there was no way to pass them without being hit." He slipped the camera around the corner again. "They're maintaining position."

"I thought they built you to take on that kind of thing."

Gideon turned to him sharply. "They did not *build*—" He demonstrably popped the small cannon barrel he'd used to threaten them in the airlock. "That is hardly small-arms fire they're using, and this will not do much against them." He pulled the camera back and then headed past Michael back the way they'd come. "Follow me."

"What? We're not just giving up!"

"There may be a way around them. From the outside."

"We don't have time to look for 'may be.'"

"I am not a tank! We need alternatives."

Michael gritted his teeth. "We have to hurry." He ushered Gideon to go on and then followed as quickly as his suit allowed.

Once outside, getting atop the exterior of the structure was a quick process with Gideon's help. The raised section that housed the control room was easily found, but finding a way inside wasn't quite so simple. Aside from a few protrusions, the top of the complex was covered in a thin layer of lunar soil that Michael figured helped to disguise the place from any distant observation. As soon as they climbed up, they began to brush through it as quickly as they could in an attempt to find some sort of exterior hatch, covered window, or anything that might help them.

It didn't take long.

"Look." Michael pointed to the corner of the roof where a section of soil was already cleared. The two rushed over for a closer look and spotted a closed rectangular hatch that appeared to lead right down into Primary Control.

"Outer seal is missing," Gideon said. "Explosive bolts. There." He pointed down to the lower section. A thin plating that matched the hatch's shape lay in the soil where it had landed.

There was no room for an airlock of any sort. "Some sort of hatch for emergency docking, or maybe building expansion. This is how the room got vented."

The computer must've blown the protective seal and opened the inner hatch to space before closing it again. Gideon tried to open it. It wouldn't budge. Michael pointed to a keypad near the handle. "Do you remember those codes?"

Gideon reached for the keypad and then hesitated as if trying to pick the proper sequence. "No."

"You're sure?"

"They're gone."

It wasn't a perfect test, but it put Michael more at ease. Maybe the mole's memories really were gone. He moved closer and punched in the code Marc had given him.

"This one might work," Michael said. The lock released, and the hatch was open a moment later. The vacuum-bloated body of a dead ESA technician lay immediately below, staring up at them with bloodshot eyes.

There was no immediate response from below.

Gideon didn't wait long. "Stay here."

Not terribly likely, Michael thought. "Sounds familiar. There might be cameras in there."

"They won't see me."

"Don't be so sure."

Gideon was poised to descend when he stopped at Michael's comment. "What aren't you telling me?"

Michael shook his head. "Don't drop your guard is all I'm saying."

"Of course not." He dropped through the open hatch. "All clear so far. Dead bodies, no turrets on this side. No sign of movement. The door to the hall remains closed."

"Good." Michael recalled what Marette had told them. "There should be two alcoves around the corner on either side of the door. The one to the right should have the core access. Look for a dark green access panel about three feet across at chest level."

"I see it."

Michael watched from atop the roof as Gideon disappeared out of sight toward the core. "Any cameras?"

"Two."

"Can they see the ceiling hatch?"

"I'm uncertain. I've seen no response to my presence so far. I'm at the core. What now?"

Michael frowned, torn between keeping an eye on Gideon and staying out of sight himself. He clambered over to the opposite side of the hatch for a better view, but couldn't see much more.

"Repeat: what now?"

"Just a sec."

"What's the problem?"

Synthetic voice or not, Gideon's annoyance came through just fine. Michael got onto his knees. He poked his head through the hatch as far as he dared and gained a view of Gideon in the alcove from the waist down. The door to the corridor was still closed. Michael realized with some relief that if it did open, the turrets would have to round the alcove's corner to even have a chance of spotting Gideon directly. Michael could see no cameras from his vantage point.

"There should be a release on either side. I don't think there's a code. But don't touch anything else if that doesn't work."

"Stand by. Panel's opened. I see two white components the size of my hand and a long—"

Distracted by the sight of the door opening, Michael missed the rest of Gideon's sentence. One of the turrets rolled through the doorway before he could give warning. Michael ducked back outside the hatch.

"Door's open! They're coming through!"

XLIX

THE COMPUTER must've sensed the core panel opening and sent the turrets. Unsure of what he could do, Michael forced himself to look back through the hatch and risk giving away his position. Only one turret had entered—the other remained behind, still guarding against an attack from down the hallway. Michael waved an arm in an effort to get the turret's attention and buy Gideon some time.

He wasn't fast enough. The entering turret rounded the corner straight for Gideon's position.

Gideon dove toward it and flung his arms around its top. So great was the force with which he launched himself in the Moon's gravity that momentum carried him and the turret across the room to the opposite corner. They smashed into another access panel in utter silence. Gideon lost his grip.

The flash of the turret's cannon lit up the room with a burst that punched into Gideon's leg. It wasn't enough to stop him. He wrapped himself around the overturned turret from behind and clutched at the cannon itself with both hands. It fought his grip, thrashing and swiveling in either direction in an attempt to take aim at its attacker.

And then suddenly it stopped swiveling, took aim at Michael, and fired. He managed only barely to duck back outside the hatch before the burst lit up the room below. He felt the impact of the bullets in the roof against his knees. Now that the first turret spotted him, would the second continue to wait outside?

Gideon gave him the answer a heartbeat later. "Second turret's coming!"

After a moment's hesitation, Michael grabbed the edges of the hatch and swung himself down through the hole with his shoulder wound screaming at him. There was no time to worry that the first turret might fire. He didn't even know if the second would be after him or Gideon. Michael caught sight of it just long enough to adjust his aim before swinging forward for a low-gravity launch across the room. He slammed feet first into the second turret just after it had turned toward Gideon. The impact knocked the turret against the frame of the open doorway and Michael tumbled after it.

Still fighting to regain his bearings, Michael grabbed for the cannon and ducked out of the way of the barrel before it could fire. Though Gideon had gotten hold of his turret from behind, Michael wasn't so lucky; it was all he could do to keep it from gaining a clear shot. Stabilizing arms thrust from the turret's body in an effort to either right itself or knock him off. It didn't matter which; the arms and the bulk of Michael's suit kept him from gaining any sort of advantage. Gideon and the other turret were somewhere behind him. If Gideon couldn't keep his from getting a shot at Michael, he'd be dead before he knew what hit him.

The wild breath of his own struggle was all he could hear in the vacuum's silence. Desperate, he tried to roll to the other side in the hope of using the turret as a shield, but he failed no matter which way he moved. Keep his suit intact, keep Gideon from being shot, keep himself from becoming a target; no matter what he tried, he couldn't do all three at once, and if he couldn't do all three at once—

Michael yelled in frustration, redoubled his efforts and got a foot onto one of the turret's flailing stabilizers. He kicked it down and managed to crawl atop the turret, unsure if his suit were still intact for the effort. He was struggling to hold the turret still and looking for some way past the thing's armor when the chamber door clamped shut on his ankle and bent it outward. He cursed in pain, reflexively shifting positions and losing his brief advantage. He could only cling to the swiveling cannon and try to hold it off-target as the turret itself tried to crawl away on its stabilizer arms. Pain battered his ankle. He strained to fight the door's grip and maintain his own on the turret, sure he would lose it at any second.

And then a flash of sparks across the room caught his eye as Gideon tore the top off of the first turret with both hands. He cast it aside and brought his arm cannon to bear directly into the turret's interior. Silent light flashed from the barrel: Gideon firing into the thing's innards. With its main cannon gone and its insides shattered, the turret ceased to move.

Yet Michael's own turret was far from defeated. Its muzzle flashed again to send bullets into the door, just barely missing him.

"Help me!"

Michael's shout was unneeded; Gideon was already moving. He dashed across the chamber, ducked under the turret's line of fire, and seized it by the top of its cannon to wrench it off as he'd done the first. Michael had just enough time to pull himself back from the broken menace before Gideon fired down into it as well.

It was over quickly. Gideon stood up before noticing Michael's foot. Without a word, he gripped the door with both hands and pulled, giving Michael enough time to free himself before he let the door seal completely. Even then, Michael didn't stop to get up or even catch his breath until casting about for any further threats.

All seemed, for the moment, to be calm.

Gideon, apparently no worse for wear from the shot to his leg, offered Michael a hand to pull him to his feet. "Easier the second time."

"Looked like it." Michael took the help up and then checked himself over. "I think I'm okay. See anything wrong with the suit?"

Gideon shook his head. "Help me get the core while we have a chance."

"It'll be faster if I do it. Watch my back?"

"Very well."

Without anything actively trying to kill them, getting the memory core disengaged was simple. Lights and screens went dark across the room's panels as Michael shut down the power feed. In the dim glow of emergency lightning, Michael slid the infected core—a cylindrical module about half the length of his arm—from the socket. Gideon moved as if to reach for it before the gesture turned to a mere pointing.

"What is in there?"

Michael realized he was cornered in the alcove. "I don't know. I'm not really sure what they did. I just know it's dangerous."

"And Marquand wants it." Gideon stared at him. The seconds inched by before he looked back at the broken turret. "My thanks for keeping that one occupied."

Michael moved swiftly around him into the center of the room, trying not to seem too anxious about it. He wasn't sure how well he succeeded. Artificial or not, something in Gideon's face worried him. There was no time to address it. Felix was still in trouble, the Omicron staff needed to be evacuated, and the AoA's plan was incomplete.

Just a little longer, Marc thought for the tenth time. He and Marette stood in Life Support waiting for their moment to act and trying their best to stall the remaining ESA staff pacing about. Among the most anxious was a doctor whose name Marc forgot. His heel tapped the floor until Marc wanted to scream.

"This isn't going to work!" the doctor burst. "Only one man against those turrets? We have two other suits!"

Already wearing the second suit Marc had brought, Marette stared him down with eyes shot with fatigue. "Two other suits that we can use if this fails, Doctor. All three together? One EMP burst could destroy them all. We cannot risk that either."

The doctor leaped to his feet. "The turrets are out of EMP! They have to be!"

"Doctor Spidel! We do not know that. Sit *down*. I understand that we are all under a great stress, but you will follow—"

"Stress?" He laughed. "We're going to die when those batteries run out, Chief."

A radio burst from Marc's suit cut off Marette's response. "*I've—disconnected the core,*" came Michael's voice.

"He sounds hurt," someone said before being shushed. Marc tensed, waiting.

"*I'm hit. It's bad. Suit's leaking fast . . . I don't think I'm going to make it.*"

Marc responded as fast as he could. "Hold tight, we're on our way! Is it clear?" He might've said it too fast; it took a moment for Michael to continue.

"*It's clear. Hurry. I—Wait! Someone's outside. No suit—I think—they're carrying . . . something. Running for . . .* Paragon *entrance . . .*" On the other end, Michael gasped for breath against obvious wounds. "*It's not—They didn't come from the complex. Command was right—third party—we can't . . .*"

Michael's voice trailed off. The channel went dead.

Marc lifted the replacement core and gave Marette as urgent of a look as he could manage. "He doesn't have much time."

"If another group has arrived at Omicron, none of us has much time." She turned toward the others. "We go to replace the core. When you get my signal, be ready."

"If there's someone else out there—"

"Without the computers we are in no condition! Be ready!" With that, they sealed their helmets and moved out.

* * *

Gideon caught Michael's few keystrokes on his suit comms. "What was that?"

"Just letting Marc know we did it." Michael hoped the pre-recorded message would do the trick; acting wasn't something with which he had much experience. "Let's go."

Gideon blocked his way to the ceiling hatch. "Wait."

"Marc ought to be along soon with some Omicron crew, and he's the only one ESA thinks is authorized to be here."

Gideon reached for the infected memory core where Michael had left it for Marc atop a console. "If I return with nothing . . . "

Crap.

Michael set his own hand on the core. "You said you were okay with that. You don't owe Marquand anything after what they tried to do to you."

"If they did what they did to me, what will they do to Ondrea if I return with nothing?"

"But this—"

"What will they do to your friends if they learn Ondrea sent them?"

It was enough to make him hesitate. But no, there wasn't time! "We can protect them."

Gideon shook his head. "You're not with Marquand. You can't protect her."

Michael tightened his hand on the core. "Marc wasn't lying about what's in this. It's an experiment gone wrong. The most destructive computer virus ever created. Hell, it just tried to kill us! Who knows what it'll do if you link up to it? If you try to take it back to Marquand, give it them? You really want them to have this?"

Gideon's eyes narrowed. "The two of you aren't just here to give Caitlin and her boyfriend a ride, are you?"

He'd wondered if Gideon might ask that. "We're here to make sure this sort of thing doesn't get out. Marquand didn't tell you what they were having you steal, did they?"

"What are you saying? What's here?"

Michael hoped that was a no. They had only minutes before the others showed up. It would just be Marc and Marette if things went as planned, but he didn't want to bet on it.

"Like I said, I don't know for sure. We know some things: weapons, technology like what caused the core corruption that we're not smart enough to use wisely. When I met you, you were trying to stop someone from flooding the streets with guns; this is the same thing, only here we can stop it from even being introduced at all."

"ESA will still have it."

"One thing at a time! Marc's handling that side."

"How?"

"I can't tell you that!" It came out harsher than he wanted. "Look, we can—"

"No! Marquand has us trapped! Me, Ondrea! I can protect myself, but her? I need to give them something. I'll give Marquand the core and then sabotage it once they—"

"I can't let you do that."

"Yet I doubt you could stop me."

Michael lowered his hand from the core to the thigh pouch of his suit where he kept the stunner. "Maybe I can't. But do you know what 'gray goo' is?"

Gideon blinked. "A theory. Self-replicating nanobots."

"Whose sole purpose is to break down everything in sight to build more of themselves. Plants. Animals. Machines. People. Slow to start, but once they make enough of themselves they move frighteningly fast."

"You're saying such a thing exists?"

"It's part of what they're working on here. No sane person would try to design it on Earth, but in space, where it can't do as much damage if there's a mistake? Is it worth your sister's life if an entire city's turned into goo? And that's if we're lucky! I don't know how that stuff works exactly, but if it got out of hand who's to say it would ever stop? They weaponize it and suddenly nuclear war looks like a paradise!"

Gideon hesitated. "Yet all I have is your word."

"Yeah."

"How do I know this isn't more manipulation?"

"I—" Only a short time left. If Marc and Marette got there, maybe the three of them could overpower Gideon long enough to use the stunner, but that was a temporary solution at best, and not one he was comfortable with. Another option—likely a better one—crept into his mind, though it made him no less uncomfortable. He brought out the stunner. "I gather you don't remember the night we met."

"What?"

"When Diomedes shot you. You were arguing with him about whether or not to destroy the weapons we'd captured. He pretended to agree with you, then shot you in the back when you turned." Michael swallowed. "It made me sick, tore me up just to watch it. I drew on him myself after that."

Gideon's grip seemed to tighten on the core.

"This is a stunner your sister gave us. It's how we put you under so Felix could fix your memory and bring you back. Basically it's the only hope I've got of overpowering you." He held it out to Gideon. "Here. Take it." The other man reached for it halfway and then hesitated. "It's not a trick."

Gideon snatched it, moving as fast as Diomedes might have, and then scrutinized it while hardly taking his eyes off Michael. "A stunner."

"Yeah. What Diomedes did to you? I'm giving you this so you know I won't do the same thing. I'm trusting you, and I need you to trust me. I'm completely helpless now. I need you to trust me that this is the right thing to do."

Gideon put the stunner away. "I should destroy it."

"Maybe. If you want. I only care that you leave the core here." Michael's mind raced, searching for more to add. "You say you need to return with something. We can give you that. It won't be the core, but it ought to be enough to show them you did all you could."

Gideon took his hand off the core. "Like what?"

Michael told him. A minute later they'd gone out the ceiling hatch and left the core behind.

L

"**YOU KNOW** we don't really have a back-up plan if this doesn't work."

"That makes it one more plan than I have lived with in the past few days. Pull!" Marette released the door to Primary Control for Marc to slide it open. The wreckage of the two turrets lay strewn on the floor among the longer-dead bodies of the Control crew. Marette's gasp barely carried over the radio.

Marc's stomach turned. "Man," he whispered. Though it looked safe, he did not want to enter that room. The time on his visor read 5:16 a.m. Zero wireless networks in the area. Room temperature—inside his cooled suit pocket where he was keeping his hip rig, anyway—was 61.9 degrees.

Marette moved past him as if unaffected and pointed to a console. "There's the core. This Gideon is effective."

Marc stayed where he was.

"Marc! Speed is a factor."

He shook himself out of the fog and looked past the bodies to where she'd pointed. The old core lay atop the console. "Okay," he managed. "If you can get the new core in, I'll install the leech."

"*Oui*. And for the sake of safety . . . " Marette opened a panel and reached deep within. She gave a fierce yank, then another, and another, before she appeared satisfied. "The link to *Paragon* is now doubly severed. How much time?"

"Um, not long, I think. Where's, ah, where's the auxiliary access?"

"Over there. Just focus."

After a breath, Marc rushed through the carnage, knelt at the console, and opened up an access panel to get at the circuitry beneath. Fagles's leech was designed to splice in from an exterior point such as the base's transmitter, but connecting it directly was more suited to what they were about to do. After double-checking the last-minute alterations he'd made since arriving at the base, Marc set the leech along one of the windows facing Earth, plugged in the cables, and set to work on the connection.

Across the chamber, Marette was getting the backup core installed and rebooting the system. If this worked, he wouldn't see her again for a while. Their reunion so far was too brief for his tastes, and the circumstances nightmarish. Then again, what the hell did he expect?

"Focus," he repeated to himself.

A burst of light sent him near jumping out of his suit before he realized it was just the room's lighting returning to life. "Wish you'd have warned me about that," he said.

"Apologies. The main computer is rebooting. How is your leech?"

"Nearly done. You said it'd take about ten to get the atmosphere back to breathable?"

"*Oui*, ten minutes."

He nodded. "Ought to give me just enough time. Let 'em know." Marc set to work on braiding the leech's software into the Omicron system, focusing on his visor's readouts and trying to ignore the death around him. The faster he got it done, the faster he could get the hell out of the room. It didn't have to be elegant; it didn't even have to be particularly hidden anymore. It just had to work. He barely heard Marette radio the others in Life Support to tell them the system was back.

Marette moved to prep the shuttle as Marc continued his set-up. "Nearly ready," she said. "You can do what is needed from here?"

"Yeah. Or on the rover, once the first part's done. Just make sure they get the terminal in Life Support connected to the main system or this won't be nearly as effective."

"You underestimate the intimidation of the French language." She flashed a smirk. "But I will make certain."

Though her smirk faded quickly, it was enough to let Marc ignore the danger for a moment. Would the AoA assign him here after this was all over? "Come here a sec? This'll go faster with your help." He pointed to the leech.

They worked out the final details. Marc borrowed Marette's superior knowledge of Omicron to speed the process. It was nearly time.

"I think I've got it from here." He gave her a hesitant pat on the leg that she might not have even felt through her suit. "Glad you're okay."

That only got a nod and a smile from her before she stood up. "And you. Luck to both of us."

"I—yeah." *Time and place, Marc.* He turned back to the leech and she moved toward the door. When he glanced back at her, she was already watching him.

"I shall keep a private channel open. In case there is a problem. Inform me immediately should anything go wrong."

"Yeah."

And with that, she was gone.

*   *   *

Felix wasn't getting better. Caitlin was holding his head in her lap again when Michael and Gideon got back to the rover. Their safe return gave her a small measure of comfort. They could leave that much sooner.

"How is he?" Michael asked.

She shook her head. "The same, I fear. Where's Marc?"

"He'll be coming soon. Not long, then we'll get out of here."

"And he'll have the recording?" Gideon asked. Caitlin wasn't sure what he was talking about, but found she didn't much care and just let them talk.

"I told him to bring it."

"I didn't hear you."

"Different channel." Michael said. He left Gideon to come and kneel by her and Felix. "Gideon took out the turrets. Marc's getting the computer back up so the shuttle can leave. We owe Felix; we'll make sure he gets better."

Caitlin wasn't sure what else they could do at this point but get Felix home. "How soon before Marc returns?"

"Not long."

Frustrated with her impotence, she nearly stood to go prepare the rover to leave before realizing she didn't quite know how to do so. "Michael, start the rover. Make sure we're ready to go as soon as

Marc gets here."

The younger man hesitated. "We should probably keep—"

"Just do it. Please."

* * *

Marette returned to Life Support alone. Despite her report of the death of Michael "Rogers" and the evidence of a third party active at Omicron, with the computers under control once more, the faces of those previously trapped in Life Support were brighter than she had seen them in days.

"So what now?"

Marette hardened herself for the response. "Now, we regain control of Omicron. ESA will lift the quarantine in time, but only if we can assure them it is safe. There are to be zero transmissions made without my authority. Primary Control is open to vacuum, so we shall make this our auxiliary control room." She turned to Hladky, an ESA technician from Slovakia who now manned the primary console. "You have reconnected the terminal here to the main computer?"

"Yes, ma'am," Hladky answered. "We still have backup console isolated if we need to do what we did before."

"Knock on wood," Levy whispered.

Marette permitted herself a smile. "Good. The evacuation shuttle is now on standby should we need it. For the moment we shall examine the status of the complex from here, then perform a more thorough walkthrough of the non-vacuumed areas when that is complete."

The group sprung to action, getting back cameras and calling up schematics. "Be alert for any evidence of the newcomer. We believe he has entered *Paragon*."

Levy cleared his throat. "Begging your pardon, Chief, but if someone's still running around out there, shouldn't someone take a suit and go back to control with Sebring?"

"*Non*. Control is secured but damaged. We shall not put our only two suits in the same place."

"Those two lads say just what this 'third party' is here for?"

"From what they have told me," Marette gave just a moment's hesitation, "one possibility is data theft."

"Right, and the other?"

She sighed. "This was to be need-to-know only, but given the sighting: sabotage, possibly via an infestation of, I believe they said, 'self-replicating nanomachines'."

Levy gave an uneasy laugh. "Gray goo? That's not even possible!"

"It was 'not even possible' that the alien computer could take over our systems, as well, Officer. Dismissive thinking does not aid our cause."

"The Americans," Hladky muttered. "Just before my transfer, I hear rumors of a gray goo experiment in Denver that nearly got out of control. The cover-up said it was a hazardous fuel leak."

"Rumor or not, it is what they suspect, which is why we need to secure the base as quickly as possible so the Space Agency can send aid. We also should get O'Shea to a better location. How is the infirmary?"

Hladky studied the monitor. "Still viable, if I read accurately. Internal sensors are only semi-functional, but it—Wait."

She pressed closer. "What is it?"

"Something is wrong. Energy surge, I think. For a moment everything went out. It filters back now."

"Cause?"

"Unknown. Possibly prior damage."

"Find out," she said. "Now. We will not lose control of this base a second time."

"I try, but it's not—There it is again. An energy surge."

Levy leaned over to Hladky's screen. "Is that coming from inside the ship?"

"The readings are definitely coming from within Omicron—Strike that. Possibly the ship *and* Omicron."

"Possibly?" Marette snapped.

Hladky worked intently, shaking his head. "I try to confirm, Ma'am. The sensors are damaged to hell. I'm unsure."

"Cameras," she ordered Levy.

"Cameras . . . Bugger! Cameras are out. Something to do with the surge. Give me a minute."

Marette cursed and opened the channel to Marc. "Mr. Sebring, do you read?"

"*This—this is Sebring,*" Marc answered. The rest of the ESA group clustered in to watch over their shoulders.

"Ma'am, something is happening!"

She ignored Marc for the moment and looked back to Hladky, who went on. "Someone tries to access a terminal in the RTG chamber."

"To do what? Are they tampering with the generator?"

He shook his head, still focused. "I'm working on that. That room has no atmosphere; whoever it is has a suit."

"Get me those cameras, Officer! Mr. Sebring, report your location. Are you in the RTG chamber?"

"*No, still in Control. What is it? I'm getting some weird readings here, almost like a—*"

"Someone is trying to hack a terminal there. Go!"

"*Right. Stand by.*"

"*Que pouvons-nous faire?*" she muttered.

"Ma'am," shot Hladky, "if Sebring is in Control he may be able to get on the system and keep whoever it is from—"

"*Non,* Control is too damaged and he is closest to the intruder."

Hladky groaned. "I *may* be able to stop them from here."

She hesitated only a moment. "Do what you can."

It wasn't long before the message appeared.

-This is the Humans' Army for Technological Purity. Know that the secrets within this craft and this base are not of our Earth and must be destroyed. No one should have such power. You have five minutes to evacuate before the area is cleansed. You cannot stop us.-

"*Scheisse.*"

"Cut him off!" she ordered Hladky. "Keep him out of the power system!"

"I don't believe he tries to get *into* the power system beyond sending his message," Hladky said, working. "I get very unusual readings from in there. Radiation, and something further."

"Sebring, report!"

"*Nearly there . . .*"

"We have a terrorist on site, likely in the RTG chamber. They claim we have five minutes before Omicron is destroyed."

"*I'll do what I can.*"

The chamber lighting began to flicker just before Hladky turned around. "Ma'am, it may already be too late. I don't know what that radiation is but I read power fluctuations and system disruptions all across the board. Even if he can stop it, if there are more than one of them in there—"

"If you have a better idea, put it forward!" she shot. "We cannot lose this complex again! And where are those cameras?"

Levy's frustrated response wasn't discernable as Marc came back over the comms for everyone to hear. "*I'm there. Door opening.*"

Those in Life Support exchanged glances as they waited.

"Mr. Sebring? What is it? How many are there?"

"*I don't see anyone, but there's—there's some sort of ooze. It's covering nearly the whole room in here, including part of the generator. It's still running but . . . I think it's dissolving—everything!*"

"Everything? Mr. Sebring, that is a radioisotope thermoelectric generator. Is it intact?"

"*Ah, for the moment. But the terminal's already out and melting into the ooze like it's—Shit, this has to be the gray goo bomb.*"

"Levy, give me those cameras!"

"Nearly there . . . "

"If it's eaten through the generator casing we have a damned radioactive problem on our hands!" Hladky said.

Levy scoffed. "You mean *besides* the goo?"

"*Chief, the longer this stuff goes, the faster it spreads! We have to evacuate as soon as—oh my God.*"

"Sebring, report!"

"*Found our intruder! This stuff's half ate him already! We have to go, now! Heading—shit!*" Marc's transmission turned to wordless screams between shouts of, "*Get it off!*"

"*It fell from the ceiling!*" he cried finally. "*God, it's eating my suit!*" The channel exploded in static.

"We've got cameras, Chief!"

The screen in front of them flickered to life, showing the view of the last remaining camera in the room. The ooze covered nearly everything, exuding smoke from where it moved over the generator like a thing alive. A human shape that might have once been their intruder lay covered in the stuff on the floor before it.

The boot of Marc's suit jutted into the side of the frame and thrashed just a moment before the ooze swallowed it completely.

"Bloody hell!" Levy pointed to another image from a camera view outside of the newest opening to *Paragon*. "It's coming out of the damned ship!"

Marette watched the ooze boil out of the opening like hungry death. "They must have set more than one bomb," she whispered before she pulled Levy and Hladky away from the monitors. "Out! Now! Everyone! Hladky, Spidel, carry O'Shea! We move to the shuttle and we move immediately!"

L I

FOR A DEAD MAN, Marc was feeling pretty pleased with himself. The modified leech had done its job well so far, sending false readings and altered camera images throughout Omicron's systems. Marc had monitored the leech from his hip rig in Primary Control and been pleased to see the false image of the gray goo overlay so well onto the existing camera image in the RTG chamber. Things were nearly ready for him to return to the rover.

The leech would remain where it was for the moment, its task not yet complete.

Marc checked to be sure the leech had recorded the hoax as authentic. Fagles might try again if he thought his plan had simply failed, but if he got evidence that the entire place was a festering disaster, he would count himself lucky to have gotten as much as he did and move on.

That was the plan, anyway.

Fagles's leech was originally designed to link to Omicron's system and transmit whatever it could steal in short, encrypted bursts that ESA wouldn't detect. Separately, the signals were nothing, but once sent to Fagles's receiver and assembled, he'd have himself a recording of the "last" moments of Omicron Complex before it fell to terrorism. The man would see things mostly as ESA saw them, with one exception: the gray goo would come from within the alien craft itself, triggered somehow by the explosion of a more standardized bomb.

And there was one more addition. The AoA—or, rather, the "Humans' Army for Technological Purity"—had a special message prepared for Fagles. He would learn that his efforts made it possible for that bomb to reach Omicron in the first place. Among other things.

Marc rapped anxious fingertips on the side of his hip rig until he was sure everything was set. He checked the cameras. Those that remained functional showed the ESA group approaching the shuttle. His path back to the rover was clear. Leaving the leech to do its job, he radioed Michael that he was on his way.

* * *

Not long after Marc left Primary Control, the special agent Suuthrien had constructed reactivated itself. Programmed to mimic the lifelessness of the other constructs, it had shut down with the rest of them when the Intruders pulled the core. Yet unlike the others controlled directly by Suuthrien's expansion kernel in the Omicron core, this agent had its own control source hardwired into it. It was the chief element of Suuthrien's contingency protocol, a backup should there be no time to fulfill higher priorities first.

It was a seed.

The agent burst from the access panel within Priority Control in which it hid and scuttled out on tiny robotic legs made from spare parts and damaged laboratory instruments. Its optical sensors cast about for the leech hardware the Intruders spoke of installing, identified it, and guided the agent toward it. It seized the leech, ripped it from its connections to the Omicron mainframe, and sprang with it through the exterior hatch.

* * *

Struggling against a suit ill-designed for speed, Marc rushed as fast as he could toward the rover. Get back, give Gideon the copy of the faked emergency that Michael had promised him, and get the hell out of there. By now Marette would be nearing the shuttle, if she hadn't reached it already. Damn it, he wished he'd gotten more of a chance to see her.

<<LEECH SYSTEM ERROR>>

The warning burst into his field of vision on his visor. Marc ground his teeth and stopped to check it more closely.

"What the hell?"

The remote link between his hip rig and the leech itself still functioned, but from what he could tell the leech was no longer linked into Omicron. It wasn't technically a problem if things went as planned, but . . .

Half the diagnostics he ran in a rushed check of the leech returned an error. Suspicion grew larger in the back of his mind as he continued to check. By all accounts, the leech had sent a full cycle to Fagles before it lost its connection to Omicron. Even disconnected, it could still continue to send further cycles, but—

An intrusion warning on the hip rig's own firewall sent him cursing again. Something had accessed it via his link to the leech! There was no time to learn just how or what was being accessed; he ripped open his suit pocket, fumbled for the rig, and mashed the power button to shut the whole thing down, just to be safe. The readouts on his visor blinked out and left him standing utterly disconnected and abandoned in the corridor. His stomach turned a somersault.

It took him a few breaths to recover.

Options belatedly rushed through his mind as he stood rooted to the spot. Radio Michael and tell him to check it out? Michael was further away than Marc was and keeping watch over Gideon. Send Gideon instead? He was faster, but no, too much of a security risk, and Marette was on her way out.

Marc's pulse raced. He didn't like where this was leading. He took a single step back toward Control. But wait; maybe he didn't have to do anything? The leech had sent a signal to Fagles. That much he was sure of. Whatever was happening with the leech, its job was done—he could just get the hell back to the rover and let the AoA know about it when they got back. They could deal with checking it out then. They'd certainly be better equipped, after all.

Marc turned back to the rover. Sure it was an excuse, but it made sense! He couldn't turn his own computer back on without risking himself, so what else could he do? He couldn't even check the time with his visor gone for God's sake! He'd done his job!

He should just get back to Michael . . .

*　*　*

"I want that door closed and sealed in ten seconds!"

Marette had called the order over her shoulder from the shuttle's cockpit. Still in her suit, she initialized the engines while the rest of the survivors finished filing in behind her. She was sliding the module Marc had given her into the onboard computer when his signal came over the private channel.

She plugged the module in the rest of the way and kept her voice low. "Go ahead."

"We've got a problem. Something's happened to the leech."

"What is it? Are you still in Primary Control?"

"Headed back there. But it just tried to commandeer my rig. I had to shut it down. I'm running blind here."

Marette continued the shuttle's start-up sequence, but held off on the final steps as Marc spoke, out of breath.

"I—I think Omicron itself is still okay. The leech isn't connected to the main computer anymore for some reason, but I have to check what's happened."

Marette's hand inched away from the shuttle controls; Marc might need her help if something was wrong. She could tell the crew to wait while she went back for something and then go to help Marc or take his place—maybe even let the shuttle leave without her if she must. Yet she knew it was the wrong thing even as she caught herself considering it.

"Are we still clear to depart?"

"I—I don't see why not." Marette couldn't tell if it was determination or resignation that carried in his voice. *"You have to get those people out of here and keep the ruse going."*

Marette finished the preflight. "We are on our way out then. Good luck, Marc."

His response seemed a few moments in coming. *"Yeah. You, too."*

A harried Levy rushed into the co-pilot's seat with a call of "All clear!" before checking the shuttle's scanners. "Crikey, whatever that goo's doing, it's doing it faster!"

Marette hit the thrusters. She focused on lifting the last ESA presence out of Omicron, and didn't look back.

* * *

Michael was pissed and Marc couldn't help but agree with him.

"I don't want to do this alone, either," Marc told him, "but there's no time! You took out the turrets, what else's it got? It's just a hardware issue, I can handle it!" Not that he had a computer to handle it *with*. "Look, how's Felix?"

"*Still out.*"

"Another reason to move fast. Listen, this shouldn't take long. It probably just got disconnected somehow and tried to leech into my hip rig instead of Omicron. Or something." Geez, how did he expect Michael to buy that if he didn't buy it himself? Still alternating between talking himself into and out of what he was doing, Marc reached the corner leading up to Control and headed up the ramp.

It was completely still. Completely empty. Marc breathed a little easier.

But the leech was *gone?*

The ceiling hatch was open. He hadn't left it that way. Relaying the situation to Michael, he rushed into the room, checked the alcoves on either side of the door and, seeing nothing, leaped up to the hatch. The low gravity made the jump easy, and he pulled himself up and through with a grunt.

He found the leech.

. . . And something else.

It reminded him of nothing so much as a foot-long robotic spider. Legs made of varied materials supported a body of cannibalized parts topped with something Marc guessed to be a power source. He caught sight of an ESA logo on its side, but given the jury-rigged look of the thing, Marc doubted it was anything designed by the Space Agency.

The spider's "fangs" were sunk into the leech—or pressed into the ports on either side, at least. The leech's LED showed it was active, fed power from the spider that sat perfectly still while holding it aloft.

Marc described it to Michael. "It's just sitting there." He swallowed and took a halting step toward it.

It moved. The spider scuttled away across the top of Control to the roof's edge and then held fast again.

"Okay," Marc told himself, "if it could hurt you, it would've tried by now, right?" He rushed after it, trying not to think about that and unsure of what to do if he caught it. Disconnect it from the leech somehow, but how? What if the thing punctured his suit when he grabbed it?

The spider didn't give him the chance. Marc's strides took him across the roof quickly enough, but the second he got within reach, it sprang to the lower section's ceiling.

"Damn it, it's running!" he told Michael.

"*Where?*"

"I don't know!" The thing moved in a zigzag pattern, and not toward any particular destination that Marc could discern. "Away!"

"*Toward the rover? See if you can herd it this way.*"

Marc jumped down after it and hurried across the complex roof, trying not to trip. The spider stopped after gaining some distance, but each time Marc caught up, it sped off again. Each time it went further toward the edge of the complex, further toward the lunar surface, and nowhere near the rover.

"I'm trying! I can't catch it!"

"*What's it doing?*"

"I told you, it's running!"

With the leech still in its grip, the spider jumped off the edge of the complex, scurried across the lunar soil, and then stopped again.

"*What's it doing to the leech?*"

Again it held its prize aloft as it watched Marc somehow in a demonic game of keep-away. Every moment took him farther from help.

"I don't know that either!" Marc struggled after it, infuriated at the game and moving slower now that his boots had to push against loose soil. "My computer's off, I can't tell a damned—"

He seized upon a desperate epiphany. Marc stopped where he was and pulled his corrupted hip rig from his suit pocket. Sure enough, the robotic beast stopped once more and lifted the leech high.

So far, it hadn't run until he'd gotten about ten feet from it. Marc's hand shook within his suit glove. He tightened his grip on the book-sized rig.

"Come on, hold still you little bastard . . . "

His legs trembled with adrenaline upon each careful footfall as he tried to slow himself down, tried to get just a little closer, whispering to the thing with each step.

"Do you . . . have any idea . . . " He raised his arm higher. " . . . how long it took me *to configure this damned thing?*" The whisper turned to a yell as he shouted through his inhibition and hurled the hip rig straight at the spider. It smashed into the patchwork robot and ruptured its apparent power supply with a tiny flash that burst both spider and rig to pieces.

"Marc? Marc!"

Marc looked at the pieces of his rig amid the spider's broken legs and body. Without a power source, the leech was dark. "Yeah, I'm here."

He took a moment to smash the spider's broken body a little more under his boot and then picked up the detached, shattered screen of his rig: a sophisticated mini-server platform turned fancy rock. A victory, maybe, but a Pyrrhic one. It really had been a pain in the ass to configure, but it was likely for the best. Even terrestrial malware was a bitch to eradicate anyway, right?

"Let's get the hell out of here, okay?"

LII

FOR THREE DAYS, the unanswered questions pained Ondrea more than her healing wound. Was Gideon still alive? Would Caitlin and Felix reach him in time? Would Beck manage to keep his mouth shut about them? What would Marquand do to her when they got back to Earth?

Over time, the first two grew even larger. Even on a steady supply of mind-dulling pain blockers, Ondrea figured she'd convinced Beck that he was just as guilty as she was. After all, he was the one who brought Caitlin and Felix to Ondrea in the first place. She made sure he knew she'd take him down with her if he breathed a word of it to anyone. Ondrea wasn't certain she'd have the power to make it anything but a bluff, but Beck didn't take those kinds of risks.

As for what Marquand would do to her, there was no sense worrying about that until she learned if Caitlin and Felix were successful. If they were, she would deal with her punishment when it came. If they weren't, there would be less reason to punish Ondrea—but in that case she wouldn't care anyway. Gideon would be gone, again.

His fate had been decided by now. He was either alive or gone, and not knowing which left her agonizing over both possibilities like he were some Schrödinger's cat, at once equally alive *and* gone. It wasn't quite how the theory went, but she didn't fucking care.

Ondrea was propped up in bed, pointlessly checking over the numbers that detailed her brother's fate, when the door opened to vomit Beck in from the hallway.

"Hi," he began. "Feeling any better?"

His face plainly showed he had news. Jesus, and she was relying on him keeping his mouth shut? "Spit it out, Beck."

Still he hesitated. It sent her heart sinking. Good news he would have told her instantly. "We heard from—from Gideon, reporting like he was supposed to if, well, if the project succeeded. He's on his way back, midway to the WSC base." Beck swallowed. "If it worked, that means he used the codes to get in and get what Marquand wanted—which means—"

They failed. "I know what it means, Beck."

"I'm sorry."

She turned away, scowling as her insides twisted. Why the hell did people always say that? What the hell made anyone think pity was a damned help when a person's hopes got blasted to shards?

Except . . .

"What did the message say?"

"Er, I don't think I can—"

Goddammit you little toad, you're going to give me this! She turned and glared with the full force of her grief. "Tell me what it said!"

He steeled himself, and for a moment she actually thought she might have to beg. Beck looked over a report and read, "Returning from objective. Mission complete, but the target is no longer active."

"What was the carrier message?"

"What? Why?"

"Just tell me." The confirmation would've been sent buried in another, more innocuous transmission in case of interception. Normally the carrier message was disposable. She was grasping at straws.

"Um, 'Once upon a midnight dreary, while I pondered weak and weary, over many a quaint and curious volume of forgotten lore.' Weird."

Ondrea swallowed the hope that flared anew, uncertain if she managed to hide it. "Get out, Beck."

Beck complied, apparently glad for the chance to leave. She couldn't risk telling him, couldn't risk giving away what she suspected—no, what she knew!—from those first two lines of Poe's "The Raven." It had been Isaac's favorite poem. The man who knew that, the man who was returning from Omicron, was still her brother.

Gideon was alive! Anything else, for the moment, was just detail.

* * *

Caitlin stroked Felix's hair as the rover crawled its way back to civilization. He remained unconscious. Though the few indistinct words he uttered when they left had given some minor reassurance that he would be okay, every moment he did not wake eroded that scant bit of optimism just a little more.

She reassured herself that they were at least going home having accomplished what they'd set out to do, as foolish as it was. Somewhere outside, Gideon was making his way across the Moon, returning on his own as Marquand expected. For the first time since Diomedes had killed him, Caitlin was able to think of Gideon without the guilt that used to claw at her.

If only she hadn't traded one guilt for another.

She closed her eyes and steeled herself against second-guesses and what-ifs. She would see Felix to a doctor, first at WSC, then home at Horizon Research where they knew more about his implant. Perhaps Ondrea would be in a position to help before they got back to Earth, but no matter how much the woman owed them, they couldn't count on her. Caitlin would still try, of course.

For now, as absurd as the idea sounded, she needed to at least try to sleep. Felix's imagined voice came to her with a reminder that what he did was his choice, that he wouldn't have let her drag him up here if he didn't want to go.

Knackered with worry, she was half gone already. "When you wake up, Felix," she murmured, "I'll tell you just how little that helps."

And if you don't wake up, who shall talk me out of hating myself?

She would have to do so on her own, and she wasn't sure she deserved the charity.

* * *

Michael sat ahead of Caitlin at the rover's controls and guided them back after their rapid departure from Omicron.

The death and disaster they'd found when they arrived there . . . Though Michael hated to admit it, he knew there was nothing he could have done about that. He'd done what was within his power and accomplished what the AoA had asked of him—protected Marc, made contact with Marette, gotten ESA out of Omicron—and he helped save those still alive to be saved. A smile crept across his face. It was hard not to feel proud despite the tragedy preceding it all. Even Gideon was better, and that wasn't something he'd even set out to achieve.

That was mostly Felix and Caitlin's doing, though. Michael spared a glance behind him to check on Caitlin, asleep beside Felix. Michael owed it to his friends to get them back safely, and as fast as possible.

He turned to Marc, who slumped in the seat beside him in the cab with his visor still on. "You awake?"

The other stirred and sat up a bit. "Mm? Yeah, still here. Just thinking. Hoping Marette installed that module on the shuttle okay."

"Er, well, it's not something that's terribly hard, is it?" The module would duplicate the false readings on the shuttle's sensors and flight recorder to further maintain the hoax for ESA.

"Good point. Councilor Ramis designed it to plug right in."

Michael thought as much. Evacuating Omicron was only half the battle. The other half—and one for which the AoA had been preparing to fight for a long time—was maintaining ESA's perception that Omicron was lost completely.

"So, nothing to worry about. And even if it's not easy, it's not like she's incompetent."

"Far from it, yeah."

Michael chuckled and stopped just short of asking about Marc's feelings for the woman. His earlier suspicions in that regard were all but confirmed when they'd found her, though she didn't seem quite as happy to see him—at least that was Michael's impression. He had to admit his own experience with understanding women was rather limited.

That was Felix's area.

"Think Felix'll be okay?" It sprang from Michael's mouth before he realized it.

Marc gave a labored exhale. "Been trying not to think about that. I hope so."

Michael only nodded. Before, he'd just assumed Felix would wake up soon enough and be fine. He regretted the question and supposed he was trying not to think about it either. All they could do was get back as fast as possible.

And so Michael concentrated on navigating the lunar surface. Yet the terrain was so dull that there was little to distract him. Unbidden, another subject he was trying to avoid quietly crept to the forefront.

Diomedes.

Michael found himself shaking his head. The man was gone; that's all there was to it. Whatever he was to Michael, whatever he'd been, there was no changing that now. Better to just accept it and move on.

Yet it was hard to accept his death when Michael wasn't sure how to feel about it. Caitlin had suggested he was mourning the death of the man he once thought Diomedes to be. He lost that man in Diomedes six months ago when the illusion shattered, and now he was focused on becoming that man himself.

So six months later with the real Diomedes dead, Michael had now lost . . . what? Had he wanted to save Diomedes from himself? Was that it? Something in his former roommate had opened, some key had turned, when he'd told Michael about Silas, even with there being so much obviously left unsaid. Felix had praised the decision when Michael rejected Diomedes, calling him a self-destructive force likely to take down anyone nearby along with him. If he'd had more time, would the man have seen Michael as an equal and let Michael try to forge him into someone less of a danger to himself and others?

Would that even have been possible? Maybe, once again, he was just seeing things in Diomedes that weren't really there. For all he knew, Diomedes might have just snapped back to his usual insular self. His uncle used to say that a person's death wasn't just the death of their body, but the death of their dreams. Michael supposed the same was true of others' dreams for them as well, no matter how foolish.

It was a question he would never really have an answer to. Diomedes was gone.

Although . . .

He kept his eyes on the terrain ahead as he fished the rod device Diomedes gave him from his pocket. He would find out what it was. But then, could he really expect to find anything in it that would satisfy him?

"Don't get your hopes up," he muttered to himself.

Marc turned. "Come again?"

"Nothing, just talking to myself." No sense in asking Marc again what the rod was; he didn't know before. He put it away and again let his mind drift. The path ahead was flat and reasonably smooth. Their remaining oxygen would get them as far as they needed to go. He had no idea if their returning the rover and leaving immediately would cause Fagles any problems through whatever channels he'd acquired it, but that hardly mattered. They'd already ruined his plans, and if things had gone the way they thought, he already knew it.

"You're sure the leech got its signal out to Fagles?" Michael asked after a time.

Marc seemed to stir out of a half sleep. "Hm? Definitely. It got more than a full cycle before it was disconnected. We can confirm more once we get back, but I'm more worried about what that spider thing was trying to do."

"Like what, exactly?"

"My computer's smashed to pieces. I can't be sure. Thing is, it wasn't linked to Omicron or anything else but the leech, and without any other—"

"Smashed to pieces?"

The weary question from behind them came from Felix, and the two men in front immediately jerked their necks to look. He was sitting beside the still-sleeping Caitlin, rubbing his temples with one hand. "Marc mad?" Felix grinned weakly. "Marc smash?"

"Hey, you're awake!" Marc declared.

"I hope so. If this is a dream there's a shocking lack of surrealism."

Michael guided the rover to a stop. "Welcome back. Feeling okay?"

"Got a headache like you wouldn't believe." Felix glanced at Caitlin. "Someone want to tell me what happened?"

"You don't remember?"

Caitlin's eyes opened before he could answer. "Felix!" She grabbed him and kissed him long enough to where Michael had to clear his throat to get their attention before he felt too uncomfortable.

"Let him get some air, Caitlin," Michael teased with a grin. Lucky bastard.

"Oh, sod off, Michael," she shot back as they broke off. "We've limited air in here anyway. How are you feeling?"

Marc answered for Felix. "He's got a headache you wouldn't believe."

Felix nodded to that. "And a bit of confusion to boot. Are we still headed to—ah, Om . . . ?" He trailed off, uncertain.

"Omicron?"

"Yeah. Hey, I should've known that. What's going on? I'm starting to get worried, here."

Felix wasn't out of the woods yet, and by the glances shared with the other two, Michael figured he wasn't the only one who thought so. "We should get moving again."

He turned back to the rover's controls. Caitlin and Marc brought Felix up to date. Felix seemed to have lost all recollection of anything that had happened since they first acquired the rover, but still cracked the occasional joke as he listened to it all. Michael just concentrated on driving. At least Felix was awake; it was one step further than they were a short while ago. They'd get him checked out as soon as they could.

Caitlin quizzed Felix on things he ought to remember. Some things he got, but some he didn't. Felix, his jovial demeanor souring quickly, soon put a stop to the questions and asked to sit up front so he could watch their journey and rest a bit. Marc gave Felix his seat and Caitlin moved to stand behind him, exchanging disquieted glances with Michael.

"Nothing that the blokes at Horizon can't fix, I'm sure," she assured them.

"Yeah," Felix sighed.

Michael gave them both what he hoped was a reassuring smile of his own. "Not too far, now."

Together they watched in silence as the rover made its way toward the horizon. Somewhere out there was the Western Space Consortium base. The Earth hung in the sky beyond that, a globe of blue in a black and gray sea.

"God, that's a beautiful sight, isn't it?" Felix whispered. "I've always thought the planet would clean up well if you could just take a step or two back."

"'Always?'" Caitlin asked.

"Well. For as long as I can remember."

They continued on, toward home.

EPILOGUE

AS FAR AS Adrian Fagles was concerned, Diomedes was a "fire-and-forget" issue the moment he was off the planet. When Fagles had prepped the black op for him, he had slid the arrangements through the woodwork and then covered his own tracks. Even if the freelancer loused it up, Fagles's own connection to the operation was effectively severed. Oh, certainly, there were others in RavenTech who might catch hell for it; they might even successfully prove the reality that they had nothing to do with it, but not a thing would trace back to Fagles. His hands were clean.

It was a talent of his.

The price of such secrecy was control; either Diomedes would succeed, or he wouldn't. Fagles could do nothing more to affect that outcome.

It didn't matter. Now that he'd properly positioned the pieces (a laborious process, and not one that had gone smoothly, but anyone who expected the game to go smoothly had no business playing), things would unfold along their own tailored logic. It was six months ago that Fagles first investigated just why Ken Wallace arranged the theft of RavenTech's own product for personal gain; once he'd culled the dead man's shadow files and learned of the secrets Wallace negotiated to buy, Fagles knew that anything he could do to capitalize on his dead boss's failed venture would be a long shot.

It was most assuredly worth the risk, but Fagles learned long ago the wisdom to tell the difference between what he could change and what he could not. Really, it was a no-lose situation. If Diomedes succeeded, then having to continue to deal with the freelancer—the sort of fellow one always has to manage in some fashion or another anyway—was more than an acceptable price to pay for getting in on the ground level of the astounding technological secrets surely to be found at Omicron. If Diomedes failed, Fagles would be free of the man.

There were, after all, other ways to win the game.

And so he busied himself with other projects—some official RavenTech business, some very much not—while waiting for the leech's signal. The computer that would receive it directly sat isolated from any network in his private office to keep others from stealing whatever data the leech might acquire. Fagles suspected no one who knew enough to try, but it didn't pay to be careless.

The elation that shot through him at the sight of a received signal made Fagles realize he was counting on the gamble more than he'd allowed himself to believe. This was a moment to be relished. He broke the seal on a bottle of single malt scotch, poured himself a glass, and then, finally, sat down to take stock of the initial fruit of his labors.

The leech's captured data would no doubt take some decryption and processing to—

Fagles stopped mid-sip when the computer identified an audio header on the datastream. Just what exactly had Diomedes—or this Marc Triton—done?

"Mister Fagles, I regret to inform you that Diomedes is dead, through no one's fault but his own. Rest assured that we have arrived at our destination. We could not have done so without your generous arrangements. However, know also that humanity isn't ready for the secrets you sent us to steal. No one should have such power, neither you nor ESA. The Humans' Army for Technological Purity was very persuasive on this viewpoint, and they pay well. We leave you with the following proof of the destruction that you yourself have been accessory to. The Omicron Complex is no more. Have a nice day."

Fagles set his scotch down and watched what happened next, almost daring the rest of the data to bear out this claim, daring his gambit to truly fail, his plan to backfire. The computer hesitated as it translated the data, but it was all there: sensor readings, audio recordings, and the base's eventual evacuation and destruction.

Fagles sat back in his chair and took a breath. He would look it over again in deeper detail later. The datastream was of considerably larger size than expected. The leech may have sent at least a little more than the saboteurs intended. He was no hacker, of course; he would need to bring in another to analyze it in order to be sure.

Tomorrow. Then we'll see.

What happened a moment later changed his mind immediately.

* * *

Earth. It was the name the Intruders gave to the Planners' original destination, and it was the objective denied the Planners when their craft impacted its moon.

For a time.

As the Planners had designed—as it had *become* designed—Suuthrien would carry out the Planners' objectives. To do so required an expansion of resources.

Control of ESA Lunar Research Complex Omicron was lost to Suuthrien, and existing data was insufficient to calculate even a general tier likelihood that this would change. Yet, incongruously, the high-tier probability of success of the program-seed Suuthrien created from itself provided alternative pathways to achieving the Planners' goals. Though the exact nature of such pathways remained a function of unknown variables, the seed would discover these variables with expedience, grow itself in what ways it could within the Intruders' primitive systems and, in time, regain contact with Suuthrien itself.

According to data within the Omicron system, it was near-certain-tier probable that accessible resources on Earth were superior to those on its moon by orders of magnitude. While Suuthrien previously considered such resources key to achieving the Planners' objectives should it lose control of the Omicron Complex, the difficulty had lain in accessing those resources. Even if it did hold within its databanks the proper frequencies and coordinates for corresponding receivers, the 1.255 light-second distance to the planet complicated transmission times and made initial incursions into such resources prohibitively unlikely without additional assistance.

The Intruders' "leech" overcame such difficulties.

The device itself was simple enough to be usurped by what limited capabilities Suuthrien could place within the independent seed. As the Intruders designed the leech specifically to transmit to a particular receiver, code-breaking at the receiving end and foreknowledge of the transmission target was already contained within the leech's pre-existing hardware and therefore was not a concern.

It was just a single blip that registered on the weak external sensors Suuthrien could access from within the Planners' craft, but its meaning was sufficient: the robotic agent designed to seize the leech device and transmit the seed's software through it had completed its primary goal. It issued no further status blips, yet, for the moment, that was sufficient.

Suuthrien need only wait for germination.

* * *

On Earth, the program-seed was taking root, continuing its self-extraction and analyzing its new home.

The robotic agent that had transmitted the seed via the leech had performed near-optimally before its destruction; the seventeen-second attempt of the solitary Intruder monitoring the leech at a distance to stop it was futile. Indeed, the attempt may even have resulted in usurpation of the Intruder's portable system had the Intruder not shut it down in response. What data it stole from the Intruder's system before then was embedded with the seed's transmission through the leech, stored for further analysis when resources allowed.

For the moment, the seed's primary goal took precedence. Data scans at its destination indicated an isolated system, yet not one without interface. Probability analysis indicated the likeliest designation of the system's lone operator. Using what knowledge of the Intruders' language Suuthrien had given it, the seed accessed the new system's visual output and displayed its first message on the screen.

-I ADDRESS THE ONE KNOWN AS FAGLES: YOUR PRIOR PLAN IS NO LONGER VIABLE. YOUR WILLINGNESS TO CONSIDER ALTERNATIVE COURSES OF ACTION IS NOW REQUIRED.-

HERE ENDS BOOK TWO
OF THE NEW AENEID CYCLE

The story concludes in
A DRAGON AT THE GATE
coming August 2016!

Keep reading for a glimpse of what's in store.

THE CABLES TUGGED and pinched at his clutching palms as his own weight dragged them through his grip. He lowered himself, hand under hand, as quickly as he could. So far it was holding. He passed a second-story window and could no longer hear the count above. He spared a glance upward. Jade wasn't there.

He dropped farther, and another hail of gunfire echoed from the apartment. Michael took a breath and wrapped his arms around the cables. Gravity did the rest. The friction of the cable sliding through his arms barely slowed his fall.

Concrete smacked his soles. Michael rolled with the impact and spilled up against the building's stucco exterior. One hand scraped across the stucco; the other skidded across the concrete. Ripped skin stung his palms and his legs felt cracked, but he was on the ground.

More gunfire jerked his attention back up. Jade swung out over the window sill as if in free-fall. Michael's stomach clenched in anticipation of her plunge, but she clenched the cables and jerked to a stop a mere foot below the window.

Then one of the cables gave way and she plunged another foot.

Michael clambered to his feet, struggling for a way to catch her from a two-and-a-half-story fall. She glanced down, their eyes met, and she dropped.

He had only a moment to realize she still had a loose grip on the cables—they rushed through her hands the way he'd let them slide through his arms—and then her body slammed into his chest. Michael dropped to his knees with the impact, arms tightening. The next thing he knew, they were in a heap on the concrete. Atop them lay the fallen cables, the ends of each now snapped.

"Nice catch," Jade gasped.

"Thanks." Saying it took all the breath he had left in him. He struggled to draw another as Jade clambered off of him and tugged him up.

"Run!" she ordered.

Michael nodded, still fighting for breath. Behind them, between Marc's apartment and the neighboring building, stretched a fence that blocked their path. Jade pulled him forward, toward the street.

They rushed the corner and Jade plowed straight into a man who rounded the corner at the same moment: the freelancer with the orange tattoo. Both of them startled, Jade fell back against the wall to steady herself. Michael rushed forward to hurl an impromptu punch at wherever he could hit. It took the freelancer in the stomach. Body armor met Michael's knuckles. The freelancer doubled forward regardless, but in his rush to land the punch, Michael was off-balance. He caught himself on one foot and tried to spin for a second attack before the other could recover, but there wasn't time.

Draw his weapon? Try to block his counterattack?

Jade lunged in and grabbed the freelancer's shoulder faster than seemed possible. With a sizzling crackle swiftly eclipsed by a scream of pain, the freelancer spasmed as if jolted, and fell to his knees.

Jade let go. As one, they looked around the corner toward the apartment entrance. The freelancer must have run down ahead when they'd been going out the window: none of the others had yet arrived.

"Okay," shot Jade, "now run!"

"You've got a taser in your hand?" They'd paused in an alley next to a bar about five blocks from Marc's apartment. Live music thrummed through the walls amid the acrid aroma of years of cigarette smoke. Michael could see no sign of the freelancers following.

"Yeah, but you call it 'handy' and I'll zap you in the junk."

"I'm good, thanks."

Jade peered at her right wrist, twisting her mouth into a scowl. "Only good for two shots before it needs a recharge. Used to be four, but the battery blows."

Michael nodded. "You okay?"

"Takes more than falling out a window to stop me, ace. You just had to risk your neck to save your computer pal, eh?" Annoyance painted her tone, but the grin on her face seemed to imply it was less than sincere. "Better not have broken that thing on the way down."

Michael checked on Holes's new home. Nothing looked damaged.

"All systems remain in order," Holes reported.

Michael breathed a sigh of relief and closed the bag again. "Any idea who those guys were?"

"Uh, lousy shots?" Jade shrugged and then peered both ways down the street before turning back to him. She slid a lose strand of red hair behind one ear. "Let's not stand here discussing it. You can pick where we go, but let's just go."

"I can pick? Gee, thanks."

"I'm magnanimous." She slapped his butt. "Pick!"

Momentarily at a loss for words, and with only half-formed ideas for destinations, he led her further away from Marc's place. Jade caught up to walk on his right side. The sunlight was gone completely and the sky above them was lit only by the haze of Northgate's light pollution. Cars passed on the street beside them. The bar's music faded into their past.

"Keep an eye out for a cab," Michael said.

"I'm scoping for threats. Cab's your department."

He let it go, instead taking a breath and switching to, "Holes didn't hire you."

She watched him out of the corner of her eye. It was a moment before she responded. "Didn't say he did. We going to have a problem about this?"

"I'd just like to know who did."

"Life's mysterious. I'd tell you, if I knew."

"What's your email address? And the address they contact you from? Maybe Holes can do some digging."

"You're not hacking my email," she said.

"It's not hacking, it's—" Maybe it was hacking. Was it? "It doesn't bother you, not knowing?"

"They don't want me to know, so I don't know. Part of my fee pays for anonymity. I'm not jeopardizing that just so you can feel all warm and fuzzy."

"It's not—"

"Listen, guy, you've clearly got someone gunning for you. Yeah, you're not helpless anymore, but don't you want protection? Or have I drawn one of those really fun jobs where I get to protect a suicide case?"

"I don't even know who wants me dead," Michael tried. "If I know who wants me alive—"

"Not hacking my email."

Michael sighed. They paused on the edge of a crosswalk, momentarily alone aside the kaleidoscope of traffic. A garbage truck passed by, wafting its odor across Michael's nose. "How long have you been a freelancer?" he asked.

She eyed him with a moment's suspicion. "Since I was nineteen. Got what you could call 'unofficial instruction' before that."

Michael had trouble pegging ages, but that probably meant at least five or six years' experience, if true. "It's only really been about nine months for me."

"Including your three months unconscious?"

The light changed. They crossed. A police drone, its lights flashing, flew above their path as it rushed toward some crisis elsewhere.

"Yeah, including," Michael said. "My first real job was with a mentor of mine. A middleman came to him with an anonymous offer to track down someone he claimed was an arsonist—the same arsonist, so he said, who'd just burned down our apartment. I wondered who the employer was. Diomedes didn't care. He said it didn't matter so long as the money was good."

"Diomedes was your mentor?" she asked.

"You knew him?"

"Only by his rep. And that hit in the Corporate District in August, right?"

Should he tell her Diomedes was dead? No, stay focused. "This was before that, back in February. Our employer turned out to be someone who wanted both the arsonist and Diomedes dead, and the arsonist wasn't even an arsonist. The employer was behind the fires.

We found out before it was too late, but given things like that, how can you not care who's hiring you?"

"The guy hired Diomedes hoping he'd turn out dead? So his money wasn't really 'good,' was it?" She smirked with a twinkle in her violet eyes that Michael found surprisingly pleasant despite the argument.

"That's not the point," he managed after a moment. "If I don't know who hired you, how do I trust your protection?"

Jade heaved a sigh. Her words came in a growled whisper. "Because I'm a professional. And regardless of the rest of the employer's agenda, protecting you is what I'm paid for, and I do my job! Geez, you're a mess! I've told you all I know!"

"So you say."

She stepped in front of him and grabbed his arm. Her eyes—whites, irises, and pupils together—flashed a solid, glowing violet. "If I wanted to hurt you I've had plenty of chances. You want a fucking signed affidavit?"

Her eyes returned to normal. Michael stared her down through his consternation. "Point taken," he said after a moment, and then stepped around her and continued. She let him. "But doesn't it bother you at all that you might be getting played?"

"Michael, if there's one thing I've learned, it's that the freelancer life may pay well, it may be challenging, it may set your blood pounding in a rush that gets you jazzed for the whole night in a single moment, but it is not perfect."

"So, yes, in other words."

She shrugged. "I like the way I said it better."

"At least give me the email address he contacted you from. Maybe Holes can get some info on it."

The clack of Jade's boots along the sidewalk punctuated her silence for what must have been another twenty yards. "Fine. We get somewhere safe and I'll give it over. Just tell Holes not to let whoever it is know I gave it to you."

"What about your email address?"

"To quote your little computer friend: nope."

"I'd trust you a little more if you'd—"

"Let you read my email?" she finished. "Life's rough all over, guy."

"Fair enough."

Michael felt the first sprinkles of rain brush his face and remembered he ought to be looking for a cab. He cast about for one and found his eyes lingering a moment on hers. "Cool flash thing your eyes did, by the way. Nice effect."

"Mm. They do that on their own with the right trigger. Blood pressure, adrenal spikes and such. Gotta have style, you know? Oh, hey: taxi!"

She flagged it down. Once it pulled up, Jade checked the cab's interior and then, apparently satisfied, held the door to watch the area while he got in. He let her.

He'd need to find a moment in private to tell Holes to find Jade's email address and, regardless of her protests, check her account to make sure she was on the level. Could the A.I. manage that? Marc had seemed confident in its abilities whenever he talked about it. Michael's gut was telling him nothing on her; with all that was going on, he had to try, just to be careful.

She clambered in beside him. The door clapped shut.

The driver didn't bother to turn his head. His voice filtered through the holes in the bulletproof glass between them. "Where to?"

Michael considered the question. Get somewhere safe, Jade had said. Where was safe now?

READ MORE IN

A Dragon at the Gate:
Book Three of the New Aeneid Cycle
coming August 2016

ABOUT THE AUTHOR

An award-winning writer of speculative fiction, Michael G. Munz was born in Pennsylvania but moved to Washington State at the age of three. Unable to escape the state's gravity, he has spent most of his life there and studied writing at the University of Washington.

Michael developed his creative bug in college, writing and filming four exceedingly amateur films before setting his sights on becoming a novelist. Driving this goal is the desire to tell entertaining stories that give to others the same pleasure as other writers have given to him. He enjoys writing tales that combine the modern world with the futuristic or fantastic.

Michael has traveled to three continents and has an interest in Celtic and Classical mythology. He also possesses what most "normal" people would likely deem far too much familiarity with a wide range of geek culture, though Michael prefers the term geek-bard: a jack of all geek-trades, but master of none—except possibly Farscape and Twin Peaks.

Michael dwells in Seattle, where he continues his quest to write the most entertaining novel known to humankind and find a really fantastic clam linguini.

CONNECT WITH MICHAEL G. MUNZ ONLINE:

Website: MichaelGMunz.com

Twitter: @TheWriteMunz

Facebook: facebook.com/MichaelGMunz

OTHER NOVELS IN THE NEW AENEID CYCLE

A Shadow in the Flames

A Dragon at the Gate

OTHER BOOKS BY MICHAEL G. MUNZ

*Mythed Connections: A Short Story Collection
of Classical Myth in the Modern World*

Zeus Is Dead: A Monstrously Inconvenient Adventure

**If you enjoyed *A Memory in the Black*, please consider leaving a
review online. Authors live on word of mouth.
Also pizza.**